an amazing, difficult book
to read! I read every word —
July 28, 2023

Twelve
Mile Limit

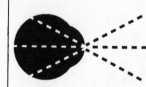

This Large Print Book carries the
Seal of Approval of N.A.V.H.

Twelve
Mile Limit

Randy Wayne White

Thorndike Press • Waterville, Maine

Published in 2003 by arrangement with G. P. Putnam's Sons, a member of Penguin Putnam Inc.

Thorndike Press Large Print Mystery Series.

The tree indicium is a trademark of Thorndike Press.

The text of this Large Print edition is unabridged. Other aspects of the book may vary from the original edition.

Set in 16 pt. Plantin by Elena Picard.

Printed in the United States on permanent paper.

Library of Congress Cataloging-in-Publication Data

White, Randy Wayne.
    Twelve mile limit / Randy Wayne White.
        p. cm.
        ISBN 0-7862-4812-2 (lg. print : hc : alk. paper)
        1. Ford, Doc (Fictitious character) — Fiction. 2. Marine biologists — Fiction. 3. Florida — Fiction. 4. Large type books. I. Title.
    PS3573.H47473 T98 2003
        813'.54—dc21   2002073229

This book is dedicated to my extended family at Sanibel's old Tarpon Bay Marina, where for thirteen years I was a fishing guide: Mack and Eleanor Hamby, George and Willy, Capt. Graeme Mellor, Capt. Nick Clements, Capt. Neville Robeson, Capt. Alex Payne, and Carlene Brennen, as well as all the guides at Sanibel Marina, South Seas, 'Tween Waters, and Jensen's Marinas who provided much good humor and help while on the water. I would also like to thank my pals Dr. Brian Hummel, Gary Terwilliger, Stu Johnson, and Rob Wells for their unfailing support and lots of great sunsets on the porch.

Finally, this book honors David Madott, Omar Shearer, and Kent Monroe, three bright stars on the Gulf Stream, wherever they may now be.

Acknowledgments

The islands of Sanibel and Captiva and the old Conquistador city of Cartagena, Colombia, are real places, and, I hope, faithfully described, but they are all used fictitiously in this novel.

The same is true of certain actual businesses, marinas, bars, and other places frequented by Doc Ford, Tomlinson, and their friends. In all other respects, this novel is a work of fiction. Names, characters, places, and incidents are either the product of the author's imagination or are used fictitiously. Any resemblance to actual persons, living or dead, or to actual events or locales is entirely coincidental.

The author would like to thank Dr. Allan W. Eckert for his friendship and his invaluable research on the Amazon Valley, its flora and fauna and its indigenous people. In South America, during my research there, William Dau, Alvaro Sierra, and Jorge Arauja were all extremely helpful. Dave Lara, Margarita Rosa, Mayra Salgado, and Haroldo Payares provided valuable social and political insights. Claudia Vinueza was helpful in translating English words into Jivaro or similar dialects.

I would also like to thank Cmdr. Larry Simmons, formerly of SEAL Team One, and CPO Bobby Richardson of SEAL Team Two for their patient assistance over the years. The good people at Mote Marine Laboratories — Capt. Peter Hull, Dr. John Miller, and J. Robert Long to name a few — were, once again, very generous with their time and expertise in the field of marine biology.

Others who contributed to this novel include Paul Rhynard, Dr. Alan Steinman, rear admiral, retired, of the U.S. Coast Guard Health Service; Capt. Denis Bluett, Ed Deloreyes, and Eric Spurlock of the U.S. Coast Guard; veterinarians Dr. Laura E. Bogert and Dr. Robert B. Miller; Renee T. Humbert for her expertise on octopi, Sue Williams, Clair Lamb, Patti Haase, Dr. Thaddeus Kostrubala, Chuck Krise of Underwater Explorers, Karen Bell of Bell Seafood, John McNeal and Bill Haney, and also Ric Antey, Barbara Scott, Vivien Godfrey, John Mann, Dorie Cox, Rick Harrison, and all my pals at Bluewater Charts in Ft. Lauderdale.

I would also like to especially thank John Camp for his excellent advice, and Bill Madott for his support and encouragement. He and other family members who braved their way through the tragic sinking, and the search that followed, have been through hell, and they prove the resiliency and brilliance of the human spirit.

These people all provided valuable guidance and information. All errors, exaggerations, omissions, or fictionalizations are entirely the fault and/or the responsibility of the author.

The Simiadae then branched off into two great stems, the New World and the Old World monkeys; and from the latter at a remote period, Man, the wonder and the glory of the Universe, proceeded.

CHARLES ROBERT DARWIN

Part One

Prologue

On Sunday, November 4, a Coast Guard helicopter was operating fifty-two nautical miles off Marco Island on the west coast of Florida, when a crewman spotted a naked woman on the highest platform of a 160-foot navigational tower.

In the crew chief's report, the woman was described as a "very healthy and fit" redhead. The woman was waving what turned out to be a wet suit. She was trying to attract the helicopter crew's attention.

The helicopter, a Jayhawk H-60, was in the area searching for a twenty-five-foot pleasure boat that had been reported overdue nearly two days earlier. According to the report, the motor vessel, *Seminole Wind*, had left Marco on Friday morning with a party of one man, three women. According to relatives, the foursome had planned to spend the day offshore, fishing and SCUBA diving, but did not return Friday afternoon as expected. The Coast Guard had been searching for the *Seminole Wind* since Friday night. The crew of the Jayhawk was looking for a disabled boat, not a naked woman waving a wet suit from a light tower.

The helicopter flew east past the tower, banked south, then hovered beside the platform. One of the crew signaled the woman with a thumbs-up. It was a question. The woman signaled a thumbs-up in return — she was okay. Then the woman wiggled into her wet suit, climbed down to a lower platform, and dived into the water. The crew of the Jayhawk dropped a basket seat and winched her aboard.

It was 9:54 a.m.

The woman they rescued was thirty-six-year-old Amelia Gardner of St. Petersburg, a passenger on the vessel that had been reported overdue, the *Seminole Wind*.

According to the Coast Guard report, the woman was given a mug of coffee from a Thermos and asked what happened. She replied that she'd been a guest on a boat that sank. When the crew chief asked where the boat had sunk, Gardner replied, "Oh dear, God! You mean you haven't found them?"

She was referring to the two women and one man who'd been aboard with her: the boat's owner, Michael Sanford, age thirty-five, of Siesta Key; Grace Walker, twenty-nine, a Sarasota realtor; and Janet Mueller, thirty-three, who lived on a houseboat at Jensen's Marina on Captiva Island and worked part-time for Sanibel Biological Supply, a business owned by a man named Marion Ford.

A Coast Guard crewman shook his head and told the distraught woman, "Nope. We've had crews searching for thirty-six hours straight and no one's seen a thing."

Gardner told the crew that Sanford's boat had swamped and capsized at around 3 p.m. Friday while anchored over the *Baja California*, a wreck they'd been diving. She said the four of them had held on to the anchor line until the boat finally sank at around 7 p.m. and they were set adrift. By then, it was dark, waves had gotten bigger, the wind stronger, and she was gradually swept away from the others in rough seas. Because she had no other options, Gardner began swimming toward the light tower, which she'd been told was approximately four miles away.

"I never thought I was going to make it,"

she told the crew chief. "I was sure I was going to die."

She said that it was a little after 11 p.m., according to her dive watch, when she finally reached the tower, climbed up the service ladder, and collapsed, exhausted, on the lower platform. She'd been on the tower since 11 p.m. Friday — thirty-five hours — and she told them she was very thirsty. She was sunburned, she had barnacle cuts on her hands and legs, and she appeared to be suffering from exposure.

When Gardner was offered the option of being flown to a hospital or remaining on station, she replied that she wanted the helicopter to continue searching. She told crewmen that all three of her companions were wearing wet suits and inflated BCD vests, buoyancy compensator devices. "We'll find them, we've got to find them," she said, and offered to help the crew get Loran — an electronic navigational system that aids mariners in determining positions at sea — coordinates for the *California* wreck from her former dive instructor, who lived aboard a trawler at Burnt Store Marina near Punta Gorda.

The crew chief told Gardner that they already had the coordinates for the wreck.

The helicopter crew, with Gardner

aboard, searched for two more hours but found nothing — nor did what, by now, was an even bigger search group that included a second H-60 helicopter, a C-130 fixed wing aircraft, the Coast Guard's eighty-two-foot cutter *Point Swift,* and a forty-one-foot utility cruiser. The U.S. Coast Guard Auxiliary and other volunteers were also providing boats and crew, but the smaller vessels could not search offshore because the wind was now blowing twenty knots out of the east-northeast.

Hopes of recovering the three missing divers remained high, however. They were all young, all in good shape, and they were all wearing wet suits and inflated vests.

As one of the Coast Guard staff assured Gardner, "Don't worry, we're the very best in the world at finding people lost at sea."

Which is true.

Chapter One

On the bright and blustery November afternoon when we first got word that our friend,
Janet Mueller, was one of three people
missing after a boating accident, I was
working in the lab of my little wooden stilt
house at Dinkin's Bay Marina, Sanibel Island, Florida. I'd spent most of the morning
testing salinity and oxygen content in my
aquaria while serving as reluctant referee in
an argument that had been going on for way,
way too many days between my friend,
Tomlinson, and my sister, Ransom Ebanks.

Well, actually, she's not my sister, and
her last name is no longer Ebanks. She's a
first cousin, the daughter of my late and
much crazed uncle, Tucker Gatrell. My
only cousin, and my only living family on
my mother's side. However, she's introduced herself as my sister so widely and
consistently to fellow islanders that I no

18

longer attempt to set the record straight. If people are willing to believe that I am the brother of a lanky, busty, coconut-brown Bahamian woman who wears Obeah beads braided into her hair and makes blood offerings on the full moon, so be it. She is smart and savvy, with a bawdy sense of humor, plus a brand of fierce independence too rarely seen in men or women, so I've come to consider the association a compliment.

What they'd been arguing about was what lots and lots of people all along the Gulf of Mexico are arguing about. It's the new save-the-manatee laws. The West Indian manatee is a horse-sized, prehistoric mammal with a fluke tail that is as slow in the water as it is slow intellectually. Because of its pug face and teddy-bear countenance, it evokes an emotional response from people, me among them. The manatee is one of my favorite sea creatures.

They have been among the favorites of many over the years — but for very different reasons. For centuries, people hunted manatee for their meat and skin, and still do in Cuba and Nicaragua — impoverished, desperate nations — and in Asia and Africa, too, where a similar species is known as a dugong.

In the United States, we stopped hunting the animal for food long ago. But we continue to kill them with our power-boats. After watchdog organizations filed lawsuits against the Army Corps of Engineers and the U.S. Fish and Wildlife Service, the feds, working with state bureaucrats, have proposed restricting or closing thousands of hectares of public waters to private boaters in an effort to save the few thousand animals that remain.

One of the bodies of water the feds want to close is our own Dinkin's Bay. If they get their way, it will mean no more power-boats, no more fishing guides. No more Mack and his marina, no more of the cast of quirky liveaboards who make their home here. No more Sanibel Biological Supply, the small business that I run, providing fish and tunicates, squid, crabs, sea stars, octopi, anemones, and a whole long list of specimens, preserved or alive, to labs and schools around the country. No more of the traditional Friday parties after Mack ceremoniously locks the gate. No more Red Pelican Gift Shop with its exotic silk and incense wares, no more fish market or fried conch sandwiches.

In short, if the laws are implemented, it will be the end of life as we know it.

Finally, the inevitable will occur far, far in advance of it being inevitable: Our small marina family will have to say good-bye and go our individual, solitary ways.

An ironic fact: As Tomlinson and Ransom argued about losing the Dinkin's Bay family, we'd already unknowingly lost one of our members, Janet Mueller. As we spoke, she was somewhere out there, adrift, alone on a horizon of gray, almost certainly fighting for her life. Alive or dead? It was a question that would take me thousands of miles from home and would get good people killed before I learned the truth — if there can be truth in such a situation.

I stood at the stainless-steel dissecting table, holding a 300-milliliter flask in my hand, attempting to concentrate on the Winkler Titration method of determining oxygen content in water, as Ransom raged at Tomlinson, "Here's what I'm thinkin'. What I'm thinkin' is, if you used your brain as much as you like to use something else you got, you'd understand a very simple fact. People, us people, we all more important than any fat no-brain creature that swim around so slow and dumb it can't keep outta the way of boats. You one sad old hippie, you can't see the truth in that."

She stood there, hands on hips, speaking with her island accent, the words joined together like musical notes, the inflection surging up and down. She was wearing a hibiscus-pink tank top and purple jogging shorts. Every day at lunchtime, the two of us had been running Tarpon Bay Road to the beach, then along the water for two or three miles and back. She'd come dressed and ready to work out but had ended up in an old argument that was becoming increasingly tiresome.

As I dipped the flask into one of my fish tanks, I watched Tomlinson's long and nervous fingers comb hair from his eyes. Blue and bloodshot eyes. Judging from all the fragile, broken capillaries behind those two wise old lenses, he'd been drinking, partying, smoking more cannabis than ever. Seeing lots of women now, too, after ending several months of sexual exclusivity with Ransom — probably another source of the woman's fury.

I listened to him reply, "My dear, dear lady, that's precisely where you're wrong. Animals, humankind — there is no *difference*. One's as valuable as the other. Like the koan my old instructor, my roshi, really flogged my consciousness with: Does a dog have Buddha-nature? Spend a few years meditating that one and your ass will go numb. So does it? Have Buddha-nature, I mean. Yes. Absolutely. Animals have Buddha-nature, 'cause as it says in the Nirvana sutras, 'All sentient beings possess it, a living consciousness, their own karma.' "

Ransom used her hands to wave away her disgust. "You crazy, man."

But Tomlinson continued right along. "It's true. Replace the word *dog* with *manatee* and you've got your proof. Does a manatee have Buddha-nature? That's exactly my point. We let them go extinct? Might as well accept the fact that we'll soon follow. All of us. People, I'm talking about."

Ransom made a grunting sound of contempt, rolled her eyes, and turned to me. Bright blue eyes looking out from her African skin, eyes that were alive, fierce. "He know lots a pretty words, but he still full of goat shit. Got his head so far up his backside I'm surprised he not walking into walls."

"He walks into walls all the time," I said. "Usually around midnight. A couple days ago, he staggered up my steps and fell into the shark pen." I was adding a manganese

23

solution to the beaker. Next would come the iodine base. Then I would titrate the solution and watch for color change.

Ransom said, "I wisht they'd eaten the crazy fool," as she looked through the window at her new skiff tied outside. A pretty little teal-green eighteen-foot Hewes with a ninety-horse Yamaha for power. She'd just bought the thing but, within a few months, might not be able to use it on the bay waters around Sanibel. Most of us are eager fans of the environment, until its maintenance threatens to inconvenience us.

The question of the manatee, however — and more and more so-called environmental causes — is. What *is* necessary maintenance? And what is symptomatic of very human and predictable attempts by government and nonprofit bureaucrats to expand their power?

The line has become so broad, so gray, that I sit way, way back and gather all the information I can before choosing sides in any environmental debate.

In Florida, considering environmental issues has, increasingly, become a time-consuming job. Truth is? Sometimes there are no good choices, and there is almost never a perfect choice.

Ransom said, "Tell him he's full of crap, my brother. All the people here at the marina, they all hate the idea of these crazy new laws 'cept this ol' rummy pal of yours, Mr. Peace Love Dove Hippie Boy."

I said, "Don't put me in the middle of this. I've got problems of my own, right here in my lab, and listening to you two bicker isn't exactly expediting a solution."

I did have problems, too. Nothing major, but problems that were increasingly perplexing and irksome. Over the last two months, someone or something had snuck into my lab and stolen more than three dozen stone crabs and seven calico crabs. Took them from the hundred-gallon aquarium where I'd been stockpiling them, and always one or two crabs at a time.

It was bizarre. At first I thought a raccoon might have found some kind of secret ingress through the wobbly wooden floor of my old house, or maybe through some unseen space between the wall and the tin roof. I searched and hunted, and found nothing bigger than a mouse-sized opening, but the crabs continued to disappear.

Maddening.

Finally, I covered the aquarium with a pane of heavy glass. If some animal were stealing crabs, a cover would certainly solve the problem, right?

Nope, it didn't. Crabs continued to disappear, one or two at a time, always at night, but in no other predictable or understandable pattern. Finally, I started sealing the lid of my crab tank with a small metal vise.

I'd begun to think some of my marina friends were playing a practical joke on me — "Hey, know how we can really mess with Doc's mind?" — but then, concurrently, my octopi began to disappear, too. Two species of octopi live in the waters around Sanibel and they are not easy to collect or keep alive, and my friends are knowledgeable enough to know that. They wouldn't mess with my octopi, not just because they are valuable creatures but also because everyone at the marina knows that octopi — like manatees — are among my very favorite animals.

I find octopi fascinating, compelling even, for a number of reasons.

As members of the phylum Mollusca, an octopus is a mollusk, like a snail or clam, but that's where all similarities end. Octopi are the intellectual giants of their phylum. They have the most complex brain of all invertebrates, and they are a hell of a lot smarter

26

than most animals that do have spines, and that includes some people I know.

Octopi have precise, uncanny long-term and short-term memories, and they learn to solve problems by trial and error, by experience. Once they solve a problem, they file away the solution and can then solve similar problems quickly.

The immediate and most striking feature of an octopus is its glowing cat's eyes. They are highly complex eyes that compare to humans' in visual acuity but focus by moving the lens in and out rather than by changing their shape. They are bright, predatory eyes that imply a rare analytical intensity, just as an octopus's ability to change skin color suggests, to some, emotional complexity. There are people who say that when an octopus's special pigment cells, or chromatophores, strobe red, it's angry. When they strobe white, the octopus is afraid.

I don't happen to believe octopi are motivated by emotion or react to emotion — people are much too quick to assign human qualities to animals — but, still, they are fascinating creatures.

Because octopi are smart and predatory, I keep them one or two to a tank and make certain the tanks are heavily lidded.

Even so, I'd now lost one small long-armed octopus and two football-sized Atlantic octopi without explanation. Like the crabs, and like Janet Mueller, the octopi simply seemed to vanish.

Now, out of frustration, I was checking the water in each and every one of my aquaria to make certain conditions were as close to ideal as I could make them before I retackled the mystery of my disappearing lab animals. Salinity had checked out at twenty-four parts per thousand, which was exactly the same as the salinity of the bay in which I'd collected the octopi, and, now, the flask in my hand began to turn a pale shade of rose, meaning there was sufficient oxygen as well.

I listened to Ransom and Tomlinson continue to bicker as I crossed the room to the sink. As I did, I noted that I was being tracked by a solitary, golden eye: The largest of the eight remaining octopi in the tanks along the wall was watching me from beneath a rock ledge.

It recognized me, I had no doubt of that. I saw an extended tentacle throb gray, pink, and brown as I passed, reacting, perhaps, to hunger stimuli. I was the man who brought it two fiddler crabs, each and every evening.

That was when, through the south window, I noticed Jeth Nicholes, a fishing guide and Janet's on-again, off-again lover, running along the mangrove path toward the wooden walkway that leads to my house. Panic has an odor, a tenor, and a visual quality that imprints on spinal neurons micro-moments before recognition touches the brain.

Jeth was in a panic.

I heard Ransom say to Tomlinson, "Okay, Mr. Vegetarian, Mr. Love and Harmony who say that we shouldn't kill no living creatures. Talk to me about the other night. The two of us out there on the deck of that sleepy white sailboat of yours smokin' that ganja. You not the man I saw jump up and squash them palmetto bugs? Man, I seen that with my own two eyes."

I was moving faster now, toward the door to see what was the matter with Jeth, and her words touched my ears as, *Mon, I seen daht wi' me oon two eyes.* A pretty accent that conjured up images of coconut palms, coral islands.

Heard her add, "What you tellin' me is, an animal got to be big before it important enough not to kill. Or it got to be cute, like a stuffed animal. Stomp, stomp, stomp! Man, I *seen* you kill them palmetto bugs. I seen you slap plenty of mosquitoes out there on that boat of yours, too, not to mention a couple bushels of no-see-ums."

I heard Tomlinson answer, "Killing insects, sure, I get some whiskey in me, something crawls up my leg, I'm gonna smack it before I take time to think. But you miss the point, lovely lady. I've killed plenty of palmetto bugs. But I wouldn't kill Florida's *last* palmetto bug," as I opened the lab's door and saw Jeth sprinting down the walkway. I could feel his weight through the vibrating wood as he ran, could see the mottled color of his face — another kind of color change that illustrated emotion.

He was frightened all right.

When he saw me, he yelled, "Doc, we've been trying to call! You got your damn phone off the hook again, don't you?"

Anger is a common derivative of fear.

I sensed Tomlinson move behind me in the doorway as Jeth, standing still now, yelled, "We've got to get all the boats we can down there! The whole marina, we're organizing, we're going to run down and join the search. But we need to hurry, damn it!"

I had no idea what he was talking about, of course, but, behind me, Tomlinson whispered, "Janet," his elevated powers of observation making the quick connection to one of the few people who could cause Jeth to react as he was now.

Which is when Jeth told us that, the day before, Janet had gone diving with three people off Marco Island, and she and her party were now eighteen hours overdue. "With that idiot she was dating, that Mike-asshole from Sarasota!" he added miserably. "The one she met at the bachelorette party. And I'm the one who let her go."

Chapter Two

The news spread fast. It had started at the Coast Guard station at Tampa, I would learn later, and beamed its way down the Florida shoreline, island to island, marina to marina, just as fast as VHF radios and cell phones could spread the news.

Janet Mueller, our Janet, was missing. The news hit me hard. Same with the entire marina community. She was one of us; a favorite member of the fun and quirky saltwater family that, on the islands of Sanibel and Captiva, is made up of fishing guides and liveaboards, waiters and waitresses, bartenders, tackle store and marina employees, and anyone else who makes a living on or around the Gulf of Mexico and its mangrove bays.

She was the quiet girl with glasses, the sisterly type, always there when you needed her, but never out front in any showy way. Janet was the one with the mousy hair and heavy hips, but a cute face; the one who liked to laugh and socialize, but who never displayed much self-confidence. If you were a man, take one look at her, and you had an inexplicable urge to protect her, just as women, on first meeting, knew they could trust and confide in her without even having to think about it much.

Janet arrived at the marina a few years back in pretty bad emotional shape. She'd been a schoolteacher in some small Ohio town. She'd had a husband who adored her, and the two of them worked hard at remodeling their house for the baby they were expecting. Janet was solid, happy, with her future securely mapped and under way. Or so she thought.

It happens very fast, sometimes, and almost always to people who don't deserve it and who never, never expect it. Her solid world began to wobble out of control, and then it disintegrated. One snowy night, Janet lost her husband in a car accident. Then she lost their baby to a miscarriage.

After a year or so of psychological counseling, she sought refuge and change by moving to Florida. She showed up at the marina one day in a little blue houseboat.

Knew nothing about the water, nothing about boats, but Janet was smart enough to realize that she needed to reinvent her own life or slip slowly, inexorably off the edge of sanity.

Ours is a small and selective community, and we appreciate raving individualists. We like small, brave people who find small, brave ways to endure and achieve. We welcomed Janet as one of us; took her under the communal wing, and she soon *was* one of us.

She started dating Jeth, fishing guide and handyman, then moved her houseboat up to Jensen's Marina on Captiva after a spat. But her relationship with Dinkin's Bay Marina continued. She'd stop by several times a week. She never missed the marina's traditional Friday party, and she was one of the few people I trusted to look after my lab and fish tanks when I was away.

Janet had found a way to find her way. Better than most and with a great deal of humor and grace, she'd done credit to the mandate of our species. She had battled back and discovered a way to survive.

Which was why it seemed so mind-boggling that she was now missing, her boat overdue. So damn tragic and unfair. We all expect life to deal us a few bad cards, but no one person is supposed to be dealt *all* bad cards. Especially not someone as decent and kind-spirited as Janet Mueller, the woman who'd come to Florida to reconstruct her soul and her future.

As Jeth stood there on the dock, with Tomlinson and then Ransom, too, behind me, I told him, "Calm down, Jeth. It's going to be okay. Let's meet down at the bait tanks and get things organized. You go tell Mack and the others."

He was breathing heavily. Not because he'd been running, but because of the panic he was in. Jeth is a big, good-looking guy with the dense muscularity and loyal face of a high school linebacker. The expression on his face was heartbreaking. The love affair between him and Janet had had its share of setbacks. But they loved each other and would almost certainly end up together. No one at the marina doubted that.

For the last couple of weeks, Jeth and Janet had been suffering through an off-again cycle, and now the man appeared to be near tears. "We've got to get going, Doc! We've got to get out there and find her!" He pounded a big fist hard against his own thigh. "Christ!" he said miserably,

"I can't believe I let her go!"

I walked over to him, put my hand on his shoulder, and told him, "She'll be okay. We'll find her. I promise."

I saw a small surge of relief come into his face. If I were that confident, so certain she would be found, then there was hope.

The first thing I did was send Tomlinson and Ransom over to the docks to meet with the others so they could start formulating a plan. With winds blowing fifteen to twenty knots, and seas four to six feet offshore, our small boats wouldn't be able to make the thirty-mile trip to Marco Island via water. Too dangerous, too exhausting. We'd have to trailer our skiffs south and hope that a couple of the liveaboards would volunteer to run down in their much bigger vessels and let us use them as mother ships.

That was assuming, of course, that Janet and her party weren't found before we got started. Which is why the second thing I did was go to the telephone and call my friend Dalton Dorsey who's a lieutenant commander at Coast Guard Group, St. Petersburg.

Group St. Pete oversees five small-boat Coast Guard stations and is responsible for patrolling several hundred miles of coastline, from Tallahassee to the Everglades and beyond. It's a massive area, but the Coasties, as they are called, do an extraordinarily good job. What most people don't know is that the Coast Guard is under the control of the U.S. Department of Transportation, not the Department of Defense, but its men and women are as well trained, as professional, and often as heroic as any military specialty group.

Which is why, when Jeth first told me that Janet was in a boat reported overdue, I wasn't overly concerned. If Janet was somewhere out there in a broken-down vessel, it wouldn't take long for the Coasties to find her.

Or so I believed at the time.

I got lucky. Caught Dalton on his cell phone outside the old St. Pete Coast Guard Administration and Operations Building. It's a whitewashed, two-story fortress, built back in the 1920s, overlooking Bayboro Harbor and Tampa Bay, just a couple of miles from the Sunshine Skyway. He was there on a Saturday, he said, because he'd scheduled a special inspection, but now he was in the parking lot, headed for his pickup truck and the golf course at McDill Airbase.

When I told him why I'd called, he said, "Our group had three boats reported overdue yesterday, and I don't remember the specifics of all of 'em, so let me go upstairs to my office and I'll check the incident report."

We talked about baseball, then a mutual friend of ours, Tony Johnson, who's a Florida county court judge but still works in naval intelligence as a reserve officer. Then I heard a rustling of paper, and Dalton said, "Okay, here's a copy. Everything you want to know. Missing small boat. The call came in at nine-ten to our Fort Myers Beach station. A woman named Sherry Meyer, a friend of the guy who owns the boat, Michael Sanford. She's the one who called. Are you friends with all these people, Doc?"

"No, just Janet Mueller. I've never met the others."

"Well . . . she's listed as being aboard. According to Meyer, anyway . . . only she said the name was spelled M-i-l-l-e-r, which I'll change right now. Her, Sanford, a woman named Grace Walker, and another one named Amelia Gardner. Four in all."

I said, "And you said there are two other boats reported missing? Three in one day, that's a pretty weird coincidence, isn't it, Dalt?"

"Not missing, just reported overdue. The other two boats, they've been accounted for already. There's a standard way we handle these things — our five stations do about two thousand SAR missions a year, so we've got it down to a science almost."

SAR — search and rescue. The uniformed branches love acronyms. A language that outsiders can't understand empowers and insulates.

He said, "The watch officers have formatted check-off sheets. When someone calls in an overdue vessel, there're standard questions and we check the little boxes off the list one by one. Where'd the vessel leave from? Where'd they park their car? What kind of car? Who was aboard? That sort of thing.

"Meyer said the boat we're talking about, the *Seminole Wind*, left from Marco Island Marina early yesterday morning and that her friends were due back at sunset because they were all supposed to go out to dinner that night at the Marco Island Inn. Ms. Meyer said — I'm reading from the incident sheet — 'Ms. Meyer said her friends had gone offshore to dive a wreck that's called the *California*.' Are you familiar with that wreck, Doc?"

I told him, "Yeah, I've dived it. *Baja California*, that's the actual name. It's not a simple dive — the thing's in, what, a hundred-ten, a hundred-twenty feet of water, and the visibility's usually not great. I don't know how experienced the other three are, but my friend Janet has no business making a dive like that. She just took up the sport. Did her first open-water dive a month ago at Pennekamp off Key Largo with a guy we both know, John Martinez. So she's a novice; the *Baja California* is way out of her league. You said they were in a small boat? How small's small?"

"Let's see . . . we've got it down as a twenty-five-footer with twin two-twenty-five Johnsons. The watch officer from Fort Myers Beach talked to a mechanic at Marco Island Marina and got a full description."

"Over four hundred horsepower on a boat that size, it sounds like a floating rocket," I said. "Who's the manufacturer?"

I was hoping to hear a name like Grady White or Mako or Pursuit or any of the other reputable manufacturers of pleasure craft.

Instead, I heard, "It's a custom boat.

Built by a little shop near Lauderdale. A semi-V hull with a blue Bimini top, the name *Seminole Wind* in big red letters on the side."

"The *Baja*, I can't remember exactly, but it's got to be at least fifty or sixty miles offshore. With winds like this, that's way too far for a boat that size."

Dalton said, "Well, according to Ms. Meyer, that's where they were headed. When they still hadn't come back by eight-thirty — they were all staying in a rental condo there — Meyer tried to call the marina, but they were closed, so she drove down and confirmed that Sanford's SUV was still there and the boat wasn't back."

I checked my watch and, for the first time, felt a surge of the same anxiety that Jeth was feeling. "That was nearly twenty hours ago, and still no word from them. That's not good."

"Maybe, but don't start worrying yet, Doc. The majority of the overdue reports we get, they've left from one marina, but end up going back to another. Because of engine trouble, or they decided at the last minute to go exploring, or because they started partying and got carried away."

I said, "That doesn't sound like my friend Janet."

"Yeah, but like you said, you don't know the others. You wouldn't believe some of the cases we work. I'll give you an example: Last month, we got an overdue report — this guy in a twenty-five-foot Mako — and we went through the whole procedure with his distraught wife. The call comes into us, we go through the checklist on the incident report. We have local law enforcement confirm the guy's car is still parked at the marina and his boat's definitely not there.

"So we call our district headquarters in Miami and discuss which of our assets to scramble. According to his wife, he was going to run offshore and fish the ledges. So we send out the big hello. No boat, no guy. So then we send out a C-130. Still nothing. Okay, now it's panic time, so we deploy every asset we have. For three days, we search — all day, all night. You have any idea how much it costs per hour to fly a C-130?

"Turns out, the guy's having an affair with his wife's sister, and they're shacked up on Siesta Key. He's got the boat hidden in a friend's canal." Dalton has a husky, beer-drinker's laugh.

"That's just one example. For seventeen years, I've been in this business. We see it

42

all, Doc. Unbelievable stuff."

"Not my friend, Janet, Dalt. She's one of the good ones. If we haven't heard from her, there's a reason. I think she's in trouble."

Dorsey told me they already had a H-60 chopper working the search, plus a C-130 flying a grid, along with their eighty-two-foot cutter *Point Swift*, and a forty-one-foot utility cruiser. Then he added, "But if you want, I'll talk to my boss and see if we can get Miami to let us send the second hello."

I told him any extra help would be appreciated, and added, "Another thing, Dalt. If you don't mind, let your skippers know that some of Janet's friends are headed down there with boats to join in the search. We'll stay out of the way, cooperate however we can, but I'd like to maintain radio contact with your people, if that's okay."

We talked for a while longer before Dalton Dorsey ended the conversation, saying, "Believe me, if your lady friend is out there somewhere in a boat, we will find her."

The next morning, Sunday, just before 10 a.m., as I was idling my skiff away from a Marco Island boat ramp, out Collier's Bay toward Big Marco Pass, a petty officer aboard the cutter *Point Swift* contacted us via VHF radio. He asked me to switch from channel 16 to channel 22-Alpha.

It was then we learned that, two hours earlier, one of the *Seminole Wind*'s passengers had been found alive, standing atop a huge light tower, fifty-two nautical miles offshore.

Idling abreast of me, in big Felix Lane's twenty-four-foot Parker, was Jeth Nicholes, listening to our radio conversation. I could see his face clearly. I watched his expression change from expectation, to delight, and, finally, anguish, when we learned that, according to the woman they'd rescued, the *Seminole Wind* had sunk early Friday evening, and she had not seen her fellow passengers since.

Unless someone had picked Janet up without notifying the Coast Guard, she had now been in water for more than forty hours.

Chapter Three

For five straight days, we searched. We searched nonstop from just before sunrise until just after sunset, and ate aboard our small boats, never pausing.

JoAnn Smallwood and Rhonda Lister rousted their doughy old Chris Craft, the *Satin Doll,* from her berth at Dinkin's Bay, and she became one mother ship. Dieter Rasmussen's gorgeous Grand Banks trawler, *Das Stasi,* became another. *No Mas,* Tomlinson's sun-bleached Morgan was a third. All were loaded with cans of gas and outboard oil, compliments of Mack at the marina, and boxes of food and drinks, compliments of Bailey's General Store.

As search vessels, we had three skiffs from Dinkin's Bay, including Ransom in her new Hewes, and Jensen's Marina sent down its water taxi and all three of its fishing guides — seven fast boats in all.

The locals of Sanibel and Captiva Islands had joined forces to look for one of our own.

Because it seemed to make sense, we anchored the mother ships in fifteen-mile increments offshore and south of the actual wreck site. My friends with the Coast Guard shared every little scrap of information they had with us, including some high-tech computer software that plotted the set and drift of the Gulf's inshore and offshore currents.

Anything adrift would travel southwest, toward the Dry Tortugas, the computer told us. The electronic drift buoys their ships dropped and monitored told us the same thing.

Yet we found nothing. Even though the H-60 choppers and search planes were using what the Coasties call FLIR — forward-looking infrared radar, which can detect the heat of a human body from nearly a mile away — there was not a trace.

It was maddening. Adding to the frustration was Amelia Gardner's story, which the Coast Guard also shared with us. According to Gardner, Janet, Michael Sanford, and Grace Walker were all wearing wet suits and inflated buoyancy compensator vests. Even if they were dead, they would certainly still be afloat. So why hadn't we found them?

On the fourth day of the Coast Guard search, Tuesday, November 8, we got a little break, a tiny glimmer of hope. About twenty-one nautical miles southwest of the wreck site, one of the Jensen guides found a dive bag and videocamera that belonged to Janet. A day later, in the same area, we found two empty air tanks and an orange life jacket with a section of rope tied to it.

But that was it. Not another piece of flotsam.

Working open water in a small boat is exhausting business. An autumnal high pressure system catalyzed steady, relentless winds, fifteen to twenty knots all day long, creating seas that whitecapped higher than my head as we surfed our little skiffs up one gray ridge, then down another, minute after minute, hour by hour, looking, searching, our eyes always straining to see. At sunset, we would return to our assigned mother ship and collapse into salon chairs, numb with fatigue, while a macrodome of silver stars revolved slowly above a black horizon.

Jeth and I stayed aboard the *Satin Doll* with Rhonda and JoAnn. I wanted Jeth

47

with me because I didn't trust his emotional condition. He blamed himself for keeping Janet at a distance because of a small infidelity in which he'd caught her — not an actual infidelity because, at the time, they were in an off-again cycle of their love affair. The few times he did speak, it was to denigrate himself or to repeat variations on a maxim that, sooner or later, we all learn to be true: "I didn't know what I had, Doc, 'till I lost it."

On the sixth day of the Coast Guard search, Lt. Cmdr. Dalton Dorsey contacted me via VHF and told me what I already knew: He'd extended the search time because of our friendship, but it had to stop. The Coast Guard and its assets had hunted more than 23,000 square miles of water on a carefully coordinated grid search, using the latest high-tech radar and heat-sensitive vector systems but had found nothing. It was as if all three people had fallen through a hole in the ocean, and vanished.

He also told me that, the previous day, marine salvage divers out of Sarasota had towed in Sanford's boat, the *Seminole Wind*. Speaking more formally because he was on the radio, Dorsey told me, "They found it in one hundred and ten feet of water, lying upside-down atop the *Baja California*. They used air bags to refloat and right it."

When I asked if the Coast Guard or the family of Michael Sanford had asked the salvage company to refloat the boat, his terse reply — "Absolutely not" — told me he was pissed off about it and would tell me more later.

That night, after the Coast Guard suspended what had been one of the most massive sea searches in the history of South Florida, JoAnn Smallwood came tippy-toe a'creeping up onto the stern deck where I was lying on the companion bench seat under a light blanket. She put her hand on my shoulder and whispered, "You asleep?"

I said, "I wish I could sleep. I truly do."

"I know, it's impossible and I can't stand it anymore. You mind some company?"

JoAnn and I have had a long and mutual sexual chemistry that we have carefully and successfully battled — dating within the communal marina family is much too risky — but this had to do with friendship, not physical attraction, so I scooched over and made room for the lady. I felt the heat of her skin on my bare legs, felt the bosomy softness beneath her T-shirt as she pulled herself close, using my chest for a pillow. Her breath was warmer than the wind as she said into my ear, "Should we go say something to him? How long can he keep that up?"

From the guest stateroom forward, muted by bulkheads of fiberglass and wood, came a booming *thud-a-thud-a-thud* backdropped by the sound of a grown man sobbing. It was Jeth, banging his fist or his head against the hull as he cried.

I said, "No. We've got to let him get it out in his own way. But after this, when we get home, we need to keep a close eye on him. There are all kinds of ways for people to self-destruct. I'd say he's a prime candidate."

She laid there quietly for a couple of minutes, holding me tight, hearing the wind, hearing Jeth, before she said, "What I hate to even think about, Doc, is that Janet's still out there. Still alive and hoping we'll find her, but that we haven't looked in the right place. God, it just kills me when I think of that! Makes me feel so helpless."

I hadn't yet said anything to anyone about what I felt the chances were of Janet surviving for even twenty-four hours adrift in the Gulf of Mexico, but now I did. Maybe I shouldn't have. I'm far from being an expert on human physiology, but because I've done a fair amount of diving, I've read the basic literature on survival at sea. Rightly or wrongly, I attempted to comfort her, because false hope is a common source of human pain.

I said, "Trust me, JoAnn, you don't need to think about that anymore. You know about tropic hypothermia? Warm water hypothermia, it's the same thing. I need to look it up again to be sure of the details, but I think I'm pretty close. Tropic hypothermia you get in water that's eighty-two, eighty-three degrees, and it feels like bathwater. Stay in for a couple of hours, and you won't even notice that your body's core temperature is gradually dropping to match the temperature of the water. But that's what happens.

"I didn't memorize the tables exactly, but in water that's in the low eighties, even a healthy person might survive for only twenty-four hours or so. I checked it our first day out — the water temp here's seventy-seven degrees. I doubt that Janet or the other two made it through the second night still conscious."

I was wrong, as I would learn later. Absolutely wrong in the face of the facts and the newest research data. Like most poorly informed people, though, I spoke with a conviction so firm that JoAnn was convinced.

"Oh God, Doc, that's so sad. But they were wearing wet suits . . . wouldn't that make it —"

"Janet showed me her wet suit before she did her first open-water dive, her new pink one with the black panels. Remember when she did that trip to Key Largo? It's a shorty, covered just her thighs and upper body. A warm-water suit. I'm not sure how thick the neoprene was, but it wasn't real thick. Two, maybe three millimeters, which is about pretty typical for tropical water divers.

"The other two people were wearing similar wet suits, according to my Coast Guard pals. Michael Sanford's was blue and black, Grace Walker's was blue and green, and Janet's, at least, was a high-visibility pink. What people forget is that human beings are not built for the water. We are land creatures. Water removes heat from the body about twenty-five times faster than cold air, and most of that heat loss occurs through the head. Swimming, thrashing around, or struggling in water increases heat loss. And you know how rough it is out here."

"Do I ever. The way we've gotten banged around, I'll be sore for a week." I felt JoAnn's body move as she sighed heavily. "Then she's dead. Janet's dead. That's what you're saying. You've known all along."

"If she's still in the water, that'd be my guess. But like I said, I need to go back and do some research. I have a friend out west who used to be the Coast Guard's surgeon general. The equivalent of it, anyway. He's done a lot of research on hypothermia, so I need to give him a call."

"I almost hate to ask, but I have to. Doc, how would it have been for her? Those last hours?"

I'd thought a lot about it. When you lose someone tragically that you care about, much of the anguish comes from imagining *their* anguish during their final moments. So I gave JoAnn an edited version. But not edited much. I told her that the body is an amazing thing — it's got lots of ways to conserve heat. When we're exposed to cool water, small blood vessels near the skin's surface automatically constrict to keep blood flow away from the outer tissues. That's true of the entire body

53

except for the brain, which needs unrestricted blood flow. Which is why the blood vessels of the head do not constrict and why heat is lost most quickly from the area of the head.

"So her first major organ affected," I said, "was her brain. She probably got confused, then drowsy. More than likely, she just fell asleep. Once her core temp got below . . . I think it's ninety-five degrees, once her core temperature got below that, her heartbeat would have become erratic, and then, finally, it would have stopped. But, like I said, she'd have been asleep by that time."

"So it wouldn't have been that bad for her and the others?"

"No," I lied. "Not that bad at all."

We lay there in silence for a time. Beyond the canvas canopy I'd rigged to keep off the dew, I could see the black horizon lifting, pausing, then falling out of a black sky. I wondered as I'd wondered before: What *had* it been like for Janet? As I wrestled with all the horrible scenarios, Janet was there in memory, her pudgy, girlish face alive in my mind and her sensitive eyes, green and kind, looking directly into mine.

I remembered the smell of the musky

perfume she sometimes wore. Remembered the distinctive cocoa-butter scent of body cream, and how, when she was excited or telling a joke, she punctuated her sentences by combing her fingers through her hair. I remembered that the first time Janet made me laugh, really laugh, was a couple of weeks after she'd been working in the lab, and she accidentally let it slip that she'd named each and every one of my fish. Janet had made me laugh many times after that, and she'd confided in me and encouraged me. She'd brought me little handmade presents at Christmas and dyed eggs with silly faces at Easter. In front of others, she'd slapped me on the ass at dock parties, and, when she knew I was stressed, she'd come quietly up behind me and massage the muscles of my neck and shoulders. Janet was a good woman, and she had been a good and true friend.

I thought that JoAnn had drifted off to sleep when, suddenly, she spoke again. "Do you hear it?"

I lifted my head slightly. "No. I don't hear anything."

"That's what I mean. He's stopped. Finally, the poor darling's stopped. Probably exhausted."

She meant Jeth.

Then, after another long silence, she said, "Doc, there's one thing I will never understand. If Janet and the other two were wearing those big, inflated vests, why didn't we find them? All those air hours, the choppers and planes, and all the boats out here looking. Why? It seems almost impossible."

I said, "I don't know, JoAnn. It does seem impossible. That's one question I can't answer."

Rhonda joined us for a bit. She came topside, sniffling and snuffing, a tall, skinny-hipped woman with short brown hair and a heart as big as Tomlinson's. Her voice was quivering as she said, "You got room there for one more?" and slid her long body in behind me when I lifted the blanket as invitation.

I've read somewhere that certain religious groups and some primitive societies practice a form of healing known, variously, as "powwowing" or "hiving" in which members of the group unite in what is, essentially, an extended communal hug. I don't believe in herbal cures or faith healing, but I have to admit that, lying between those two women, sandwiched by people whom I've come to respect and love, I felt better than I had since the end of our second day searching for Janet. Why? Because by the end of that long day, I was pretty certain that Janet was gone.

The sense of respite didn't last, though. The two ladies returned to their own beds a little after midnight, and I still couldn't sleep. Couldn't get the question *What had it been like?* out of my mind. It was a haunting question to consider.

I am not an overly emotional person. Indeed, I believe that once a decision has been made, or an event has occurred, any investment in or concession to emotion is a waste of time and energy.

Even so, Janet remained a lucent image, her private eyes staring into mine. There was a shyness in them, and a brand of kindness that comes only from deep pain. Finally, I realized that there was only one way to come close to understanding what she had experienced the night that she and the others were set adrift.

I have an orderly mind that sometimes insists on factual, experiential input. So I threw off the blanket and walked to the boat's transom. I was wearing running shorts, no shirt, and the deck was damp beneath my bare feet. Except for the wind and the creaking of wood and braided line, it was quiet now. Below, JoAnn and Rhonda were either asleep or trying to sleep.

High in the sky was a quarter moon. It was all the light I needed. I rummaged through a stern storage hatch, tied a mooring line to a life ring, and tossed the line astern. Then I slipped over the transom into the sea.

You might expect water that's seventy-seven degrees to be warm, but it isn't, and the sudden chill caused my lungs to spasm momentarily.

I allowed my body to submerge, which seemed to warm it, then I held on to the line as breakers freighted me outward. Now, six days after the sinking of the *Seminole Wind*, conditions were still almost exactly as they had been the night that Janet and the other three were set adrift. The wind was fifteen to twenty knots out of the east-southeast, seas building.

I felt my body contort rag doll–like as the first big wave flooded over me, then lifted me: big waves without rhythm on a windy night. I could feel them rolling past, lifting, suctioning, then tumbling me under. Even with the quarter moon, I couldn't see the waves, but I could hear them coming — a keening sound, the sound of wind over ice — and their approach was felt as an expanding buoyancy.

Janet's first night out here was one day into a waxing moon. I'd checked the tide tables. On the previous Friday, the day her boat sunk, sunset was at 5:38 p.m.; the setting of the frail lunar crescent was exactly fifty-eight minutes later. Hers would have been a blacker night with stronger currents.

Still drifting outward-bound on the line, I turned away from the *Satin Doll*. Miles to the east was a flashing light. It was the 160-foot-high navigation tower to which the lone survivor, Amelia Gardner, had swum after being separated from her companions, and where she'd been found by the Coast Guard chopper thirty-eight hours later. From the crests of waves, the light was an explosion of white; from the troughs, it was a milky concussion. Every four seconds, the light flared: a visual hypnotic that penetrated to the brain, oscillated the pupils, eroded equilibrium.

If I stared at the light too long, I lost all depth perception. The tower might have been three miles away or it might have been a satellite flashing from outer space. When I forced myself to continue staring at the light, I began to feel a sickening sense of unreality. Where did the sky end and the sea begin? Was I looking up at the stars, or looking down from them in the midst of some disturbing dream?

I have made many long swims in open water at night, yet it was unpleasant, even for me — the wallowing darkness of being in a wave's trough, then suddenly vaulted starward only to be temporarily blinded by that distant strobe. I found the prospects of trying to make such a swim scary as hell. Janet was a novice diver and an average swimmer. For her, it had to have been an existential nightmare — not the first living nightmare of her tough, tough life.

An Olympic ski racer once told me that the most frightening aspect of the sport was pointing her skis downhill. As a waterman, I had had to scan awhile to find the empathic equivalent. I decided that pointing a small boat offshore, out of sight of land, was similar. Both acts were expeditionary; both were a kind of voluntary untethering. I described for her how the wheel torques at the hands, trying to veer shoreward. She said, "Yes, yes — it's the same with skis." We might have been discussing mountains: Hers was white, mine gray.

Dread of the abyss is communal among outdoor people. It is not the fear that unites us, but the potential that anything, absolutely anything, can happen. It creates a kind of congenial freemasonry — perhaps because feelings of dread, like nightmares, usually vanish when exposed to light.

For Janet, though — if she survived it — enduring such a night would not have been mitigated by the first pale streaks of a windy dawn. The Gulf of Mexico had been slowly killing her, killing her without conscience, and she would certainly have been aware that there was no escape.

I now knew some of the sensory components she had experienced. But rolling there on a black sea, beneath a black sky, I found myself troubled on a deeper level. The phenomenon that is human existence can be described in a number of ways, and one of those ways is chemical. There are ninety-two elements found in nature, and sixty-six of those are found in seawater. Blood and human protoplasm, the salty components that are the source of life, contain many of those elements in the same precise proportions as our major oceans.

As I drifted, I felt reduced. I felt clinically defined, though not insignificant because the word *significant* implies a judgment of worth, and I had no worth. Nor did the life and death of Janet Mueller. Nor the horror she had endured. I was hydrogen, sodium, chlorine, sulfur, potassium, and carbon. I was a soup of electrolytes that fired a brain that, inexplicably and absurdly, had evolved beyond the requirements of base survival and reproduction. I was skin over a scaffolding of lime-hardened skeleton that I'd inherited from the calcium-dense oceans of Cambrian time.

Perhaps Tomlinson was right. Perhaps humans are no better, of no more value, than dogs or a fish or manatees. For reasons I cannot comprehend, he seems to find that philosophy freeing. I meet more and more people who feel similarly. They apparently find some level of peaceful, spiritual equity by viewing all life as homogeneous and equal.

Not me.

My view of existence is neither romantic nor sentimental. But on this night, adrift and mourning the loss of my friend, Tomlinson's judgment seemed, at once, valid and terrible. Eons ago, the first one-celled animal developed a circulatory system in which its lifeblood was pure sea-water. I was not that much different, nor, it seemed in this moment, were the best of the many good men and women I've known.

I'd put myself in Janet's place, and I'd learned a little. But I also knew that I would never understand intellectually or emotionally what she'd felt that night. It was impossible, because the circumstances were so different and we were such dissimilar people. A few months back, to celebrate a birthday, I'd swum four miles of open water, St. Petersburg to Tampa. When I'd told Janet, she'd marveled: "My God, I've driven across the Sunshine Skyway, and that bay is huge! You actually *swam* across it?" Now I was still tethered to a floating boat that had a bed and blanket waiting for me. Aboard were people who would answer if I called for help. Aboard the boat were VHF and single sideband radios. I was in the water, but I was still safely, securely connected.

But my friend Janet had experienced the bottomless void. She'd been swept away by a mindless thing that we all dread. Which is possibly why human nature won't allow an individual — or three — to vanish without explanation. Blame and reason are contrivances to which we cling for comfort, a way of imposing order. When one is dealing with deep ocean, however, all acts are expeditionary, and even the most mundane untethering — such as pointing a small boat offshore — carries risk.

How can you blame the sea? At night, alone, waves are as indifferent as wind, or the void that is the backdrop for a flashing light at sea.

I'd learned enough, and what I'd learned was not comforting. I could never share that knowledge. I would never share it. As Janet's friend, I would do what she would have wanted me to do: Protect her friends from the truth.

I climbed back aboard, found a towel, and stripped naked, drying myself. Then I stood in the wind, hands on hips, feet set wide for balance, looking at the star streaks and comet swirls of two unfathomable spheres: sea and space. The constellations Orion and Cassiopeia were bright in the autumn sky; the Pleiades, a hazy, crooked A-shape. At home, from my stilted house, those star-shapes were familiar guideposts. Out here, sixty miles at sea, they seemed gaseous and foreign, insensible with their vacuum chill.

I continued to stare into space, drying myself, and then I stopped, as I was drying my hair, surprised to hear a polite clearing of the throat behind me. I turned, still scrubbing away, to see JoAnn standing in the companionway. There wasn't enough light to decipher her expression, but there was a weary, weary smile in her voice, as she said, "Leave it to you to find a way to get my mind on something else. Out for a late-night swim, were we?"

I wrapped the towel around my waist as I told her, "I had to know. I had to find out for myself what it was like for Janet and the other two." In the moment of my speaking, it seemed irreverent to leave Janet's companions nameless, bodiless, so I added, "Michael Sanford and the other woman, Grace Walker. All three. So I got in the water."

JoAnn stepped over to me and laced the fingers of her right hand into mine, palm up, and gave me a shake of mild reproach. "Don't do that, Doc. Don't try anything like that ever again, not at night, not unless you tell us! I couldn't bear it if you disappeared out here, too. Christ, I always thought I loved the Gulf, but I'm coming to despise it. It scares the hell out of me like it never did before."

JoAnn has a flexible, expressive voice, and it stumbled a little as she then asked a question that she wasn't certain she wanted answered. "So how was it once you got away from the boat? In the water at night, I mean. God, I *can't* imagine."

I told her, "It's colder than I thought. That surprised me, but it's a good thing for us all to know, so I'm glad I used myself as a guinea pig. After getting in there, I'm convinced that in the first hours after their boat sank, they were probably still in pretty good spirits — you know, confident they were going to be rescued at dawn. Then sometime the next day, they just drifted off to sleep, one by one. It was so gradual, they probably didn't even realize what was happening."

I was wrong, so very, very wrong — but it was an unintentional lie, an attempted kindness.

I felt JoAnn squeeze my hand. "Thanks. No wonder you've never married. You're such a terrible liar, no woman could depend on you to lie when she needed a little ego boost."

Then, as she pulled herself closer, she added, "Rhonda sent me to ask you. We talked about it. After what happened to Janet, after being in this freaking wind for

66

six days, all the polite little rules and laws; all the social-moral crap about how we're supposed to behave, and what we're supposed to do and not supposed to do, it . . . *everything* just seems like a bunch of bullshit. I mean, this makes all our silly little worries seemed stupid. We're alive! And we're alive for such a short time, why not have fun? Why not be with the people you care about and make them feel great?"

She was bouncing around, not tracking clearly. I said, "Well . . . sure, very short lives. Yeah, I guess."

Her voice took on a small, rueful quality. "Does what I'm saying make any sense? Or am I just making an ass of myself because of what I'm asking?" She was stammering now. Standing there in her thin white T-shirt in the chill wind, brown hair tinted amber in the moonlight, oddly embarrassed.

I said, "No, I have no idea what you're getting at. Rhonda sent you to ask me *what?*"

She tapped fingers to her forehead. "You mean I didn't say it? Jeez, my brain really is scrambled. Turns out she gave Jeth two Valiums, and he's out like a light, the poor babe. So Rhonda and I want you to come down . . . to, well, basically to hang out with us."

I chuckled, pulled her to me, and kissed her on the top of the head. "Know what? Our little hugging session actually did make me feel better so, yeah, I'll come down to say good night. Give me a minute to get some dry shorts on and a T-shirt."

She touched her fingers to my shoulder, stopping me as I turned away. She stood there looking up at me in the moonlight — a friend I'd known so long and so intimately that I no longer saw the features of her face, only the warmth of her expression. "Don't make this hard on me, Doc. What I'm telling you is, you don't need your shorts or your shirt. Come just the way you are."

I said, "JoAnn? Are you asking . . . wait a *minute,* do you mean — ?"

She said, "Yeah, ol' buddy. That's exactly what we mean."

I stood there, mouth agape, until she took my elbow and tugged.

"We've got wine," she said.

Chapter Four

Florida has the population of a fair-sized nation, and the disappearance of three people grabbed some quick headlines. But, very soon, it was business as usual on what Tomlinson once described as the "Disney Peninsula — a multitonomous fantasy that features every brilliance of the racial rainbow, along with every human fakery and illusion."

The media wave peaked with interest momentarily but then flooded away just as fast, once again indifferent to the fact that three people had lived and died.

Physically and metaphorically, Janet and her companions had been swept out of sight, and the news gatherers went on to more current matters: On Thanksgiving Day in Miami's Liberty City, members of a ghetto gang called the Spliffs stopped four Canadians in a rental car and shot them to death because the Canadians had made the outrageous mistake of taking the wrong exit off Interstate 95, and then onto the gang's neighborhood street.

In the gorgeous country town of Arcadia, a Brahma bull busted out of its loading ramp and gored three rodeo fans as they walked to their cars, but the fans refused the entreaties of clamoring personal injury attorneys to sue. As one fan told a reporter from the *St. Petersburg Times,* "Rodeo'n's risky business whether you're in the ring or in the stands. That's the way we like it."

And on the main sawgrass plain of the Everglades, immigration police arrested forty-seven illegal aliens of various nationalities who'd been jettisoned off the uninhabited Ten Thousand Islands and left to wade ashore by flesh merchants who'd smuggled them into U.S. waters from Colombia. The illegals were dehydrated, cut all to hell by the coral rock that lies at the base of the sawgrass, and starving. In the November heat, many days without good water, it became a death march of sorts. Three of the weakest fell and were left to the vultures. Another died shortly after being hospitalized. One of the survivors, though, was quoted as saying, "Why did I risk my life to come to America? Because here I can live as a person, as an individual with dignity, not as a beast of burden. I am a woman, not a thing!"

It was the sort of story that gave one hope.

The effects of the *Seminole Wind* tragedy did not fade nearly so quickly on the islands of Sanibel and Captiva nor on the islands and water places that comprise a back bay community that is separate from the rest of Florida's Gulf Coast communities. Talk of the three missing divers continued to be the main topic of conversation on Cedar Key, Siesta Key, and Venice Beach, on Don Pedro, Palm Island, and Gasparilla, on Cabbage Key, Useppa, and Estero Island, on Vanderbilt Beach, Bonita Beach, and among the boating community of Naples, too.

The refrain was familiar: How was it possible that three adults in wet suits and inflated vests were not found? It just didn't make sense.

At Dinkin's Bay Marina and Jensen's Marina, the pain was palpable, so much so that our communal Thanksgiving dinner was more like a wake. Which is why, two weeks later at Dinkin's Bay Marina's traditional Friday party — the Pig Roast and

Beer Cotillion, as it is called — Dieter Rasmussen, the German psychopharmacologist, herded us over to the big sea grape tree near the boat ramp and gave us an unrehearsed lecture on what might have been titled, "Dah Five Stages of Mourning When Vee Haf Lost a Loved Vun, Yah!"

Dieter is a wealthy German who loves the lazy, kicked-back lifestyle of Dinkin's Bay, but he is also an internationally respected physician who's an expert on human behavior and the chemistry of the brain. There were about fifteen of us, beers in hand, platters of steamed shrimp and fried conch on the picnic tables nearby, and at the center of our little group was Jeth. Jeth with the Cherokee black hair and Beverly Hillbillies accent, wearing filthy khaki fishing shorts and shirt, a plastic cup in his hand that we all knew was filled with vodka plus a little fresh grapefruit juice from the grapefruit tree behind the shell shop. Jeth, who'd once had a mild stutter, but who had not stuttered once since Janet's disappearance. Not that he'd said much at all after our little fleet returned from Marco Island. He was sleeping too late, not bathing, and drinking way, way too much. Lots of red flags.

Standing while the rest of us sat, Dieter

spoke in a guttural, booming Teutonic accent and used sweeping arm gestures. He outlined the list — numbness, yearning, and disbelief, then disorganization and denial, before anger kicked in. Then came the final stage, which was the beginning of the healing process.

Jeth, I was not surprised to realize, was displaying all the symptomatic stages except for the last.

He was not healing, nor did he seem to have much interest in allowing himself to heal. Janet was dead because he'd insisted that they date other people. She'd been with Michael Sanford on that Friday dive trip because Jeth had refused Janet's pleas that the two of them go away for the weekend and attempt to sort out their problems.

That was the way he saw it, anyway, and why he was clearly punishing himself.

I listened to Dieter say, "Emotional numbness, if unresolved, can impair a person's ability to be deeply intimate or to interact with people and situations in a spontaneous manner. In other words, my friends, you will not haf fun anymore! In fact, you will be the pain in my ass, and we have enough pains in my ass on this island!"

We all laughed. Everyone except Jeth, who yawned, took a gulp of his vodka, and watched a pelican collapse its wings in mid-flight and crash like a crate into the bay.

As Dieter talked about the second and third stages of mourning — deep yearning, disbelief, and then denial — I noticed a green Jeep Cherokee pull into the shell parking lot and a lean, leggy redhead get out. It was Amelia Gardner. I recognized her from photos I'd seen in the newspaper and from television, too. For the brief period in which the disappearances got a lot of press, she, as the lone survivor, was the center of attention — Gardner and the families of the three people who'd vanished. As a group, they'd held press conferences and commented jointly on what they believe happened to the pleasure boat *Seminole Wind* and had issued occasional opinions on the job the Coast Guard had done.

Their comments about the Coast Guard's efforts were always positive, and deservedly so, yet their group hadn't wanted the search to end when Dalton Dorsey and his superiors pulled the plug. I didn't blame the families. Even if the three were dead — and there seemed no other possibility — their loved ones wanted the remains found because they desperately wanted and deserved closure.

As Dalton told me on the phone, "I don't blame them one tiny little bit. But we're in the business of saving lives, not recovering bodies. People don't realize, you get out there in international waters, beyond the twelve-mile limit, there's only so much help you can expect."

Janet's representative family consisted of a younger sister, Claudia Kohlerberg, who was a stockier, more athletic version of Janet. She'd traveled down from an Ohio farm town called Bryan, returned home two days after the search was ended, and now was back again to see to Janet's personal effects. She'd been staying on the little blue houseboat at Jensen's Marina: a nice woman with a strong smile and a jock-like informality, but who clearly showed the pain of her sister's disappearance. There was a familial similarity both in appearance and depth of sensitivity, but Claudia did not give the impression of shyness, as Janet had. I had the feeling that, under happier circumstances, Claudia would have been the rowdy partier and the sisterly confidant of a long list of guy friends.

Claudia seemed to like Dinkin's Bay,

and we all liked her.

I wasn't the only who recognized Amelia Gardner. Tomlinson and Ransom — who'd apparently hammered out a separate peace during their six days at sea — stood and walked toward the parking lot to intercept her. Dieter was saying, "When we lose someone we love, there is a deep yearning for what was lost followed by a desperate search for a way to replace that person.

"This can be a very dangerous time! We blame ourselves. We say, 'If only I'd done something *different*.' We have many regrets. Then we do a very human but stupid thing. We rush into bad rebound relationships. We try to replace the person with alcohol or drugs. During this period, we feel we have a hole inside ourselves that cannot be filled, a thirst that cannot be quenched."

I watched Tomlinson and Ransom introduce themselves to Amelia Gardner. Watched her nod as Ransom gestured to our little group, then as she leaned into her car and retrieved a small backpack, then walked with an easy-hipped grace across the white shell.

She was a wearing a red tank top, khaki shorts with starched pleats, and thin sandals. A woman as tall as Ransom, but flat-chested, with pale Irish skin, freckles, and curly red hair clipped boyishly short. The bright red of her tank top made her hair the color of old copper. Take one look at her and you assumed certain things from her appearance, the muscle tone, and the way she carried herself: She probably had green eyes, didn't tan, was a high school athlete, maybe competed in college, too. Good at endurance sports, almost anything outdoors, and had inherited a family passion for St. Patrick's Day through her father, whom she probably adored. Not unusual among women athletes.

There was something else I knew about her, even though we'd never met: Amelia Gardner was a survivor. On a black and windy night, out of four desperate people, she was the only one who'd made it to the light tower.

Dieter finished by talking about "free-floating" anger that seeks physical relief and how, if we dealt honestly with our emotions and recognized them for what they were — symptoms of loss — it would enable us to pull wisdom and meaning from pain. "It will deepen and strengthen our relationship with ourselves and increase our resilience in living. That is

Janet's gift to us, but we must choose to accept her gift."

Jeth, at least, seemed to hear that. I saw him sit a little straighter, listening.

Then it was Tomlinson's turn, just as we planned. He stood and tugged at his ratty, gold paisley surfer's shorts, his sun-bleached hair hanging long, and stood scratching at his goatee until he had everyone's attention. Then he held up his hands for quiet and said, "The party's gonna be a little different tonight. The rules are the same — you put ten bucks in the bucket, then eat and drink all you want. But one thing everyone needs to know. This party's going to be in Janet's honor. We are going to celebrate the life of our sister, that good, good woman, and it is going to be one hell of a party!"

A couple of people hooted and there was gradual applause, then louder applause.

Tomlinson raised his voice a little. "I already talked to Claudia about it. It's time to stop feeling bad about Janet being gone and start talking about what a great life she had. About what she contributed to the lives of us all. Man, I miss her! Damn right I do! Janet Mueller was a spiritual horse. There was no load so heavy that it took the light out of her eyes. She had energy, my children, a great karma, and here's what I can tell you: Energy *can't* be destroyed. That's a fact of physics. Janet may have taken a different form, but her energy's still here."

I'd heard Tomlinson make this point before. In fact, after trailering my skiff when we'd returned to Marco Island, I'd stopped at the island's tiny cemetery where, awhile back, he'd once spoken very similar words at the funeral of a young girl. The child's second funeral. Exhausted from my days at sea, I'd sat for nearly an hour alone, next to the girl's headstone, before starting the long trip back to Sanibel.

Now Tomlinson said, "Janet's still with us and loving us and looking over us. Which is why we are gonna party our asses off tonight. Just to get things warmed up, I here and now challenge Doc's sister, Ransom Gatrell, to a limbo contest. And, ladies? I'll be wearing a brand new sarong, a hand-painted Cartier from New Orleans, so get your seats early. Zamboni and the Hat Trick Twins are back in fighting shape and ready to *rumble*."

My friend continued, "I want to send out a special invitation to all the waitresses at Mucky Duck, Green Flash, Chadwick's, and Sanibel Grill. As always, there will be a topless division. For the last seven years, that very popular division has been won by the Davis sisters from Mason City, Iowa, Andrea and Kristin, and God bless their family genetics. But one of the sisters has gotten married, so Andrea is at half strength. Ladies, the time to strike is *now*."

I noticed Jeth drop his head, shaking it, maybe laughing, maybe fighting back tears, I couldn't tell. Saw Amelia Gardner smile as everyone hooted and applauded. I also saw Gardner turn suddenly, scanning the little crowd until her eyes found me. Then she stopped, as if she recognized me, before returning her attention to Tomlinson, who was using his hands to call for silence.

"One last thing," he said. "Day after tomorrow, Sunday morning, here at the marina, we're going to hold a service for Janet. I talked to Claudia about this, too. It's time to say good-bye, my children. It's time for some closure. We can shed all the tears we want on Sunday. We can bawl like babies, but tonight, damn it, tonight we are going to kick a little cosmic ass. Tonight we're gonna live the hell out of every single, drunken moment, and love each other like the family we are!"

When he said that, I found my eyes turning involuntarily to my left where

JoAnn and lanky Rhonda sat side by side on a picnic table. I saw, to our mutual amusement, that their eyes had swung automatically toward me. I nodded at Rhonda's smile but pretended not to see JoAnn's bawdy wink.

I did notice that Gardner was moving in my direction, but gradually, as if she didn't want to divert attention from Tomlinson.

As Tomlinson said, "There's a very powerful woman I need to introduce right now," Gardner stopped walking, giving me a brief, pointed look that maybe meant something, maybe didn't. Then she waited as he continued, "We didn't expect her, but the timing couldn't be better. We all know the story. Four people were set adrift, and only one of them made it to the light tower. If you think we've been through hell, imagine what she went through. That woman's here right now. She came here because she wants to talk to the people who care about Janet and answer our questions.

"Out in the parking lot, she told Ransom and me that she's made it a point to go to all of the families, one by one, and try to clear up any misunderstandings. We're Janet's family, and I think we all know what the lady means. That's why I de-

81

scribed her as a powerful woman. I watched her get out of her car in the parking lot a few minutes ago, and she had an aura so bright it damn near hurt my eyes. She's got a strong and caring heart, so let's welcome Amelia Gardner to Dinkin's Bay."

He nodded to Gardner, who was smiling, but not giving it much, keeping herself within herself, as people applauded politely. "Amelia, you mind if we adjourn to the main docks? We'll do it any way you want it, but I suggest you grab a beer, get some food, relax, and make yourself at home. Then you can talk to us as a group, if that suits you. Afterward, you're welcome to stick around and drink heavily with the rest of us. But I warn you — you may never be the same woman after you see the limbo contest."

Gardner's laughter had a jazz singer's rasp, and her voice was a foggy alto that did not mesh, at first, with her Boston accent. She was articulate and polite, and seemed slightly nervous speaking to a group of strangers, which was understandable. "The only favor I ask," she said, "is that you don't hold anything back. I want to answer all your questions. I want to set the record straight as best I can. I don't care what rumor you've heard, no matter how outrageous, I want to address it.

"There's a thing called 'survivor's guilt,' and I know I've got a bad case of it. This is my way of trying to help all of us. So, you bet, I'd love a beer. I'll meet you over on the docks."

A couple minutes later, as I walked alone across the shell parking lot, toward the mangrove path that leads to my house, I was surprised when Gardner came up behind me and said, "You're not leaving, are you?" Then, when I stopped and turned to face her, she added, "You're Ford, right? Dr. Marion Ford?" Her tone was business-like, formal, and confident.

I said, "That's right. How'd you know?"

"Dalton Dorsey described you. From Coast Guard St. Petersburg? I'd like to speak with you privately, Dr. Ford, after I've talked to the group. Commander Dalton said you'd be the perfect person."

"The perfect person for what?"

"I want someone to help me find out why that boat sank. Every single little detail, so I can make it public." She dropped the formality then, the tone of her voice communicating pain, as she added, "The rumors are killing me, Dr. Ford. I don't know what makes people so mean that they're saying these kind of things, but none of it's true. I didn't know the other three people very well, but those poor souls aren't even here to defend themselves, which is absolutely infuriating."

"That's understandable," I said. "Some of the stuff floating around is pretty silly."

"I'm an attorney. I know that the best way to fight a lie is with the truth. I've met my share of private investigators, but I've never met one who was qualified or equipped to do the kind of research it's going to take to find the real facts and make them public. Commander Dorsey told me that you might be just the guy."

I said, "That's a compliment. Dalton's a good man."

"I like him, too. Very professional, plus, my guess is, he's got a little circus going on inside him, which I tend to like in people. When he told me about you, first thing I did was look you up on the Internet. No web page — which I found surprising — but you've published a lot in journals, and enough of your fellow scientists have quoted your work, so there was plenty to find."

"I had no idea," I told her. "Awhile back, I had an interest in the Internet. I still use

it, but just for research. So I haven't bothered to check out what's on there about
me."

She was nodding, pleased to be sharing
information. "The thing I like is, you're
not attached to any agency. No government funding. You do your own work in
your own way, and you obviously know
your way around boats and the water. So
I'm inviting you to help me figure out what
the hell went wrong out there. Your
opinion would carry a lot of weight with
people who live along this coast, and the
media, too. I want my reputation back, Dr.
Ford, it's as simple as that."

I looked into her face. The late winter
sun burnished her skin with a klieg-light
gold. In that harsh, parchment light, I
could see how she would age; how she
would look in ten, twenty, even thirty
years. Amelia Gardner was not pretty. She
had never been pretty. But she possessed a
handsome, prairie-woman's plainness that
is uniquely American, and that I, person-
ally, find far more attractive than the predictable, painted masks of film stars and
beauty queens.

Hers was a good face with a strong jaw,
eyebrows darker than her red hair, full pale
lips, no makeup at all, and a corn-silk

down that grew below her temples. There were a few pores visible, and a faint acne scar or two that implied a difficult adolescence. She was an outdoors person with horizontal sun wrinkles on her forehead and at the corners of her eyes; the tennis-player, mountain-bike type who was also a professional. She had a sloping nose shaped like a ski jump and, yes, cat-green eyes. In that brilliant light, her eyes glowed as if illuminated from within, showing little specks of blue and bronze.

I said to her, "I'd like to help, but I've got a job, Ms. Gardner. The one person who I could trust to take care of my lab, Janet Mueller, is gone now. I'm sorry."

I was surprised when she reached and put her hand on my shoulder, a fraternal gesture not often used by women, particularly women strangers. "I want you to think it over. Listen to what I have to say about what happened three weeks ago, then talk to me later. I'll stay as late as you want. The thing is —"

I said, "What?"

She had her arms folded now, looking at me, and, from her expression, I knew she was trying to decipher the most productive approach for the brand of person she was dealing with — me. How was I best handled? What would be the fastest, most effective angle? It is an increasingly common phenomenon, a calculated brand of assessment and manipulation that may well be taught in business and law schools, yet I find it offensive.

Finally she said, "I have to follow my instincts. So here it is: There's something I want to tell you, but you have to promise me not to tell the others. You'll understand why later. If you promise, I'll take you at your word. I don't meet many stand-up guys these days, but maybe you're one of the few."

"Stand-up guy, huh?" I didn't say it, but I assumed that what she had to say had something to do with her behavior after the sinking, some guilty secret, a burden she now needed to share.

She seemed surprised by my tone. "Is there something wrong with me thinking you're trustworthy?"

"We just met."

"Like I said, I'm going on instinct."

I was shaking my head. "Sorry, Ms. Gardner. I've known the people at this marina much, much longer than I've known you. I respect what you did that night, but talking to me privately is the same as speaking to the entire group. If there's some secret you want to share or maybe even confess, I suggest you contact a priest. But please don't tell me."

I could see that it irked her that I'd correctly deduced her religion, and she was clearly annoyed that I was questioning her intent. A friend once told me that newborn redheads ought to by law come with a warning tag on their toe.

Amelia Gardner had a temper. I saw her face flush, her eyes glitter, as she lowered her voice to say, "First of all, pal, I don't need some oversized, sun-bleached nerd with Coke-bottle glasses to tell me when to see my priest. And second, I've got nothing to confess. I'm going to tell you anyway, and if you want to risk hurting Janet's friends, go right ahead. But I will not play some little role you've dreamed up."

She took half a step toward me, an aggressive move, hands set on broad hips, her nose not much lower than mine, as she added, "This is it: I can't prove it, but I think there was another boat out there that night. Early that morning. A boat without lights. I saw it. I'm sure I saw it. And I think it may have stopped.

"Commander Dorsey says I was probably imagining things, but I know what happened, I was there. I think it's possible that they got picked up, Janet and the others. Why else didn't we find them? What I'm telling you, Mister Doctor Marion Ford, is that I think there's a chance, a very slim chance, they might be alive." Then she spun and stalked away, pissed off, demonstrating it by refusing even a chance of additional eye contact.

I stood there, watching her, and gave a private little whistle.

Tomlinson was right. A powerful woman.

I went to my house to change shirts before rejoining the party, reviewing Amelia Gardner's words as I walked, her nuances of speech, wondering if she really might have seen a boat. Was it possible?

The woman was still much on my mind when I peeked into my lab and flicked on the lights. My pattern of thought shifted instantly. Aloud, I said, "What in the hell is going on in here?"

Two more stone crabs were missing. I'm so familiar with my stock that I knew right away. The heavy glass lid was on the tank, but the little metal vise I'd used to seal it fast lay on the lab's wooden floor, in a streak of water. I stooped and touched my finger to the tiniest fleck of crab shell in the water.

Someone *was* sneaking in and stealing my specimens. Someone too sloppy or hurried to replace the vise. Who and why, I couldn't fathom.

But my eight remaining octopi were still in their covered tanks. That, at least, was a relief. As I checked them, I sensed the solitary, golden eye of the largest Atlantic octopus tracking me from beneath its rock ledge. Its extended tentacle was still throbbing gray, pink, and brown as I switched off the light and locked the door.

Chapter Five

Before we met, as a group, and listened to
Amelia Gardner's story, we made the sunset
rounds in a marina caravan that increased
the number of partygoers with each stop.

There wasn't much doubt why. Word
was out that the lone survivor was with us.
Everyone on the islands wanted to hear
what happened from Gardner's own
mouth.

We stopped at Jensen's Marina for
Claudia to join us. Seeing her come out
the door of Janet's little blue *Holiday Mansion*, with its curtained pilothouse windows, gave us all an emotional jolt. It
wasn't just the family resemblance, though
that was part of it. It was the fact that
Claudia was wearing a pale, peach-colored
beach dress and makeup, and she had a
bright red hibiscus bloom fixed behind her
right ear.

It was exactly the sort of outfit that Janet typically wore to our Friday parties.

I was standing beside Jeth when Claudia made her entrance. I heard him whisper, "Jesus Christ, that's almost too much to handle."

I patted him on the back. "Nothing's too much. That's one of the things Janet taught us."

We stopped at McCarthy's Marina and boarded the *Lady Chadwick* for drinks, then we mobbed our way to the Green Flash, and then the Mucky Duck for sunset on the beach. Milled around swapping stories with Pat and Memo at the bar, listening to John Paul on the guitar before returning to Dinkin's Bay.

The entire time, I noticed that Gardner kept her distance from me, still mad, apparently. Ransom, though, she liked. The two women fast became a pair.

Once, passing behind them, I paused to listen as Ransom, speaking in her musical Bahamian accent, told her "Amelia, darlin'. Let me tell you something 'bout these nice titties ah' mine. They changed my womanly life, they surely did, and don't let no man tell you he doan care about your boobies. A woman deserve to look how she want to look, my sister! Yes sir! I reckon they cost me four, maybe five, blow jobs apiece, and that cheap, girl! Very cheap! I were kind'a sweet on that lil' doctor man anyway. I'd a' made him feel good for free, no problem!"

I liked Gardner's unembarrassed laughter — then she noticed me. She said to Ransom, "This big goon really is your brother?"

"Oh yes, oh yes, he one of the very few white ones in our family. He can be kind'a mulish sometimes when it come to women, but he good. Doan you doubt that. My brother, he a good man."

Long after sunset, several dozen of us sat quietly listening to Amelia Gardner. She was sitting cross-legged atop one of the picnic tables, behind Dinkin's Bay's Red Pelican Gift Shop, facing the docks. Sitting to her left was Claudia. Ransom to her right.

The windy, high pressure system that had made our search so exhausting was gone now, replaced by a balmy, tropical low. Through the coconut palms, beyond the yellow windows of my house and lab, I could see drifting clouds and oily star paths on black water. Woodring's Point and the mouth of Dinkin's Bay were a charcoal hedge of mangroves two miles north.

It was a very warm night for late November. Even so, Gardner had gone to her Jeep for a jacket, as if affected by memories of the cold that night three weeks earlier. It wasn't easy for her to talk about it. There was no mistaking the emotion in her voice, and I admired the way she fought her way through it.

I was holding a plastic cup of beer poured over ice, plus a wedge of squeezed lime, and I took a sip now, as she said, "I met Michael Sanford and Grace Walker when I was in the Keys, then again at a dive club party on Siesta Key. You guys ever eat at the old mullet restaurant there? That's where the party was. They were with a woman by the name of Sherry Meyer, who was supposed to dive the *Baja California* with us. Lucky for her, though, she had a cold and didn't make the trip. I wish to hell we'd all had colds that day —" She touched her hand to Claudia's arm as she said that; Claudia patted Gardner's hand in return. "But I guess destiny has its reasons and there's no going back now. Janet was a friend of Michael's, and I didn't meet her until I got to Marco. He'd rented a three-bedroom condo — him in

94

one room, we four women in the other two — and we went to bed early Thursday night so we could get up early Friday."

Because I'd seen still shots of them in the newspapers and on television, I had a fixed mental image of both Sanford and Grace Walker, and impressions of both of them that may or may not have been valid. Michael Sanford could have been a fashion model — six foot four or so, probably 220 pounds, with the jaw, the dimpled chin, and dense, curly black hair that photographs well. Walker was his female, African-American counterpart — busty with makeup and lots of jewelry, a business-woman in her thirties who was making money and fighting for causes in which she believed. They both knew how to look into the lens of a camera and smile.

Gardner told us that the four of them had left Marco River Marina in Sanford's twenty-five-foot boat at around 8 a.m. and were headed out Big Marco Pass when Sanford noticed that one of his 225-horse-power Johnsons was overheating. They returned to the marina and had a mechanic switch out a thermostat, which solved the problem.

"Michael bought a second thermostat just in case," she said. "I suppose most of you've heard the rumors that Michael — maybe all of us — ran offshore and sank the boat intentionally for the insurance money. Well, check with the marina. Why would he have bought a second thermostat if he'd planned on sinking his own boat? Why would he have bought a second thermostat if we'd planned on rendezvousing with a drug boat, sinking the *Seminole Wind*, and escaping? That's another theory you've probably heard."

Around me, I could see the island fishing guides — eight of them, sitting in their own little group — thinking about it, nodding their heads. Yeah, it didn't make any sense. If you were going to sabotage your own vessel, you might buy new canvas or pay for a new paint job, just to make it convincing. But a backup thermostat? Very unlikely.

Gardner, an attorney, was already doing a good job of making her case.

On their way offshore, the four divers stopped at a wreck called *Ben's Barge*, which is about three miles off Marco. Sanford, a fisherman, wanted to catch some bait so the four of them could fish the *Baja California* after diving it.

Using tiny hooks and bits of shrimp,

they filled the stern's bait well with small bluegill-shaped fish called pinfish.

"While we caught bait, we discussed what we wanted to do," Gardner told us. "We were listening to the weather channel on the radio, and Michael told us it wouldn't be real nice out there, but it should be okay. A couple days ago, I had got my hands on the actual forecast from NOAA. It was 'small craft should exercise caution, wind out of the east southeast, fifteen to twenty knots, seas four to six feet, with bay and inland waters choppy.' "

She saw the guides react, and said, "I know, I know. We shouldn't have gone. The temptation is to put the blame on Michael. It was his boat, he'd made the dive several times. But that's bullshit. We were all adults, all certified divers, and we all agreed. We wanted to dive the *Baja California*, and, because we were still close to Marco Island, I guess we figured we would be protected from an east wind. It seemed fairly calm three miles out. What I didn't know at the time was that you don't measure a wave from its trough. You measure it from sea level. So, when we were anchored on *Ben's Barge*, I thought the two-foot waves we were seeing were actually four to six feet high. That changed pretty quickly."

Amelia said the seas were considerably worse once they were fifty-two nautical miles offshore and reached the Global Positioning System numbers (GPS) that marked the wreck, but the waves still didn't seem overwhelming. She remembered Michael Sanford telling the group that it sometimes took him three or four times to get the boat anchored just right, but on that Friday, he dropped the anchor, fed out line, and nailed it first try.

"We could see the wreck on the screen of his electronic bottom recorder," she said. "The bottom was flat, then all of a sudden there was this long geometric shape jutting up. It looked like a small, flat mountain. Michael explained to us that the little floating shapes we saw above the wreck were fish. There were fish all over it. Like a cloud. Because of that, we decided to fish first, then dive."

Once again, the guides began to shake their heads. It was not a wise thing to do. Hooked fish send out stress vibrations. Stress vibrations attract predators. Why attract predators before getting into the water?

Amelia said, "We fished for maybe an hour. You know how barracuda will crash a live bait right by the boat? The girls had fun with that. But it was getting a little rougher out and Grace started to feel sick, so we decided to gear up and get into the water because we thought she'd feel better then."

Gardner said that she paired up with Janet, and Sanford paired with Walker because she and Sanford were the two most experienced divers. "Plus I really liked Janet," she said. "We hit it off the first time we met. She is . . . Janet *was* the sort of woman you know you can trust after just talking to her for a few minutes. With her, there wasn't going to be any of that catty crap that so many men and women pull. No bitching, no whining. Right away, just being with her a couple of days, I was thinking that the two of us could start doing some dive trips together. Maybe some of you know, but good dive partners are hard to find. Especially women divers, the independent types willing to do some traveling."

Before they got in the water, according to Gardner, Sanford told them that one of the rules of diving is that you never go off and leave a boat unattended. But, because the *Baja California* was so deep — it was in 110 feet of water — the divers would only have about fifteen minutes of bottom time, so maybe it was actually safer for them all to go at once. It might be wiser to have four divers together on that deep wreck than go in two isolated sets.

"It's not like Michael called for a vote or anything," Amelia said. "But nobody stood up and said, 'Hey, absolutely not. Someone has to stay in the boat.' I've seen other divers go off and leave their boats lots of times, and, the sad thing is, it was the first time I'd ever been with a group who did it.

"We were fifty miles offshore, there weren't any other boats around, and I, or Janet, or Grace, should have put a foot down. It wasn't just Michael's fault. We all screwed up. But that mistake we made . . ." Amelia laced her fingers together and bowed her head slightly. "That mistake, leaving the boat alone, it's when things really started to go south. We had the dive flag up and it never entered our minds that, in fifteen minutes, so much could go wrong."

The four entered the water together, but when they got to a depth of about thirty feet, Grace Walker indicated that she was having trouble equalizing the pressure in her ears. "We followed Michael and Grace up to ten feet or so and waited until she decided to try it again. But Grace's ears were still hurting her, I could tell. Michael indicated that he and Grace were going to return to the boat, and I signaled 'okay.' Janet and I watched them go to the surface, then we continued our dive."

Gardner told us that she and Janet spent approximately thirteen minutes on the wreck, then started back up. When they were fifteen feet from the surface, they made a safety decompression stop of about three minutes. Then they surfaced. Gardner said she was shocked by what she saw.

"Only about three feet of the boat's bow was sticking out of the water, and it was capsized. I couldn't believe it. Janet was in shock, too, and we started swimming toward the boat. We couldn't see Michael or Grace, and Janet started yelling out Michael's name. Michael finally answered, but we still couldn't see them because of the waves. The seas were running about four feet now which, as I told you, meant they were eight feet high or so from the trough. When you're out there swimming . . . when you're out there alone in the water, trying to swim, you spend a lot of time in the trough."

I didn't realize how quiet it had become until Amelia paused, then stretched her legs cat-like, giving herself some time, perhaps, to regain emotional control. There was a light breeze drifting out of the mangrove bog from the southwest, carrying the tumid odors of sulfur, tannin, iodine, and salt. The breeze touched the halyards of sailboats, caused a random, indifferent tapping, and carried across the water the *sump*-sound of the pump to my big fish tank.

No one was talking now. There was no fidgeting. All attention was on Amelia Gardner and the words her lips formed, everyone seeing the scene, the slow tragedy of it re-creating itself inside the minds of us all.

She said, "Janet swam straight to the boat while I swam toward Michael's voice. When I got closer, I could see Michael and Grace in the water, drifting away. They both had their BCD vests inflated, with the tanks still attached, but they weren't wearing them; they were using them as floats. They couldn't get back to the boat because they weren't wearing flippers, and the waves were pushing them farther and farther away. It was awful."

Gardner told us that she and Janet swam

to Michael and Grace, grabbed them, and helped the two jettison the tanks from their backpacks and get into their inflated vests. They then swam back to the boat, jettisoned their own weight belts, and hung on to the exposed length of the anchor line that was attached to the bow. There, Amelia said, she checked her watch. It was 3 p.m.

I didn't want to interrupt, but had to. It was an important point. I asked her, "What color was your weight belt?"

She looked at me oddly. "Orange," she said. "Why do you ask?"

I said, "Janet's weight belt was a kind of blue-green. Teal, I guess you'd call it. Were the weight belts found? Did anyone go down and look?"

Now she was nodding, realized the implications. "Weight belts are so heavy, they would have dropped like rocks. If my story's true, they'd be side by side. That's what you're saying. Maybe on top of one another." She paused, still staring at me. "No. No one has gone down to confirm my story."

I knew she was thinking about what we'd discussed earlier, but she didn't say anything about it. Instead, she continued.

"So . . . after we surfaced, and when

things settled down, our first question, of course, was, what happened? Michael said he didn't know. He said that he and Grace climbed up the dive ladder at the back of the boat and took off their vests and fins. Then he went to the front to take off the rest of his stuff. When he looked back, he said he was shocked to see water coming in over the transom where the engines were attached. The salvage divers told me later that, when they found the boat, it was still in gear. What must have happened was, Michael had Grace run the boat while he set the anchor, and she must have switched off the engines while they were still in forward. As most of you know a lot better than me, a boat won't start when it's in gear.

"But that still doesn't explain why the boat was sinking, of course. Michael couldn't figure it out. He talked a lot about that later, when it was dark. He said maybe the bilge pumps weren't working, maybe one of the scuppers got plugged or something. He just didn't know. With water flooding over the transom, he said the boat immediately started to tip sideways. He said it happened so fast, just like that, and that he and Grace jumped overboard. They didn't have time to make a call on the radio, nothing. I remember thinking to myself that, when we were back on land, we'd find out exactly what happened."

As Gardner spoke, I was calculating in my own mind what might have happened. My guess was, the boat was already sinking when they arrived at the *Baja California*. Or, at the very least, already had water in the inner hull. Why else would it have turned turtle after only a few minutes of inattention? If someone had stayed aboard, the results might have been very different.

I listened to Gardner say, in a weary, weary voice, "When we came up, though, and saw that the boat had capsized . . . it was awful. That began the longest night of my life."

The four of them floated there, hanging on to a rope that was connected to the swamped boat, which, in turn, was held fast by several hundred feet of anchor line. The wind had picked up even more, and the waves, Amelia said, seemed a lot bigger than they had that morning.

Their plan was simple because they had no alternatives: to hang on to the rope, stay close to the boat, and wait for the Coast Guard to come and get them. Back on Marco, Sherry Meyer knew where they planned to dive and was expecting them back in time for dinner. She'd figure out soon enough that something was wrong and call for help.

For the next four hours, Gardner told us, she and her three companions floated on their backs alongside the boat, staying close to one another to keep warm. They tied an orange life jacket and a white bumper to the end of the rope, and Walker looped the rope into her flotation vest. The sun set at 5:38 p.m., and the crescent moon set an hour later. It was a black night, with stars hazed by tumbling clouds.

"By the time it got dark, the wind was blowing pretty hard. I was scared like I've never been scared in my life. I was shaking, my whole body was shaking down to the bones. I didn't understand then if it was because of the cold or because I was just so absolutely terrified. I know the others were scared, too. But we kept the conversation light and tried to keep a cool head about everything. It's weird, but when you know everyone's fighting to stay calm, it sort of validates what you're pretending to do. We talked about how this would be a story to tell our grandchildren. Someone said that we'd be best friends all our lives after this."

Claudia hadn't spoken a word, but now she did, and everyone leaned a little to hear her, because she talked in a small, small voice.

"How was my sister? How did Janet react? Did she maybe talk about something that I ought to know about?"

Emotion has a contagious component, and I watched Amelia wrestle to control herself, then gulp back Claudia's tears. I watched her sit there, eyes shining, taking slow, deep breaths before she answered, "She was unbelievable, Claudia. I'm not saying that to make you feel good. I knew her for, what, two days, and I consider her one of the finest people I've ever met, just because of the way she handled herself that night. Janet, Grace, and Michael, they were all good people. I know that especially because . . . well, I'm going to admit something to you. It's something I haven't told the other families. I hired a private investigator to do background checks on them. That's how paranoid I got when I started hearing all the nasty little stories about why we were out there. I wondered if the three strangers I'd met had somehow involved me in something I knew nothing about.

"I'm glad I did, too, because I got confirmation of what I learned about them that night at sea. They were very caring, productive people. They gave a lot and they had a lot more to give. Michael was a high school English teacher. He coached football and did a little modeling on the side. Grace was a Sarasota realtor who was very involved in community projects. Voluntary stuff, like charities. She was a black woman, very proud of her heritage, and she took her commitments seriously. Janet worked here, on Sanibel, for Doc Ford, who, I guess, almost everyone here knows and likes."

Gardner paused to give me a brief, meaningful look when she said that, before continuing, "The point being, just through blind luck, I couldn't have chosen three better people to be adrift with. That night, the way Janet behaved —" Gardner placed her hand on Claudia's arm once again. "She was calm and brave as hell. There was something about your sister, Claudia, a real inner strength that seemed to make us all a little stronger, a little braver.

"When we were floating there, hanging on for our lives, Janet talked a lot about this crazy little marina of yours." Gardner had matched faces with names, and now she looked from person to person to person as she said, "She talked about you, Doc. You were a common topic of conversation. And about Rhonda and Mack, and about you, Jeth. About how you two had your problems but that she loved you and couldn't wait to get back to you, and about how pissed off you were going to be because she'd gone so far offshore in a small boat without you driving. She told us you're a professional captain, right?"

I couldn't bring myself to look at Jeth. He sat off by himself, a silhouetted figure beyond the dock lights. Everyone around me, I noticed, had turned their eyes away, leaving him alone to whatever was going on inside him. He responded, finally, with a muffled, "I'm a guide, yeah."

As Claudia sniffed and touched a finger to her eye, Amelia was shaking her head, close to tears. At last, she said, "After what happened, it didn't seem like it could possibly get worse. But it did. I learned one lesson out there on the Gulf that I'll never forget: On the water, one bad thing leads to another and, once it starts, it happens way too fast to do much of anything to stop it. The momentum, I mean. You're screwed unless you're prepared way in advance. And we weren't. We weren't prepared for anything like what happened next."

★ ★ ★

At 7 p.m. Amelia heard Janet yell, "Hey! Where'd the boat go?" and the anchor line they were holding was ripped from their hands, pulling Grace Walker, who'd tied a life jacket and the anchor line to her vest, under water. The rope pulled Sanford under briefly, too, and he used his dive knife to cut both himself and Walker free.

"He saved her life," Amelia said. "How he managed to react so quickly, I don't know. But he did. I'm aware that a lot of you helped during the Coast Guard search, and you probably heard that someone found a cut line tied to an orange life jacket more than twenty miles southwest of where we started. Well, that's the story behind it. I guess the only reason the boat stayed afloat as long as it did was because some air pockets got trapped in it when it capsized. Once those air pockets were gone, though, it sank like a stone."

So there they were: four people adrift in heavy seas on a November night. At first, there was a general panic among the group. Sanford was yelling, Walker began to cry. But then they got themselves under control once more.

" 'We're going to make it,' Janet kept telling us. She kept saying that we'd make it, we'd all make it, but we had to stick to-gether."

Staying together, though, wasn't easy. Because of the drag of their inflated vests, the waves kept knocking them apart, even when they linked arms to stay together. Worse, because the wind was out of the east, the waves were sweeping them farther and farther from shore. One by one, they began to doubt whether drifting aimlessly was the best thing to do.

"It was Michael's idea to swim to the light tower. He told us he'd fished it before, and he guessed it to be three, maybe four miles inshore of where we were. Out there, it's the only light around. When we were on the top of a wave, it was so bright it was like seeing a camera flash go off. Civilization, that's what it seemed to represent. And safety. So that's what we decided to do. Swim for the tower."

But if drifting as a group was difficult, swimming as a group was even harder. One reason was that Grace and Michael were no longer wearing fins. They'd removed theirs just before the boat capsized. Another reason was that neither Grace nor Janet was a strong swimmer.

"Grace kept saying she didn't think she could make it, and Janet just kept telling her that we had to make it because we didn't have a choice. She told Grace to think about all the weight they were going to lose, burning all those calories. Funny stuff to keep our spirits up.

"So we just plugged along, side by side, with me on one end and Michael on the other, Janet and Grace between us. I don't know how long we swam. But we didn't seem to be getting anywhere. We'd kick toward the light, then a big wave would come out of nowhere and knock us back."

Amelia said it was then that she lost all sense of time. They may have swam for only a few minutes, maybe half an hour.

"I'm sorry," she told us, "that part is all hazy to me. I remember wondering, 'Is this really happening?' Like maybe it was some terrible nightmare. All I could see was that flashing light, and sometimes it seemed like it was a hundred miles away and sometimes it seemed like it flashed right in the middle of my brain. I became completely disoriented. Maybe we all did. But I really started to lose it. I was crying, but not loud, because I didn't want the others to hear. I'd been swallowing a lot of salt water because it was so rough, and I couldn't stop shaking. I knew we were in a lot of trouble. Then something happened to me that I've never felt before."

Amelia Gardner experienced a cerebral gearing-down, like the arcing of a spark, that keyed the most primitive of our instincts, the fight-or-flight response. There was what she described as a tangible "wave" of fear followed by an inability to catch her breath, then overwhelming panic.

"I stopped swimming to try to get myself back under control, and I turned away from the others because I didn't want them to hear me crying. Then there was a big wave, and another big wave. When I turned around, they were gone. All three of them. I heard Janet yelling to me, yelling, 'Don't leave us!' and I could hear Michael calling, too. I swam toward their voices, but they were gone. I couldn't find them. I kept calling, screaming their names. It was black and windy with a lot of big breakers, and I hope I never experience another moment like that in my life. I felt like I'd just fallen over a cliff and there was no way back. That's when I thought I was lost for sure."

Her only hope of finding her friends, and safety, she realized, was to somehow make it to the light tower. So, once again, she turned eastward and started swimming. Once again, though, because of her inflated vest, the waves kept knocking her back. Still terrified and panicked, Amelia Gardner then did a very brave thing — not that she described it to us as brave or gave herself any credit. What she did was take a leap of faith. She decided that she might well die, but she was going to make at least one last and final best effort to find a way to survive. She jettisoned her vest, her only guaranteed way to stay afloat. Then she turned into the waves and began to swim again.

Four hours or so later, she washed into the girder-sized pilings of a 160-foot light tower, far off the Everglades coast of Florida. It took her awhile to locate the service ladder, and then she climbed up onto the tower's lowest deck. "I laid down on the platform just to sort of reassure myself that I'd really made it," she told us. "It was still like some terrible dream. But, after awhile, I got up and started calling for the other three. As the night went on, I kept thinking I heard their voices, heard them calling to me for help. The wind makes strange sounds out there. I kept getting up and calling back, calling their names.

"I expected them to arrive at any minute," she added, once again struggling

114

to keep her emotions in check. She paused, took several slow breaths, before finishing, "They . . . the three of them . . . those three good people . . . they never did show up. I was there alone for another day and another night, and I kept screaming for them, calling their names. But they never answered, they never came."

Tomlinson stood, suddenly, walked to Amelia, and touched his palm to the back of her head as she sat there, face now in her hands, still taking slow, controlled breaths. The woman needed a break. Her voice had gotten softer and softer, as if revisiting that tragic night, the horror of it, was once again leaching the strength out of her. There was no way she could continue to talk without breaking down completely. For reasons I don't understand, the stronger a person is, the more painful it is to watch them founder.

Which is why we were all a little relieved when Tomlinson said, "That's enough for now, Amelia. And thanks for the courage it took and the love it took to come to us and tell us what happened."

He stood there, patting her head, as he then looked to us and said, "This woman's our guest and we need to take good care of her. So here's what I suggest. She can tell us more later, if she feels like it, or maybe tomorrow, if Ransom or the good ladies of the *Satin Doll* can talk her into spending the night with us here at the marina. But I warn you right now, Amelia, stay at Dinkin's Bay tonight, and you're in for an evening of blissful excesses . . ." He smiled at her, his haunted eyes telling her something, offering comfort, perhaps, as he added, "Blissful excess or maybe even some wholesale debauchery. We'll have all the food and drink you can handle."

Right on cue, people hooted and applauded.

That quick, he'd changed the mood. Amelia lifted her face from her hands. He'd earned a little smile.

Chapter Six

Later that night, what started as a typical bar fight nearly escalated into a riot, and, as I told Tomlinson later, we should have both seen it coming and found a way to put a halt to it before it got started.

"How was I supposed to stop anything?" he asked me. "I had a pitcher of margaritas in me, four Singapore slings, three *grande mojitos* made with delicious fresh mint, a six-pack of Corona, plus two joints of very fine Voodoo Surprise. There also may have been pills involved — I remember very distinctly speaking to that lady anesthetist from Englewood. We both know she tends to be overly generous with her recreational pharmaceuticals. No telling what poison that Asiatic brute may have put into my hands. My friend —" he was shaking his head, being serious, "it is impossible for one to impose social order when one is lying facedown, puking, in the sand next to the totem pole at Jensen's Marina."

Then he pointed out: "I do remember that you seemed a little drunk yourself, Marion. That's not something we see in these parts very often, Doc Ford out of control. I don't think you were in a position to stop what happened, either."

Well . . . not out of control, but I did have too much to drink. Tomlinson was right. It's something I rarely do. Alcohol poisoning makes it impossible to do the quiet, articulate work in my lab at night or to enjoy my run or ocean swim the next morning.

But like everyone else at the marina, Amelia's story had ripped the emotional bottom right out of me. I'd believed everything she'd said, which is why in retrospect her confidential assertion to me that a boat might have picked the others up really knocked me off my own personal tracks.

I'd already accepted the fact that Janet was lost. She was dead and gone, and I'd said good-bye to her in my own private way.

Now, though, Amelia Gardner had opened a tiny little corridor of uncertainty and hope. I was so shaken by it that I immediately understood her wisdom when she asked me not to share the information with the others.

There is nothing in life so unsettling or so painful as the unknown.

Alcohol is a favorite analgesic for both.

The traditional Friday parties at Dinkin's Bay are usually relaxed and conversational, with pauses for music and maybe a little dancing. Fifteen or twenty people mingling on the docks, discussing esoterica that would be of interest only to those of us who live on the islands.

This party was different, though. It had a different attitude and a different feel, probably because of the stress we'd all been under — not just because of Janet, but because, for the last many months, we'd all been living with the knowledge that Dinkin's Bay soon might be closed to all powerboat traffic.

If that happened, the feds would come in, rip down the old Florida fish camp that is Dinkin's Bay, and replace it with some sterile, pressure-treated, and poured-to-form clone of the government's idea of a marina. They would equip it with regulation buildings and docks. It seemed unlikely that, on Sanibel, they'd be able to find and hire the breed of seniority-system employees such buildings required, but that was a sad possibility, too.

For one or both reasons, everyone at the marina that night seemed more intimately aware that life is brief and that our interaction with the people and places we love is temporary. Those feelings caused the party to move with a complex intensity and at a much faster pace.

A final contributing factor to the near riot that occurred may have been presaged earlier that day by Dieter Rasmussen, who'd told us that the fourth stage of mourning usually included anger with a potential for violence.

What began as a celebration of a good woman's life later turned very violent indeed.

By the time the limbo contest started, I'd had four or five tumblers of fresh grapefruit juice and vodka and was enjoying myself very much. First time I got a chance, I went up to Amelia Gardner and apologized for apparently suggesting that she had some guilty secret to confess, explaining, "It's not that I was suspicious of you, I just don't know you well enough. When someone asks me to keep something confidential, I need to know who and what

I'm dealing with for a very simply reason — if I give my word, I *will* keep the information confidential."

It seemed to mollify her, put us back on friendly footing again, which pleased me more than I expected. I liked her rangy looks, her private, businesswoman's grin, the way she moved from group to group, socializing comfortably. Liked her plain, handsome face, her Irish hair. Liked the way she stood, hands on hips, one knee bent slightly — a cattle wrangler's stance — and the way her expression narrowed, focusing, when people spoke to her, giving them her absolute attention. She was a person alone among strangers, but one who could take care of herself, no problem.

One thing I was unable to do was get her by herself long enough to ask about the boat she said she'd seen. At one point, I tried, and she touched a finger to her lips very briefly, and said, "Later, okay? I'm going to spend the night with your sister. She said she has a house near here?"

True. Along with her Hewes Bonefisher, Ransom had used the inheritance from her father, Tucker Gatrell, to buy a tiny little bungalow just down from Ralph Woodring's place, off Woodring's Point, near the mouth of Dinkin's Bay. Ralph let her keep the skiff at his dock, so she could run back and forth to the marina anytime she wanted.

"Okay," I told Amelia, pleased that she was staying. "We'll get together late tonight. Or tomorrow, maybe, for breakfast."

The big fight began at Sanibel Grill, moved to the Crow's Nest at 'Tween Waters Inn on Captiva, then spilled out onto the deck of the pool bar, spreading to the little beach that angled into the bay.

It started an hour or so after the limbo contest, which Tomlinson won, though I did not see the finish for the simple reason that I preferred not to watch. When Tomlinson limbos, he wears nothing but his sarong, which is why Mack, Jeth, and I, along with most of the other fishing guides, made it a point to stroll out on the docks and talk among ourselves — unless it was Ransom's turn. Except for me, there wasn't a man at the marina who didn't want to watch her.

Which is why I tend to be overly protective of her, and overly suspicious of any man who shows an interest in her.

There is no denying that Ransom is a stunning-looking woman. I'm not certain of her age. She refuses to confide even in me. With her long, sprinter's legs, dense muscularity, and skin the color and texture of chocolate toffee, she could be thirty-two — or forty-five. No telling. What I do know is that, a few years back, she got tired of being overweight and out of shape and, in her own words, decided to take back her "womanly life." She started working out, watching her diet, and now she is mostly muscle and sinew, but with all the appropriate angles and curves, and she has become my devoted running and weight-lifting partner.

Tomlinson often refers to her as living proof of his own private theory: The world's most beautiful women are always well into their thirties, forties, or fifties because only the experience of living and prevailing day after day can provide the necessary emotional texture and depth of understanding that Tomlinson's definition of "beauty" requires.

Ransom is smart and beautiful and funny, too. But she is no man's toy and no person's fool. So there's something I have to keep reminding myself: My cousin is very capable of taking care of herself.

By the time the limbo contest ended, it

was a little after nine. Still early, so we decided, as a group, to walk along Tarpon Bay Road to Timber's Restaurant, which is just a couple hundred yards from the shell lane that leads to Dinkin's Bay Marina.

In late November, there's a little post-Thanksgiving tourism lull. Even so, the restaurant was busy — people standing in line at the fresh-fish counter — so we pushed tables together at Sanibel Grill, the adjoining sports bar, and sat together, a dozen of us crowded in tight. Nice bar with dark wood, good ventilation with palms outside the windows and a Gulf wind breezing through, orange Converse basketball shoes holding condiments on the tables — yes, basketball shoes — ceiling fans, walls a museum of sports memorabilia and photos of the restaurant's gifted, idiosyncratic owner with a garden variety of famous jocks.

Jeth and I exchanged our empty plastic cups for fresh beer, and he said to me, speaking very softly, "I don't know why, but I feel a lot better after listening to Amelia. It kind of shook me out of my funk about what happened and the way it happened. She talked about me, Doc. Janet, I mean. The night their boat sunk, I was the one she was thinking about."

124

After a long pause, he said, "I miss her like crazy. I never realized what a prize I had until she was gone, but the fact that she told the others about me — the guy I thought she was dating, Michael — the fact that she told him and the two women that she loved me, it makes me feel closer to her than I maybe ever felt before."

He thought about it for another moment, the noise of the bar shielding us from people sitting nearby, and then added, "I believe the story Amelia told us back at the marina. At least, I want to believe her. Or maybe . . . what kind of worries me is, you think she'd make up some of that stuff just to make me feel better?"

I told him, "I think she'd probably stretch the truth to make it easier on us as a group. Sure. But lie just to make you feel better? When they were in the water, unless Janet really talked about you, how else would Amelia know your name, that you and Janet were lovers? No. She wasn't lying. I know Janet . . . I *knew* Janet, and I know how much she cared for you. I don't doubt for a moment that Janet's last words, her last thoughts, were about you."

Jeth was holding a bottle of Bud Light in his big right hand. I watched his fingers fade bloodless, white as he squeezed the bottle, showing the frustration, all the pent-up sorrow and anger in him, seeking release. "I was an idiot," he said, then repeated what he'd already told me many, many times. "She asked me out that weekend. She wanted the two of us to go to Palm Island, rent a beach house there, wanted to talk about our future. So what do I tell her? I tell her I've already got a date, and she should go find a date of her own."

He banged the bottle down on the table, and I could see then that he was drunker than I realized — it was a gesture that was far out of character for this man I knew well.

It was then that JoAnn reached across the table and tapped me on the wrist. "Hey, Doc, you recognize the guy Ransom's talking to?"

Sitting near the end of the table, next to Tomlinson and Claudia, Amelia said, "I do. I recognized him right away."

I followed her eyes to the bar, where Ransom was speaking to a group of three men sitting on stools. Successful professional types dressed in clothes chosen to make a statement about wealth, leisure, style. Chambray and Ralph Lauren, pleated khakis, waxed Topsiders, watch bracelets by Rolex and Tag Heur, something theatrical about the careful, windblown hairstyles of all three. Either actors, politicians, or realtors, I decided — although the best people in those fields wouldn't have pushed the look so hard, made it so obvious. So I wasn't surprised when JoAnn added, "That's Gunnar Camphill. As in *the* Gunnar Camphill. The *film* star."

When I didn't respond immediately, she shook her head, her expression suggesting that I was hopeless, a hermit alien out of touch with the modern world.

Amelia said, "You're kidding me. You don't know the name? The guy's been in only like four or five absolute box-office smashes." She waited for a moment before adding, "You really *don't* know what I'm talking about. I can see it. Know something, Ford? You are an unusual man."

Then Amelia named some titles, a couple of which seemed familiar, but I don't have a television and don't go to movies, so I'd never seen the films. I sat there as JoAnn, still staring at the actor, explained to me, "He does these great action-adventure movies. Lots of car chases, or he'll be like a Navy SEAL trapped on a hijacked airliner, only no one knows who he really is. I read this article. He actually is some kind of martial arts expert, only I don't remember the Japanese name for whatever it is, and he pisses off a lot of people because he's a big political activist. Environmental stuff mostly. He speaks at rallies and led some kind of boycott a couple months back. You know, very outspoken." She paused, smiling. "Damn, he really is good-looking, isn't he? And a lot bigger than I thought. Actors, I've seen a bunch of them, they're almost always a lot shorter than you expect."

Rhonda was listening now, the two women leaning shoulder to shoulder, having fun with it, ogling the film star. Claudia was right there with them. Fresh from Ohio, her first night in the tropics, and here was this movie icon. JoAnn said, "So out of all the women in the bar, who does the famous actor pick out to hit on? Ransom, of course. That sister of yours, Doc, we love her, you surely know that — but, speaking for Rhonda and me, we marina women don't exactly need any more competition."

Beside her, Rhonda laughed, nodding. "We're not getting any younger —" she nudged me with her elbow, then whispered so no one else could hear, "not that we're exactly over the hill. We still got some bounce in us. Which I guess you'd vouch for, huh?"

I smiled — *no comment* — pleased that these two friends of mine were happily starstruck. On the islands, we get a lot of vacationers from films, television, sports, music, and politics, men and women who are famous nationally and internationally. You get used to seeing them at Bailey's General Store, or on the beach, or in the little shops and restaurants. No big deal. People who come to the islands can depend on their privacy being respected. So I was surprised that JoAnn and Rhonda were impressed, and I took it as a measure of the actor's fame.

I was still smiling when JoAnn said, "Maybe we should stroll up to the bar and see if Ransom will introduce us. I've never asked for an autograph in my life, but . . ." which is when I stopped smiling and JoAnn stopped talking because we both saw the actor, Gunnar Camphill, reach out and touch Ransom's arm, saw Ransom pull away. Then we watched Camphill reach again and this time catch her arm and try to pull her to him, but Ransom yanked her elbow back once again and said something to him, her expression cautionary, not yet angry but getting there.

I was pushing my chair back, but Jeth was already on his feet, moving across the bar toward Camphill as the actor held both hands up, palms out to Ransom — he was surrendering — laughing at Ransom, a concessionary posture, but Ransom wasn't smiling back.

I got there just behind Jeth, whose eyes were moving from Camphill to the men at his side, and I heard him say, "What's the problem, this guy giving you a hard ta-ta-tah-time?" Nervous, his stutter had suddenly returned.

As Ransom told us, "This white gentleman getting very, very close to getting his pretty face slapped," one of the men next to Camphill — he was much smaller, with a pointed face and coarse black hair, holding a cigar with the paper ring still on it — said simultaneously, "Jesus Christ, it's Porky Pig to the rescue," meaning Jeth with his cartoon stutter.

That stopped Jeth, changed his expression, an insult so obvious, and he moved a step closer to the man, Ransom backing slightly to his right as he said, "What dah-dah-did you just call me, mister?" angry and drunk enough to punch the guy right there, his stutter getting worse because he was furious.

Then Camphill — large boned, muscular, with blond hair, square chin, tough-guy eyes — stepped in. He stood and moved between Jeth and the bar and said, "Look, my friend, what we'd really like to avoid here is causing a scene. Doesn't that make sense? So what I'm going to ask you to do right now is back off a few steps, give us our space. A little room for us all to breathe, huh? Then here's what I suggest: I will apologize to your nice lady friend for misreading something she said. Entirely my fault. After that, you go back to your table like a good boy, and all of us, we go our separate ways and forget the whole thing."

Jeth didn't step back; he seemed frozen, his fists clenched, staring at the smaller man, hyperventilating, while pointed-face, the man with coarse black hair, sat there sipping his drink, eyes moving lazily around the room, smiling as if Jeth were invisible or too small to see — an insignificant problem, something for the hired help to deal with, nothing at all to worry about.

Camphill's voice had an actor's resonance, and he knew how to make a statement using his body, posing. He was playing a role now, and the role was that of the rational adult, the peacemaker — a person big enough to take all the blame, even though he didn't deserve it — but his hand gestures, the way he held himself, his vocal intonations said: Don't push it, make nice with me right now, or I'll have to change character and do something I don't want to do.

"Did you hear me, my friend? Back off just a little bit. You understand what I'm saying? We're *apologizing*." Camphill reached to touch Jeth's chest — move away, please — but I got my hands on Jeth first, worried that minor physical contact might cause him to snap. I've known the man for years, and I'd never seen him so angry, so close to losing all control. I turned Jeth and moved between him and the bar, my back to Camphill and the others. "Jeth Jeth, listen to me. Let me handle this. Go back to the table, I'll find out what happened."

Behind me, I heard the man with coarse black hair say, "First Gilligan with an Afro Mary Ann, and now the Professor. Where the fuck's Skipper and Ginger?"

Jeth was looking past me. "Hey . . . wait a minute, did that guy just call me

Gilligan? You jerk, I don't look anything like Gilligan!"

"Drop it, Jeth. Let it go." I was herding him gently away from the bar. Behind me, I heard pointed-face say, "Watch out for that razor intellect of his, Gunnar. He's a sharp one, very sharp."

I turned and, over the noise of their laughter, said to Ransom, "What happened? Why'd the guy grab you?"

Camphill said, "I was chatting with the lady —"

Angry myself, and feeling the alcohol in me, I leaned and put my index finger within an inch of the actor's nose. Held it there for a moment before I told him, "I'm talking to *her*. Not you." Stared into his eyes.

It took all the noise out of the bar. I stood and listened to a shuffling of feet, heard someone cough. I expected Camphill to knock my hand away. Instead, he took a huge breath, making a show of controlling himself, letting everyone around know this wasn't easy for him, still playing the peacekeeper's role, as the man to his right — a slim blond tennis player type — said, "He doesn't know who you are, Gunnar. Better drop it. We know in twenty, thirty seconds, you could put him in the hospital, kill him, whatever, but you're the one with the career — not the Professor here."

I lowered my hand slowly, looking at Ransom, who was already talking, her voice easy to hear because the bar had gone so very quiet. "The way it happen, my brother, this pretty gentleman, he start a conversation with me. Very nice at first, then he say he give me two, three hundred dollars, whatever I want, if I come to their hotel and make his friends feel very good tonight. Told me his two friends, they'd never had them a black girl. It so good he wanted them to know what it like.

"I told 'em he and his friends, all three of them, they probably used to trading blow jobs with each other. Or maybe little boys —" Several people at the bar laughed at that. "So why they want to bother a nice colored woman like me?" She was shaking her head, smiling, giving them a dose of her contempt before she added, "That's when this pretty gentleman, he grab me."

I turned once again to the actor, some inner awareness reminding me that I'd had too much to drink, that I needed to be careful, cognitive, keep things cool, so I said, "You're right, mister. You need to apologize to her. *Now.* Then we go our separate ways."

He thought about it, staring at me with his tough-guy eyes, nodding, creating drama because he knew how to do it, and then threw his head back and laughed. "Okay, Professor! I'll blink first!" He stood, took Ransom's hand, bowed at the waist, and kissed the back of her hand regally. "Lovely lady, I was wrong to say what I did. I hope you'll accept my apology."

Then he stood there as if maybe expecting to hear some polite applause, but there wasn't any. Everyone around the crowded bar was staring at him, mostly locals, their expressions saying he was a jerk, maybe they were a little embarrassed for the famous man, too.

Which got to him. I could see it in his expression. So he had to get the last word, contrive a dominant gesture, so he leaned and put his index finger near my nose — payback time — and said loudly, "And you, my friend, you don't know how very, very lucky you are that I'm in a good mood tonight."

Looking into his eyes, I let the words hang there for a moment before I answered softly, "Just for the record — I am *not* your

135

friend." I waited for something to happen, and, when it didn't, I shrugged and turned away.

I thought that was the end of it.

It wasn't.

Because then Gunnar Camphill focused on Jeth's T-shirt. It was a T-shirt that had quickly become popular with Florida's sports fishermen. On the back is a silk-screened cartoon of a dead manatee lashed to a spit, roasting over a fire. Beneath the cartoon are the words: *Any Questions?*

The irony of the T-shirt — and the situation — is that Florida's sports fishermen have, for years, been among the state's most vocal and powerful environmental advocates. Now they were being labeled "antienvironmentalist" by groups pushing to get fishing boats off the water. The long and careful defense required to disprove broad, buckshot accusations, such as "racist" or "communist," is incapacitating — exactly the reason such charges are so commonly made and why they are so effective.

Thus the popularity of this angry T-shirt.

"What the fuck is that?" said Camphill, pointing.

Jeth looked down, looked up, and said, "Yeah, what about it?"

Camphill made a blowing nose with his lips — was this guy really so stupid? "You're kidding. You really don't know why I'm here? SAM — the Save All Manatees group — flew me in for the conference on Captiva. They've got about a half million members, and I'm their national spokesman, which is why, Gilligan, you either need to strip that T-shirt off right now or get the hell out of this bar."

Chapter Seven

If Matt, the owner, hadn't intervened, it would have started right there. Jeth was ready to go at him, and as for myself, this guy, Camphill, his behavior really was noxious, and I was drunk enough to bypass the obvious, rational options — as most drunks will — and had decided to see just how far he was willing to push it. It's a truism: Almost all bullying behavior is symptomatic of bedrock cowardice, and there was plenty of evidence now that Camphill was a bully.

But then Matt was there. After twenty-some years in the business, dealing with drunks and pissed-off tourists, he knew just how to handle the situation. First he went to work on Camphill with adulation — "You're really *the* Gunnar Camphill? My God, I love the work you do" — as he positioned himself between Camphill and us. Then he fed him some man-to-man

stuff, first giving us a meaningful look —
*Stay calm, he's an asshole, but let me deal
with it.* "Don't worry about Jeth. Our locals, they tend to be . . . *different.* Just
goofing around — the manatee roast? It's
kind of a local joke. We're all very pro-environment on the islands." Matt was
steering him away, toward the bar. Then he
added a bribe, saying, "I just got in a half
dozen jars of Russian Malossol caviar.
Gray beluga. My own personal stock.
Would you and your friends mind trying a
couple of ounces, giving me your
opinion?"

That quick, Matt had Camphill's full attention. "Malossol? How did you know I'm
a connoisseur of caviar?" Close enough to
the bar now for his friends to hear, he
added, "When I was studying aikido in
Japan, I fell in love with the stuff. My
master, Ueshiba Morihei, he got me
hooked on the gray beluga. Had it shipped
in once a week from Vladivostok, just
across the Sea of Japan. Unpasteurized, the
finest. There's an art to serving it, of
course."

Truth is, Matt has an amazing memory
for trivia. He probably saw the bit about
the caviar in some magazine and filed it
away.

Meanwhile, out of the corner of my eye, I saw Tomlinson stand up, use his fingers to comb his hair back. He gave Amelia a reassuring wink before he walked toward Matt. Tomlinson had been uncharacteristically silent during the confrontation, and now I watched him place his hand on Matt's shoulder — this was a *friendly* intrusion — then stand there in his flower-print sarong and black Hawaiian shirt, smiling mildly. Looking at Camphill, he spoke briefly in what, after several slow seconds, I finally realized was fast Japanese. Friendly tone. Very animated. He might have been welcoming him or extending an apology.

Pointed-face grinned toward Tomlinson, saying, "Ginger! Finally, here she is. I *knew* Ginger would make an appearance!" For the first time, Camphill seemed momentarily at a loss. But he recovered quickly, also looking at Tomlinson. He placed his palms together and gave a slight oriental bow, saying, "My friend, I think it's very rude to converse in a language that others in the room don't understand. We'll chat in Japanese another time," then turned away from Tomlinson, using Matt to emphasize the new focus of his attention.

End of conversation.

Back at our table, Tomlinson took a heavy swallow of his drink, then another before he nodded at me, and said softly, "The actor, he has a very young spirit. Very young and immature — the number of incarnations he's made into this world I'm talking about. In his mind, no one on earth actually exists but him. Every other sentient being is simply a bit of fleshy furniture or decoration. That's the way they are during that stage."

Tomlinson then added, "Plus, he's a liar. He never studied with Ueshiba Morihei. My friend, the great master, Ueshiba, doesn't speak English, and the actor doesn't understand a word of Japanese. Even his *gassho,* the way he placed his palms together, was a poor imitation."

A little too loud, Jeth said, "The guy's an egotistical pah-pa-prick."

Amelia added, "Little boy in a man's body. I see them all the time in court."

Camphill and his two friends, pointed-face and tennis player, all raised their heads a little, hearing their words, feeling them, then all emphasized the depth of their reactions by trying hard not to react. Matt had effectively insulated them with a forced truce, but it wouldn't last beyond the last glass of vodka.

There was little doubt in my mind, then, that Camphill would have to do something to save face, to reinforce his big-screen persona. His friends were going to take this story back to Hollywood, and he couldn't allow that.

We should have left then.

Half an hour later, when we did walk out the door, we were all a little drunker.

Over there drinking vodka shooters and eating caviar, so were Camphill and his pals.

Timber's Restaurant and Sanibel Grill are built high on wooden stilts over a parking area that opens onto Tarpon Bay Road, near a sanctuary of lakes and trees, not far from the beach, and only a quarter-mile or so from my house and lab, which is on the bay side of the island.

I was the last of our group to leave. I stepped out onto the wooden deck and had only taken three or four steps when I felt the double doors behind me burst open. I glanced over my shoulder, and there was Gunnar Camphill in his khakis and black Polo shirt, biceps showing, walking fast, his two shorter friends following along behind like ducklets.

Camphill's friends' faces were flushed

and mottled, a mixture of excitement and expectation. There was going to be a show, a little slice of real-life adventure theater, and they were the great star's sidekicks, their man the good-guy hero who won every fight.

Camphill was calling as he walked, "Gilligan? Oh . . . Gilligan-n-n-n-n," giving it a loud, humorous read.

JoAnn, Rhonda, and Claudia were already in the parking lot. Jeth and Tomlinson were halfway down the steps, and Amelia was just a few paces ahead of me. I turned when I saw Camphill, then moved sideways to intercept him when he tried to brush past me.

I said, "Hold it . . . hey! You're not going anywhere." I had my hands up, palms up — stop right there — and was backing away just a little to demonstrate that I didn't want to initiate contact.

Behind Camphill, pointed-face, his voice strangely husky, said, "Kick his ass, Gunnar. The Professor with his thick glasses made you look like a fool in there in front of all his redneck friends."

Camphill stopped and leaned, his face a few inches from my nose, and I could smell the alcohol on his breath as he said, "Your little friend needs to take off that

T-shirt and throw it away. It's offensive to me and anyone else who gives a damn about this earth and the creatures who live here. So he takes it off right now, tosses it in that Dumpster, and he walks away, no problem."

Behind me, I heard Jeth yell, "You want to threaten me, mah-ma-mister? Then come down here and do it to my face!"

Camphill called back, "That's what I'm *trying* to do, Gilligan. So tell your bookish friend here to move his ass, get out of the way, so we can discuss this man-to-Gilligan." The humorous inflection again, telling his friends to enjoy it — it wasn't going to last long.

He'd been looking over my shoulder. Now he looked into my face as he added, "Okay, Professor. This is your final warning. Get out of my way. Or . . . or here, I'll tell you what I'm going to do." He thought for a moment, making a show of the process, smiling because he had so many options. He glanced back at his friends as if in some wordless conferral, before he said, "Okay, what I'm going to do is, I'm going to put the heel of my right foot dead square on the right side of your temple. No . . . your jaw; I'll go easy on you. Kick you on the temple, I could kill

144

you. It's going to happen so fast, you may hear it coming, but you won't see it.

"Now, what I'm worried about is, I might knock you over the railing. It's sure as hell going to drop you. I don't want to hurt you — it goes against all my training, my entire commitment to nonviolence — but if you don't move your ass?" He shrugged. "You've forced me. I have no choice. And know what the funniest thing is, Professor? There isn't a damn thing you can do to stop me." He paused, giving it a few beats, as if speaking lines for the camera. Then: "Final warning. Get out of my way. *Now.*"

I heard Amelia and Claudia, their warning words melding together: "Ford, I don't think he's kidding. I've read about him. Me, too . . . he's got all kinds of black belts, he really does . . . His hands, he had to, like, register them as weapons or something. . . . It's no big deal, just let him go. . . . Doc!"

Camphill liked that. He puffed up a bit, his smile broader. "Do us all a favor, Professor. Listen to your little girlfriends. Move."

Without looking at Amelia or Claudia, I said, "No, I don't think so. That kick he just described? I'd kind of like to see if he can really do it."

"Okay, friend, I warned you. Everyone here's a witness."

"I'll testify on your behalf," I said softly.

Then I watched Camphill take a half step back, knees bending, fists clenched low for balance, and I knew he was preparing to do a spinning back kick, my head as his target.

A few years back, I was having dinner at Mack's bayside home, and he talked me into watching one of those pay-for-view extravaganzas. It was the "world championship" of something I think they called "Extreme Fighting," as if there were any other kind, or maybe it was "No-Holds-Barred Fighting." I didn't pay enough attention to remember.

Mack was very excited about it because the "Professional Bracket" included six of the world's most famous and feared martial arts experts from Asia, Europe, and Africa. Films and documentaries had been made about two of the masters; one of the experts supposedly had a cult following. There was also one heavyweight boxer who was ranked in the federation's top five. The hype was massive, the purse hefty, and the ring an enclosed cage from which only the winner could exit.

The promoters made a very big mistake, however. They allowed four "amateurs" to buy their way into pairings against the number-one seeds.

Apparently, it was a feed-the-Christians-to-the-lions gambit in the minds of the producers — a way of feeding easy meat to the audience before the real fighting began.

One of the amateurs might have been another boxer, the other might have been a martial arts expert, I don't know. Two, however, were mildly successful former collegiate wrestlers, one from the University of Wisconsin, I think, and the other from a little Pennsylvania school by the name of Slippery Rock.

In the first bout, Mack was shocked when the kid from Slippery Rock — he couldn't have weighed more than 170, 180 — had the famous Ninja on the mat, gasping for air, within less than a minute. The Ninja couldn't breathe and tapped his lone free hand on the canvas in pain and for mercy.

The kid seemed a little surprised. He'd hardly broken a sweat.

Then the wrestler from Wisconsin — big guy, two hundred plus — had the heavy-weight boxer down and unconscious before anyone had time to understand what had happened, and the boxer might have died if doctors hadn't come charging into the caged ring.

Neither of the wrestlers used holds that were legal in amateur wrestling, but every experienced amateur wrestler soon learns all the illegal stuff, all the dangerous and dirty little tricks, and they know how to use them.

It went that way all night. One martial arts expert after another was quickly eliminated and unfailingly humiliated — a big letdown for the promoters, but no surprise to me. Out of all the so-called "fighting" disciplines, there are only two groups who actually fight. They fight it out, toe to toe and hand to hand, day after day after day. Those two groups are wrestlers and boxers. The other disciplines pose, they practice and play-act — which is why they are sufficiently naïve about actual combat to take themselves too seriously.

Boxers work hard, but no sport requires more discipline, courage, or mental toughness than amateur wrestling (and that's why it's a national tragedy that colleges are eliminating wrestling because of a misused but well-intended piece of legislation called Title IX). Only wrestlers and boxers actually fight for a living. The rest are interesting and often stylish pretenders.

Which is why I did not take Amelia's advice, why I did not move aside.

When Camphill shifted his weight toward me, preparing to jump, spin, and kick, I reached across and grabbed his right wrist and bicep, moving with him. I pulled and ducked under his arm and leg, then came up behind him just as his feet returned to the deck.

My hands on his shoulders, controlling his body, I said into his ear, "You missed," as I reached around and pried his mouth open, avoiding his teeth by using only the middle fingers of my hands.

Then I hooked a finger into each corner of his lips, applying pressure, pulling his mouth wide, until he arched backward, and I heard him making a hoarse, gasping noise, shocked and in agony, his nails scratching at my wrists as I kneed him hard, twice, on the coccyx at the base of his spine, the very sensitive and easily bruised remnant of our primate tail.

The next morning, I knew, Camphill would have trouble walking. If he *could* walk, and it would probably be impossible for him to sit.

Had I wanted to rip his face from ear to ear, I could have done it easily. Drunk as I was, mad as I was, that wasn't my intent. I was giving him a signal — letting him know that, if he continued, the consequences would be serious. There is nothing pretty, heroic, orderly, or theatrical about a real fight. It is brutal, messy, and damn dangerous.

Pointed-face and tennis player were screaming at me. It seemed as if I were in a vacuum, yet a few of their words and phrases pierced through: "Kill him, Gunnar . . . what are you waiting for! . . . My God, Gunnar, your *face* . . . there's *blood*. You're hurting Gunnar's face!"

The harder Camphill tried to pry my fingers out of his mouth, the more pressure I exerted, so there was some blood, a slight ripping of tissue, but not much, and, finally, he stopped struggling.

Still speaking into his ear, I said, "I'm going to let you go. If you try to fight back again in any way, I'll put you down on the deck. Then I'll put you in the hospital. *Count* on it."

I slid my fingers out of his mouth.

I thought he'd heed my warning. He didn't.

As I released him, wiping my hands on

my fishing shorts, he relaxed and shrugged — a decoy posture — then exploded, side-kicking me hard on the left shin, which hurt like hell, and tried to spin his right elbow back into my ribs. I managed to catch the main impact of the blow with my arm. Even so, it put a little wheezing sound into my breathing, caused me to double up momentarily. It also infuriated me.

When he came at me again, I locked my hands on his right wrist, got myself behind him once more, and, without giving him time to react, bear-hugged, lifted, and launched him up over my head, as I arched backward steering his body — a potentially deadly wrestling throw called a "suplay."

Had I continued arching backward, I would have pile-driven the top of his skull into the floor. Instead, I did a fast quarter-turn so that only the side of his face slammed down onto the wood. Then I pinned him there, using my right elbow to burrow into his neck until I finally heard him wheeze, "*Enough*. No more!"

I stood and waited to make certain he wasn't going to leap to his feet. Then I turned and limped toward the steps, hearing pointed-face say, "You're going to let him do that to you, Gunnar? He got lucky, for Christ's sake. Go get him!" as

Amelia took my arm, helping me.

The side-kick had been nasty. I'd be feeling a burning sensation in my shin for a week, maybe longer.

I turned to her when she squeezed my arm and saw an intense, appraising expression on her face. A little bit of surprise in there, too, as she said in a low voice, "My God, you're something. Professor — I figured, yeah, the perfect nickname 'til watching you just now. Like he was a sack of corn or something, that's the way it looked when you threw him. *Un-damn-be-lievable.*"

I used peripheral vision to make certain Camphill wasn't rethinking his surrender. "He's a sack of something," I said. "You want to get another drink?"

Chapter Eight

And it still wasn't over.

We stopped at the Green Flash because it's a good place, then walked along the narrow beach road to 'Tween Waters Inn, the Gulf off to our left, a vast lens of starlight and black water without horizon.

Everyplace we stopped, we collected people; old friends and fishing guides and islanders out for a Friday night, more than willing to help us honor Janet. On the islands even a bad reason is good enough for throwing a party, and this was a great reason. So by the time we got to the Crow's Nest at 'Tween Waters, there were more than twenty of us, and the place was already crowded.

One look told me why. The bar has an extended dining area that can be partitioned off from the elevated dining room. The partition was closed except for a door-sized space through which I could see tables of men and women wearing name tags. A sign on an easel read: "Save All Manatees."

Welcome SAM members!

Damn.

I remembered Camphill saying he was the national spokesman, which meant that he was bound to show up sooner or later. In fact, they probably had him housed in one of the little cottages out back. I took Rhonda and JoAnn aside and told them, "I think we ought to collect our people and get out of here."

But Rhonda was already locked in animated conversation with Wally, the chef, and Janice behind the bar, so, as she hurried back to them, she said, "Doc, you worry too much. You think Mr. Hollywood is going mess with you again after you put him in orbit? I don't think so."

That wasn't what I was worried about. I didn't think there was much of a chance that Camphill would give me another try, but the dining room was filled with SAM people, and there was Jeth in his barbecue-a-manatee T-shirt, plus most of the Dinkin's Bay family.

Something I saw underlined just how irrational and mean the issue had become.

The Crow's Nest is built around a hardwood bar in the shape of a broken L. At three corners of the bar are hand-carved manatees — a classy, ornate touch in a classy sportsman's bar. Really beautiful pieces of work. On the belly of one of the manatees, though, someone had recently used a black marker to draw a bull's eye, complete with an arrow. Above the arrow were the words, "Save a Fishing Guide, Kill a Sea Cow."

A disturbing bit of graffiti.

I worked my way through the crowd and finally found Tomlinson holding court next to the fireplace beneath a mounted tarpon. When I tried to talk to him, though, he was slurring his words so badly that I gave up.

I decided that, if there was going to be trouble, there was nothing I could do to stop it.

Turned out I was right.

Frieda Matthews, one of Florida's best biologists and field researchers, motioned toward the lighted building and told me, "I'm supposed to be in there speaking tonight, but they fired me."

I said, "You're kidding."

She smiled. "Nope. But I still get paid.

In our line of work, that's what counts, right?"

Feeling claustrophobic among all those people, I'd stepped outside and spotted Matthews leaning against a palm tree, sipping a fresh beer. I'd met her years ago at a symposium near her office in Tallahassee and had come to respect her work — particularly her articulate field-research papers. She's a fine observer and has a gift for precise, lucid, declarative sentences. Unlike an unfortunate and growing number in our field, Matthews is an advocate of science, not a scientist who advocates a particular point of view. She is generally regarded as a leading expert on Florida's sea mammals. Thus the manatee connection.

I asked, "They canceled your talk? Why?"

She was still smiling, a healthy-looking woman with a good jaw and short hair wearing a dark business suit with a pale blouse. "Why do biologists and expert witnesses usually get fired? Because their employers doesn't want to hear what they have to say. The thing that really irks me is, their so-called experts in there obviously haven't read my recent papers. If they had, they could have fired me by telephone, and

I could've saved myself a trip. We're swamped in Tallahassee, plus I had to leave my husband alone with our four-year-old."

The implications of her sudden dismissal were interesting. Suddenly, I wished I'd brought a notebook.

"Let me get this straight," I said. "The SAM people paid you to come here, but now they don't want you to speak? I don't get it."

So the lady explained it to me. I stood there fascinated, listening, as Frieda listed the accumulated data as she knew it. She spoke softly, but as articulately as any of her fine papers.

She and her staff had spent the last five years collecting manatee data, she said, performing necropsies, doing manatee counts by plane and helicopter on both the Gulf and Atlantic coasts of Florida, yet it was only in the last three months that her team felt they had sufficient information to publish their partial conclusions.

"All valid biological data," she told me, "indicate that the population of our West Indian manatee is increasing, not decreasing. Not only that, the population has been increasing for the last twenty-five years. The manatee should be taken off the endangered species list. It doesn't belong there, and our research proves it. Florida has plenty of environmental problems, and that's where the money should be spent. But the manatee people don't want to hear that."

I listened to her explain that the minimum manatee count has increased at a rate of 6 to 7 percent per year but that it was really probably closer to 10. "You know me, Doc. I always use the most conservative figures possible. I take my work damn seriously. I'm not going to manipulate or exaggerate the figures for anyone. At the cost of what? My professional reputation? No way."

She went on to explain the data in detail, and the bottom line was that the sea cows were back and doing well. I didn't say what I was thinking, though: I'd recently read a report issued by one of the federal agencies that said exactly the opposite. Boat-related manatee deaths had risen from 25 percent ten years ago to 33 percent now, and the increased death rate far outstripped the slow-growing manatee population. Furthermore, in that same ten-year period, Florida had registered more than a hundred thousand new boats — bad news for anything in the water that was big and slow moving. But here was Dr. Frieda Matthews telling me about her own work, her own observations. It was not the time to debate.

Instead, I said, "That's great news. So why's this the first I've heard it? There ought to be headlines. Instead, they're trying to close down a whole hectares of the water around here."

She shrugged. "I've got a private theory about that, but I'd hate for you to get the impression I've gotten old and cynical. Don't get me wrong, Doc. Manatees should continue to be fully protected, but they've recovered to a level where, clearly, they're no longer an endangered species. Fish and Wildlife ought to down-list them from endangered to threatened, at most.

"This afternoon, I expected SAM's board members to clap and cheer when I told them what I was going to talk about. They've done a hell of a good job getting the word out, educating boaters on what to look for and how to avoid contact. They deserve a fair share of the credit, right along with another club, Save the Manatee. I was going to tell them congratulations, score a big win for the good guys. Instead, I watched their jaws drop open, and they looked at me like I was a heretic. They couldn't get me out of the room fast enough. The club's president — get this, Doc — she's afraid of big bodies of water, won't get on a boat, but there she is, running the whole show. She actually screamed at me. Called me a liar and . . . what was the phrase?" Matthews tilted her head, thinking about it. "She called me a 'stooge for the boating industry,' that was it.

"Doc, we don't get a cent from private enterprise. You know that. She has to know it, too, but it was like, because she said it, that made it *true*. So now a couple hundred people in there are convinced our entire project was bought and paid for by boat manufacturers. Their president has spoken, and that's that. I had to be discredited, and that was the only way she could do it." Matthews was shaking her head, frustrated and angry.

"God spare me fat, middle-aged, neurotic do-gooders!"

I said, "So why are they doing it?"

I watched her take a sip of her beer, eyebrows furrowed. She said, "Just between you and me? After they booted me, I went back to my room and used my laptop to do a little online research. The question seemed obvious to me: Why would any group continue to manufacture and promote an endangerment crisis that simply does not exist?"

"Money," I said. "Group survival or some political agenda."

"Probably all of the above," she said. "You catch on quick. Save All Manatees was started by two people who had good reasons to be worried about the well-being of that animal. They worked their butts off raising money and expanding the membership. So now, fifteen years later, the membership's grown to about half a million nationwide. It's got an annual budget of a couple million. They've got a paid staff and a stable of attorneys on retainer. SAM isn't just a club, it's a growing industry. Same with a couple of state and federal jobs created to keep tabs on this particular animal. The department heads now employ assistants to the assistants of their *assistants*.

"So what happens if the manatee is all of a sudden taken off the endangered species list? They're all out of business. So SAM, at least, has stayed aggressive. They file lots of lawsuits. People are going to stop donating if Fish and Wildlife down-lists the manatee, so they keep them on the defensive — that's my guess, anyway — and, to get new members, they base their arguments on emotion, not science. Most of the bay areas they want to close to boat traffic have never had a manatee fatality in the thirty years we've been keeping records. That's a fact. I went back and checked."

"Like Dinkin's Bay?"

"Like Dinkin's Bay."

"So you're saying they don't need to close down the marina and kick us all out of there. The trouble is — and I'm sure you're aware of this — there are a number of very good biologists around who are going to disagree with almost everything you've just told me. People I know and respect. So who am I supposed to believe?"

With her hands, she made a nothing-I-can-do-about-that gesture. "I'm just giving you the data, Doc — which are now part of public record. Look 'em up. From everything our team has learned — this is my opinion, of course — but closing Dinkin's Bay is absolutely unnecessary. I wouldn't tell you that if I didn't believe it was true."

She went on. "I used to think that I was as radical and green as they come. Not anymore. I don't know the board members in there well enough to say, but lately I've been meeting more and more so-called environmentalists who aren't really pro-environment. What they are is anti-human. Anything that has to do with people, they hate. They want to rope it all off, exclude everyone — except for themselves, of course. They're enviro-elitists, not environmentalists. And just like SAM's leaders, hysteria is their favorite tool. So see, Doc? I *have* gotten old and cynical."

I smiled at her and said, "Join the club, pal."

"I know, Doc, but it still bothers me. I've worked so damn hard all my life to get it right, to do my science properly — follow the data faithfully and without expectations wherever they may lead. Isn't that what the really good professors taught us?" She looked at me and snapped her fingers. "One thing they didn't teach us, though, is — *that quick* — one big, public lie can completely taint the work. I don't doubt that most of SAM's members are good people and honestly care about protecting the environment. But who are they going to believe, our science or their own president? See my point?"

I was about to say I did, but instead, we both stopped talking because of a growing noise coming from inside the Crow's Nest — raised voices and screaming. Then we watched as the double doors came flying open and out poured a running, tumbling, shoving mob of people, a many-headed pointillist swarm that seemed to have one frantic body.

It took me a moment to understand what was going on. Because they were both a little taller than most of the others, I saw that Jeth and Gunnar Camphill were at the center of the crowd, shoving each other and swearing, the familiar preface to a bar fight.

Already moving, I told Matthews, "I need to see if I can break this up. But do me a favor. Don't get too close."

Studies have been done on multigroup violence, and the template is fairly standard and shares an odd and surprising symmetry with tornado storm cells, of all things.

As fighting between the combatants intensifies, little skirmishes will begin to occur on the outskirts of the main fight, much as large tornadoes at the center of a storm spawn a minion of smaller tornadoes on the borders. Like the smaller tornadoes, the skirmishes are energized, concentrated, but dissipate quickly, only to reappear at another place along the outskirts.

Which is why I told Frieda to keep her distance, and why I didn't go charging right in.

We followed the mob down the sandy drive, past the pool bar, and then under the condo parking to the beach where rental kayaks and canoes were neatly stacked by the water. I kept looking and looking, and finally picked out JoAnn, Rhonda, Ransom, Claudia, and Amelia moving along with the mob, in their own tight little group. I ran up behind them, grabbed Ransom and JoAnn by the arms, and yelled to them above the noise, "You ladies come with me. We're going to watch this from the docks." Meaning I didn't want to risk some drunk taking a swing at any of us.

Ransom wouldn't budge, though. "Mister pretty man and his friends, they all jump on Jeth at once. Know how it started? One of their guys, he drunk, and he find out who Amelia was, and he ask her, right out loud, 'Tell us the truth about the drug deal that got your buddies killed. Everybody in Florida know you're lying.' That's when Jeth step in. Then their women friends, they try to rip Jeth's shirt off him. You think I'm gonna let them city trash get away with something like that?"

165

"Ransom, please! As a favor to me. Okay?"

She didn't want to follow me, but she finally relented, allowing the mob to move away from us, and I led the five of them — Frieda had wisely vanished — up the ridge to the docks where we could watch the scene from the aspect of open water.

It was not a pretty thing to watch.

They'd torn off all of Jeth's T-shirt except for the collar and a patch of material down his back. He was faced off against Camphill while a few men but mostly women stood around them in a ragged circle, screaming. In peripheral skirmishes, I noticed that a couple of our guides, big Felix Lane and Javier Castillo — a Cuban immigrant — were moving from fight-cluster to fight-cluster, separating the combatants until they could tell who was who, then systematically cold-cocking anyone they didn't recognize as one of us, an islander — something else that was not pretty to watch.

But the main event was Jeth Nicholes, the local fishing guide who'd just lost the love of his life, and Gunnar Camphill, the film hero.

So far, it looked as if Jeth had gotten the worst of it. His face was swollen, and blood

166

was pouring from his nose. I watched Camphill use his nasty side-kick to batter Jeth into the canoe rack, then almost drop him with a spinning back elbow to the ribs. Jeth staggered, nearly fell, but managed to keep his feet.

I badly wanted to help him, but I couldn't. You can't fight another man's battle. Jeth wasn't going to quit, and he would have taken my intrusion as an admission that he was beaten.

But he wasn't.

I watched him take a deep breath, charge Camphill, and manage to wrestle his arms around the man's chest. The actor knew all the pressure points, all the dangerous places to hit. But Jeth held on and, with the slow determination of a boa constrictor, worked his way upward until he got Camphill's neck cradled in his strong right arm, then used his left hand to apply pressure — a headlock.

That's when the momentum began to turn.

Jeth grabbed a fistful of Camphill's hair and levered him over his hip onto the sand — a weird thing to see because a cap-sized patch of the actor's hair actually came off in Jeth's hand. Jeth looked at the thing, shocked, and then flung it into the water.

It made no sense at first, but then I realized — a small crown toupee. Camphill wore a hairpiece.

Maybe the psychological impact of being exposed had something to do with it, or maybe Camphill was just exhausted. Whatever the reason, Jeth ended it quickly, using his fists to pound away at the man's face until Camphill rolled into a fetal position, hands protecting his head, calling, "Enough! Enough! I quit, goddamn it!"

Jeth stood shakily; he seemed a little surprised that it was over and he had won.

But it wasn't over yet. He still had a small mob to deal with, pointed-face and tennis player among them, plus a couple dozen women and men. The little mob began to walk toward Jeth as he retreated, backing away faster and faster until he was running as they pursued him.

He chose exactly the right escape route. I watched him vault over the railing of the dock where we stood, then sprint toward us, not realizing, at first, that we were there — he probably had planned to jump into the water to get away.

His expression, when he saw us, was touching. It's a frightening thing to have a mob after you, and his face registered panic, then puzzlement, as his brain scanned to identify us and analyze the situation. Then his expression changed to pure relief.

I pushed him past me, saying, "You okay?" not expecting an answer. Then I began to walk shoreward, toward pointed-face and tennis player, who were leading the mob.

Both men stopped abruptly when they realized who I was. The men and women behind them suddenly went quiet, perhaps sensing pointed-face's uneasiness. They saw the way he was looking at me, seeming to get smaller as he took a step back, then another, retreating as I continued to walk toward him, his little mob bunched up behind him now, blocking his escape.

When I was just a couple of paces away, hearing sirens warbling in the distance, he yelled, "Stay away from me, damn you! Don't you touch me!"

He looked at me blankly when I asked, "Can you swim?" Then I lifted him and vaulted him into the bay.

Chapter Nine

Amelia told me, "You've sobered up a little — maybe we all have — but not enough for me to talk about the boat. The one that maybe picked up Janet, Michael, and Grace."

"You're absolutely certain you saw it?"

"It wasn't light yet, but it wasn't dark. You know that time of morning when it's powdery gray, like fog? I hadn't heard the Coast Guard helicopter in awhile, or the search plane. Like maybe they'd gone back to base or something to refuel. That's when it went by, maybe a mile off. No lights, like a ghost ship, and it stopped out there. But what I think might have happened, the way I feel about it all, let's save for the morning. Maybe because I'm a public defender, dealing with all those indigents in trouble, I've learned never to discuss anything serious when I'm drinking. That's what nails them each and every time. And this is about as serious as it gets."

It was a little after 3 a.m. We were back at Dinkin's Bay, a couple dozen of us, bruised and scarred a little, but the whole group intact, no one arrested, no one hospitalized, although Jeth was going to need a doctor to check out that crooked nose of his. Camphill had almost certainly broken it.

We were in a small open area of grass and sand by the seawall near the boat ramp and canoe racks. A couple of the guides had built a fire of driftwood, piled the wood on high, and now we all sat around it, feeling the heat, watching sparks comet skyward, little pockets of us set off in shadows, the familiar faces of friends suspended like orange masks above the flames, a tribal effect. There was a tribal feel, too. We'd drawn blood and been bloodied together, and now we were back in camp, our secluded mangrove village.

The feeling was not unknown to me. But it had been a very, very long time since I'd experienced it.

Only two of us were missing: Tomlinson and Ransom. After leaving the 'Tween Waters docks, I spent half an hour searching

171

around, convincing myself that someone hadn't knocked him unconscious during the brawl and left him to die in the condo parking area or facedown in the shallows.

Instead, I found Tomlinson near the water facedown in the sand at Jensen's Marina, passed out at the base of the palm tree totem pole there everyone calls Queenie. When I rolled him over to make certain he was still breathing, he pulled a curtain of scraggily hair away from his face, struggled to focus, and, after a few beats, finally realized who I was. "Ah . . . my *compadre*. Back from the Crusades, I see. Did Jeth slay the black knight?" He slurred the sentences together, wincing as if it pained him to form words.

Ransom came up beside me, as I said, "Yeah. His nose is a few inches off center, he took some bad shots, but he won."

"You realize that actor's handlers are never going to look at him the same again. In fact, man — *poof,* like *presto-chango —* his career may be over once words gets around. Him and his small, teenager soul. See? Good sometimes *does* triumph, Marion. Not always, but sometimes. You should find that reassuring."

I took his arm. "We need to get you up and back to the *No Mas.*"

He shook his head. "No. I want to lay here and feel the earth. I'm hurting, my friend. Deep, deep in my Bodhi-mind, my *Dharma-kaya*, the pain, my God, the *pain*. All my life, I've wondered how I stand it. But no matter how many times my heart breaks, it still refuses to turn to stone." He burped, burped again, then made a groaning sound before he added, "So I've just got to lay here and suck it up until the fat lady finally sings." From the sound of his voice, the look of his face, I could see that he'd been crying.

I said, "What? You're so drunk you're making even less sense than usual."

"Hah! 'Cause you don't understand, Marion. It's Janet. Our Janet. She was still out there when the Coasties called off the search. I know it. I could *feel* it, man, Janet's strong vibes. That's why I stayed at sea for a couple more days. I could communicate with her spirit, but I couldn't find her physical body. Maddening!"

I said slowly, "You mean her dead body. Her corpse."

"No! She was still alive!"

I don't believe in fortune-tellers or parapsychology, but I've been around Tomlinson long enough to know that his intuition and perceptions are sometimes

173

eerily accurate. How he does it, comes up with some of the things he knows, I don't pretend to understand.

I said, "What about now? Do you think she's alive now? It's been three weeks exactly."

He groaned again as he got up onto one elbow. "I don't know. I can't find her anymore. Her spirit, I mean. The first week after the boat sank, she'd come to me at night, in dreams, if I'd really smoked a lot of my good Colombian and chanted the *Surangama sutra*. Janet and the two others. I could see what happened, what they were doing, how they felt. I could even hear what they were saying. Phrases. Snatches of emotion. That's why I overmedicated myself tonight. I was trying to break through again. I'm still trying to break through, trying to find her, but no luck."

I told him, "I can't leave you here. You get sick when you're passed out, you could choke and die."

Tomlinson used his hand to wave me away, then settled himself back in the sand, eyes closed, curled in a fetal position. "Demon rum," he said. "Not a bad way to go. Only thing I'll miss is going into town and playing ball come Sunday."

We both played Roy Hobbs baseball, a

174

fairly serious brand of ball.

Beside me, Ransom said, "I'll stay with him." She sat herself in the sand, using Queenie the totem pole as a backrest, and combed her fingers gently through Tomlinson's long hair. "Poor old bony hippie man. This boy drive me crazy, but he in my heart and ain't nothin' I can do about it." She looked at him for a moment, shaking her head. "He got a toothache in his soul, my brother, and there ain't nothin' I can do about that, either."

I said, "Yes, he does. I think he probably always will."

I left the two of them to sleep in the sand, because that's what they wanted, and headed back to Dinkin's Bay, determined to get Amelia alone long enough to ask her about the boat. Maybe it *was* possible. Maybe Tomlinson and Amelia were both right — there was a chance Janet had been picked up and was still alive.

Now, sitting by the fire, Amelia said to me, "I'm going to stay at your sister's house — if we ever get to bed. She says you're a runner. How about we go for a run tomorrow, and I'll tell you all about it. A couple miles along the beach, maybe?"

I told her that would be just fine. She

was probably right. Certain subjects are appropriate for drunk talk, other subjects are not. The fate of three missing people deserved elevated status. So I asked her about something she probably would feel comfortable talking about — how the fight started back at 'Tween Waters.

"I've almost gotten used to it," she told me. "I was sitting at one of the big tables with Jeth, Ransom, and the two women who live here — JoAnn and Rhonda? — and Claudia, too. Claudia was asking me more questions about Janet. What did we talk about when we were hanging on to the anchor line? She asked a lot of little details about what went on after we were set adrift. That sort of thing.

"I don't know how they found out who I was, but a couple of guys from the bar came over and introduced themselves. Part of the SAM crowd, one was from Jacksonville, the other from Palm Beach. The moment the first one opened his mouth, I knew how it was going to go, that's how many times I've been through it in the past few weeks. The ones who don't believe my story, they always start out very polite — like, hey, congratulations, what an honor to meet you. They've read all about it, know all the details. Which fooled me the first couple of times, but not anymore.

"It's something in the tone of their voice. That's how I can tell. Way too friendly and impressed, trying to make me feel important, but what they're really trying to do is set me up, trap me, like amateur interrogators. Tonight, the guy from Palm Beach — and he was pretty drunk, too — goes on for ten minutes or so, making backhanded accusations by telling the story to his friend, until finally he stops, looks at me, and says, 'Lady, how stupid do you think people really are? You're telling us that three adults in inflated vests just vanished off the face of the earth? Bullshit. Okay, so pretend like we're not all idiots here and tell the truth. What happened was, you cooked up some drug deal with some badasses from Miami or maybe South America, and they wasted your three pals to make it nice and clean. Somehow you had an in with them. Maybe one of the drug bosses had a taste for redheads, so they let you live.

'Or maybe what happened was, you and your pals decided to sink the boat for insurance money, and something went real wrong. They weren't wearing their vests, like you said. Something else I heard was about you and the others maybe being involved with some kind of porno ring. . . .' "

Amelia let the sentence trail off, and I noticed that her hands had gradually clenched into fists. After a moment, she said, "That's when I stopped him. I'd had enough. It's true that I once had to defend this porno slimeball, and the case got a lot of press, so that's where that nasty little rumor got started. But no way was I going to let him associate the other three with that.

"You know how they say redheads have a temper? I can't speak for the others, but I'll only let someone push me so far. So I stood up and let the guy have it with both barrels. I know all the words, and how to use them. I realize I'm no great beauty, but I've had to back off enough of the casting-couch macho types to know exactly where to aim, and the guy didn't like where my words hit him. So that's when Jeth stood up and got involved. Then, out of nowhere, the actor was there, right in his face. Gunnar Camphill to the rescue, take two. It was a damn ugly thing to watch, wasn't it, Doc? Makes me feel sick inside to think about the sound their fists made when they were hitting each other. The flesh-on-bone sound."

I'd known her for, what? less than eight

hours, but I'd already accepted her as what Tomlinson once defined as a PBR — a person who is reality based. One night, over beer, we'd kicked around the definition and more or less refined it. A PBR wasn't just a brand of blue-collar beer, it was also someone who was not dominated by neurosis, ambition, or ego. It was a person who was relatively honest, rational, and reasonable most of the time; a man or woman who had a general sense of his or her own worth and limitations, who acknowledged the worth of others, who demonstrated a sense of humor, and didn't take him- or herself too seriously.

With a definition so broad, you'd expect to meet lots and lots of PBRs.

Instead, I seem to be meeting fewer and fewer.

In my opinion, Amelia Gardner qualified, and I would trust her until, if, and when she did something to make me think otherwise. Now I reached over, put my hand on her arm, and squeezed gently. "That remark you made about 'great beauty,' I hope you're not suggesting you aren't attractive. Because you are. But you're tired, I can see it in your face. Know what might be a good thing for you to do right now? It doesn't look like Ransom's

179

going to be back any time soon, so let me walk you over to my house, change the sheets, and put you to bed. I've got a big hammock strung on the porch. A starry night like this, no bugs, I'd rather sleep out there anyway."

Laughter can communicate a variety of emotions. The amused sound she made was shy, a little weary, but pleased. "I was always the lanky, gawky tomboy girl. All elbows and legs, with no chest at all. I kept waiting for my body to change, but it never did, so now I'm the lanky, gawky attorney lady, all elbows and legs and still no chest at all. But thanks anyway. It was a nice way to tell me I look tired." She stood, stretched, and yawned, still smiling. "Let me say my good nights, and I'll take you up on the offer."

I waited while Amelia fetched an overnight bag from her car, then I walked her to the house. Gave her a quick look at my lab — no octopi or crabs missing — and then took her through the screen door into the cottage and showed her how things worked. Little propane stove for tea. Small ship's refrigerator if she wanted a snack. If she couldn't sleep, there were books on the shelves and a shortwave radio near the

Celestron telescope that was angled toward the north window. I laid out fresh sheets and towels, then returned along the mangrove path, back to the marina, to give her some time and privacy to use the outdoor shower and change into the XX T-shirt I'd loaned her to use as a nightgown.

I expected the party would have ended. It was well after three by now, but Mack and Jeth, most of the liveaboards and guides, were still there, still sitting around the blazing fire, laughing softly, talking in early-morning voices. Still riding that emotional, adrenaline high, replaying the events at 'Tween Waters. We'd won the battles and won the war, and each and every member wanted to cement his or her role in the way things had transpired, secure their place in the marina's oral history here and now, at the edge of the fire, before memories were tarnished by the edge of the first morning light.

For how many hundreds of centuries had this ceremony been repeated, on every continent, by men and women sitting around burning wood at the water's edge?

The scene touched some atavistic chord in me, created the illusion of ancient memory, but, illusion or not, it was a moving and pleasing scene to behold.

There were people milling around on the deepwater docks, too, I noticed. Four, maybe six. I couldn't tell. I walked past the sumping-aerator hiss of bait tanks, beneath the sodium security lights, and out toward the darker fringes of A dock, sailboats with halyards a-tapping off to my left. I heard a splash, then another splash. Then heard JoAnn's alto whisper. "Doc? Hey Doc's here!"

With the security light behind me, in the blue light of a waning half moon, I could now see JoAnn and Rhonda standing on the dock, naked but for bikini panties. JoAnn, short and Rubenesque; Rhonda, tall and stork-like with skinny hips and hair clipped short. They had their arms wrapped around themselves, for the night had turned cool. But as I neared, JoAnn dropped her arms to her side, heavy breasts right there for me to see, and said, laughing, her voice fluid with alcohol, "We decided it was a night to break marina rules. We're all gonna go skinny dippin'! No exceptions, pal!"

I stopped and placed hands on my hips, smiling. Down the mangrove shoreline, at my house, I could see the solitary figure of Amelia Gardner lifting her arms, head back, washing herself beneath my outdoor shower, her body long, lean, and milky-white when touched by the moon. Because of the direction my cottage faces — all water and mangroves — anyone using the shower gets the impression of total privacy.

Not always.

To JoAnn, I said, "Looks like I've got some time on my hands," as I unclipped my belt and stepped out of my sandals.

Chapter Ten

In the mangrove heat of an autumn after-noon, Amelia and I ran along the marina's shell road that tunnels through prop-roots, tidal swamp, out into the light and traffic of Tarpon Bay Road, then straight to the beach. We were on the late November cusp of tourist season, so there were a lot of rental cars, metallic bubbles in crimson, bronze, white; a noticeable increase in the number of license plates from Ohio, Michigan, New York, Canada.

The first ten minutes or so, we talked about how crappy we felt, how shaky.

"I'm not going to drink any alcohol for a month," she said. Her tone told me that she was angry at herself, disappointed, too, and communicated to me on a deeper level so that I could be certain it was uncharac-teristic behavior.

In a similar tone, I said, "Couldn't agree

184

more. What an idiotic waste of time. It ruined my whole damn morning. I slept for a couple hours, woke up at seven, went straight to the lab, but didn't get any work done at all."

Later, watching the sunset from the patio outside the Mucky Duck, me holding a draft beer, her with a glass of wine, we'd both laugh at our own weakness and hypocrisy. Now, though, we were determined to get ourselves clean again, to take control, and physical penance seemed like an appropriate start.

If you run or swim much, you can tell very quickly if an unfamiliar workout partner takes either discipline seriously. Amelia clearly did — she ran with a long, pure stride; she seemed to glide as I pounded along, big and muscle-dense, at her side. When I asked her, "Okay with you if we pick up the pace a little?," she answered, "Seriously? I'd love to," with an edge that made me think, *Uh-oh.*

So we punished ourselves. Got the sweat going, hearts pounding, the lungs burning. Got the tiny little voice of reason that lives on the outskirts of the modern brain whispering couch-potato lies: *Slow down. Why push yourself? Listen to the pain. Listen to your body, not your instincts! Stop fighting against the inevitable!*

We ran southeast on the sand ridge that is higher and harder than the actual beach. To our right, the Gulf of Mexico was mineral green, dense with salt, swollen with autumnal light. There were beach umbrellas, bikini swatches triangulated on strawberry breasts, oiled thighs, boom-box Margaritaville music, and bearish men sleeping facedown, their white skin seared the color of ham. Off to the left were sea oats and condos and expensive hotels with pools and package deals, outdoor cabana bars with familiar names: Casa Ybel, Sandal Foot, Snook Inn, Westwind.

After slightly more than twenty minutes of pushing myself way too hard — we had to have gone at least three miles — I took a couple of big gulps of air in order to speak, and said, "What I'm worried about is, if you don't know CPR, I could collapse right here and die."

She guffawed, broke stride, held out her palm to me, still jogging, and we shook hands. "That was a hell of a five-k. We had to be running sub-sevens. And in this damn sand!"

"I know, I know. Mind if we walk until my legs stop shaking?"

We turned back toward Tarpon Bay

Road, and I listened as she made small talk about her work. She'd graduated from South Florida, got her law degree from Stetson, then went to work for the state, representing migrant workers in Immokalee and Belle Glade.

"My dad, God rest his good, good soul, always told me that I was born to be a rescuer. I so wish he'd been right."

I said, "You're being pretty hard on yourself, lady."

"I know, I know. I keep hoping it will go away. That feeling keeps coming back, survivor's guilt."

I decided it was as good a time as any to bring up the subject again, so I asked her, "Any chance the guilt is so strong that you might have imagined seeing the boat? The one you think could have picked up the other three, the boat without lights?"

"No . . . no, I don't think so. At least . . . well, I probably did go a little crazy sitting on that tower for two nights, but not that crazy. The mind can do funny things, but I know in my heart that I saw something. It was there. I could hear it. I could *smell* it even before I saw it. Even with all the dried bird guano on the tower, the air out there is so clean, the smell really stuck with me. Diesel fumes and cigarette smoke and something else . . . a kind of . . ." Her nose wrinkled, remembering it. "Stench. A stink. That's the only word that describes it. Not just old fish. The boat had this really foul odor. I've never smelled anything like it before. Worse than garbage. Which means I couldn't have imagined it."

I told her, "So I accept your earlier offer. I will listen to everything you say and keep it in confidence — Tomlinson is the only exception. Sometimes I need to bounce things off that big brain of his. If that's okay with you, tell me all about it. In return, I'll promise to help you in any way I can."

She pursed her lips, giving it consideration, then held out her hand again to shake on it.

We did.

Probably because I've spent so much time in port towns and small coastal villages around the world, I've heard many stories about survival at sea. There are the epic tales, such as those of Shackelton and Bligh, as well as the more modern accounts of Steve Callahan's 72 days adrift or the Baileys, who survived for 117 days in a rubber raft, eating raw turtle and trigger fish, and of the Robertson family, who endured 37 days in a raft after their sailboat was damaged by a whale.

I'm also familiar with a dozen or more accounts of SCUBA divers who surfaced only to discover that their boat had sunk or, more commonly, the charter boat they'd been on had gone off and left them, almost always because of some bored dive master's sloppy head count.

It happens a lot. Way more often than most sport divers realize and more than most busy charter companies care to admit. Worldwide, there are dozens of similar incidents reported each year, which is why smart divers always make it a point of introducing themselves to several strangers when outward bound on an unfamiliar dive boat. Even if you're the shy, quiet type, make very damn sure that other people aboard know who you are, where you're from, and that they find you and your partner unforgettable.

The modern world and its complicated series of safety nets have orphaned us from the exigencies of fundamental survival. To be adrift in a lifeboat or to be adrift in the water, floating and alone, legs dangling down into the abyss, are two very different propositions, though neither is enviable. It is the stories of the lost divers, though, that

I find the most chilling. There are some heroic stories and some horrific stories, although few lost divers live to tell the tale.

Here, jogging along at my side, was a woman who had found a way to survive. I gave her my full attention, asking only the occasional leading question to prod her along when necessary. I also made little mental notes that I would later detail on paper when I returned to the lab.

When you meet one of the rare strong and good ones, a small request for help is not an imposition, it is an opportunity. Sometimes it is also an honor.

Amelia told me that at around 11 p.m., after four hours of swimming fixedly toward the light, the steel girders of the 160-foot navigational tower took shape in the blackness. When she was near enough, she let the waves wash her into the metal service ladder, then fought with the last of her strength to hang on. She held herself there until she had the waves timed, then used one of the swells to boost herself up onto the rungs, and climbed to the tower's lowest deck. It was only about 8 feet above the water.

"I felt like I was dreaming," she said. "The only time it was bright enough to see was every four seconds when the light at the top of the tower exploded. You know those strobe lights they use at parties sometimes when people are dancing? It was kind of like that. Very weird, nightmarish. My muscles were quivering, and I knew the barnacles had cut me up pretty good. But, after awhile, I got up and started calling for the other three. As the night went on, I kept thinking I heard them. The wind makes strange sounds out there. I kept getting up and calling back, calling their names."

Around midnight, Amelia saw what she correctly believed to be a Coast Guard helicopter off in the distance, with its searchlight fanning the water.

"My eyes just kept following the helicopter," she said. "It went east, then south a bit, and I moved with it around the tower. I watched it for a long time, the helicopter's flashing lights, and then it seemed to settle over an area near where I guessed our boat went down, but a couple miles too far west. Like it was too far out, understand? Right on the edge of the horizon. I thought, 'There's no way I could have swum that far.' "

We were back on Tarpon Bay Road now, walking shoulder to shoulder, me getting the occasional whiff of girl sweat and the morning's shampoo. Every few minutes, she'd pull her T-shirt up to wipe her face dry, a jockish mannerism that I found endearing. I told her, "It's tough to gauge distance over water. Sometimes things seem closer than they are, sometimes they seem farther. It's doubly hard at night. The chopper probably used GPS coordinates to settle down right over the *Baja California*."

She touched my arm, communicating her agreement. "That's exactly what I finally decided. The copter had found my friends. Why else would it hover like that? Which made me feel good. I didn't stop to wonder why Janet, Michael, and Grace had swum back to the wreck site or how they could have even found it. See? My brain wasn't working right. I was exhausted and cold and just not tracking."

At about the same time, she also saw the lights of what she believed was a large boat. "It was out there in the same general area, several miles to the west, only it didn't seem nearly so far out as the helicopter."

I said, "But not the mystery boat? The boat with the foul smell, the one you say went by the next morning."

"No, absolutely not. I'll tell you how I

know in a second. But seeing boat lights out there, the way my mind processed it, the helicopter had found Michael, Grace, and Janet, and they'd called a boat in to pick them up. A Coast Guard cutter. That's what I wanted to be happening. But after a little bit of time, the boat seemed to head off to the southwest, so then I figured, after rescuing those three, they'd found my inflated vest. The one I'd taken off because I couldn't swim with it. So they'd found the vest, couldn't figure out where I was, and were now looking for me. I started jumping up and down, screaming and waving my arms, trying to time it to the strobe. Yelling 'Here I am, I'm okay!' As if anybody could see that far. Or hear."

She made a soft noise in her throat, a sound of despair, or of visceral pain. Then she was quiet for a few moments before she added, "Out there, your mind has no familiar reference point, so it plays weird tricks. I was trying to make sense of what the boat was doing because I wanted to believe it so much. In real life, your boat doesn't sink. Your friends don't vanish. People aren't swallowed up by the dark, leaving their loved ones back home wondering what in the hell happened."

She made the same sad sound again, and

I listened to it become a soft chuckle, then fade. "At least, that's the way my reality was. Every story, every event has a rational, plausible ending, right? But not this one. Which is why my life has seemed a little unreal . . . sometimes like some really bad dream ever since." Amelia stopped and looked at me. "You want to hear something ironic? Something way too damn tragic for me to even want to think about it?"

She told me the irony was that the boat she saw that night wasn't a Coast Guard vessel. It was the *Ellen Clair*, a ninety-foot charter boat out of Fort Myers Beach. Captain Ken Peterson, with a party of ten aboard, had stopped to fish the *Baja California* while en route to the Dry Tortugas, fifty miles away. The Coast Guard had contacted the *Ellen Clair* by VHF and weeks later Lad provided Amelia with a telephone number for the boat's captain.

"I've been trying to put all the pieces together," she said. "I'm trying to figure out what happened and why it happened. That charter boat was a tiny little piece of the puzzle of that night. So I called Captain Peterson on the phone. He told me that he first spotted the helicopter when he was about ten miles north of the *Baja Cali-*

fornia. It had its spotlight on, in a search pattern. The helicopter did a fly-by of his boat, contacted him on the radio, then continued searching.

"So here's the ironic thing. Peterson anchored on the *Baja* at around 1 a.m. and they sat there and fished for about an hour. Had some soft drinks, looked at the stars, the engines off. If Michael's boat had stayed afloat for just a few hours longer, they'd have found us. If we could have found some way to stay in the area for just a littler longer, they would have found us. Michael, Janet, and Grace would be here now. Or someplace in Florida. We'd probably all be laughing about what a great adventure we'd had."

Amelia, who hadn't had anything to eat or drink since Friday morning, spent the next thirty-five hours on the tower, hearing noises, waving to boats, planes, and helicopters that never saw her until 9:45 Sunday morning.

One of the boats, she said, was the mystery boat. The boat without lights, the boat with the strange odor, the vessel she could smell before it was close enough to see.

"It came from the opposite direction the wind was blowing," Amelia told me. The

195

boat came out of the southwest, she explained, heading toward coastal Florida, maybe Marco Island, or the Ten Thousand Islands, a mangrove maze that fringes the Florida Everglades. "First I heard the engine, way off in the distance. Then the stink. That's how strong it was. The wind wasn't strong enough to blow it away. It was an hour or so before sunrise. Over the noise of the wind and that creaking tower, the engine kept getting closer and closer."

We were back in my house now, cooling down from the run. Sitting on the upper deck outside my lab drinking water from plastic liter bottles that were cold from my little ship's fridge. I've got a few cane-backed barstools on the deck (the higher the elevation, the easier it is to see fish when looking down into the water) and a couple of old rockers. We sat in the rockers, Amelia staring out over the bay, still inside herself, reliving the tragedy as she spoke.

That first night, she didn't sleep at all. Suffered through a couple of more panic attacks similar to the one she experienced while in the water. She continued to hear her friends' voices, too. Imagined voices.

"As crazy as I was that first night, though," she said, "the boat's engine was real. You know how, just before first light, way before sunrise, the sky seems to turn a misty charcoal color? There's no light in the sky. Even the stars fade to gray. But *things*, individual objects — the frame of the tower I was on, the face of a wave — solids and liquids seem to have a little bit of light inside them. Not strong. Like a sky so black causes friction, so anything that moves sparks a little. That's how I saw the boat. But that's also why I didn't get a good enough look to describe it."

Amelia told me the boat passed within a quarter-mile, probably less, but there was no way to judge for certain.

"At one point, when the strobe flashed, it was close enough that I'm pretty sure it had those steel booms you see on a certain kind of boat. Just the silhouette. That's all I saw."

I said, "Do you mean the kind of booms found on shrimp boats?"

She nodded. "Yes, I think so, the kind they use for dragging nets. The booms were up, folded like wings. Only I can't say for sure it was a shrimp boat. It was pretty good size, though. Not moving fast but pushing a lot of water. No lights at all, not in the cabin, none on the deck. No navigational lights, either. It went sliding by in the night like a ghost ship or something, that big strobe light showing me nothing but shadows and angles way out there on the edge of a white circle. It seemed like the boat was coming right at me. Then, all of a sudden, it turned away. Headed north, running parallel to the coast."

I asked, "What time was that?"

She touched a hand to the stainless dive watch on her left wrist. "It was 5:50 a.m. That's when the boat was real close and I checked my watch."

"Was the Coast Guard helicopter still on station? Were they still searching, I mean?"

She shook her head. "No. They hadn't been out there for a couple of hours. I found out later that the Coast Guard suspended the air search between 2 a.m. and sunrise, and the cutter they sent wasn't even close yet. Which means it was just me out there. And the others — me on the tower, them in the water, and that boat. Which is why the Coast Guard didn't see it. Never knew it was there."

So far, I didn't doubt the woman's story. By law, between dusk and dawn, all vessels are mandated to show running lights, but it's common for skippers to ignore the law and run dark. On black nights, white anchor lights, even red and green bow lights, interfere with night vision. It's easier to see random waves without them. As to other boat traffic, there's usually not much at night, particularly in stretches of seldom-traveled wilderness water, and the water space off the Ten Thousand Islands is about as wilderness as it gets.

Even so, something was missing from the story. Had to be. By my judgment, Amelia was a rational, logical person, and thus far, her story contained a major omission. I said, "Okay, you saw a boat. The boat wasn't showing lights. Trust me, it's not unusual. It slipped through a little hole in the Coast Guard search schedule. I don't doubt that, either. So the question is obvious: What makes you think that boat may have found Janet, Michael, and Grace? It was dark. There was no way for people aboard to see three people floating in the water."

Amelia took a sip of her water, turned her head, and looked at me. She had eyes the color of spring grass, a lucent green, and they seemed to be set slightly deeper into her face, as if having retreated from the emotional beating she'd taken over the last several weeks. "The boat stopped, that's why. About twenty minutes later, the sky had changed from charcoal to a kind of pearly gray. It was way to the northeast, but it was out there. I could see it. Out there, floating, but not moving forward."

"Could you hear its engines?"

"No. It was too far away by then. I'm sure you've seen the tower I was on. It has two platforms. One just over the waves, and the other about twenty feet above that. I climbed up to the highest platform to get a better look. It was cold up there, windy. Doc, I'm telling you now exactly what I told the Coast Guard. There was a boat out there. I'll swear to it. And it stopped. For the first time, it showed lights. I saw it flashing a spotlight around. Then it started moving again toward shore and was gone. It'd stopped for five minutes, maybe ten."

She paused for a moment, building her case, letting me think about it before she added, "All three of them were wearing inflated vests. If all those search boats and helicopters didn't find Janet, Grace, and Michael in six solid days and nights of searching, doesn't it make sense that someone else did? Someone picked them up. My God, someone *had* to. That's the only reasonable explanation. We didn't find them because they weren't there!"

I said, "I'd like to believe that — and so would you. So would we all. But it's a big ocean, Amelia. You know that better than most people will ever know it. Drop the average adult diver into the Gulf of Mexico, and he or she is proportionally reduced to the size of about one molecule in the atomic structure of a very large animal. Easy to miss, and sometimes almost impossible to find."

She was nodding, anticipating my response, way ahead of me. "I agree. But it should be easy enough to prove there was another boat out there. At least that there is a possibility they were picked up. It's like I told your friend at St. Pete Coast Guard, Commander Dorsey.

"I told him that everyone knows the government has all kinds of satellites flying around the sky, up there to monitor weather and drug trafficking and who knows what else. Maybe a satellite flew over that night and there's a photo of the boat somewhere, a way to identify it."

"What did Dalton think about that idea?"

"He thought it was great, but he said the Coast Guard couldn't help me. No access to that kind of classified information. Not officially anyway. It had something to do with them not being a branch of the military, which was news to me." She seemed to make it a point not to look in my direction when she added, "Commander Dorsey suggested that I mention the satellite idea to you. When I asked why, he didn't say. Just sort of ignored the question. Like there was something he knew but wasn't going to tell me. Does that make any sense to you, Doc?"

I was thinking: *Satellite images. Good idea.* But I said, "Nope. I have no idea why Dalton would say such a thing. But look . . . well, what we should decide here, as far as me helping you, Amelia — of course I will. Count on it. What I'm not clear on is what you want me to do."

Now she turned to look at me. "I want you to question every detail of my story. This is the lawyer in me talking. Trying to prove me wrong is the only way I can be proven right. Come to some conclusions, write them out, and Commander Dalton said he would attach it to the Coast Guard file, which will make it public record. What I really want? I told you before. I want you to help all four of us get our reputations back."

Chapter Eleven

I listened to my old friend, colleague, and confidant, Bernard Yeager, Ph.D., say to me over long-distance telephone, "Satellites? So why should I know a satellite from a submarine? Tell me that if you don't mind very much."

Patiently, I replied, "Bernie, this is me at the other end. If you can't talk, just say so. I wouldn't ask if it wasn't important. Surveillance satellites: I need some general information, and maybe a little piece or two of specific information — if it's available."

"Trust me, it's not available. Even if I had access to that kind of data, it's not available. Which I don't."

I sighed and stared at the shelf of aquaria along the wall of my lab. It was feeding time, and eight football-sized octopi stared back at me from their individual tanks, while aerators in each created the sweet molecular odor of ozone and a soothing chorus of bubbles. I said, "Won't you at least listen?"

"I'll listen, I'll listen, already! But first things first. You say you are Marion Ford. I know your voice well. You are my old friend. But these are dangerous times. Did you know that there are certain computer magicians who can record another person's voice, download it, and then use microphone active software to make their own voice sound very similar to the one they've recorded?"

"Nope," I said. "Never heard of such a thing."

"It's true! So maybe it's you, maybe it's not. What it could be is some *nebbish* playing a trick on poor old Bernie, showing I've gotten so old I trust my ears, not my brain. Which is why I want you to speak a few more words, and let me make certain you are who you say you are."

I pictured how it would probably be on his end of the line. He would be in the office of his desert adobe outside Scottsdale, Arizona, talking on the newest generation of high-security scrambler phones. The telephone would somehow be hooked into the bank of computers on his desk and around the room that he'd assembled lovingly by hand and interconnected. On one of the monitors would be a series of voiceprint images, old and new, but all of them seismic renderings of my voice.

All voices are distinctive, the uniqueness of each determined by the size of throat, nasal, and oral cavities, and the shape, length, and tension of the vocal cords. The manner in which speech muscles are manipulated is distinctive as well. Bernie would be using some esoteric program to confirm that my voiceprints matched. Presumably, he was using the same sophisticated computer system that made it possible for me to dial a Virginia area code yet end up speaking with the rotund and brilliant retired National Security Agency department head. How? I have no idea. My guess is, the same way you can dial a special seven-digit phone number and reach the security station at Kwajalein in the middle of the South Pacific. More of Yeager's electronic wizardry.

Bernie is still a legend among the elite intelligence community familiar with the man's work. It was Bernie Yeager who single-handedly unscrambled the Soviet nuclear subcode progression. It was Yeager who invaded and compromised computer communications between Managua and

Havana during the Sandinista wars in Nicaragua. It was Yeager who discovered that, for years, the Mossad had the key to many code transmissions between the United States and Panama, compliments of a Mossad agent named Michael Herrera who Manuel Noriega had, amazingly, put in charge of his Panamanian air force. Next time you see a photograph of the former dictator in uniform, note the inverted paratrooper wings of the Israeli army — an honor bestowed on Noriega by a grateful Herrera.

All true.

And it was Yeager who consistently interrupted and intercepted radio and Internet communications between the Taliban in Afghanistan and Islamic terrorists in the United States. I'd heard through mutual friends that he had become obsessed with unmasking and destroying them individually and as groups. I knew that Bernie had lost both parents in Nazi concentration camps, so it made sense when our mutual friend said that Bernie considered the Islamic fanatics to be the Nazis of the new century. Nor was it surprising that he would become obsessive about destroying them.

Many of my friends in the intelligence

community share the same obsession.

Bernie's is not a name that is found in newspapers; he has never been invited to appear on national television and, hopefully, will never be asked. Yet he has done as much as any one person to safeguard the security of his adopted nation.

Several years back, I did a favor for the man because I like, admire, and trust him. His sister, Eve, the young mother of a three-year-old son, had a evening of silly, injudicious behavior. On a lark, at a party with a couple of former college roommates, she tried a street drug that they were told was "coca candy."

It was crack cocaine.

As a upper-class professional woman, she'd never experienced anything like it. A few days later, Eve rationalized a reason to contact the friend of a friend who had the stuff, and she bought a little more.

Slightly more than a year later, at Bernie's request, I tracked his sister across four states to a suburban crackhouse outside Boulder, Colorado. It took me a couple of days to size up the hierarchy of males who exploited the women there and provided them with drugs. It took another couple days of research to find just the right way to leverage the crackhouse chieftain. I got her out without much trouble, and we got her into a superb rehab program. We gave it a month before we told her the bad news: Her distraught husband had divorced her in absentia and had secured custody of their son.

I stayed in close touch. I liked Eve very much; Bernie and I gradually became close friends. I joined the two of them, by telephone, for a small celebration the night Eve's ex-husband said, yes, he was willing to try again. It should have been the storybook ending to an American tragedy. Unfortunately, storybook endings are seldom associated with the white rock. After more than a year of apparent domestic tranquility, Eve vanished. Bernie asked me to go a-searching once more. I found her in Colorado again, the same suburb, the same crackhouse. This time, she refused help. She was found dead a few months later.

I rarely impose on Bernie for favors. Friendship is based on loyalty, not on behavioral bookkeeping, quid pro quo. But when I do ask a favor, he never refuses.

After I told him the story of Janet Mueller and her two lost companions, Bernie said to me, "Awful! Tragic! In such a terrible mishmash, who wouldn't want to help? Unfortunately, and as I keep telling you over and over, I don't have access to the kind of data you need. But just out of curiosity, do you have the lat and long of the wreck they were diving? Or GPS numbers, perhaps?"

I was taught to think in terms of latitude and longitude and still prefer it over the more modern Global Positional System numbers. For some reason, it's simpler for me to picture our planet covered with imaginary lines called parallels and meridians, or lines of longitude and latitude. It's easier for me to calculate distances in my head, too. It takes the earth twenty-four hours for a full rotation of 360 degrees. Thus, every hour we rotate 15 degrees longitude, or one time zone. For the sake of precision, the imaginary lines are broken down into degrees, minutes, and seconds. There is exactly one nautical mile per minute, and there are sixty minutes (and sixty nautical miles) between degrees.

I told Bernie that the wreck of the *Baja California* lies at 25 degrees 21 minutes 60 seconds north latitude and 82 degrees 31.97 minutes west longitude.

"And you said the Coast Guard had found debris from the wreck, but not a trace of the divers themselves?"

I told him that, besides Amelia Gardner, all the Coasties had found were a length of manila line tied to a life jacket, as described by Amelia, a camera bag, a water jug, and two empty tanks, all scattered to the southwest.

I found it very reassuring when Bernie asked, "I don't suppose you have the lat and long for the most distant item found?"

I told him an empty tank was found floating at 25 degrees 19.60 minutes north latitude and 82 degrees 46.50 minutes west longitude. The rough math was easy — twenty nautical miles or so southwest of the site of the wreck.

I heard him say, *"Humph,"* as if preoccupied, his keyboard clattering in the background, working on something else as we talked. Then he said, "So tell me what you know about satellite surveillance systems. Wait, I withdraw the question. Me, the computer nerd asking you, Mr. Live-in-a-Hut-Hermit. So let me tell you what is public information, which is why there's no harm in me giving you a little crash course in what it is you're asking. I tell you certain things, you judge for yourself if the satellite data you need are maybe available. Not that I can provide them."

I said, "Understood and agreed."

Bernie said, "Okay, so stand outside, look up at the night sky, and what you're seeing is the makings of a junkyard. You laugh. The man thinks I'm joking. About satellites, I never joke. There are nearly ten thousand man-made objects up there orbiting this little planet of ours. More than three thousand of those objects are satellites, operative and inoperative, plus garbage you wouldn't believe. Up there, we got nosecone shrouds, lens covers, hatch covers, rocket bodies, payloads that have exploded, junk the astronauts or cosmonauts threw out or forgot. All sorts of stuff.

"But the U.S. intelligence agencies also have some very amazing birds up there. I've *read* about this, understand, I got no firsthand knowledge. Not that anything is such a great big secret anymore. Our military shoots off a rocket, the world's watching. The Chinese, the Saudis, everyone, they know that if the rocket goes east or west, it's probably an electronic eavesdropping satellite. If it goes north or south, it's most likely a photoreconnaissance satellite, doing what they call a polar orbit or figure-eight orbit. The photorecon satellites, that's what might interest you."

No longer gazing at the octopi, concentrating on what Bernie was telling me —

telling me with words, and without words — I said, "Exactly. Satellite photographs. How good are they?"

"Even back in the 1960s, when the CIA first starting launching them, even then, they were pretty good. CORONA Satellite Photography, that was the name of the operation. Keyhole photography we . . ." Bernie paused, catching himself. "Every satellite had a KH, keyhole, designation. Carried large spools of seventy-millimeter film into space, great big panoramic cameras. After photographs were taken, the satellites jettisoned the exposed film, which was then snared in midfall by military planes. Amazingly complicated, but it worked pretty good."

I said, "But it's better now."

"Better? Remember the old rumor that NSA could read the number on a license plate from outer space. That was ten, fifteen years ago. Bunk! Three-meter resolution, that was about as good as it got. So the rumor was complete nonsense up until a few years back when we launched a couple of ultra-high-tech birds, KH-12s and now KH-13s. Absolutely fabulous resolution . . . which is what I've read, anyway. Pictures are so sharp, they can count the rivets on equipment coming out of Iraqi factories. They can pick out a human face in a sea of people. And the KH-13s, what they can do is still classified so, of course, how is someone like me supposed to know a thing or two about something like that? Spectacular reconnaissance, that would be my guess. With all the improvements in sensor development, maybe they can see through clouds. At night. In a heavy fog. I'm not saying it's true, but in such a world, name one little thing that's not possible."

Yep, Bernie definitely had access to the satellites, and the satellites had the capability. That's what he was telling me. I found his line, *a human face in a sea of people,* at once subtly evocative and also haunting. Was it really possible that he could pull up photos that might isolate Janet, Michael, and Grace *after* they were adrift?

I said, "Just for argument's sake, let's say I wormed my way into the right department, filled out all the forms, jumped through all the hoops, and managed to get official authorization to check the satellite data banks —"

"Marion, Marion! *Forget* it. Don't waste your time. It could never happen. If this country allowed intelligence satellites to be used in even one missing person's case, the floodgates would be opened. You know how many people go missing every year? Not to mention the breach of security. The whole system would be compromised. It would be disastrous. Even if you were a U.S. Senator, the governor of a state, it wouldn't matter. They wouldn't release that information to you, or even admit they had it."

"But let's say I *did* manage to get access. What are the chances that one or more satellites flew over the area the night my friends were set adrift? That photographs were taken?"

Yeager's voice changed slightly, had some emotion in there — additional reassurance. "The chances? A man so naturally lucky as you, what do you care about odds? I'll put it this way. There is now in place a keyhole system called 'Lacrosse' that is part of the old Star Wars initiative. With the satellites they have, U.S. intelligence people are able to see all parts of Russia at the same time, twenty-four hours a day, no problem. We've got newer birds on station now. Could be, our people want to keep a close eye on Cuba. Or Panama, maybe. I wouldn't be the tiniest bit surprised if that included the Gulf of Mexico, the Florida Keys, the whole kit 'n' kaboodle. Isn't that where you live, down there in the tropics? Coconuts and alligators, tourists wearing those horrible shirts. All that rain and humidity. Every summer we used to have to visit my aunt on Miami Beach. Whew! It's yours, you can have it." He was laughing now.

Yes, there would be photographs available, and Bernie could find them.

We talked for another fifteen minutes. We traded old stories, spoke of old friends. I mentioned the Islamic terrorists, and he went on a ten-minute tirade. "They have asked for a dirty war, and we are giving it to them!" he said more than once.

Yes, he was fixated on them, despised them.

Bernie was wrong when he said I have no appreciation for the electronic niceties of this century. I much appreciate the fact that I now have access to instant communications worldwide with people about whom I care deeply. Pick up a telephone, punch a few buttons, and we have an immediate conduit to those individuals who have made a mark upon our lives. Much of technology is a response to the loneliness of the human condition. Drums and signal fires, cell phones and Internet cafés —

methods change, but our wistfulness, our rebellion against isolation, does not.

Finally, Bernie told me how well Eve's son was doing. He was in high school now. Getting straight As and he'd almost aced his SATs on his first try. Sports, too. He was a superb point guard and played baseball as well. The proud uncle going on and on.

As we chatted, me standing in the lab, watching the octopi with cat-gold eyes watching me from their lighted tanks, I had an idea. Missing stone crabs were not nearly so compelling as three missing people, but the oddity of it still troubled me.

I said, "Hey Bernie, maybe you can give me some advice about another little problem I'm having. Someone or something is sneaking into my lab at night and stealing specimens. How hard would it be to rig a little night-vision camera in here and keep track of what happens when I'm away?"

"So, finally you ask for a favor that I can help you with! What I'm going to do is loan you a little digitized video camera. The night-vision lens is already attached, so what you're going to do is mount it on the wall, plug in the converter, and walk away. Simple as falling off a whatever it is people say. A barrel? There's a timer you could probably figure out on your own after futzing with it two or three hours, so it's better if I program it here. How's it with you I set it to come on at midnight, off at six? With enough memory to film nine, maybe ten, nights before you got to go to the menu and delete."

"Perfect," I said.

"Not a problem, old friend. You will be getting something from me in the next few days."

I wasn't certain if he meant the camera or satellite photographs.

The next night, Sunday, a cool, clear Pearl Harbor anniversary eve, Tomlinson came puttering up in his little rubber dinghy. I could hear him swearing fraternally at the ancient Japanese kicker that missed, coughed, sputtered, and threatened to stall. He'd had the thing for years, refused to get rid of it because, he said, it dependably sapped all the aggression right out of him each and every time he used it.

"The goddamn thing is an emotional laxative," he explained. "A bad karma purge with a carburetor glitch that Jesus Christ himself plus the twelve disciples couldn't solve if their holy asses depended on it. I still think it's a bad diaphragm, by the way. Reminds me of my ex-wife, the ball-breaking dragon lady. Dealing with that rice-burning piece of crap is like meditation in reverse. It's cheaper than therapy, plus I'm never in much of a hurry, so what do I care?"

Now I felt the rubber boat bump my inside dock, then felt and heard the *clomp-slap* sound of Tomlinson's bare feet as he swung up onto the deck. Heard the heavy rustling of paper bags, so I flipped on the outside flood, then held the door wide as he came in, arms filled with two bulging grocery sacks. I don't have air conditioning — don't like it, don't need it. Just ceiling fans and lots of big windows with screens. Even so, Tomlinson came in pushing a pocket of mangrove-dense air, hotter than the air inside, and rich with sulfur, iodine, and the oil fragrance he always wore, patchouli. Something else, too: the sappy sweet odor of marijuana clinging to his baggy surfer shorts and tank top, plus a hint of a familiar woman's perfume, Opium. Opium was my sister, Ransom's, favorite perfume. Apparently, they were keeping company again. I fanned the air away as I pulled the door closed and hooked it tight.

"Dinnertime, compadre. You eaten yet?"

I looked at my watch. It was more than an hour past sunset, nearly 7 p.m. Through the west window, I could see a quarter moon, coral pink among December stars, drifting seaward. I'd checked the *Farmer's Almanac*: Moonset was at 10:46 p.m. A good, black night for stargazing if I decided to break out the superb Celestron Nexstar 5-inch Schmidt-Casselgraine telescope that stood angled on its tripod by the north window, next to my reading chair and lamp. It is an amazing piece of optics. With its built-in computer and GPS, all you have to do is point the barrel of the scope north, punch in the approximate lat and long, and you can then select from a menu of many hundreds of celestial objects, stars, and planets. Choose any one of them, touch a button, and the telescope will automatically find it.

I said to Tomlinson, "Amelia didn't head back to St. Pete until after four, and I just finished working out. So the answer's no, I haven't eaten."

He was taking objects out of the sacks, bunches of fresh herbs — parsley, basil, cilantro — a handful of Persian limes. "Did you run? Or go to the school and

219

swim laps? They're keeping the pool open late, I hear."

"Both. Kind of. I went down by the old landing strip and ran a couple of miles along Algier's Beach, then swam out to the jet-ski buoy and back."

"You're shitting me. This time of year, man, the water's getting cold. Has to be in the mid, maybe low seventies."

I said, "I don't care. After the Gulf, the water in my cistern shower seems warm. I like it." I looked at the counter as he unloaded his sacks on to it, noting that, along with food, they contained a pilot chart of the Gulf of Mexico, wirebound, plus a sheath of what looked to be printed material from the Internet. I picked up the pilot chart, then looked into Tomlinson's deepset and sad blue eyes. "You called your buddies at Blue Water Charts in Lauderdale."

"Yep, Rick and Dorie. They knew just what I needed and FedExed it over."

"So explain. Are we making dinner or doing research?"

"You got any fish? Maybe some shrimp, something like that? I'm going to make a Panamanian *chimichurri* sauce."

I loved Tomlinson's *chimichurri* but could never seem to duplicate it exactly:

diced bunches of parsley and cilantro, one clove of diced garlic, one small diced chili pepper, a pinch of kosher salt, a little drizzle of balsamic vinegar, the juice from half a fresh lime, plus a cup or more of olive oil. Sometimes he added tomatoes, sometimes he didn't.

I nodded. "Jeth dropped off a couple of nice kingfish steaks. He says the mackerel are running two-ten off the lighthouse in thirty-five feet of water."

Tomlinson was at the sink now, washing the greens, the veins in his biceps implying the tubular network linked beneath his skin, the complicated hydraulics of human physiology. We are delicate machines, indeed, fleshy pumps, electrodes, and cartilaginous wiring. He said, "In that case, we're making dinner *and* doing research."

Chapter Twelve

Tomlinson and I discussed it, going back and forth until we agreed that there were only three possible explanations for why Janet and the other two weren't found. One: The people aboard the planes, helicopters, and search vessels missed them. Two: Someone, something, or some incident had removed them from the surface of the water before or during the search. Three: They were never adrift to begin with.

Sitting at the little teak table on the porch outside, an oil lamp burning between us for light, Tomlinson took a bite of his mackerel in *chimichurri*, and said, "Okay, but the working premise is that Amelia Gardner's story is mostly true. We start with that, then presumably eliminate the other possibilities as we go along."

"Agreed," I said.

Tomlinson was getting into it, his brain

firing, generating enthusiasm. We'd had the memorial service for Janet that afternoon at Jensen's Marina. It was an emotional affair. Some crying, some laughter, the ceremony — like all funeral ceremonies — underlining the fact that our lives are brief and that the impact an individual has on the life of another is never realized until the association has forever ended. Apparently, Tomlinson had converted his own sense of loss into a determination to salvage Janet's reputation. It'd been awhile since I'd seen him so focused and lucid. Now he said, "Our job is to compile all the data we can. Objectively, I'm saying. If we go into this as advocates, *hermano,* we forfeit our credibility. We're both scientists. We both know that."

"Of course. I wouldn't do it any other way."

"Not that I don't have my own biases. Some of the crap they've been saying about what happened out there? It was a drug deal gone bad. It was murder. It was some military snafu that the right-wingers are trying to cover up — that one, at least, I'm willing to consider. Like maybe the three drifters were out there and saw the military doing something top secret. Whatever happened, we need to collect all the data we can and just have faith that Amelia's story is mostly true."

That word again: *mostly*. It surprised me. "Did I miss something? I didn't find any holes in her story. Everything seemed consistent. An emotional event that was tough to talk about, but she seemed to do her best to lay it all out there. To be honest."

Tomlinson started to speak, hesitated, choosing his words carefully before he said, "It's just a feeling I've got, man. You know me. I collect information on a whole different level. Let's face it. I'm clairvoyant. Psychic, whatever small label you want to use. Clairvoyant, anyway, 'til it comes to love affairs, then I turn into a hundred percent numb-nuts fuck-up. But, if I'm not in love, I know things about people without them having to say a word. I just have a sense that Amelia didn't tell us everything. Intuition. But it's more than that."

"If you think she's lying, you need to tell me. What's she have to lie about?"

He said, "I think it has something to do with the way she got separated from the others. Something she's ashamed of. Not that she should be. Under those kind of circumstances, your boat sinks, you're set adrift at night, no one has a right to question or criticize someone else's behavior."

"But that's exactly what you're doing right now. Did you catch her in some kind of factual error in her story? Or are you just guessing?" I said.

I felt relieved when he said, "Intuition, just like I said."

"Okay, your concern is noted. But let's stick to the facts. You're the one who brought up the importance of credibility."

"Just because it's anecdotal doesn't mean it's not factual. There are all kinds of ways to collect data. When I was out there alone aboard the *No Mas*, three extra days searching, I dropped into a very deep meditative state. It was a heavy scene, man. I was right there with them the night the boat went down. Janet, Amelia, Michael, and Grace. I saw what happened. I saw what happened afterward. The whole dark vision. Like an electric current pouring into my brain. My own little movie running, close enough to them to see their faces, hear their voices."

I almost allowed him to lure me off the subject and back into our old debate on parapsychology, ghosts, the whole mystical question. I'd like to believe such things happen. Who wouldn't? If certain people really can foresee the future or read the minds of others, it adds substantial weight to the proposition that there is symmetry and spiritual purpose to the human experience. I would like to believe that, but I don't.

I've heard Tomlinson's so-called proofs often enough, but I have yet to see proof myself of mystical, extrasensory powers. Tomlinson has an eerie ability to read people and quickly perceive what few others can — that, I don't argue. I suspect he does it by interpreting body language, voice intonations, who knows, though he's very good at it. But could he really know what happened the night the *Seminole Wind* sank without being there? That I did not believe and would not accept.

I took the pilot chart off the deck and folded it open beside my plate. "So if you perceived all that through meditation, tell me how it was. What happened to the three of them after they got split up from Amelia. Are they still alive?"

Tomlinson smiled patiently and tugged his scraggily blond hair back with his left hand, letting the question hang there before he answered, "Marion, sarcasm is your least attractive quality. You resort to it so rarely, I sometimes forget."

I was cleaning my thick glasses, wanting to see and understand all the little symbols on the chart. I pulled the oil lamp closer as I said, "I'm sorry. So I withdraw the offensive tone, but the question's the same. What do you think happened? Why didn't we find them?"

"What I think is, one of the reasons is right there in front of you. Actually the main reason. Look at the current arrows. It's all right there on the chart."

Pilot charts are superb tools for the bluewater voyager or the gunk-holing cruiser. They give a lot more information than the much more commonly used U.S. government or NOAA nautical charts. Published by the Defense Mapping Agency, their aim is to help the mariner select the fastest and safest routing for any offshore passage at any time of the year. The charts provide information on weather conditions for very specific areas. They note prevailing winds and calms, average wave heights, typical barometric pressure, average currents, air and water temperatures, and recommended routes.

This pilot chart was for the Gulf of Mexico, Campeche, Mexico to Cuba to New Orleans and Florida, the entire, massive basin dotted with symbols and navigational data. The chart consisted of twelve pages, one for each month of the year, and I had it open to the month of November. I found Marco Island, found the little cross-hatched egg-shaped icon at 25 degrees 21 minutes 60 seconds north latitude and 82 degrees 31.97 minutes west longitude: the wreck of the *Baja California.*

As I studied the chart, noting the feathered arrows that marked prevailing winds and the serpentine arrows that indicated ocean currents and tidal currents, Tomlinson said, "When the *Seminole Wind* sank, all the detritus drifted southwest. The life jackets, the empty tanks, everything we found. So it's very natural to assume that three swimmers wearing inflated vests would also drift southwest."

I was nodding, enjoying the food, enjoying the concise data on the chart, the way they accurately distilled the wild ocean into an orderly and predictable rendering of numbers, graphs, directional arrows. I said, "It's more than an assumption. All of the data-marking buoys the Coast Guard dropped — what? There were half a dozen or so of them? DMBs — they all drifted southwest. Covered five or six miles every twenty-four hours, which . . ." I paused. "Now that I think about it, and this is the

228

first time I've checked a pilot chart, that *doesn't* seem right. It says here the prevailing ocean current runs at about two knots. Anything floating, adrift, should have covered at least thirty, maybe forty, miles in twenty-four hours."

"Exactly. I was struck by that, too. The figures don't seem to work out. I spent the afternoon holed-up in Mack's office doing research on the computer, calling sailor buddies of mine, a couple of shrimp-boat captains who do a lot of dragging in that area. You ever seen a data-marking buoy?"

I had, but I let Tomlinson talk.

"They're sealed canisters, about three feet long, flat on both ends, painted bright orange, and heavier on the bottom to make them float upright. There's a GPS antenna on top. Self-locating data-marking buoys, that's the official name. They send a signal directly to a satellite that tracks their movement. So it's got to be accurate."

I said, "Very accurate. Which is why I hadn't stopped to question the math before. So why did the buoys drift so slowly?"

He stood, came around behind me, looking over my shoulder at the chart. Tomlinson has huge, bony hands with nails bitten down to the quick. Now he touched an index finger to the icon that represented the *Baja California*. "Okay, this is where they dropped the DMBs, right on the wreck site. All along this line. According to the chart, the prevailing winds are out of the northeast — and they were that night, blowing fifteen to twenty. Prevailing current moves east-southeast at about two knots. The wind was blowing slightly against the current, and that would have reduced the speed of drift. The DMBs covered only about six miles a day. So far, it's just like the Coast Guard and all the rest of us figured."

I said, "Three people wearing vests would have blown southwest with the wind, but slowed quite a bit by a current trying to push them to the east. Then that explains it. They would have traveled the same direction and at a similar speed as the buoys."

Tomlinson said, "Not necessarily. Last night, I took this chart with me when I crawled into my bunk. Kept looking at it and looking at it. You know how when you look directly at a star too long, it disappears? I did that with the area around the *Baja California*. I just let it blur until it vanished, and that's when the whole current system came into focus. I'm talking about for the entire Gulf of Mexico. Try it.

Let your eyes go wide, imagine the current arrows are in red. Let them stand out and see what happens. The big picture is what you need to see."

I looked at the chart momentarily, tried to let my eyes blur, but then shook my head. "My imagination isn't that good. Save us both some time and just tell me what it is I'm supposed to see."

"Okay, first thing you see is a big salt-water lake, more than a thousand miles wide between Florida and Mexico. The Gulf of Mexico." He moved his finger down to Cuba. "The saltwater lake has only two openings. There's a 20-mile-wide opening here between the Florida Keys and Cuba. There's a 125-mile opening here between Cuba and the Yucatan Peninsula. Those are damn small openings for ocean currents to squeeze through. Take a garden hose, squeeze the end with your thumb, and the water speeds up. Like a jet."

I said wryly, "I'm aware of that. It's called the Venturi effect. Constrict flowing water or gas, and its velocity increases."

"That's precisely what happens in the Gulf. The arrows here tell the whole story. The equatorial current and the Guiana current come flowing into Cuba, get squeezed between Cuba and the Yucatan, then blast into the Gulf, directly toward Louisiana, the Mississippi River Delta country. The current's so strong that it ricochets off the southern shallows and breaks into two great looping currents. Those currents break into a series of crazy spirals, smaller loops, like gyres."

He began to tap the chart with his finger. "There's one here . . . a gyre here . . . here. They're all over the place. One side of the gyre flows more or less south, the other side flows more or less north. They're like big, slow-motion whirlpools floating around out there at sea. Oval-shaped rivers that, in the fall and winter, flow at one, maybe even two knots, and faster in summer. Ultimately, most of them exit and gain speed at the stricture between Key West and Cuba."

"The Gulf Stream," I said. "That's what you're describing. The source of the Gulf Stream."

He said, "It all contributes, yeah, the Gulf Stream. But do you see what I'm getting at?"

Tomlinson is a teacher with extraordinary gifts, and now, for the first time, I could see that what, at first, appeared to be a random but consistent flow of water was, actually, a series of symmetrical loops. According to the pilot chart, in November, historically, a particularly small but strong gyre existed between Sanibel at the northerly extreme and Flamingo to the south. Offshore, water flowed southeast. Inshore, water spiraled northward.

"Datum marker buoys can't swim," Tomlinson said softly. "Janet, Michael, and Grace could. I think that accounts for the difference, and why we didn't find them. Remember the big charter boat that Amelia told us she saw that night or whose lights she saw, anyway. The *Ellen Clair*? The captain, Ken Peterson, told her later that he'd anchored over the *Baja California*.

"I called him this afternoon, Doc. I told him what we plan to do. Find the *Seminole Wind* and figure out why she sank. Dive the *Baja* and collect anything we can that corroborates Amelia's story. We talked for maybe half an hour. Nice guy. Feels terrible that his boat was so close and he couldn't find them. Just like the rest of us.

"So I was asking him how it went once he got to the Dry Tortugas, how the fishing was, and he said something that made all the little lights come on. He said the trip back to Fort Myers Beach was a lot faster than the trip out because he ran closer to shore where there wasn't as much wind . . . and there was a hell of a strong northerly current pushing him along."

I'd stopped eating. Did not feel like eating anymore. "So they swam east toward the flashing light, Janet, Michael, and Grace," I said, "just like Amelia. They probably got close to the tower. Maybe real close. But then they stopped swimming for some reason."

Tomlinson walked to the window above the little ship's stove. Stood there staring at the lights of the marina. People moving around out there on the docks. Silhouettes, shadows, and muted voices. All Sundays dampen noise, particularly a memorial service Sunday. "I've thought and thought about it," he said. "It's plausible, possible, maybe even probable . . . and it's so goddamn sad I can barely stand it."

He continued, "We assume that Amelia's story is mostly true. So why didn't we find them? If the three hooked up, stayed together, they would have been a larger mass, easier to see. If they separated, the chances of spotting at least one of them increase proportionally. The Coast Guard was using forward-looking infrared radar; those things register body heat from a mile away. So it's damn unlikely we could have missed them unless I'm right. They swam east toward the tower but stopped. They got caught on the edge of the gyre. Just like Peterson told me: where there was a hell of a strong current pushing them north. At one, maybe two knots, they'd have been off Marco by first light, fifteen maybe twenty miles away. Way the hell north of the *Baja California*."

I said, "I wouldn't call a two-knot current that strong. Those were his words?"

" 'A hell of a strong northerly current.' That's what he said. I agree with you. The pilot chart for November shows one to two knots for this particular gyre, but maybe it was stronger. Who knows? Things change fast out there, you know that. But that's what the man said, and he's been captaining for fifteen years."

Now I was feeling sick. The Coast Guard, all of us, we'd all searched from a few miles north of the wreck site, then forty miles and more to the south and southwest.

Tomlinson said, "Powerboats are machines, but a fine sailboat has more in common with a divining rod. The *No Mas* kept trying to take me north. My sailboat, the wheel, she tried and tried to turn, to show me the way. I was a fool. I wouldn't let her.

"Our last three days out there, alone, that's when I finally let the *No Mas* take control. I gave her the wheel, just like you sometimes give a horse free rein, and she took me way north and west, far out to sea. But it was too late. Too late."

His voice became a whisper as he added, "At night, when I meditated, I could see what happened, how it happened, everything. Their voices, I could hear their words, see their faces, could feel Janet's fear, her horror. What Janet saw, I saw, and I knew then just what I know now. They were still alive. They may *still* be alive."

Part Two

Chapter Thirteen

Stars, planets, streaking satellites fell toward her, propelled by the buoyancy of each cresting wave, then stars were yanked skyward again as the wave collapsed, dropping her body into a black valley . . .

Floating on her back, eyes focused overhead and clinging to a universe of blazing starlight, Janet Mueller used her left hand to grip a section of anchor line hitched to the bow of the *Seminole Wind* while the fingers of her right hand touched the thin gold crucifix she was never without. It was a gift from her late husband, Roger, who'd been killed in a car accident years ago, only three months before their first baby was to be born.

They were to have a boy. They knew it from the first ultrasound — an infant so obviously a boy that it was the subject of many whispered bedtime jokes.

Thomas Roger Mueller.

Janet barely survived the shock of her husband's death. Their child did not. She went into labor prematurely, and the doctors could not save the boy, though young Thomas fought valiantly to live for three nights and four days, rabbit-sized, tiny fists clenched, lying inside the oxygen spherical in the preemie ward, Toledo General Hospital.

Her husband was killed the day after Thanksgiving. Thomas Roger died one week later, the first day of December. That was seven years and a different lifetime ago, it had come to seem. Almost as if it had happened to another person, a person with her name and face who'd dreamed all those peaceful times with Roger, and then, still sleeping, slipped into a nightmare that was the deepest of horrors.

That was Ohio. This was Florida. Her new life. The elementary school teacher who, to save her own sanity, traded in expectations of a suburban house and conventional family for a quirky little houseboat at a quirky little marina. Her new life in the tropics with parties, devoted friends, great sunsets, and, finally, a second good man — though she and Jeth had had their problems. Everyone did.

Once browsing through the library of her friend, Marion Ford, she'd found a chapter in a book about certain lizards, members of the Iguanid family, that could change colors as required, even grow new tails if they'd been injured — chromatic transformation and cellular regeneration. Janet felt an unexpected kinship with those creatures because she had learned that, if sufficiently traumatized, a woman must employ chameleon capabilities to endure.

Janet Mueller had lost her heart but was slowly growing a new one in this, the life of her own invention. A good life, too. Until this day. Until this dive trip.

She would survive it. She had to. She'd survived worse.

Now, holding on to the rope, frightened to the point of emotional exhaustion, Janet repeated the prayer that had become her bedtime mantra, her savior during those worst of times: *I am strong. My faith is stronger. I am strong. My faith is stronger.* Over and over in her mind, she spoke the words by rote. There was another mantra that she'd sometimes used during the day when the pain threatened to overwhelm her. It was one of her favorites because it was both reassuring and assertive: *This evil stands no chance against my prayers.*

She switched to that mantra now, finding comfort in the old, familiar rhythm of the words, repeating the phrase silently as all four of them clung to the rope in single file.

This evil stands no chance against my prayers!

She'd been in the water now for nearly four hours, and her body was beginning to complain, give her little signals that it was time to step back on to the dock, get into a hot freshwater shower, then change into clean clothes, something dry and warm.

If only she could!

Janet wore a pink neoprene shorty wet suit. Beneath that, she wore what divers call a "body skin," a one-piece undergarment made of nylon and lycra that's soft and stretchable. Even so, the wet suit was beginning to chafe at the ridged areas where the seams were glued, under her arms and on the inside of her thighs. The nylon was also beginning to chafe around, her nipples, which were naturally supersensitive, anyway.

Salt water made the chafed areas burn. Janet's neck-length, chestnut hair was caked with salt, too, and salt was so heavy on her tongue that her breath now had a metallic odor, which she could taste when she swallowed.

Still, she repeated her strong assertion: *This evil stands no chance against my prayers!*

Janet was closest to the bow of the boat. Holding on to the line behind her were Grace, then Michael, then Amelia. Amelia had volunteered to take the end of the rope because she said she'd been a competitive swimmer in high school, and so was probably the best swimmer of the group. Plus she, like Janet, still had her fins. If a wave knocked her away from the rope, she'd have the best chance of making it back without requiring someone else to release the rope to help her.

For Amelia to volunteer to do such a thing, when they were all so frightened and in such danger, impressed Janet tremendously. She'd known Amelia for only a few days but liked her, trusted her on a level of perception that was qualitative, and now her trust was confirmed. Amelia was a strong woman who felt an obligation to the welfare of others. Someone who could be relied on to act and who wasn't afraid to take charge.

When Amelia made the offer to take the last space, Michael protested, but in a way that said he was actually grateful. He still seemed to be in shock. It was his boat that had sunk; his responsibility, not to mention what had to be a terrible financial loss. Janet had known Michael for more than a year. They'd had a brief sexual fling — which was very unlike her, but Michael was gorgeous; no one could argue that — and she still enjoyed his company because he was sociable, quick to laugh, and thoughtful in ways that she sometimes found touching. Plus, remaining friends mitigated the probable remorse of a one-night stand — something she'd never done before and would never risk again.

Janet had never seen Michael like this, though. In the nearly three hours of daylight after the *Seminole Wind* first swamped, the fear in the man's face was unmistakable in the mottled skin, the glazed eyes. Every few minutes, it seemed, he'd mutter, "I can't believe this is happening. This can't really be happening, can it?" When he did try to make conversation, his voice was strained. He couldn't seem to concentrate or complete a sentence.

None of them, however, was more frightened than Grace. Janet had known Grace for nearly as long as she'd known Michael. He always introduced her as "my closest lady friend" and she almost certainly was.

The only thing they didn't do together was dating and sex — or so they joked — and they were hilarious when they'd get into one of their black woman versus white male mock bickering matches, which had become a kind of shtick, they were so good at it. It was like a comedy routine, they were so darn funny, him the big jock football coach-teacher and not the smartest guy in the world, Grace the successful realtor and black community activist.

It was a friendship that seemed unlikely but really wasn't. Five years earlier, only a month or so apart, they'd coincidentally bought adjoining duplexes on Avenida del Mare, just across the canal from Palm Island and only a couple of blocks from Siesta Key Beach. Both were trying to restart their lives after ending ugly, destructive marriages. Both were wary of beginning new relationships, both loved cooking, fitness training, lived far from their own families, and each owned a dog — Grace, a miniature Doberman; Michael, a yellow lab named Coach.

After a wary few months, they entered into a mutually beneficial acquaintance-ship that began with dog-sitting and gradually became a more dependent and far more complex friendship. By the time

Janet met them, Michael and Grace had become indispensable, each to the other, as confidant, advisor, protector, and as the quick and dependable judge of potential lovers who circulated in and out of their own small, stable orbit. They were workout partners, swing dance partners, and safe, steadfast escorts in those social situations when an escort was needed but a decent date couldn't be found.

The two were so clearly at home with each other that they quickly put people around them at ease. Almost everyone they allowed to be a part of their friendship said variations of the same: You two should form a comedy team. You two should have your own television show, because you're such a riot!

Grace and Michael hadn't made any jokes in the last few hours, though. Soon after leaving to make the dive, Janet knew it had been a mistake to bring Grace. A mistake for any of them to come so far offshore, probably. Especially, though, for the Sarasota realtor.

What was immediately evident as they headed out Marco Island Pass, into the rolling seas, was that Grace was nervous and uncomfortable in a boat. It was plainly seen in the way she hung next to Michael Sanford, often grabbing his arm when jolted by an unusually big wave, and in her repeated questions: "Are you sure it's okay for us to be out here, Sandman? You sure it's safe? You get the Princess Grace hurt, Sandman, the Princess is going to open up a can of whoop-ass on you, my friend."

Despite Grace's use of the pet names reserved for their private use, as if making light of their situation she was scared, no disguising that. A couple of times, Janet and Amelia made eye contact, eyebrows raised, both acknowledging that Grace was frightened, didn't like boats, didn't like water. She wouldn't be here at all if Michael hadn't made it his special project to teach her to SCUBA dive. He'd taken her through the PADI classes, then on a couple of dives to the Dry Tortugas, and recently a weeklong trip to Key West and the reefs of American Shoals.

That had been her favorite dive trip, American Shoals. All the great coral heads and big fish at Looe Key and Western Sambo, then eating and drinking at the Green Parrot in Key West, that old pirate town, with its shipwright houses and widows' walks. On the charter boat to Looe Key, they'd met Amelia and formed a diving friendship. American Shoals was where their little group started. That kind of diving, she liked: glassy, flat seas, and water so clear it was like looking down into outer space, a whole aqua-bright universe of color and light.

This, though, Grace hated. Big waves, gray water. Too much wind and salt. This wasn't like the Keys where there were lots of boats, lots of fun. This water was wilderness, alone and open to the sky. It terrified her.

Her discomfort was even more obvious when she got into her dive gear and jumped off the boat. Grace not only wasn't a good swimmer, she didn't enjoy being in the water, all those waves lifting and rolling, spraying salt water into her face, beading in her African hair, causing her to squinch her eyes tight, this tall, muscular woman making faces like a little girl.

Once again, Amelia had demonstrated her strength by risking offense when she tapped Michael on the shoulder and said, "Are you sure Grace is up to this? Maybe she should stay on the boat and just the three of us dive." But Grace interceded immediately, saying, "I'm not staying up here on the boat alone. No way, sister! Big wave could come along and suck me right outta there!" And Michael had agreed, laughing, saying, "You think I'm going to let anything happen to the Princess? Where I go, she goes." Waiting while Grace rinsed her face mask and pulled it on, Michael had shouted, "We're a team, right, Gracie?"

Once again, Janet and Amelia communicated via eye contact only: No way was Grace going to complete this dive.

They were right. Pulling themselves in single file down the anchor line, into the green dusk below, Grace had stopped at about thirty feet. She knew the hand signs from her classes: Her ears wouldn't clear. She'd have to go back up. She *wanted* to go back up.

Michael returned to the boat with her, of course. On the buddy system, buddies stick together.

The two of them were still together when Amelia and Janet surfaced nineteen minutes later to find the *Seminole Wind* upside-down, floating bow-high on its taut anchor line, wind sharpening out of an afternoon sky with a horizon the color of winter clouds, like moonlight on ice.

During hurricane season in that year, July through November, there was less activity than usual in the southern meridians.

There were seven tropical storms but only two became hurricanes, which is significantly below the average of ten tropical storms and six hurricanes during that five-month window. Also, there were no major hurricanes (category three or higher on the Saffir-Simpson scale, meaning winds greater than 110 mph), which is also unusual — though one storm did approach that strength, Hurricane Gordon.

On an average, there are two major hurricanes in a season that make hard landfall somewhere in the tropics. There are death tolls. There are estimates of property damage. There are coordinated relief efforts that include many agencies, sometimes many countries. The year that Janet and her friends disappeared was an exception.

As far as tropical weather, it was a rare, peaceful season — with the exclusion of one short period, the first week of November, the week that the *Seminole Wind* sank. It was during the last week of October and the first seven days of November that the season's only two hurricanes formed, and they formed almost simultaneously.

Hurricane Florence began to take shape on November 2 as a subtropical depression at latitude 23.20 and longitude 47.70, which is on a line with Cuba and west of Florida Channel, that tight water exit between Key West and Havana.

At the same time, above the Isthmus of Panama and east of the Miskito Reefs of Nicaragua, Hurricane Gordon began to gather heat and convective energy, the slow formation of its tropospheric circulation visible to Tropical Satellite Analysis and Forecast (TSAF) weather monitors along its track. Gordon followed an unusual, erratic path over Nicaragua, the western Caribbean Sea, then drifted toward the Gulf of Mexico's second constricted water space, the Yucatan Channel.

By November 4, the day that Janet, Michael, and Grace were set adrift, both narrow entrances into the Gulf of Mexico were dominated by these two massive and conflicting low-pressure systems, though the effects on the Gulf were not obvious in terms of wind and rain. Between November 1 and 3, Florida residents from Sarasota to Marco Island awoke to read similar, repetitive weather forecasts in their daily papers: partly cloudy, chance of showers. Highs in the upper eighties, lows in the upper sixties. Winds east to southeast, fifteen knots, seas one to two feet, bay and inland waters a moderate chop.

It was good boating weather, nothing obvious out there to fear.

On Friday, November 4, the weather grew more brisk, although newspapers still predicted winds only to fifteen knots. The forecast that Michael Sanford and the others heard that morning on the VHF radio as they left Marco Island was slightly more severe, and more accurate. A recorded voice for NOAA Weather Radio repeated several times each hour: "From Cape Sable to Tarpon Springs, and fifty miles offshore, small craft should exercise caution. Winds will be out of the east fifteen to twenty knots, seas four to six feet, with bay and inland waters choppy."

It wasn't ideal weather, but it wasn't terrible, either. In his custom twenty-five-foot boat powered with twin 225-horsepower Evinrudes, Sanford could still blast through waves at thirty-five miles per hour or faster, which put the wreck of the *Baja California* less than two hours or so from the light buoy off Big Marco Pass.

Something else that Sanford may have considered is that weather forecasts for the Gulf Coast of Florida are notoriously unreliable. Fishing guides often joke about them with a bitterness born from losing family income because, each season, clients cancel trips after listening to erroneous forecasts predicting foul weather. It's not because the Gulf region lacks excellent meteorologists. Weather here is difficult to predict because the Gulf of Mexico is a complicated body of water, sensitive as a barometer, and influenced by changes in global weather, both subtle and strong.

The influence of the two gathering hurricanes on the Gulf was invisible but indisputable. The erratic, swirling currents and gyres of the Gulf are driven by diverse factors that include wind, heat, and oceanic currents. During a normal week, the great trade wind currents of the Caribbean push through the Yucatan Channel, into the Gulf, rivering along at speeds that can exceed three nautical miles per hour during the fall and winter. When Hurricane Gordon began its slow counterclockwise lumbering, however, the trade wind streams began to pile water massively off Cuba and the Yucatan Peninsula, pressuring it through the Yucatan Straits at more than twice the speed of normal flow — in excess of six knots, or more than seven miles an hour, which is twice as fast as an Olympian can swim.

Off the Florida Straits, the effect of soon-to-be Hurricane Florence was proportional, but in reverse. As the Gulf of Mexico's great loop current flows eastward along the Florida panhandle, then southward along the Florida peninsula, it rejoins a smaller but more powerful current loop off the northern coast of Cuba. These two saltwater rivers combine to form an inexorable surging of water called the Florida Current. This is the beginning of the Gulf Stream, which Juan Ponce de Leon described in his ship's log as "the current more powerful than the wind." The Gulf Stream transports 80 million tons of water per second along the coast of the United States, then east toward Europe, its warm waters profoundly affecting the weather of the British Isles and Europe.

Because the Florida Current is severely constricted by the Florida Keys and Cuba as it exits the Gulf, it flows hard even in normal weather, sometimes nearly four nautical miles per hour. However, with Florence hanging off the stricture, sucking in heat, wind, and water, both the velocity and mass of the Florida Current were amplified.

Hurricane Gordon was pushing water from the west; Tropical Storm Florence was pulling water from the east. The swirling, mobile, and complicate gyres whirlpooling within the Gulf were energized proportionally, gathering speeds of up to five, six, perhaps even seven knots, though no one knows for certain.

As the velocity of the currents and gyres increased and conflicted with wind flow, seas became heavier, more volatile, with occasional rogue waves large and out of keeping with normal seas abraded by twenty-knot winds. Even during calm weather, boat traffic is never heavy offshore of Florida's Gulf barrier islands. There are more fish and more fun to be had gunkholing around the bays. When the weather turns sloppy, though, boat traffic is almost nonexistent, and the Gulf becomes an uninhabited desert of gray.

There is an additional factor to be considered when contemplating the fate of three lone souls adrift in rivers that have no horizons. Oceanographers have determined that wind blowing across open water can sometimes alter the direction of the fluid's movement — a phenomenon known as "wind drag," the effects of which are defined as "geotropic flow."

Wind moving over water creates friction, and the influence of that applied friction can cause objects on the water's surface to drift at a 45-degree angle to the wind. Thus, wind blowing from the northeast will gradually create its own northwesterly water current. If the water is already flowing north, the velocity of that current will be increased and its direction altered only slightly.

Under such rare conditions, wing drag might have more influence on an inflated buoyancy compensator vest, which floats mostly atop the water, than on a data-marking buoy, which floats mostly beneath it.

Hurricane Florence formed quickly, swirled out to sea and vanished. Gordon had an impact on the Atlantic coast, though it was a hurricane for only about a day while southeast of the North Carolina Outer Banks. Most of its havoc was wrought as a tropical storm, its driving rains producing flooding and mud slides, which were particularly deadly in Haiti. Estimates of the death toll ranged up to two thousand. In Florida, seven deaths were attributed to Gordon, and there was significant agricultural damage.

If judged by similar elements, factors that can be consistently measured and recorded, the effect of the two hurricanes on the Gulf of Mexico, however, was negligible — unless you were one of three people out there in a gyre, floating and alone, being swept away.

At 7 p.m. on that moonless, windy night, Michael Sanford heard Janet make an abrupt mewing sound, then heard her scream, "Hey! My God, where'd the boat go?"

Moments later, the anchor line he and the others were holding was ripped away.

The anchor line had been in his left hand. In his right, he'd been holding Grace Walker, had her spooned against his body, trying to comfort her. Was trying to find some comfort himself, too — there was reassurance in the act of reassuring. When the boat went down, the anchor line snatched him under, vibrating with the intensity of a piano wire. He let go instinctively and stroked his way toward the surface, up through the blackness . . . and felt Grace sliding down his body, clawing at his abdomen, then legs, her fingernails gouging into the flesh of his feet as the boat dragged her toward the bottom, 110 feet below, while he ascended.

Gracie!

Even before he reached the surface, he

understood what had happened. To make Grace feel more secure, he'd tied a conventional life jacket to her BCD, and then he'd looped a bight of the anchor line into the life jacket. She been terrified of losing her grip on the rope and drifting away. What would happen if he fell asleep? Who'd come get her? Being tied to the life jacket and the anchor line seemed to calm her.

But now the *Seminole Wind*, the boat he'd help design, the boat that was a favorite symbol of the lifestyle he embraced, had belched the last of the air pockets floating its fiberglass hull and was finally sinking, pulling the anchor line and Grace down with it.

Still underwater, Sanford deflated his BCD by yanking the dump valve cord at his right shoulder, then jackknifed downward, eyes open in the black water, seeing only the iridescent streaks and swirls of phosphorescence. A couple of yards below him was a strumming, greenish light that he hoped was the anchor line, and now he swam wildly toward it.

With his fingers outstretched, he found the line and clamped his left fist tight around the rope, while, with his right hand, he fumbled for the stainless-steel dive knife in the plastic scabbard strapped to his ankle. Ironically, the knife was a birthday gift from Grace, an expensive blue tang made by Underwater Kinetics.

He drew the knife — nearly dropped it — then severed the anchor line with three fast sawing strokes and was instantly catapulted to the surface by the buoyancy of Grace's inflated vest. Came up right beside her, the two of them already wrapped tight in the other's arms, both of them coughing water and vomiting, each calling the other's name, while Janet and Amelia, from out of the darkness, shouted, "Michael? Grace? Michael? Gracie? Where are you?!"

Sanford yelled, "Here! We're over here!" then began to inflate his BCD again, holding the valve open with his trembling fingers, blowing into the valve, seeing nothing but black waves, canyon-sized, and Grace's silhouette floating beside him, his heart panicking inside his ribs, as he heard her scream, "I'm scared, Mikey! I'm so scared, and I don't want to be here anymore. Please take me home. *Please!*" The childlike quality of her voice was so touching and painful that he groaned, groaned again, then began to shake uncontrollably between breaths.

When his vest was inflated and he could speak, he hugged Grace tight to him, as she whispered over and over into his ear, "You saved me, Sandman, you saved me!" and him not hearing because he was speaking into her ear, whispering: "I'm so sorry about this, Gracie. I'm so goddamn sorry about this I could cry."

Then he did.

Amelia had left them. Intentionally or accidentally, they didn't know. For the last half hour, she'd been right there at their side, one of four gray shapes in the darkness, a hand to grasp as, together, they battled their way toward the flashing light that fired on the horizon.

If they were riding a cresting wave, they could see the light clearly: a detonation of white, every four seconds. The light was about three miles away — Michael told them that. Not such a far swim, Amelia kept telling them that, too. Told them that when she was in high school, their swim team workouts had sometimes been five, even six miles. "Three miles," she said. "That's nothing. We'll just take it steady and easy."

They talked back and forth that way, shouting over the whistle of wind and keening waves, trying to bolster themselves with lies no one really believed: The swim would be easy. There was no danger. Sooner or later, a boat would come along and pluck them out. Michael kept saying the *Baja California* was a popular wreck. It attracted a lot of fishing and diving traffic. This would be a funny adventure story to tell their grandchildren. Some day, they'd all look back and laugh — no one really believed that, either.

Only Janet seemed to have any real confidence as she said over and over: "We're going to make it. They're going to find us. If we stick together, we'll all make it." Once she told them oddly and without explanation, "This evil doesn't stand a chance against my prayers. Trust me. It doesn't stand a chance."

It was very slow going. They were southwest of the light tower. The wind was blowing even harder now, whistling into their faces out of the northeast. Waves rolled toward them from that direction, so it came to seem as if each wave was a purposeful attack, one after another, intentionally blocking them from their destination.

At first, they tried to swim individually, but that didn't work. Janet and Amelia still wore fins, but Michael and Grace had lost theirs when the boat swamped. There was no way that the barefooted swimmers could keep up. It was Amelia who suggested that she and Janet each give the other two a fin to wear. "We've got to share!" she yelled. "None of us are going to make it at this rate!"

But that wouldn't work, either. Both women wore full-footed fins, Amelia's fins expensive and made by Force, Janet's a much cheaper set made by U.S. Divers. Janet was a size 6, Amelia a size 7. Grace was a big woman, and Michael was a very big man. The fins wouldn't fit them.

They juggled the order, getting mauled by waves, and finally settled on a method that was at least better than what they'd tried before. Michael and Grace, arms locked, floated on their backs, kicking, while Amelia at one end and Janet at the other used their fins to paddle their tiny human raft along.

The four of them would battle their way several yards up a wave, only to be smashed back that distance or more by the wave's crest. Worse, their inflated vests, while keeping them afloat, were also acting as effective sea anchors, slowing their progress. Wearing an inflated BCD in those conditions was like being strapped to a small parachute in a wind tunnel. It was maddening. It was exhausting. In time, as they one by one realized how unlikely it was that they were going to make it to that far tower, the situation became terrifying.

The psychology of group hysteria is well documented, its roots predictable — *la participation mystique,* Carl Jung termed it. Hysteria can begin when one member of a group is overwhelmed by a fear or an illusion so powerful that all rational thought processes cease, sparking brain activity in the frontal lobe and the primitive limbic system. All primates are deeply coded with the instinctive fight-or-flight response. When one group member displays that limbic response, other members react immediately, and for good reason — survival is the only inviolable mandate of our species. Panic is contagious because it effectively speeds reaction time.

None of the four could ever be certain who panicked first, nor would they have reason to wonder. There was a big wave, then a second big wave that covered them like a waterfall and separated them, then a third, mountain-sized wave that sucked them down, down into blackness, tumbling them, contorting their bodies and nearly drowning one of the swimmers, so it was possible that they all panicked independently as they surfaced, one of them surfacing slightly later than the other three.

There were screams and swearing. A mouth opened skyway, begging for deliverance: *Dear God! Please help us, God!* Two of the swimmers vomited salt water. One independently reached out, seeking elbows and bodies, and drew a person toward her.

That's when Amelia disappeared. One moment she was bobbing with the group. Then she was a wave ahead of them, and soon, two waves ahead. Then she was gone, like a small mist that had dissipated in blackness, leaving the shouted pleas of her companions to feather away in the wind: *Don't leave us, Amelia! Amelia, come back!*

Now, it was just the three of them . . .

The panic had passed, replaced by a resolve that was part numbness, part survival instinct. The flashing light was their only hope. On that wide dark ocean, beneath its black rolling sky, the explosion of light was their only link to civilization, to the safety of their homes, to the reality that had abandoned them, the security of their daily lives.

Each time one or two of them faltered and began to panic again, or to lose confidence, another became assertive, assumed the leader's role, and rallied the group's spirits. There was no choice. They knew independently and as a group that, if they lost control again, stopped fighting and gave in to their fear, they were dead.

Endure. They had to keep struggling. They had to continue kicking, kicking, using their hands to pull them into wave after wave after wave as the sea rolled toward them. There were no other options.

It was Janet who most consistently provided encouragement and comfort. Each time they stopped to catch their breaths, or after they'd been washed by an unusually large wave, she'd remind them: "We're going to make it. We'll all make it. We've just got to stay together and keep swimming."

Michael had regained his self-control. As an assistant junior varsity football coach of a Sarasota high school, he was accustomed to motivating people as part of his job. So was being tough and showing a tough face. He reverted to that mindset and those skills now, and the results were unexpected: By assuming that old and familiar role, he actually did begin to feel stronger and more confident.

He would yell comments such as "Teamwork, ladies! Harder we work together, the faster we get to the tower" or "Last one to the light has to buy breakfast!"

Most heartening, though, in those first four hours adrift was that Grace Walker reassumed the personality of the woman she'd been back on land: fiercely goal-oriented and fearless. The terror and the panic she'd experienced after being dragged underwater and almost drowned by the sinking *Seminole Wind* had done something to her. In some inexplicable way, being so abruptly confronted with her own death had exhausted her flight response, leaving only her determination to fight. The woman was a survivor — no one who knew her ever doubted that.

With Amelia gone, they'd abandoned the human-raft technique. Janet simply wasn't strong enough to push all three of them along with her fins. Now they swam side by side with Grace in the middle, everyone doing a slow breaststroke, riding up the front side of waves, swimming harder down the backside. They tried to keep enough distance between themselves not to bang arms but still remain close enough to be heard over the noise of the wind. For the first hour, Grace said nothing, used what energy she had left to try to keep up with the other two. But when she finally did speak, it was with the same self-assured voice people had come to expect from her: "Call me crazy, Sandman, but I think we're getting closer to that light. I really *do*, man. We're covering some ground, brother. I believe we're gonna make it!"

Michael was so grateful to hear the confident, familiar tone, he actually shouted as he replied. "Damn right we are, Gracie! We're kicking ass, baby, and I feel great!"

"Yeah? Well, that's something funny 'cause I'm feeling pretty good, too. Strong, that's the way I feel. Maybe getting stronger."

"All of us! Lady, we're *all* getting stronger. Know what? When we get back, I'll do your laundry for a month to make this up to you. You can lay out by the pool, I'll bring you drinks, whatever you want. We're going to make it, sister!"

For the first time that day, Janet smiled as Grace replied, "Sandman, when we get back, the only water I want to see is in a whiskey glass. Or a fucking shower. Don't you be mentioning water to the Princess 'till we get this shit way behind us!"

That rallied them. Kept them swimming hard for the next hour without a pause. The light was getting closer. Grace had said so. Little by little, stroke by stroke, they were fighting their way back to civilization, back into their understandable, orderly lives.

Attached to his BCD vest, Michael Sanford had a small plastic board called a navigation slate. Built into the slate was an illuminated compass. When they finally did stop to rest, Michael lifted the little board in front of his face and sighted it like a rifle toward the flashing light. Twice before that evening, he'd checked their course heading using the same simple technique. On the first sighting, the light had been at 64 degrees, which was slightly east of north. On his second sighting, the light was at 62 degrees, which meant they had drifted slightly to the south but were still making progress. Now, as he sighted the compass, he looked, then paused. He tapped the compass with his fingers as if it were not working, then took another sighting.

Janet was watching him and sensed that he was puzzled by something. She called over, "What's wrong, Mikey?"

Sanford said, "I think this compass has gone crazy," and aimed the slate at the light tower a third time, studied it again before he adding, "We were drifting

268

slightly south — the current, I'm talking about. Out here there's always some kind of ocean current. But in the last hour or so, we're suddenly way north. The tower's almost due east, 45 degrees. I mean we are *flying*."

"The tidal current is taking us, that's what you're saying?"

"An ocean current, yeah. That's what it's gotta be. A really strong current."

Grace said, "Is that good? Sandman, you better be telling me that's a good thing."

Michael paused too long, thinking about whether he should tell the truth, wondering if he even knew the truth, before he spoke. "It doesn't matter either way. We still have to swim to the tower. That's exactly what we're going to do."

That was at a little after 10 p.m. For two more hours, they battered their way eastward, and each time Michael stopped to check his compass, the tower was farther to the south. Their rest stops became longer, the time they spent swimming became shorter and shorter. Hobbyist runners train for months to do a first 26.2-mile marathon, and many run the distance in between four to five hours. The three of them had now been swimming for more than five hours, their own terrible marathon of survival, and one by one, their bodies began to fail them.

They were dehydrated, though did not yet feel the terrible thirst, and their muscles began to cramp. Because Janet was wearing fins, her calves and thighs began to cramp first. For Michael, it was his jaw and neck if he yawned with fatigue or nervousness, and then his legs began to cramp, too.

It was Grace who finally said what they had all come to realize but not yet admitted. "Know what I think, ladies and gentleman? I think we're better off saving our energy and just drifting 'til morning. Planes, boats, there's gonna be all kinds of stuff out here tomorrow morning looking for us. Probably helicopters, too." There was still strength in her voice, some confidence, as well, when she added, "Let the bastards come to us. What do we care if they find us in the water or on that damn light tower?"

They were all chilled, and the black wind felt colder now, after midnight. Once again, they locked their bodies together to form a tiny human raft. Floating on his back, Michael spooned Grace into his arms, as Janet slid in behind Michael and held them both close to her breast.

The three of them drifted. They dozed. Once, they even laughed when Grace told them, "I just peed in my own wet suit, and man, it feels warm." Their teeth started to chatter, and, finally, the slowest sunrise of their lives began to form on the eastern horizon: a radiant blackness over the Everglades, then a smear of gray, of white, of tangerine.

They stared at the horizon, anticipating the gaseous bloom of light, anticipating its heat, when Michael jerked his head around abruptly to the south. "Jesus Christ!" he yelled. "Do you see it? My God, it's a boat! You see the boat?"

It was almost upon them, a ghostly figure of rust and steel, net booms swung high, rolling out of the morning sea spume, the heavy wind shielding the noise of its engines. Janet had spent enough time around marinas to recognize it as some kind of trawler — maybe a steel shrimper, but it had a foreign look and she wasn't certain. Its hull was black, wrinkled with blistered paint, rust, grease. Some kind of workboat, filthy.

The boat was already so close they could see that its high, beige wheelhouse was covered with people, that there were men and women, children, too, jammed tight and standing on the vessel's long stern deck. Dozens of people, maybe a hundred, their faces sickly, African faces, brown faces, a confederation of misery bound by something terrible: seasickness, exhaustion, fear, or some other dark, nameless thing. Then the vessel was close enough that air molecules from the boat began to mix heavily with the wind, and the stench of the boat drifted down on them, a terrible odor, so inhuman that it could only be human, the stink of feces and vomit, of disease and dying, diesel fumes mixed in, the density of oil floating it all, causing it to linger above the sea.

Janet whispered, "Am I dreaming this? Please don't let me be dreaming this."

It was a bizarre vision: three desperate people now looking into a herd of desperate faces; faces that created a hundred dark, ocular vacancies staring back at them, a man and two women in the water adrift, shouting at the vessel to stop, screaming at the mirrored windows of the wheelhouse as dark faces began to yell back, the mass of them sprouting bony arms and hands that pointed at them in reply.

Michael shouted, "They see us!" and

Grace began to weep, saying, "Thank you, God. Oh thank you, dear God!" watching the vessel slow, then turn in the heavy seas, wallowing in the troughs of waves, hammering geysers of wake as its bow swung toward them.

Janet, Michael, and Grace were all waving their arms wildly as the vessel came about, and they watched the door of the wheelhouse slide open. A huge, very fat brown man came through the door — a man so wide that he could only fit through the opening sideways. He was followed by a tall, cadaverous man who had a shockingly white face shaved smooth, his flour-pale skin covering sinew linked by bone. Draped over his head, as if to shield him from the heat, he wore a dirty-looking rectangular cloth that was folded diagonally and held in place with a headband.

An albino person, Janet realized.

Michael called up to them, "Drop a ladder down! Our boat sank and we've been adrift all night!"

The albino and the fat man stood holding on to the steel railing, looking down at them, and they seemed to be conferring, talking back and forth.

Michael shouted, "If you don't have a ladder, throw us a rope. We can climb up!"

Still, the two men did not react, continuing to talk among themselves — a disturbing hesitation. They seemed indifferent.

"We need help! *Please*. We'll pay you. We'll pay you whatever you want!"

Then Janet said, "What's he doing? What's he going to do with that?" as the albino ducked into the wheelhouse and came out holding a rifle.

Because she'd been worrying about it all night but had not allowed herself to mention it, Grace now said what was in her mind. "Maybe we have sharks around us. Maybe that's it. Probably got it to keep sharks away, don't you think, Sandman?"

Then all three watched, weary beyond shock, as the albino snugged the rifle against his cheek and shoulder, then swung the barrel seaward, taking aim at Michael Sandford.

Chapter Fourteen

We were dropping down, down through the diatom gloom of the Gulf of Mexico — Amelia, Tomlinson, and me — descending onto the wreck of the *Baja California,* when the shark materialized. A tiger shark, probably ten, maybe eleven, feet long.

The short, pointed snout of a tiger is distinctive. So are the requiem shark's unusual recurved teeth if you are lucky enough — or unlucky enough — to get close enough to see them.

Tiger sharks are a tropical species, and the young have characteristic bars on their backs and upper sides, thus the name. The mature animals, though, lose the camouflage decoratives because they are not needed. A fully grown tiger shark has few enemies in the sea.

This one was a mature female, probably weighed close to a thousand pounds: a half-ton illustration of adaptation and natural selection in battleship colors, gray on bronze.

Amelia was above me; Tomlinson was above her, his long blond hair, normally scraggily, now undulating like seaweed in the current. We all stopped, holding on to the anchored descent line we'd dropped upon arrival. Our heads turned as one as we watched the shark cruise by.

I did a quick survey of facial expressions. Through his face mask, Tomlinson's eyes were childlike: He was delighted to see the big tiger. Amelia appeared worried, but she relaxed noticeably when I put thumb and index finger together and signaled, telling her everything was okay, nothing to worry about.

With the exception of certain specifics of physiology concerning the bull shark, *Carcharhinus leucas,* I don't consider myself a shark expert. I know too many real experts to indulge in that pretense. I am, however, a great admirer of these extraordinary animals.

I have dived with great white sharks off South Africa and Tasmania and with bulls and tigers and hammerheads all around the world. One thing I have noticed is that the really big sharks always appear in the same surprising way.

This large female tiger was no different. At first, on some primary level of perception, I was aware of motion in the distance where there had been no movement before. Then I noticed two unexpected black vacancies in the green murk, strange voids not instantly identified by my brain. The voids were horizontal, consistently spaced, swinging slowly back and forth, growing larger, vectoring.

Strange. What trick of light was this?

Then the black holes were skewered by a conical nose, beneath which was a grinning apparition. It was a fixed, fanatical grin, as meaningless as the grill of a car, yet it lent an impression of all that is mindless and unsympathetic and inevitable. A million years of energy were distilled right there in front of me: wind, water, light, current.

The huge tiger glided toward us, then banked slightly, black eyes passing us without interest or expression. The impression given by her indifference was probably accurate: The animal knew all there was to know about us, and there was *nothing* to be known. We were meaningless; we were irrelevant because we were not prey. We were a gathering of protoplasm, healthy seals or fish or manatee. Perhaps something would occur to change that. We might be wounded, show distress, or the shark's own precise feeding instincts would reclassify us because of hunger.

It was an indifferent process. A biologist from Sanibel? An unreformed hipster who lived on a sailboat, who believed in God, who crossed his 7s, read his horoscope, and was a devotee of reincarnation?

Such things did not exist. Water, light, tide: all else was delusion. We were wind in the void. We were matter without purpose. It made no difference who we were, what we had accomplished, who we loved. Our fast hearts had a silly, finite number of beats remaining. There was always other prey.

We watched the shark drift past, descending, and saw her vanish over the diatom horizon.

Observing Tomlinson, I had the distinct and accurate impression he wanted to go after her, to be a part of whatever life adventure the tiger shark was on. So I grabbed his elbow, holding him until she'd been gone for a couple of minutes. Then I touched Amelia and Tomlinson both, signaling.

We completed our dive.

Using Dieter's Grand Banks trawler, *Das*

Stasi, as a dive platform, we spent Tuesday and Wednesday, December 9 and 10, a day, a night, and part of this next day over the wreck, diving and assembling evidence that, piece by piece, did much to confirm Amelia's story. Salvage divers had already refloated and towed the *Seminole Wind*. But what she dumped when she sank was still below, and that debris told a story.

Because the *Baja California* is in 110 to 120 feet of water, we kept careful track of our bottom time and made each and every safety decompression stop longer than it needed to be. We calculated data from our personal dive computers but did not log the data until our figures had been re-checked and confirmed by at least one other person.

I have spent much of my life in the water and on the water, yet I have never become so comfortable that I allow myself to be sloppy. When we were under, our second dive team, consisting of Dieter, Jeth, and Dieter's nubile, Jamaican secretary Moffid Seemer, stayed attentive topside. We did the same when they were down.

I also insisted on one very simple safety precaution that would have saved the lives of Janet, Michael, and Grace, had only one of them done the same: I asked that each member of our team attach a little, plastic strobe light to his or her BCD vest. The strobes are cheap, they come with long-life batteries, and, when activated, they can be seen at night from at least three miles away. Anyone who travels over water in foreign lands, aboard foreign vessels, or who dives, should carry one. Few boat passengers or sport divers expect to be in the water after dusk. But all sunny days over a reef ultimately darken, and accidents are never planned. Which is why, each year, a surprising number of passengers and sport divers are set adrift and die. A strobe is the cheapest possible insurance against disaster.

So we did the dives methodically, safely. I kept a close eye on Amelia. So did Dieter, a psychiatric physician. It had to be a hell of an emotional experience to return to the scene of the tragedy, and only thirty-five days after she'd made that long midnight swim.

She had some quiet moments. There were periods when her vision seemed to glaze, and her attention wandered to some faraway place. Generally, though, she handled herself well. The more I was around the lean redhead, the better I liked her. She was a competent dive partner, and she did more than her share of the menial labor aboard *Das Stasi*. Under crowded conditions at sea, a person's core personality asserts itself quickly So far, she'd contributed much to a successful, productive trip.

Mostly, we all focused on collecting the remains of the *Seminole Wind*, which now lay atop the remains of the much older *Baja California*.

Dieter, with his German obsession for precise information, had provided us with some interesting history. The *Baja California*, he told us, was a 214-foot freighter built in 1914, and sunk with a single torpedo on July 18, 1942 by one of his country's Nazi submarines, U-boat 84. The *Baja California* was under way to South America with a general cargo of tobacco, baby bottles, mercury, and American military vehicles. Three crew members were killed.

Now this place was the site of a second wreck, and it was an eerie experience to dive through 110 feet of murky water, then come upon the colorful detritus of an event that led, most likely, to the loss of three more lives. The old freighter was a fissure of rubble, the stillness of which implied a furious animation halted long ago.

It might have been the remnants of a rock slide. It might have been a graveyard. Atop the rubble, scattered all around, were items that had once been aboard the *Seminole Wind*.

The day before, we'd arrived early enough to make two dives. We'd found much, and catalogued those items carefully. Lying among the debris we'd found a big tackle box and two smaller tackle boxes. They contained several hundred dollars' worth of equipage and lures, including some new lures still in cellophane.

One of the rumors being parroted around South Florida was that Sanford had intentionally sunk the *Seminole Wind* for the insurance. Why would a man who planned to sink his own boat invest money in new lures? We also found the new thermostat that Amelia had told us about, the one Michael purchased as a backup the morning of November 4, the day they headed offshore. The thermostat was still in its now-sodden box, lying near the chassis of a military vehicle. You don't buy backup parts for an engine you plan to scuttle.

No, the sinking certainly had not been intentional.

Another rumor, and one of the most

popular, was that the foursome had not traveled offshore to fish or dive but actually to finalize a drug deal. From the evidence we gathered, that seemed unlikely.

Near the tackle boxes, we found several fishing rods, rigged and ready. Two of the rods were light tackle spinning rods, and one was still rigged with a number 3 hook — commonly used for catching bait, nothing else. Amelia had told the Coast Guard and us that they'd stopped on the way out to catch bait. The rod added credence to her story and implied a more general truth: No one would have gone to the trouble to rig a rod specifically for catching bait if their real intention was to rendezvous with a drug boat. If they wanted to costume themselves as fishermen, rods with standard-sized hooks would have sufficed.

Something else: Why the hell would they choose the *Baja California* as a meeting place? Wrecks attract divers and fishermen no matter how far offshore. There was no way they could have been certain that another boat wouldn't have come along and surprised them out there. Any other GPS way point in international waters, beyond the twelve-mile limit, would have been a far more logical and likely choice.

We'd also found one SCUBA tank filled

with air. Amelia told us that they had carried eight, which a Marco Island dive shop confirmed by telephone. The salvage divers had already retrieved five tanks that were nearly full (or they would not have sunk), and the Coast Guard had recovered two air tanks drifting miles from the site. Air tanks that are empty, or nearly empty, float. All tanks accounted for. It supported Amelia's story that only she and Janet had completed the dive.

In my mind, the report that Tomlinson and I would submit jointly and simultaneously to the Coast Guard, as well as to several newspapers, was already taking shape. We had the credentials to be taken seriously, and we were assembling some compelling data.

The day before we boarded *Das Stasi* and left Dinkin's Bay, Tomlinson used my truck to drive to Fort Lonesome, an agricultural crossroads northeast of Sarasota where there was a small marine salvage yard. The salvage divers who'd refloated the *Seminole Wind* had done it without the permission of the missing Michael Sanford or his family. The group had been bitterly criticized in the press and by the public for what many saw as outright theft from a grieving family.

Legally, though, the salvagers didn't need the approval of Sanford's relatives or anyone else. Since the Key West pirate days of the 1700s, marine salvage has been a controversial but legitimate enterprise in Florida. Success relies on the misfortune of others, and salvage captains don't go into the business to make friends. Because a powerful animosity already existed, I worried about my old hippy pal venturing into Florida's gun-rack and cattle country interior to investigate.

But Tomlinson told me, "Rednecks, man. Except for some of their politics, amigo, I love their spirit; the music, the history, the whole social scene. Hank Williams? Garth Brooks? Those dudes both make me cry like an American baby, plus Garth plays baseball, just like you and me. The folks around Fort Lonesome are gonna greet me like a brother, so don't you worry your little head."

Turned out that he was right, as usual. He returned with his own detailed assessment of the *Seminole Wind* — lots of precise measurements and numbers — including digitized video. Also, he'd stopped to see Dalton Dorsey at Coast Guard St. Pete and, after filing a handwritten Freedom of Information Act request, obtained the official report of the marine surveyor hired to inspect the *Seminole Wind* after her sinking.

I was surprised when he told me, "You know what qualifications you need to have to be a marine surveyor in Florida? Nothing, nada, zero, zilch. Drive down here from Kansas, print up some business cards, pay for an operational license to run a business, and you, too, can be a so-called 'licensed professional marine surveyor' without ever touching your toes in salt water. What a scam. In some cases, anyway.

"You need to tell your buddies at the Coast Guard that the woman who wrote this report, the so-called marine surveyor, needs to take a basic boating course or two. Or they need to start hiring people who actually know something about marine architecture. I think they're going to be very interested in what my report has to say."

Tomlinson's fervor for the mission had not waned. It was "our final gift to Janet," as he said more than once.

I still wanted to make a dive beneath the light tower where the helicopter had found Amelia (one especially absurd theory among local gossips was that drug runners or military-intelligence types had killed the other three and sunk their bodies but had spared Amelia for reasons unknown). I also wanted to interview a real expert on human physiology and tropical water hypothermia. It had been years since I'd read anything, and I wanted to confirm that what little I did know was still accepted fact.

It was a much-discussed question that begged for a final answer: How long could the three have survived while adrift?

Our work here on the *Baja California*, though, was nearly done.

Now, on this, our final dive, Amelia and Tomlinson followed me down the line, taking it slow, giving each other plenty of time to clear their ears and adjust to the increasing water pressure. Water has weight; it squeezes the tissues, and, at a hundred feet, bubbles from a regulator change pitch, as if issued through strained vocal cords.

An alien space has been breached. Your body knows it. Your ears know it. The change, the unfamiliarity, suggest an edgy potential.

There is a transformation of light, too. It's not just that there is less light in a hundred feet of seawater, though that is certainly true. The gradual change suggests a density of darkness and an intransigence of gray that is defining and permanent. This is a world separate from others — if other worlds actually *do* exist.

Beneath ninety feet of water, the sunlight or "white light" that land dwellers know has been reduced in its radiant strength by 90 percent, and it has been leached of every spectral color but green. What remains is a primal green, a chemical and cellular green, as if one has been ingested by something massive, alive — some photosynthetic being. Human eyes become feeble collectors and undependable interpreters. Four atmospheres beneath the wind is no place for a primate to linger.

With fingers interlaced, arms folded across my chest, I did a slow-motion flutter kick, the whip of old Rocket fins powering me over the rubble of the ruined steamship. There were cables, bent railings, barrel-sized storage tanks crushed, mangled — all still exhibiting the physics of Nazi percussion, and hosts to a thick, living skin of veined, jellied, clustered, and copper-gray benthic growth, hairy with broken fishing line and byssal thread.

Ahead was a cloud of thread herring,

glittering like coins. The cloud became a curtain, parting to let us pass, then closed again behind us, giving the illusion that we'd just swum into a trap and that the trap had been sprung.

There was a school of forty-pound amberjacks moving as one body in perfect incremental spacings; a predatory tribe, each member the size of a pit bull, scouting, hunting, as, beneath them, gray snapper did nervous figure-eights. There were tropicals, too: clown fish, butterfly fish, and sergeant majors, all drab at this depth, and barracudas stacked at the edge of visibility like helium swords.

The working freighter, *Baja California*, was long dead, killed by a German torpedo in a great war. The wreck of the *Baja California* was intensely, inexorably alive.

We'd found most of the wreckage from the *Seminole Wind* just beyond the barnacled framework of some kind of World War II vehicle. Now I touched the vehicle's steel fender, stopping myself, and I signaled Amelia and Tomlinson to assume our familiar search formation: Amelia in the middle, Tomlinson and me on either side, each of us about nine feet apart.

We swam to the edge of the wreck, turned, respaced ourselves, then swam back over the wreck.

It was Amelia who made our final discovery. Deep in a crevice hollowed out in the body of the ship, she spotted Michael Sanford's black weight belt, and then, a few meters away and nearly on top of each other, there was Janet's chartreuse weight belt and Amelia's own orange weight belt.

Grace Walker's weight belt had already been retrieved by the salvage divers who refloated the *Seminole Wind*, so now they were all accounted for.

It was just as Amelia had told us: When she and Janet resurfaced after completing their dive, they'd helped Sanford and Walker get into their BCDs, returned to the swamped boat, and dumped their weight belts together.

They were side by side, exactly where they should have been.

I looked into Amelia's eyes when she first pointed to her discovery. Her face showed the kind of intense emotion seen in old silent films. Back at Dinkin's Bay, one of the first questions I'd asked her was if their weight belts had been found. How those belts were distributed on the bottom would say much about what really happened that tragic day.

For Amelia, it was a vindication of sorts,

at least as far as her relationship with me was concerned. Her jade eyes peered out through the lens of her face mask, into my eyes, and then she gave me a quick and unexpected hug.

I checked my air gauge, checked my watch. I tied the weight belts onto a float bag, used my regulator to inflate it, and sent the belts to the surface.

Chapter Fifteen

That night, as we sledded and wallowed our way toward Sanibel at an unvarying twelve knots, Amelia and I sat on fly bridge captain's chairs, high above the black sea, letting the autopilot steer the boat while we chatted and gazed at the star stream above.

Tomlinson, Jeth, Dieter, and his secretary were below. It was late, nearly midnight, so they had probably drifted off to the fore or aft staterooms to bed. Or maybe they were still in the air-conditioned salon playing liar's poker on the octagonal, teak dining room table. Or watching a video in the teak entertainment center. Wherever they were, whatever they were doing, they were comfortable.

Dieter's forty-six-foot Grand Banks Classic was a model of useful luxury. Everything was inlaid, beautifully fitted, and multifunctional. The floors were teak parquet, the salon was surrounded by glass with the sides curtained, and there was a sea view forward. The U-shaped galley was on the port side, the steering station with instrument and circuit breaker panels on the starboard side next to the hinged deckhouse door. The staterooms were plush, the heads and shower stalls massive. The interior smelled of fine wood, lacquer, brass, and electronic circuitry. A very nice combination, indeed, if you are a yachting type.

Even so, I preferred to be topside, in the wind, where I could see the stars and smell the open Gulf. The Gulf of Mexico has a more complex mix of odors than other ocean places, perhaps because it is more intimately adjoined to its landward influences.

Even thirty miles offshore, the wind carried trace remnants of the Everglades. There were brief baloonings of denser, warmer air. A hint of mangrove sulphur. A touch of frangipani, sawgrass, and feral jasmine. Out there, beyond the horizon, were shell mound outposts — Chokoloskee, Everglades City, Dismal Key. The wood ash and citreous lime odor of those places clung to the occasional, abraded air molecule, touched the nose briefly, then was gone.

I'd volunteered for the early morning watch. Had been up there alone for nearly an hour when, surprise, surprise, Amelia slid into the chair next to me, bringing two iced cans of Bud Light, a thoughtful gesture. Along with her floated new odors, the good, bedtime girl-odor of shampoo, toothpaste, soap.

"Mind some company? I'm the night-owl type even when I'm home."

I told her that she was most welcome — very true — but I also sensed that there was something on her mind.

There was. It was a possibility we had all thought about, even talked about briefly, but had never fully and openly discussed because the subject was too terrible.

She began by saying, "I can't get the image of that shark out of my mind. I've never seen a tiger shark, and nothing even close to that big. The way it came gliding in, like a big plane about to land. I know what you told me this afternoon, but you have to admit, that's what could've happened to them. Sharks."

What I'd told her is what I'd told many people since Janet had disappeared: The possibility of a shark attacking one of the three divers was unlikely but not impossible. A fatal attack, however, was *extremely* unlikely. Sharks in the Gulf are very good at what they do, and what they do, aside from copulate and give birth, is eat fish. In very murky water, they will sometimes mistake a human hand or leg for something that should have scales, but that is rare. The probability of a shark or sharks attacking all three was so unlikely that it was statistically insignificant.

I'd thrown in some data that I'd gathered in my own work with bull sharks. Worldwide, there are normally between fifty and eighty unprovoked attacks a year, according to the International Shark Attack File, and only a dozen or so of those attacks are fatal.

When you consider the many millions of hours that humans spend in, on, and under salt water, that is a telling statistic.

Records also show that nearly 80 percent of all attacks occurred in shallow water, while divers and snorklers account for only 18 percent of attack victims. Something I didn't mention was that attacks do seem to be increasing slightly, and laws protecting sharks from certain types of fishing may be increasing their numbers while populations of fish upon which they feed decrease. Didn't mention it out of pure and simple self-interest: I *like* sharks.

Water depth was an issue, so I said, "It's a generalization, but, in my experience, deep water tends to be clearer than shallow water. In shallow water, rain, wind — things like that — drainage, they have an immediate effect on turbidity. That's not true offshore, so sharks are less likely to make a mistake in deep water. Once again, Gulf sharks are experts at finding and eating fish, not people."

She repeated herself. "But it *could* have happened."

I took a sip of beer, rocking back in my chair, and said, "Okay, it's a possibility, sure. You're asking me to shift from what is probable to what might have happened, which is something I try to avoid, frankly. You know that as an attorney . . . what's the legal term you folks use? *Speculation.* Plus, I don't see the point in a useless emotional exercise."

"I wish I could stop thinking about it. Maybe it's because I was out there with them. Because it could have happened to me. Or maybe it's like Tomlinson told me. We were up here last night talking, drinking some wine. He was telling me about you, what kind of person you are. You've got a lot of admirers, Doc. But one thing he said was that you find the sensitivity of others surprising because it's a weakness that you refuse to recognize in yourself. Only he didn't say weakness. He used another word. A . . . *frailty*, that was the word. A frailty that you refuse to recognize in yourself."

I smiled. "You're insisting. Okay, sharks. Let me attempt to be sensitive then."

I said, "Let's take your question and think it through aloud, though neither one of us is going to like it. Let's see . . . three people adrift at night, their legs hanging down, kicking in a hundred feet of water, and one or more sharks head for the surface, drawn in by the vibrations.

"No matter how big they are, sharks tend to be skittish, easily spooked. So they take their time. Maybe even do a couple of bump and runs. Finally, one shark makes a mistake, hits what it thinks is a fish. If that happened, the best-case scenario — and the most *likely* scenario — is that the attacking shark would immediately realize that it'd made a mistake and would bolt. The other sharks would have followed. That's what usually happens when shark bites man. Remember a few years back, near Daytona, when they had all those minor injuries, sharks biting surfers? The numbers were way higher than normal, but no one was badly hurt. Same thing. One chomp and they were gone."

"And the worst-case scenario?"

I'd been looking northward, through the darkness, at a distant, flashing halo of light that reflected off clouds. Probably Cook Key light near Marco Island — not long ago, I'd spent part of a terrible night there. Not a good memory to linger over. Now I turned and looked at Amelia. "Are you sure you want to hear?"

She nodded. "Sorry, but yeah. Facts are about the only thing we attorneys allow ourselves to trust."

"All right. One shark makes a mistake, rolls, takes a bite of a foot or an arm, and the other sharks react. There's blood in the water, then a blood trail forms. One by one, the sharks arch their backs in a feeding display, and the frenzy is on.

"For Janet and your two friends, it would have been the horror of all horrors. Worse than any nightmare. One of them gets hit, screams and keeps screaming. The other two try to help, but there's nothing they can do. They have to float along beside the victim and wait, knowing that something is beneath them, feeding.

"If they *were* attacked by sharks, the

trauma would have been to their legs, maybe their arms. They would have bled to death, and probably pretty quickly. Massive blood loss, shock, then a sleepy unconsciousness. Thing is, their inflated BCDs would still be afloat, probably with their heads and torsos intact. There would have been plenty left for the Coast Guard to find. Or us. Or some random boater during the last month."

Amelia sat a little straighter. "Jesus Christ, Doc, no wonder you didn't want to talk about it." She made a shuddering, guttural sound. "What a terrible thing to imagine."

"I know, I know — but remember, what I just described almost certainly did *not* happen. You weren't satisfied with the answer I gave you this afternoon, and you weren't satisfied with the same answer a few minutes ago. It told me you either wanted to be reassured or that you genuinely wanted to explore the most extreme possibilities. I haven't known you for long, but I know you well enough to respect your intellect and your character. So I told you the truth. An extreme and unlikely truth. My version of it, anyway."

"Character," she said, with a hint of self-contempt. "Don't be too sure about that one. Believe me, I don't have any more character than the next person."

I remembered Tomlinson saying that what Amelia had told us was "mostly" true. I don't believe that he's a mind reader, but I have come to trust his judgment. Was she offering to share some secret with me, a detail yet to be confided?

I said, "Anything else you want to discuss?" then waited several beats for her to answer before I added, "The first day we met, you asked if you could confide in me. I didn't know you then. I do now. So the answer is yes. A blanket, unconditional yes. Whatever you want to tell me, any damn private thing you want to say."

Her reaction surprised me. She cupped her hand around my leg, then leaned and placed her head against my shoulder. "I can see why Janet loved you and all your crazy friends. What you've done for me, all the effort you've put in. I don't deserve it, Doc. I really don't."

The tone of self-contempt again.

Not much doubt now. There *was* something she wanted to tell me. I said slowly, delicately, "That night more than four weeks ago, big seas, no moon, the four of you adrift. Out here, not far from where we are right now. Each of you had a responsibility to yourselves to find a way to survive. Not to the group. To yourselves."

In the darkness, the glow of running lights, I heard her issue a weary sigh.

I added, "There're a couple of old navy expressions that are supposedly based on some archaic military law: When your ship's in trouble, use one hand for yourself, one hand for your ship. After that, it's every man for himself." I waited again through another long silence before reminding her. "Your ship, Amelia, was gone."

She replied softly, "I wish they bottled people like you and Tomlinson. I really do. And I wish I could make myself believe that what you just said is true."

Two days later, Friday, December 12, a package arrived at the marina office via private courier, a sturdy box in brown paper wrapping, heavily taped, with no return address.

I knew that it had to be from Bernie Yeager.

I carried the package home and into my lab and placed it on my stainless-steel dissecting table, which runs the length of the north wall. To my right, beneath the east windows, on a similar table, was the row of working, bubbling aquaria, octopi and fish therein, and more glass aquaria above them on shelves. To my left, along the east wall, near the door, were more tanks, all heavily lidded because they contained the mysterious, disappearing stone crabs and calico crabs.

A quick glance told me that the lids were still in place, my population of crabs undiminished.

In the center of the room, I'd installed a university-style science workstation: an island of oaken drawers and cupboards beneath a black epoxy resin table, complete with a sink, two faucets, electrical outlets, and double gas cocks for attaching Bunsen burners or a butane torch.

Now, from the top drawer, I selected a 5½-inch Mayo dissecting scissors, placed it atop the autoclave, then touched the play button on my wall phone recording machine as I returned my attention to the package.

The recorder is a recent concession to an increasingly integrated, digitized world, and to the growing demands of my small business, Sanibel Biological Supply.

I had more than a dozen messages. I listened to them as I carefully opened the package.

Ransom had bought a little cracker house out on Woodring's Point. Her toilet was plugged. Could I equip Tomlinson with a plunger, toilet paper, a six-pack of beer, today's paper, and send him out on my skiff, ASAP?

I smiled. My cousin has the same duplicitous streak as her father. She wouldn't come right out and say she was lonely, that she wanted the man's company. She had to attach her private wishes to other needs.

From Colorado College, Colorado Springs, I had an order for two dozen whelk or conch shells, sectioned, cleaned, and bleached. From Davenport Central High in Iowa, I had an order for a hundred live fiddler crabs — what in the hell were they going to do with a hundred live land crabs?

I stopped to jot down the details of several more orders before I heard the voice of Amelia Gardner say: "Hello, Dr. Marion Ford, my new friend and old pal. Greetings from the fifth floor of the Criminal Justice Building, Sarasota, which is a heck of a change from where we were a couple of nights ago, so I'm walking around in kind of a daze. If I sit still too long, the floor starts moving — *seriously*. Hey, Doc, I want to thank you again for what you and

Tomlinson are doing, so maybe you'll let a nice single lady buy you guys dinner this weekend to celebrate. Or . . . or just you, if the Stork can't make it."

The way Tomlinson looks, the way he behaves, invites nicknames of endearment. Aboard *Das Stasi*, Amelia had christened him Stork.

What we had to celebrate was the completion of our investigation into the sinking of the *Seminole Wind*. Behind me, atop the steel military-surplus office desk, stacked neatly next to my black manual typewriter, was the rough draft — twenty-three pages of facts, figures, interviews, and conclusions.

Tomlinson had spent the morning with me, pacing as he dictated from his notes, gesturing wildly when he got excited, while I hunched over the typewriter, banging away with two fingers. We both agreed that the false theories, the nasty rumors that Amelia found so hurtful, could not be addressed directly. The written word has power. To detail those rumors on paper was to give them fresh life, a life of their own. The best way to debunk the rumors was to reveal the facts, simply and concisely. There was no need for advocacy.

The data spoke for themselves.

Tomlinson and I wrote it as we would have written a scientific paper. There was a summary, an introduction, a description of methods, then the results of our investigation. We ended with conclusions and a few recommendations. Everything was footnoted with supporting materials listed in an appendix. It all went together quickly because we knew the material intimately, plus we've both authored and published many, many papers.

There were some key issues.

Well into the body of the text, I'd written: "The tower to which Amelia Gardner swam is a 160-foot tower, located in the large Naval Operation Training Area north of Key West and southwest of Marco Island. The tower is part of the U.S. Military's Air Combat Maneuvering Instrumentation (ACMI) system. ACMI towers are equipped with strobe lights, electronic discs, and antennas, and they are maintained by the U.S. Department of Defense through private contractors. The towers are used by both the Air Force and the Navy as electronic way points for a variety of training exercises.

"The towers are shown on some but not all charts, but the waters in which they are located are not off-limits to civilian boaters, and clandestine military operations do not take place in the area. Indeed, there are seven other such towers in the Naval Operations Training area, and they are commonly described in popular sporting magazines as excellent places to fish and common destinations for boaters.

"Our investigative team searched the bottom beneath the tower where Ms. Gardner was found. We found no debris that could be associated with the *Seminole Wind*, nor with any of the vessel's passengers."

In notes Tomlinson took when he did his survey of the salvaged *Seminole Wind*, he'd written: "The boat was built and rigged five years ago by a small Miami manufacturer. It is twenty-five feet, two inches long with a beam of eight feet. Boats over twenty-two feet are not required by law to have flotation in the inner hull. The *Seminole Wind* did not have flotation.

"The boat's back end, or transom, was cut very low to the water. Twin 225-horsepower Johnson engines, weighing 455 pounds each, were mounted on the transom. Abutting the transom were three deck hatches. Port and starboard hatches each contained 37-pound marine batteries.

The center hatch was a bait well plumbed to hold approximately twenty gallons of water, but would hold thirty gallons if the overflow tube was plugged — an additional 160 to 240 pounds.

"Rigged the way she was, the *Seminole Wind*'s stern was weighed down by more than 1,200 pounds of water and hardware. Only eleven inches of freeboard plus a folding fiberglass spray curtain separated the cockpit from the open sea.

"There is a boarding ladder mounted aft. When Michael Sanford and Grace Walker reboarded the vessel after their aborted dive, they, plus their dive gear, could have added four hundred-plus pounds — nearly a ton of weight on the back of the boat.

"A well-designed offshore boat could have sustained this weight. But the *Seminole Wind*'s scuppers (holes on the rear deck through which water escapes) were not covered by flanged flaps, which means that water would flow freely into the boat if those scuppers dropped below sea level. Also, the port scupper gutter was not only a half inch off true, it was drilled a half inch lower on the transom than the starboard scupper. What this means is that there were several ways for water to come into the boat, but almost no way for water to flow out.

"There are several possible scenarios that could account for the sinking of the *Seminole Wind*: A dead fish plugged the bait well, yet the bait pump continued to pump, and gradually flooded the inner hull. If Sanford and Walker had climbed on to the stern at the same time, the additional weight could have swamped the hatches and shorted the batteries, thus inactivating the bilge pump. Maybe one of them pushed down the fiberglass curtain to get their equipment aboard. Because the vessel had no flotation, one or all of these factors could have easily caused the inner hull to fill and the boat to roll over."

Tomlinson's conclusions were uncharacteristically succinct: "The only thing surprising about the *Seminole Wind*'s sinking on November 4 was that she hadn't already sunk long before. The vessel has several dangerous design flaws. It is no surprise that the company that built her has gone bankrupt. We found absolutely no evidence that the boat was intentionally scuttled."

Our report's most surprising — and painful — revelations were gathered by me the night before when I finally made telephone contact with Dr. Aaron Miller, retired rear admiral of the U.S. Coast Guard Health Service. For years, Dr. Miller served as the equivalent of the surgeon general for his beloved Coast Guard, and no one anywhere knows more about hypothermia than he.

I'd been trying to reach him for personal reasons. From what I'd remembered reading about tropical hypothermia, I'd convinced myself that, adrift, Janet and her friends couldn't have survived, or suffered, for more than half a day, or twenty-four hours at most. That was what I badly wanted to believe.

I was so surprised by what Dr. Miller had to tell me that I decided to include it in the report as a reply to those who had criticized the Coast Guard for extending its hugely expensive search over six days.

Dr. Miller — Aaron, as he insists on being called — is a nice man with a dry and mawkish sense of humor. He's fifty-six years old, still good at social sports, works out devotedly, and, because he is a scientist, he is apt to describe his current health and fitness level in terms not normally used by laymen.

"I'm still at twelve percent body fat,

Doc," he told me from his home in Washington state. "Cholesterol's low, blood pressure perfect, so I'm not doing too bad for an old fart."

We ping-ponged information about old friends, old acquaintances, before I finally told him why I was calling. His response was characteristically direct and clinical.

"Tropical hypothermia, yeah, that's what we used to think before we started accumulating all the studies and building good computer models. A two-day limit, that was the rule of thumb." I felt a trickling sense of dread as he added: "But that's all changed. In fact, the Coast Guard will soon be issuing a whole new set of guidelines for SAR groups. You've been out of the business for a long time, Doc, and you're way behind in your reading. That includes newspapers, apparently."

I said, "Newspapers? What could newspapers have told me?"

"Same thing they told us — that the old tropical hypothermia theory was wrong. A couple of years back, you may have read the story about the Navy pilot off Jacksonville, Florida, who ejected into the Atlantic. He had no life vest, no wet suit, no flotation of any kind. This was in the fall — maybe even November. Water temp

310

was in the low seventies."

I almost hated to ask. "How long was he in the water before they found him?"

"More than sixty hours. Two and a half days. He was exhausted and dehydrated. He knew drown-proofing, which is how he stayed afloat. Other than being tired, he was in pretty good shape. Then there was the guy who went into the water and survived off the Oregon coast. He was a big Norwegian sailor, six foot eight, nearly three hundred pounds. Same thing: No wet suit, and the water temp was fifty degrees. According to the tables, he should have been dead within a few hours. But he was fine when they picked him up twenty-four hours later. It told us we needed to do some more research. Nationwide, we — the Coast Guard, I mean — we deal with close to a thousand boating related fatalities a year, and hypothermia and drowning account for three-quarters of those deaths."

Dr. Miller told me that the information they had now was far more accurate and that an excellent software program, Cold Exposure Survival Mode, had been created by Dr. Peter Pikuisis, a Canadian physician.

"I've got my laptop with me. Tell me

about your friend who disappeared," Dr. Miller said, "and I'll plug in the numbers."

First, he asked for the water temperature — seventy-eight degrees. Then he asked for Janet's age, approximate height and weight. From that, the software program calculated her amount of body fat.

"Subcutaneous fat is the best-fitting wet suit in the world," he explained. "A skinny person can have up to nine times the cooling rate as a fat person."

He told me that at five foot four, and approximately 145 pounds, Janet probably had 25 percent body fat, or a quarter of her total body weight. He was a continent away, but I could hear the noise of his typing over the phone line, then I listened to him say, "You're not going to like this, Doc. Just in terms of hypothermia, she could have lasted three or four days, possibly longer. *Probably* longer. Were the other two young and fairly fit?"

I told him yes.

"Then the same is probably true of them as well. There's still some debate whether women survive longer than men because they typically have a greater percentage of body fat. That's true, but women also have a smaller surface area relative to volume, so I don't happen to accept that theory.

How long the three would have lasted would've been fairly similar."

I made a involuntary groaning sound. "I had no idea, Aaron. It had to be hell for them if they lasted that long. Four or five days? Do you really believe that's likely?"

"Let's review the facts, Doc. They were wearing shorty wet suits. That's decent insulation, plus the suits would have added eight to ten pounds of buoyancy. They were also wearing BCD vests. More insulation and ten to fifteen more pounds of buoyancy. Staying afloat would've been no problem, plus they wouldn't have had much trouble maintaining what we call 'airway freeboard' — the distance between the water and a swimmer's mouth.

"You might know this, but most people don't: It requires a heck of a lot more energy to swim in cold water because cold water is denser, more viscous than warm water. Water that's, say, forty degrees has a viscosity nearly 70 percent higher than water down there in palm tree country. So your friends had optimum conditions for staying afloat and staying alive."

We discussed the possibilities for a while longer, before Miller swung the conversation back to hypothermia.

"The clinical definition of *hypothermia* is

a core body temperature below ninety-five degrees. But you don't really begin to see the effects of cold on the body until the classification *mild hypothermia* is reached, which is when the core temp drops into the high eighties. Even then, thermoregulatory mechanisms — shivering, I'm talking about — and all other bodily functions continue to operate, although there may be ataxia, some apathy, maybe even amnesia."

When I asked, he told me *ataxia* was the medical term for "confusion."

"The body's ability to shiver is hugely important," he added. "Body heat produced by shivering can reach levels five to six times our resting metabolic rate. If you're cold and you stop shivering, that's when you know you're in trouble. With wet suits, in water that warm, it would have taken a long time for your friends to reach that stage. That's why I doubt if it was hypothermia that killed them, Doc."

I said, "They couldn't have lasted out there indefinitely. In your opinion, for those three people, what would the end have been like?"

"I'm not going to insult you by lying. It would have been awful. It would've been a horrible survival experience. Mental toughness is difficult to predict, but it is the most important survival tool that a person has. Back in the old days, when we could still experiment on lab animals, some researchers used shaved and anesthetized dogs to learn about the effects of cold water on physiology. But the data weren't much good. In survival situations, animals react consistently. People don't. Maybe that's one thing that separates us from animals. We react *very* differently. There may be a spiritual component — no one knows. How badly did your friends want to live? Some people fight with every fiber. Others get depressed and give up."

I told him, "My friend, Janet, was one of the tough ones. She'd been through a lot in her life. She wasn't the kind to give up without a hell of a fight."

The sympathetic tone of his voice was a reply to the distress in my own voice. "Then I'm very sorry, my friend. It would not have been pleasant or easy. In the end, their fatigue would have been accentuated by dehydration. Fatigue, that's probably what caused their deaths. Their neck muscles would have been so cramped and tired, they wouldn't have been able to hold their heads up. One or two big waves in a row, they would have aspirated water, and that would have been it. Two days, three days, six. No way of knowing how hard they would have fought to stay alive."

I hated it. Hated hearing it, despised writing it.

But I had to. Including Dr. Miller's information in the report was unpleasant duty, but I saw it as a duty because Janet, Michael, and Grace would not be the last to be set adrift in the Gulf. Despite the cost to taxpayers, a six-day search by air and sea was not a futile exercise. One or all of them could have been found alive. Way down the road, on a similarly tragic day, maybe some stranger would benefit from the pain I knew the data would cause Janet's friends around the islands and to the families of her lost dive companions.

I'm not prone to depression, but the conversation with Aaron Miller leached some of the spirit out of me. When horrible things happen to good people, you begin to ask the big questions, questions that do not lend themselves to comforting, clichéd answers. Ask those questions often enough, and the small, affected trappings of humanity can seem feeble, silly, meaningless.

That night, for the first time in a long time, I wrestled and sweated my way through a familiar nightmare: There came into my memory the iridescent faces of two men, as seen through a Starlite night-vision scope. The scope was attached to the weight and length of a Remington 700 sniper rifle.

Two Russian faces. The Mongolian angularity was distinctive. In this old nightmare, I watched as the faces turned slowly toward me, losing flesh in slow transition.

Like those dreams in which you try to run but your feet will not move, my right hand was frozen on the rifle's trigger guard. My index finger refused to flex.

Then, suddenly, the faces were skulls, and their all-seeing black eye sockets peered deeply into my eyes, and they knew the evil that was in me, and the guilt, before there was a thunder-blast that echoed through a rain-forest darkness . . . then a second shot . . . and, just as suddenly, both faces were once again human, but only for an instant, as they were vaporized in a scarlet, slow-motion cloud that ascended like a nuclear mushroom, then fell to the earth as mist.

On that cool December night, with a Midwestern breeze blowing through the screen window above my cot, I sat upright, sweating, trembling, my heart pounding.

The running shorts I wore were soaked. So were the sheets.

I threw the sheets back, then stood on shaky legs.

Chapter Sixteen

It was impossible to sleep after a dream so terribly vivid, so I went outside and took a cold shower, using a double ration of rainwater from my wooden cistern. I dressed, slipped into my sandals, then I went to work in the lab, writing up our report.

It was long before first light, just after 4 a.m. Fish and octopi in their tanks were watching me. Outside, there were stars in a black sky, and familiar, back bay sounds: the distant tapping of a halyard, the sump and whine of bilge pumps, the cornfield rustle of wind through the mangroves.

I wrote all morning. The only breaks I took were to walk to the marina for coffee, as I do almost every morning, then I returned there again around noon to pick up mail. On this particular day, I decided to have lunch at the marina. So I was sitting in the shade near the bait tanks, eating one of Joyce's excellent fried-conch sandwiches, when Mack stepped out of the office door and called to me, "Hey, Doc! There's some bloke here says he's got a package for you. Won't let me sign, won't leave it at the desk. It must be important because he says he's got to put it directly into your hands."

Which is how I happened to receive the reinforced box from Bernie Yaeger that I now opened.

Inside was a Styrofoam cover, which I removed, then a layer of bubble wrap. Beneath, fitted into another cradle of Styrofoam, was a small, silver video camera not much bigger than my hand. There was a brand name and model designation on the side — Sony DCR-TR — and a typewritten note taped to the camera.

It read: "Doc, these directions are so simple even a lug like you can't mess it up. Notice the wall bracket. Mount it no more than ten feet from the area you want videotaped. The camera has an infrared component, and it operates just fine at 0 lux, otherwise known to you hermit types as total darkness. The timer has already been programmed, and the memory stick has been inserted. Don't touch anything! After you have mounted the camera, plug in the

12-volt converter. In the event you have a power outage down there in Hurricane Land, there is an info lithium battery backup. Try to install this beautiful little camera without crushing it in your big paws or dropping the damn thing!"

My attention intensified as I then read, "Also, I enclose several photographs that may be of interest. I'm sorry the series of images is not more complete, but these are the best data available. I wish your lost friend only good things, though I fear the worst. There is no doubt in my mind how you will react, and so I wish you safe travels as well. Ours is a dangerous world. It would be good to have you back working with us again. We need you. Shalom!"

He wished me "safe travels"? What the hell did that mean?

There was a final, short paragraph and no signature: "The container is vacuum-sealed. The proof sheet enclosed has been treated via a process with which you are familiar, and the images will vanish within one hour or less after the seal is broken. They are for your eyes only, and, of course, you must not divulge to anyone that these images exist. Viewing the images requires medium-power magnification capabilities."

I glanced into the box and saw what appeared to be a heavy, ignition-walled Pyrex test tube that was capped with a black stopper. I held the tube up to the bulb of the goose necked lamp and saw three, maybe four, tiny strips of paper therein. Each strip was a series of miniature photographs, and each image was no bigger than the head of a nail.

I walked to the middle of the room and pulled the wooden swivel chair into position, then removed the cover from my Wolfe zoom stereomicroscope. Finally, I hunted around for a notebook and pencil before checking my watch, removing my glasses, then sitting down at the microscope.

The Pyrex tube made a suctioning sound when I unscrewed the cap. I used dissecting forceps to mount a strip on the viewing stage — and noticed that my fingers demonstrated a slight tremor. I turned the scope's revolving nosepiece until I found the most satisfactory objective, and the first of several photographs came into sharp focus.

I looked at four different images before I whispered: *Oh . . . my . . . God.*

What Bernie Yeager had sent me were twelve photographs in three individual strips. Two of the strips contained four photos taken minutes apart. After some confusion, I realized that the third strip contained only one photo, but in various degrees of enlargement. The photo had been reproduced from the second contact sheet.

They were undoubtedly satellite images, although the source numbers and altitude information normally imprinted at the top of each image had been blacked out, as were the GPS coordinates. The date and time line at the bottom, though, had been left.

Each photo was dated November 5, and the time span was 6:15 to 6:39 a.m.

Amelia hadn't been imagining things. There *was* a boat, and it was just as she had described it: a steel-hulled shrimper, maybe sixty feet long, booms folded high, rust streaks fouling the vessel's name, which was painted on its stern. One of the images was an enlargement of the name:

Nan-Shan
Port of Cortez Florida

The most striking thing about the vessel, though, was that it carried a human cargo. The deck and the wheelhouse were jammed with bodies. The resolution was so fine and sharp that I could distinguish individual faces. There had to be a hundred people aboard. It reminded me of various refugee boats I've seen around the world: Vietnam, Cambodia, Mariel Harbor, Cuba. When people are sufficiently desperate, they will risk any means to escape to what they hope is a more tolerable existence. It makes them easy prey for flesh traders and profiteers.

The *Nan-Shan* was in the flesh trade. U.S. citizens do not ride willingly atop the wheelhouse of a trawl boat in twenty-knot winds. These were illegal immigrants, of that there was no doubt.

I remembered Amelia commenting on the stench that blew from off that vessel. Now I understood. I understood because I know that stench. I've suffered it in many of the world's dark places. It is the stink of fear and of sickness. It is the stink of animal despair.

The photo keyed a vague memory awareness. It took me a few moments to isolate the reason. Finally, I remembered a newspaper story I'd read several days after Janet disappeared. The story said that immigration police had arrested a couple dozen illegal aliens of various nationalities who'd been jettisoned off the uninhabited Ten Thousand Islands and left to wade ashore.

Thirty of them? Forty? I couldn't recall the figure. They'd been carried by flesh merchants who'd smuggled them into U.S. waters from Colombia. The people they'd arrested were in bad shape: dehydrated and starving. Several had died.

Suddenly, Bernie's words — *Safe travels. Ours is a dangerous world* — assumed meaning.

He had already assembled information that I, presumably, would gather, which was not surprising. And I thought to myself: *not South America. Not again.*

The obligation to return there, though, was now an uncomfortable prospect. Between 6:23 and 6:31 a.m. on November 5, my friend Janet Mueller was still alive. In a series of four photographs, I could see a shrimp boat closing on three small dots, people adrift.

In the first shot, the three of them were alone in an expanse of gray. The second shot was from the same aspect, but the shrimp boat had intruded into the upper corner of the frame, its bow pointed in the direction of the swimmers.

They'd been spotted, apparently, and the

boat was returning to pick them up.

In the fourth frame, the boat sat abeam the three dots.

It was this photo that had been reproduced on the third contact strip in various degrees of enlargement. The resolution was not as good as in the other photographs, so each photo was grainy and indistinct.

The first image was a tight close-up of the three swimmers. I could distinguish Janet's pale, farm-girl face. Grace Walker and Michael Sanford were close beside her in a tight cluster, faces turned upward, their BCDs still inflated.

There was now no doubt that they were all still alive at the end of that first long night adrift.

Janet's expression was heartbreaking. She had both hands out of the water, waving, her mouth open wide — perhaps shouting something to the boat but maybe grinning, too.

The next three shots included the vessel.

Aboard the shrimper, among the mass of people, standing at the door of the wheelhouse, was a man wearing a baggy dark cap. Or maybe he had long hair. I played around with the magnification and still couldn't be certain.

Hair. Long hair. That's what it seemed to be.

The man was holding something in his hands. He appeared to be reaching out with it to the three swimmers. It was an elongated shape, dark — a boarding hook, perhaps, but thicker. But that didn't seem right, either, because of the way he held it.

I stopped, turned away from the binocular tubes, rubbed my eyes, then looked again.

Could it be a rifle?

That made no sense. Why would he have a rifle?

My brain scanned for possible explanations. Okay, so put yourself in the place of longhair. He owns the boat. He's smuggling in refugees. Once they've made contact, the three swimmers become witnesses. So he shoots three defenseless and desperate people?

I have witnessed terrible acts of inhumanity in my life, have even participated in a few, but nothing ever as callous as that.

It couldn't be a rifle.

Or *could* it?

No . . . almost had to be some kind of pole or boarding hook. What almost certainly happened was, the boat stopped, the crew fished Janet and the others out of the water, then continued on to the remote backwaters of the Ten Thousand Islands where their human cargo was offloaded.

Then what?

Obviously, the three were not released there. Not alive, anyway — we'd have heard from them. If the vessel had returned to its home port of Cortez, same thing. They'd all be home by now.

Conclusion: Janet, Grace, and Michael had either been killed, or they were being held prisoner, or they'd been abandoned on some remote island where they could not make contact with friends and family.

The indirect linkage came into my mind again, and the word sucked some of the light out of the room: *Colombia*.

The fourth and final frame gave no clue: water and just the stern quarter of the shrimp boat, with the name in white — *Nan-Shan*, Port of Cortez. No people. No faces.

I was still studying the third frame twenty minutes later when the images suddenly darkened, faded, then disappeared as the strip of paper turned black.

Speaking on his cell phone, Cmdr. Dalton Dorsey said, "What I don't understand is, why this sudden interest in a shrimp boat named the *Nan-Shan*? I'll help you any way I can, Doc, but you need to be upfront with me."

An unavoidable consequence of involvement with the intelligence agencies is the obligation not only to lie, but to lie convincingly and plausibly.

I was never good at it, not even when I was duty-bound to lie. I'm still not good at it, so I loathe any social or professional situation that requires it. However, back in the days when lying was a necessary part of my day-to-day life, I came up with a technique that, at least, made duplicity manageable. The method is simple: Speak factually, but omit the larger truth.

It had taken me nearly an hour to reach Dorsey. Now I was outside by the big fish tank on the lower deck of my stilt house, pacing nervously. I said to him, "The reason I'm interested in that particular boat has to do with a newspaper story I read a few weeks back. I don't know why it took me so long to make the connection. Do you remember reading about those illegal aliens the immigration people found down in the 'Glades?"

"Sure, our people worked the cleanup search. There were forty-seven out there lost, mucking around in the sawgrass.

Three ended up corpses, and the vultures didn't leave much. One of them was a child, only three or four years old. Two more adults died later. So what's the connection?"

"The time window. I'm not certain of the exact date, but the feds — maybe your people — found the refugees a week or so after the *Seminole Wind* sank."

"A private plane spotted them, and Naples air traffic control forwarded the information to Immigration. Yeah. Okay, I see where you're headed with this. The coyote boat that dumped them in the Ten Thousand Islands was in the area at the same time the three victims were adrift."

I said, "Coyote boat?"

"The boat that brought the illegals. The question is," he said, "what gives you the idea the coyote boat was a shrimper named the *Nan-Shan*?"

A perceptive man, my Coastie friend.

"I can't tell you, Dalt. I would if I could. But it's good information. You've got to trust me on this one."

A familiar professional restraint had crept into his voice. In the uniformed services, duty always comes before friendship. "I trust you or we wouldn't be talking. So what are you asking me to do?"

"I'd like to get some information about the boat. A boat that size, it's a registered vessel. Who owns her, who runs her? And those refugees — where are they? What do I have to do to interview them?"

Dorsey seemed to relax a little — that's all I was asking? "As far as the boat goes, you could call the federal documentation office in Miami, but I don't think they'd help you much. Or I can run what we call an EPIC search. That stands for El Paso Intelligence Center — which I suspect you already knew."

I did, but said nothing. In fact, I'd once had reason to visit that high-security facility out in the New Mexican desert. I remembered soundproof rooms and a forest of satellite antennas.

"The EPIC maintains a database system," Dorsey said, "that all the federal agencies use. Particularly the agencies that deal with drugs, refugees, that sort of thing.

"Let's say the shrimp boat you're interested in was stopped and searched for drugs, five or ten years back. All the information goes into the EPIC database, whether drugs were found or not. Vessels that we know the bad guys own, or vessels we suspect are dirty, all go into the computer, too. Nothing has to be proven. There's a lot of interesting reading in that file. Can you confirm the spelling of the vessel's name?"

I did, then added, "And what about talking to some of those refugees? If they saw three people adrift, they have no reason not to tell me about it."

"You're out of luck, there. I happen to know the whole group was transported to the Immigration and Naturalization Service facility in Miami. The State Department has the process so streamlined that it takes less than a couple of weeks — unless the refugees happen to be Cuban, and there's a question of political asylum. They get fingerprinted, photographed, then a quick physical. Couple days later, once the State Department has gotten the okay from the home country, they're herded onto a military transport and shipped back to where they came from. In this case, it was Colombia. Probably flew them into Bogotá."

"That's what I was afraid of."

Dorsey told me he'd check the computers and give me a call in an hour or two.

I stayed busy in my lab assembling the

digitized video camera system. My old stilt house is constructed of heart pine, solid as a small ship, built by the long-defunct Punta Gorda Fish Company back around 1920 — many hurricanes ago. I used a rechargeable drill to fix the bracket to a wooden beam in the corner of the room. As the screws burrowed into the beam, they augured yellow wood to the surface, releasing pine resin nearly a century old. That pleasant pine smell mixed with the ozone odor of the lab.

When the bracket was solid, I threaded the camera onto the male base, then toyed with it until the view through the lens, at its widest angle, included the crab tanks, the door to the lab, and some of the aquaria along the eastern wall.

I had to use an extension cord to plug in the 12-volt converter. Finally, I touched the camera's on switch, allowing the computerized timer mode to take control.

Nothing or no one could come through the door, approach the crab tanks, and avoid the lens of that camera.

I was standing there, admiring my handiwork when the telephone rang. Commander Dorsey had some interesting — and troubling — information.

"Turns out your intel about the *Nan-*

333

Shan may be right," he began, then laughed. "So why am I not surprised?"

He went on to tell me that the vessel had been searched by the Coast Guard twice in the last six years, suspected of carrying drugs, and once by agents from the INS because the owner was suspected of being involved in the people-smuggling trade. No arrests were made.

"Internationally, people smuggling gets bigger and bigger every year. Big financial return with a minimum of risk. That's not my area of expertise, but I've got a State Department briefing paper on it. I can send you a copy if you want."

I told Dorsey I would be very interested in reading the report, then made notes as he told me that the owner of The *Nan-Shan* was a man named Dexter Ray Money of Sarasota County. The EPIC had him flagged as a career criminal who'd been arrested and charged with crimes that, over a span of two decades, included grand theft, drug trafficking, extortion, assault and battery, and manslaughter.

"Money got off on everything but the drug-trafficking charge. He spent seven years in Raiford for that, but he's been out for more than ten years. He's a suspect in three murders, including the manslaughter charge, so I don't think running illegals would bother him much at all. He owns three trawler boats, all out of Cortez. The *Nellie*, the *Rebel Witch*, and the *Nan-Shan*. A very bad man."

I said, "Do they have an address listed for him?"

"Whoa, whoa, wait a minute, pal. Do yourself a favor. Do my conscience a favor. Please don't go looking for Mr. Dexter Ray Money. I don't know him, but I know his type. The EPIC has him listed as armed and extremely dangerous, approach with caution — those are the exact words from the data bank. You want to talk to him, do it over the phone."

I kept my tone light. "Give him a call — yeah. Jesus, murder, extortion, plus he's smart enough to keep getting off. After what I've just heard, that sounds like good advice."

"Doc, how reliable is your information? You tell me the source, let me look into it. If we find probable cause, we'll go talk to Mr. Money."

I answered, "I wish I could. I really do." And meant it.

I asked Dorsey one last question before signing off. In his opinion, if Janet, Grace, and Michael had been picked up by a vessel smuggling illegal aliens, why hadn't we heard from them? "Give me some possible scenarios," I said.

"I can think of two right off the top of my head, neither one very pleasant. A bad actor like Money? He kills the man and keeps the women. He keeps them to use for himself, then probably kills them both when he's done. Or decides to make a profit on them. The white slave trade is no joke. Drug smuggling gets all the press, but the flesh trade is a multibillion-dollar business. You read the report I'll send you. There's big money in selling women in places like Brunei, North Africa. Hell, Amnesty International just issued a paper criticizing Israel because people're kidnapping women from outside the country, smuggling them in, and selling them over there."

He added, "Either way, the guy's dead. If someone picked them up — Michael Sanford? — he'd be the first to go."

Chapter Seventeen

When I hung up the phone, I immediately dialed information and asked for the number of Dexter Money, Cortez, Florida. I wasn't exactly sure how I was going to work it, but the first thing I had to do was establish the man's whereabouts. How I would contact him, I'd decide later.

I was relieved when the automated voice responded with the ten-digit number.

Caller ID has mitigated some of our modern problems, and it has created others. I wrote the number on a sheet of paper and walked to shore, then up the shell road to the Hess convenience store next to the old Sanibel Police Station. There's a pay phone there. I went inside, exchanged dollar bills for coins, then dialed the number.

I listened to it ring several times before a girl's voice, in a rush, said what sounded like, "Obie, you ain't got no use to keep callin' here, pesterin' me, and if you doan stop I'm gonna set daddy loose on your ass, boy!" A harsh, Dixie-girl accent, very nasal, but with an adolescent, hormonal rasp.

Playing it as I went along, I answered, " 'Scuse me, miss, but this ain't Obie. I'm callin' for Dexter Money."

She made a deprecating noise of chagrin. "Aw, I'm sorry, mister. That damn Oberlin Carter, he been calling and calling, just won't take no for an answer, so that's who I . . . well, that don't mean nothing to you. You want my daddy, right?"

"If your daddy is Dexter Money, yes, miss, I'd like to speak with him."

"Does it have somethin' to do with pit bulls?" For some reason I got the impression she was asking me two questions, not one. Respond with the correct password or signal phrase and I'd be recognized as part of the inner sanctum.

I gave it a try. "I'm a big fan of that particular breed, yes I am, miss."

Wrong answer. In a flat voice, she said, "He's down working on one of the boats right now, something about one of the flopper-stoppers busted. So I can tell him to give you a call when he gets back to the house."

"That's okay, dear. I got a few things to do, I'll try later."

"Maybe he'll be here later, maybe he won't. You want to talk to my daddy or don't you?" When I didn't answer immediately, some of the aggressiveness returned. "I don't believe you told me what your name is, mister."

"It's not important. I can call back. What you think, maybe an hour or two?"

Families that live outside the law are naturally and pointedly suspicious. The girl said, "I think you best give me your name and number, and let Daddy decide who calls who."

As if I hadn't heard her clearly, I said, "Okay, about two hours then," and hung up.

I'd gotten only a few steps away when the pay phone began to ring. Yep, Money had caller ID.

There was no reason to put the father or daughter on guard, so I answered the phone and listened to the girl say, "Mister, you best tell me who the hell you are and what it is you want."

I said, "Oh, I'm sorry, miss! No need to get upset. My company gives me a list of potential clients, and I'm down here on Sanibel, gettin' ready to swing north. Your

339

daddy's name's on the printout sheet they give me. That's all."

"Oh, really? What kind'a business you in?"

I tried to add a solemn note to my voice when I said, "I sell full memorial packages, miss. From the funeral to a final resting place, and on easy monthly payments. None of us are too young to plan ahead and spare our loved ones the pain of dealing with financial details during their time of grief."

The girl thought that was hilarious. "Mister, you walk onto our property and say that to Daddy, he put *you* in a hole. Your final resting place be right here!"

I was relieved when she hung up.

I checked my watch: 2:15 on a Friday afternoon. I looked overhead: The sky was a December blue with a few cumulous clouds suspended in isolated plateaus over the mangroves, motionless. No wind. I'd already listened to the VHF weather that morning, the maddening computer voice predicting winds to ten knots, seas calm. It's difficult to imagine what kind of idiotic agency would employ an indistinguishable computerized voice to communicate information so valuable.

In my six-cylinder Chevy pickup, it

would probably take me two and a half hours to drive the eighty miles to Cortez. In my new twenty-one-foot Maverick flats boat, though, I could chop a lot of miles and half an hour off the time, and the trip would be a hell of a lot more enjoyable.

Another consideration was that, if need be, I could more easily escape unnoticed in a boat, and there was less chance of being intercepted by law enforcement. No way of telling how Money would react to my questions or what I'd have to do to get information.

At the marina, I topped off the fifty-gallon fuel tank and the oil reservoir, then loaded on block ice, beer, and liter bottles of water. In the big hatch beneath the swivel seats, I'd already stowed extra clothes, a tent, minimal camping gear, and several MREs — the military acronym for meals ready to eat — in their rubberized, brown bags.

At just after 3 p.m., I turned my skiff toward Pine Island Sound, the massive 225-horsepower Yamaha rumbling like a Harley Davidson roadster, and touched the throttle forward. There was a rocket sled sense of acceleration as the skiff reared, lifted, and then flattened itself on plane, rising slightly in the water, gaining buoyancy and speed as I trimmed the engine upward. At nearly fifty miles an hour, the blue horizon rushed toward me, and I left the safety of Dinkin's Bay rolling in my slow, expanding wake.

At Redfish Pass, I cut along South Seas Plantation, waved at Johnny, the resort's enduring tennis teacher — he was wearing a Santa's hat, of all things — then exited into the open Gulf and turned parallel to the beach.

After that, it was beach all the way: the glitter of mica-bright sand, palm trees leaning in windward strands, high-rise condos in schematic rows, and seaside es-tates in the shadows of hardwoods, secure behind walls, on their own grounds.

It was Gulf Coast Florida: part tropical idyllic, part Shaker-Heights-by-the-Sea, part theme-park deco.

I love the region and love being on a fast boat alone. I cracked a cold beer, sat back in the swivel seat, and watched the barrier islands slide past — Gasparilla, Manasota Key, Venice, and Siesta Key — sunglasses on, ball cap pulled low, feet up on the con-sole, steering that solid skiff with one bare toe.

Cortez is a village of four thousand or so

souls, a settlement of piling houses and gray docks clustered on Sarasota Bay, south of St. Pete and just across the bridge from Bradenton Beach.

Just before 5 p.m., I raised the bridge. I banked east through Longboat Pass, its riverine tide fast beneath my hull, the water tannin-stained, a perfect place for snook or bull sharks on a feed. Ahead was Jewfish Key, a few tin roofs silver in the late sunlight beneath a canopy of palms. The bridge was to the north; Cortez a clutter of buildings and docks to the northeast.

Cortez is among the last of Florida's old-time fish camps. Among the last, because increasingly stringent fishing laws and bans are gradually squeezing independent fisher families out of business, leaving international factory ships to strip the sea bottom and supply the world's demand for seafood. An irony of government intervention: By disabling the people it can control, bureaucracy empowers the people and nations it cannot control.

Because the village is built out and isolated on a mangrove peninsula, Cortez has a time-warp feel. The firestorm of development that is strip-mall Florida might have blazed past without noticing the little fish markets and piney-woods houses. Back in the 1930s, the men and women of Cortez wove their own nets, grew peppers and pineapples and mangoes; they wholesaled mullet and stone crabs caught from boats that they had built up from wooden stringers and glassed themselves.

Things hadn't changed much. But they would.

As I dropped down off plane and began to idle toward the docks, I noted mountains of wooden stone crabs traps stacked behind buildings, curtains of shrimp net strung to cure or dry. The air smelled of creosote, diesel, and exposed barnacles.

Ahead was a two-story warehouse made of white cement, a massive blue fuel-storage tank beside it. The sign over the docks read: A. P. Bell Fish Company.

It was a big commercial operation. Inside would be freezers, perhaps even a blast freezer, and container-sized holdings of every variety of salable sea life. From this small place of debarkation, the wealth of waters adjoining Sarasota Bay would be shipped around the world.

Next to the warehouse was Star Fish Company, a two-story building that was spray-creted white. The sign read: Retail Sales & Restaurant. Beer on Tap, so I tied up at the dock and went through the door into the air-conditioned market. Nice little place: snapper, grouper, sea trout, clear-eyed and fresh, lined in the display case on a bed of ice, plus oysters, clams, and shrimp, too. Someone had gone to the trouble to hand paint the tiles that decorated the little room. Behind the counter was a nice-looking woman, her brown hair tied back with a red handkerchief, wearing a white apron that read *Don't Kiss the Cook!*

I laughed as I said, "If I promise not to kiss you, can I get something to eat?"

The woman had a nice smile and the sort of country-girl face that reminded me a little of Janet. "Skipper, you got here just in time 'cause I was getting ready to shut down the grill. There's the menu. What'll you have?"

I ordered a dozen oysters, raw, the grouper sandwich, and a beer with ice. I took the beer out to the picnic tables beneath the awning and sat there looking at the line of commercial boats moored to the docks. There were bay shrimpers, purse seiners, crab haulers, deep-water shrimpers, and maybe thirty grouper boats. A couple had just gotten in — sea gulls screamed overhead in a cloud while fish were offloaded. A couple of vessels were getting ready to head back to sea — men in stained T-shirts muled boxes of groceries, cigarettes, and beer aboard. Most of the boats, though, were stolid, empty-looking, as they sat motionless on the black water. A few had been decorated for Christmas: lights in the rigging, reindeer and plastic Santas waving from wheelhouse windows.

One by one, I checked the names of the oceangoing boats.

There was no *Nan-Shan*.

When the woman brought my food, I invited her to have a seat. She hesitated, then did; she sat down gratefully, as if her feet hurt.

Her name was Stella. An old-timey name that matched her old-timey face. I sat there and ate the good, cold oysters and listened to her tell me about Cortez, the kind of place it was. How it'd changed since they tore down the Albion Inn to build the Coast Guard station, and now there were banks and 7-Elevens sprouting up out east on 648. The village people were still holding it together, trying to save what they could and preserve their own dying history.

Stella said, "They want to put something on the Endangered Species list? They ought to put the independent commercial fishermen. Now there's something darn near extinct." She paused and looked toward the docks. "That your Maverick skiff, skipper? It sure is a pretty boat."

I nodded.

"Hope you don't take no offense. I know you sport anglers got a different view of things."

I told her no offense taken, then used that as an opening to say, "Truth is, a couple of friends and I are thinking about investing in a commercial boat, maybe let someone run it as a shrimper. That should come close to making the payments, and we can use it occasionally for long trips to the Tortugas, or maybe even Belize. I hear the fishing's pretty good over there."

"Sounds like a pretty smart idea, skipper," she answered affably.

"That's one reason I'm in the area. Someone told my partner that a shrimper named the *Nan-Shan* might be on the market. Owned by a guy named Dexter Money. He's the friend of a friend, I guess. You know where I can find him? Or maybe get a quick look at the boat?"

Her demeanor changed instantly, and so did the expression on her face. It was as if I had just strung together all the foulest words in the language. "The *Nan-Shan*," she said, deadpan. "You say you're interesting in buying the *Nan-Shan*?"

I said, "Maybe. I haven't seen her. We'll be looking at a lot of boats."

She stood abruptly. "Well, sir, I'm not in the boat-selling business, so I guess I can't help you." Her tone was now chilly, formal, and I was no longer "skipper." I was "sir."

I held up an index finger, asking her to give me a minute. "Stella, would you please explain something to me. We were getting along great, having a nice conversation, then, suddenly, it's like I'm poison. Did I say something to offend you?"

"I have no idea what you're getting at, sir. Is your food okay? I've got to get back to work."

I smiled at her. "Come on, now, somehow I just screwed up. Can't you give me just a hint about what it was I said?"

She looked at me for a moment, pressed her lips together, thinking. Reluctantly, she said, "Okay, I'm probably being a dope again, but I'll take a chance. You really do seem like the nice, solid sort, so I'll risk it. You said you got friends who are friends of Dex Money? Well, mister, you're keeping the nastiest kind of company, then. And you ain't got no friends in Cortez if you're fixing to do business with that kind'a scum. Forgive my French. Or maybe you're one of the feds after him again, sneaking around trying to get information. Either way, something ain't right."

I said softly, "I've never met the man, Stella. I meant it when I said I didn't know where to find him."

She jerked her head north toward a wooded point on the other side of the bay. "You'll find him on the far side of Perico Island. He's got some land there, a couple houses and some docks."

"I take it you don't like him. You and the people of Cortez."

"We don't claim him, if that's what you're asking. Let's see . . . it's Friday night? So at his place tonight he'll be having dogfights — he raises pit bulls, lets 'em fight 'till their bellies are ripped open. Or snortin' up coke with his redneck pals, shooting guns. Or that daughter of his, Shanay, she's only fifteen or sixteen, and the word that describes her, I won't say. Shanay's a party girl and she may have her friends over. Which is maybe understandable what with Dex putting her mama in the hospital so many times she finally just run off and disappeared. Do the people of Cortez like Dex Money? No, sir, we do not."

Her expression became grim when I asked for more detailed information about where the man lived. She said, "Just past Boca del Rio Marina, there's a mangrove river cuts in. He's up the river. Got a little boat way, his own docks. You'll see the warning signs at the mouth. Keep out. Do what you want, you're a grown man, but if you're smart, you'll do what the signs tell you."

I paid, and took care not to overtip. The woman had described me as solid-looking when, in fact, she was describing what she valued in herself.

I liked her, wished it hadn't been necessary to lie to her. A woman like this would not react kindly to the slightest suggestion that I was paying her for information.

I got my first look at Dexter Money just after sunset. The soft December light did nothing to soften the man's features, or his manner. He came swaggering parallel to the docks, shoulders thrown back, belly pushing a black T-shirt away from his skinny hips, sleeves rolled to show his biceps, two bat-eared pit bull dogs trotting along behind, tongues lolling.

His was a territorial display. There was no doubt who the man was, who owned that land.

The guy was gigantic. Closer to seven feet tall than six, he had to weigh more than three hundred pounds, with a shaved, butter-bean head and a florid, alcoholic's face. As he approached me, his right eye was squinched, a cigarette between his teeth. He carried a green bottle of beer, and there was something else, too: He had a holster clipped to his hip, the butt of a chrome-plated revolver showing. One of the big ones. Maybe a .357.

"Buddy ruff, you either can't read or you one dumbass Yankee! You didn't see them signs at the mouth of the river you just come up?" He had a coarse, curiously high-pitched voice, a fried-okra twang; an accent that was intentionally emphasized to communicate his contempt for me, an outsider.

I'd seen the signs. Saw one at the mouth of the deepwater mangrove cut — No Trespassing! This Means You! — and a second sign just before I rounded the bend at dead idle and saw the two CBS houses through the oaks elevated above the river, an airboat and a couple of ATVs, a junked GTO, another GTO gray with Bondo up on blocks, a bunch of new pickup trucks parked in the shade, dog cages in the back, men with ball caps milling around as country music played, and a hulking, rusted shrimper tied adjacent a machine shop, *Nan-Shan* in white letters on her stern.

He'd been by the house when he noticed me, a foot or more taller than the other men. He turned, then ambled down the hill to intercept me. Now here he was, Dexter Money, a big man and a bigger disappointment — a disappointment because he was not one of the two men in the satellite photos. I would have recognized him. Did he hire people to run his boats?

I fixed a smile on my face as I turned the bow of my skiff toward the riverbank, Money still walking toward me, the two of us separated by only ten or fifteen yards, as I called to him, "I saw the signs. I thought they meant don't come ashore. What I'm doing is, I'm scouting for snook spots, won't harm a thing." When he didn't respond immediately, I added, "I didn't know a person could own a river."

He stopped at the bank, and his tone was without inflection, his eyes were glassy, drug-bright, fierce: "That's where you wrong, buddy ruff. This river's *mine* — and you just had your last warning."

I started to reply — "In that case, I'll . . ." — but didn't get a chance to finish because

Money pivoted, cocked his arm, and rocketed his beer bottle at me. I ducked as it shattered against the console, glass shards everywhere. Heard him scream, "Get the fuck outta here! *Now!*"

I have dealt with enough Dexter Moneys in my life to know there is no point in dealing with them. But I'm not immune to anger, either. I stared at him for a moment before I jammed the throttle forward as if to run my skiff ashore, then spun the wheel hard so that the stern skidded toward him. The hull of the boat dug deep as it turned, plowing a high, waking wall of water that washed over Money and sent his two pit bulls running.

I stopped the boat, engine still idling, and looked over my shoulder. His clothes were soaked, his cigarette smoldering. Christ — he had his revolver drawn but was pointing it at the ground — a man who could snap that quick. "Motherfucker!" he said, his voice trembling. "I have killed men better than you!"

Before I touched the throttle again, planing away, I said in a voice low enough to force him to listen: "Mister, I hope that's the only thing we have in common."

I came back that night just after 3 a.m.,

the graveyard hour, when even the worst of insomniacs are asleep.

To the west, magnified by the horizon's curvature, the moon was huge, the size of a setting sun, a disc of platelet orange, a scimitar fragment missing in earth shadow. The river reacted to contact with the moon, becoming a lighted corridor in the darkness, its water red.

I shut the engine down far from the mouth of the river and poled my way in, no noise at all, just the creaking of mangroves and water dripping onto reflected stars. A dog barked somewhere. There were owls conversing in the shadows beyond.

That afternoon, I'd argued it back and forth in my head. Stay or not to stay. How important was it that I got aboard the *Nan-Shan* and had a look around?

Could be pretty important, I decided. Even the most poorly run vessel keeps some kind of log. And if the operators were too sloppy to maintain records, they were usually sufficiently sloppy to leave behind some form of identifying spore aboard.

Yeah, I needed to have a look around.

With my evening free, I considered finding an open stretch of beach and camping. December's a good time to be outside in Florida, looking up at the stars.

But I was feeling sociable and in need of a hot shower, so I ran across the bay to the backside of Anna Maria Island. The Rod & Reel Marina was booked full, so I found a slip among the liveaboards at Bradenton Beach Marina and walked two blocks to the Pelican Post Inn. A rental cottage was available: a little place on stilts with knotty pine paneling, kitchen, couch, swivel chair and TV, plus an independent bedroom with a mattress that seemed firm enough. I called Amelia on the chance she was free for the evening, and I got lucky.

"Doc?" she said. "You don't know how great it is to hear your voice! Damn, am I *glad* you're here."

We met for a drink at the Bridge Tender, then walked to the Gulf side for seafood at the Beach House.

I was touched by the fact that Amelia appeared to have taken special care in the way she dressed for the evening. Black dress and stockings, red hair brushed to a sheen, and makeup, too, a touch of eyeliner, peach gloss lipstick. The first time I'd ever seen her wear makeup.

She seemed surprisingly glad to see me. A lot of warm eye contact, a lot of brief nudges and illustrative touching after we'd greeted each other with a long hug.

At first, I thought the most frustrating part of the evening would be that I couldn't tell the lady about the satellite photos I'd seen, about why I was there. No one was more deserving then Amelia to know there was a slim chance that Grace, Janet, and Michael might still be alive.

Wrong. There was an entirely unexpected source of frustration. When the relationship between a man and a woman changes, or there is a potential for change, there begins a multilevel variety of communication that is unmistakable but not easily pinpointed. Because there is a risk of embarrassment, the form of communication requires that one meaning must necessarily be concealed by another, more innocent meaning. Some of the exchange is verbal, some physical.

At the Bridge Tender, we sat at a table overlooking the bay. The moon was high and bright, and the lady looked very attractive indeed. Once, she used her index finger to tap the back of my hand before she said to me, "I'm so glad you called. I've been dating a couple of different people off and on, and just this week, I made the decision, no more, that's the end of it. Nice guys, but the attraction isn't there, and I found myself feeling lonelier when we were together than when I was off by myself. Life's too short to waste it pretending."

A little later, she said, "Something happened to me those nights when I was stranded. After being on the tower, I don't even have patience for my own lies. I'm a healthy, physical woman. I've finally admitted that to myself, too — not easy for a single Catholic girl."

Was there a hidden message there?

At the restaurant, she told the waiter she wanted a half-dozen oysters, but the waiter didn't hear.

"A dozen, miss?" he asked.

Amelia was looking at me when she replied, "No, a half dozen. I just want sex. I mean . . . six." Laughing at herself as the waiter walked away, her eyes averted now, blushing, too — maybe the first time I'd ever seen an attorney blush — as she dabbed at her face with a napkin and said to me, "My God, talk about Freudian. I've got to start getting more exercise, go for a long run. *Something*."

It set up a fun, unspoken sexual tension. When she'd finished her wine, we walked out onto the Bradenton Pier. It seemed the most natural thing in the world when she slipped her arm through mine and then, later, when I placed my hand on her waist as we walked. I could feel the pivot of her hips, the sharp blade of her pelvic bone. There were men fishing, lovers tangled together in the shadows.

Near the end of the pier, we stopped, me looking down into the water, fish moving through the circles of light, her with her head pillowed against my arm. It surprised me when she said, "I don't want to be obvious here, but there's something we've never talked about."

I said, "Oh?"

"Yeah, it's your social status. There used to be little symbols. Wedding bands, bracelets . . . tattoos." She chuckled. "Who belongs to who. But now you have to ask. So I'm asking: Do you belong to anyone, Dr. Ford?"

"Nope. Never been married, never been engaged. I have a long list of female friends who are just that — friends. Nothing serious going on right now."

"Does that include JoAnn and Rhonda from Dinkin's Bay? I got the impression there was something special between you and . . . well, frankly, both of them."

An insightful, perceptive lady. But I said, "No, we're all three buddies, that's all."

"Ah, the independent type, the male rogue."

I turned to look at her, smiling. "I used to tell myself that, and for a time I believed it. Like you, the thing you said about lying to yourself? I don't have much patience for my own lies anymore, either. I've come to the conclusion that I live alone because I am, at the core, an essentially selfish person. It's taken awhile for me to admit it. My lab, the work I'm doing, it always comes first. All loving, devoted relationships require compromise in terms of how time is shared, and I'm too self-interested to compromise. No woman's going to put up with that for long, and I don't blame 'em."

"My God, and you're honest, too."

I thought about the lie I told her, explaining why I happened to be in the Sarasota area — research at Bell Fish Company — and replied, "Just because I've lost patience for my own lies doesn't mean I don't tell them to others. Nope, I'm not particularly honest, either."

That seemed to touch her on some deeper level. "I can relate to that, my new friend. One thing I've learned is, you can't pray a lie, which maybe, in a way, makes sinners of us all. So, from one sinner to another, how about I walk you back to your cottage?"

In the darkness of banyan shadow near the motel, Amelia stopped, and I turned her toward me, looking down into her face. Then I kissed her softly, feeling her lips move against mine, feeling her rib cage pressing washboard-like against my stomach. As her hands moved up my sides, her mouth opened, tongue searching, my hands began to move, too.

Open-palmed, exploring with fingertips, I felt body heat radiating through the sheer material of her dress, felt the stricture of latissimus cordage beneath her arms, swimmer's muscles. Then felt her mouth open very wide, heard her moan softly as my fingers found eraser-hard nipples, her breasts flat over bony sternum. Felt her pull away long enough to whisper, "I hope you don't like the busty type. If you do, you're in for a disappointment."

I found the self-deprecation touching, almost sad. If we men were required to wear sized penis stockings outside our pants, our discussions of women's breasts would be markedly less frequent and our preferences more vaguely defined.

I wrapped my arms around her hips and lifted her chest high as I whispered my reply: "The way your body feels, I like just fine. There's less distance between my lips and your heart." Then I kissed her neck, and each nipple, feeling her swell and arch beneath the black dress, breathing heavier now, making soft sounds.

"Doc . . . we have a perfectly nice cottage right there. If you keep doing what you're doing, I'm going to rip those shorts off you. Indecent exposure — the cops'll arrest us both. Me, an officer of the court."

Which is when it finally dawned on me that I couldn't allow this to go any further. I do so many stupid things so often, it should no longer surprise me. Sometime that night, way after midnight, I had to go a'calling on Dex Money's shrimp boat, the *Nan-Shan*. If Amelia went upstairs to my bed, there was a good chance she'd stay over. How would I explain a lengthy disappearance?

I lowered her to the ground, held her away from me. "You are one spectacular woman," I said.

Her voice had an unmistakable huskiness. "I can barely hear you, my heart's pounding so loud."

She took my hand and pulled me out of the shadows, into a circle of streetlight, toward the cottage. I hated the way her expression changed when I stopped, refusing to follow her, and I said, "Amelia, let's . . . let's not do this. Not tonight, anyway. Let's give it some time, date for a while, see what happens. Why risk the friendship?"

She said very slowly, "Give it . . . some *time?* You're kidding, right? Please tell me you're kidding."

I badly wanted to tell her just that, but couldn't. "I'm trying to look down the road, anticipate what's best for the both of us." Then added lamely, "We really don't know each other that well, when you think about it," and I hated myself for sounding so prudish and insipid.

"Uhh-h-h, excuse me." She laughed, an attempt to mask embarrassment. "I'm looking at you, not believing what I'm hearing, but you *do* mean it. You really *don't* want me to come up to your room. Sorry, Amelia, request for service denied, Amelia. That's what you're telling me."

"No, no, absolutely, it's not like that at all. It's just that I don't want to rush you into something you might regret."

Her face had gone from flushed, swollen, and sleepy to a pained look of surprise. "What you really mean is, you don't want to risk doing something *you'll* regret. Well, Doc, just for the record . . . let me put it this way: I want to set you straight about something, just so you don't get the wrong idea about me. Before I get in my car and drive away, which is what I'm about to do.

"When it comes to men, I've never rushed into anything in my life. I don't go around hopping from bed to bed. This is as close as I've ever come in my life to throwing myself at someone, and, believe me, sir, it's something I'll never risk again. It's been nearly a year for me, and it may be another year before I find a man I like enough and trust enough to join in bed. But that's one thing you don't have to worry about, Dr. Ford, it *won't* be you."

The woman had a temper. I tried to call her back as she walked away. She never turned, never looked, never replied.

Chapter Eighteen

There's an alarm on my watch, which I set, and I set the alarm in the cottage's bedroom, too — both for 2:45 a.m.

But I didn't need either one of them because I couldn't sleep. I laid awake in the darkness with a Gulf wind blowing through the screen, berating myself for my insensitivity, my stupidity. Why hadn't I the foresight to come up with a more plausible, less insulting lie?

Twice I dialed Amelia's home number, got the machine each time.

Clearly, she didn't want to talk to me. The woman had taken enough cheap shots over the last few months, and now I'd added to her pain and humiliation.

At 2:30, I dressed and checked the duffel I'd packed for the boat. Inside were military BDU pants with tiger-stripe camo, my old black watch sweater, Navy blue stocking cap, leather gloves, mask and snorkel, Rocket fins, and a small water-proof flashlight. Back in Dinkin's Bay, I'd decided against packing my 9mm SIG Sauer semiautomatic handgun. That was before I'd seen Dexter Money and his pit bulls. I regretted that decision now.

I carried the bag to the marina, stepped into my boat. On one of the liveaboard yachts, I noticed a silhouette pass across the disc of the porthole — someone in there awake — and so I didn't risk poling my skiff away from the docks. At that hour, people who try not to make noise are suspicious people. Instead, I started the engine and idled out into the bay.

There was still sufficient moonlight to read the markers, so I didn't use a light. I ran north, then turned my skiff east toward Mead Point and Perico Island.

Somewhere out there, beneath the blackness, beyond the flashing markers, I hoped that Dexter Money and his dogs were asleep.

I pushed my skiff upriver, staying close to the bank, where the water was shallow. My push pole is made of fiberglass, similar to a vaulting pole, and it bent beneath my weight as I levered it against the marl bottom. Standing above the engine, pole in hand, I watched the moon flatten itself over a black plateau of mangroves. Then the moon vaporized in a striated cloud of rust.

Nearing the final bend, I could see the yellow glare of sodium lights reflecting off the water. Security lights. I'd noticed the poles on my first visit, which was why I brought my swim gear.

Time to get wet. I moored the skiff's stern to a prop root and stripped off my T-shirt and shorts, ears straining to hear: tidal drainage and wind in leaves. Nothing else. I continued to listen as I dressed myself in BDUs, sweater, and stocking cap. I had a pair of Five-Ten rubber-soled climbing shoes and fit my Rocket fins over them. Wearing mask and snorkel on my arm like a bicep band, I bellied over the side into the water. Brackish water, just a hint of salt and oil. This far up in the swamplands, the river felt earthy, warm.

I swam with my eyes above surface level. When I rounded the bend, I could see the big shrimper, the *Nan-Shan*, motionless beneath the security lights. Could see rooftop angles of the two blockhouses through the trees, part of an outside wall. No lights showing in the windows, no sign of life. I stayed close to the bank, in the shadows.

Once, I stopped, held myself erect, treading water. Was that a log floating on the surface up ahead of me? Or maybe an empty fuel drum?

I decided that my eyes were playing tricks and continued on.

When I was beneath the docks, I held on to a crossbeam, looking up through the deck, listening. Now I *could* hear something unusual. It was a faint whining noise, a weak animal sound. Maybe the sound of an injured bird . . . or a pump with a bad rotor. I wasn't certain if the noise came from near or far, but it couldn't have been human.

I pulled myself up onto the dock. Stood there crouched long enough to feel confident I was alone. Then I removed my fins, walked along the dock, and stepped over onto the deck of the shrimp boat.

The odor of an ocean shrimper is distinctive: petroleum-based net coating, diesel and paint, the protein rot of sea animals stuck in nylon mesh or in small crevices that are impossible to clean thoroughly.

This vessel smelled of shrimping, but of something else, too. I have been in places of war where battlefield sanitation required that personnel attempt to destroy the stench of death with disinfectant.

The boat had that odor, the odor of flesh masked by strong chemicals. Someone had tried hard to scour the stink out of this vessel. I tested the door of the wheelhouse and stepped inside: The smell of bleach, pine cleaner, and ammonia was nearly overpowering.

I closed the door behind me, waited a few moments in the darkness, accustoming myself to the fumes before taking out a rubberized mini-flashlight. I rotated the bezel until I had a little flood beam and then began a methodical search.

It didn't take me long to find the ship's log. It was a mess, nearly illegible. Entries sometimes included weather as well as the GPS numbers of where the boat was fishing at the time. Sometimes the entries were signed, sometimes not. The last entry into the log had been made in October, three weeks before Janet and the others were set adrift, signed by someone named Baker.

I made a mental note of the name. If Dexter Money hired Baker to drag for shrimp, maybe he hired Baker to run refugees, too.

I ducked down the companionway steps into the galley. It was the standard layout: propane stove, sink, icebox, dinette table that collapsed into a settee berth. Despite the smell of disinfectant, the place was a mess. Greasy dishes, empty beer bottles, dented peanut cans filled with cigarette butts, *Penthouse* magazines strewn around the tiny head, soiled linen in the master's quarters. The only personal items I found — subscription labels, a locker filled with prescription medications — were in Dexter Money's name.

One time I stopped, frozen and listening for more than a minute. Had I heard footsteps on the dock outside?

Nothing.

So I continued my search and had an unexpected stroke of luck. When slovenly types want to trash a document they don't want found, they invariably wrap it in something innocuous and throw it away. On a boat, you'd expect them to toss it overboard. But here, someone had packed in a hurry, not much worried about covering his tracks.

In a trash bag in the master's quarters, I found an empty, crumpled bag of Starbuck's coffee — expensive tastes for a commercial fisherman. I opened the bag

369

and found therein a series of digital photograph rejects. They were badly printed on standard computer paper and smeared. Each shot was graphically pornographic, featuring a tall, thin, naked albino man in a variety of poses with two naked, Latin-looking women. Oral sex was the consistent theme.

Because the shots were badly framed, I got the impression that one of the three had probably placed the camera on a desk, touched the timer button, then rushed to get into the picture. Strictly amateur.

In one of the photos, both women stared into the camera's lens, moistened lips and sloe-eyed, their expressions so obvious and salacious that they might have been parodying stage sensuality. Because of certain grotesque characteristics of the man's physiology, and because the woman looked to be no older than their late teens, I guessed them to be prostitutes. Women doing things they'd never do unless they were getting paid. Because of the man's dull, glossy stare, I made another deduction: He was very drunk during the session or on drugs.

The rattan furniture in the background had a commercial look, suggestive of a hotel.

The inference got some support. Crumpled with the photos, I found a brochure for a place called Hotel de Acension, Cartagena, Colombia.

I knew the hotel, had even been in the bar a couple of times. High marble ceilings and European prices. It had been a cathedral during the time of the Conquistadors. Now it was a notorious hangout for drug cartel people, informants, and State Department types on the make. With the brochure was a copy of receipts for a one-month stay made out to someone named Hassan Atwa Kazan. He had expensive tastes and liked room service. Moët, smoked salmon, Dunhill cigarettes.

I turned and checked one of the peanut can ashtrays.

Yes. A quill of Dunhill butts in there.

I considered the name: *Kazan*. Probably Middle Eastern, possibly Islamic, though I have a friend in London named Kazan, and she's Italian.

Even so, the face did not mesh with the name. Albino or not, the man in the photographs had facial characteristics common to mountain Europeans and certain North Africans.

I stood, studying the receipt, holding the paper close to my face, but then I stopped reading. Stood there listening for a moment, then extinguished the light.

Footsteps?

I decided that, once again, it was just my imagination.

I stored the papers in a waterproof bag, stuffed the bag into my cargo pocket, and retraced my steps up the companionway.

I was just opening the door when the wheelhouse lights suddenly flashed on. I stood with my hand on the knob, frozen.

Behind me, a woman's voice said, "What I may do is shoot you. Or jes' feed you to Daddy's dogs. Sonuvabitch, I'm sick to death of you leeches actin' like you own the place, hurtin' me like I ain't got no feelin's at all."

I turned to see a high school–aged girl holding a sawed-off 12-gauge with a pistol grip instead of a butt — a weapon known as a "street sweeper" because of the pattern it fires.

The girl had brown hair layered shag style, cutoff shorts. Abdominal baby fat bulged beneath her midriff T-shirt. Her face was narrow, pinched around thin lips, and the divider that separated her nostrils — the columella — was creased. She was a type: skinny hips, heavy breasts. Physically mature by thirteen or fourteen, emotionally old before thirty; a producer of fertile eggs and barroom dramas.

The girl squinted at me for a moment before saying, "Hey — you ain't one of Daddy's dogfight buddies. I don't remember seein' you here when they decided to have their fun."

Her piney-woods accent was familiar. I'd heard it earlier that day on the pay phone. Shanay Money, the girl who was having trouble fending off a kid named Oberlin Carter, only her voice was different now. Some of the steeliness had gone out of it. Her arms and shirt, I noticed, were smeared with blood, and her eyes were bleary, red, perhaps from crying. The intensity with which she held the weapon, the tone of her voice, her expression all communicated a resonant hysteria. I got the feeling I'd stumbled into something very personal. Catch a burglar on any other night, she'd have probably called the cops. Or her father. Tonight, though, she was ready to use the shotgun.

I decided to take a chance. "You've never seen me before, Shanay, because I've never been here before. Never met your father. But, from what I've heard, I wouldn't like his friends. Probably wouldn't like him, either."

That earned me a bitter smile. "I suppose you man enough to want to say that to Daddy's face?"

"I'd prefer not to."

"Hoo-eee, I bet you wouldn't! I once saw him strip one of my boyfriends naked, pants and undies, then spank him like a baby! He likes hurtin' people, my daddy does. His sick friends, they ain't no better." The hysteria in her voice now had acquired a shrill edge.

I said, "Tell me about the blood on your shirt, Shanay. I'm not here to harm you. But I might be able to help you. What happened here tonight?"

She jabbed the barrel of the shotgun at me, as she used her head to gesture vaguely toward shore. "There ain't nothin' you or anybody else can do to help my ol' Davey dog. He's up there bleedin' to death right now. *You're* the one who needs to do the explaining, mister. If I thought for a minute you was one of 'em, I'd blow your damn head off!"

I raised my hands slowly, palms out. "Your dog's injured? Then wake up your dad, call a vet."

"You don't call a vet for animals hurt in

a dogfight. Not unless you want the law stickin' their nose in, and my daddy's so fucked up on that powder of his and liquor, he didn't wake up when I was screamin', and he ain't gonna wake up now."

I put my hands down and took a step toward her. "Then I might be able to help. I'm a doctor. I'm telling you the truth. Take me to your dog, and I'll tell you why I'm here. Then you tell me what happened."

She lowered the shotgun, tears now dripping down her face. "You a people doctor or an animal doctor?"

I opened the wheelhouse door, holding it for her, saying, "An animal doctor. Sort of. I specialize in fish."

Dexter Money was in the dogfighting business, in a big way. Because I'm an obsessive reader, I know that Florida is one of a very few states in which it is legal to own, train, and promote fighting breeds, though it is a felony to actually stage a dogfight — a gigantic legal loophole that the public would not tolerate if some organization, the manatee people, for instance, adopted it as a cause.

I also know that, each and every

weekend, there are dogfights taking place somewhere around Florida, and that championship purses have exceeded $100,000. The drug dealer types like owning vicious dogs because they offer an added layer of personal protection, so fighting their dogs, betting on the outcome, is a natural extension of that illegal activity.

I followed Shanay along the dock, through a door into the old machine shop. It looked to be made of cypress, open ceilinged, two stories high, rafters showing, bleachers built around a sawdust pen, bare lightbulbs dangling overhead on cords. Stacked in the far corner of the pen were the corpses of five, maybe six dogs. Most of them were brindled, brown, gray, and yellow, their skin ripped off in places, blood crusted black in their fur. They hadn't been dead long.

"Davey dog's over here," the girl said, as she walked around the pen to the back of the building and knelt, then threw back a blanket. Her voice cracked as she added, "I hope he's not dead already. I've had him since I was a little girl."

The whimpering, whining noise I'd heard earlier was Davey. He was a yellow Lab, maybe eighty pounds, gray hair showing on his muzzle. He was still alive. Barely. His left ear was gone and part of his tail. When I touched my palm to his ribs, testing for a pulse, the dog opened his eyes slightly and thumped his stub of a tail, acknowledging me.

"Can you save him, mister? It'd break my heart to lose him. It purely would."

I said, "Are you sure we can't call a vet?"

"Daddy would kill me. He'd beat me 'til I couldn't walk. It's the law. The vet would have to report us, and Daddy ain't goin' to jail again. He already told me that."

I said, "Okay, so we've got no choice. I'll do my best." I told her what supplies I thought I needed. She came running back with most of what I asked for. From her father's own kennel supplies, she brought Acepromazine, an animal sedative, and a length of clear plastic tubing. She also brought several surgical cutting needles, a roll of unflavored dental floss, peroxide, and a bottle of Gatorade.

When I asked for the Gatorade, she seemed surprised and said, "If you're thirsty, I'll get you a beer. Anything you want."

I'd already seen gauze, tape, peroxide, and the antibiotic cephalexin aboard the *Nan-Shan,* and she brought those articles, too.

"The only thing I couldn't find is that spray can stuff you wanted. Lanacane? Can you get along without it?"

"I need something, some kind of anesthetic, or your Lab isn't going to hold still for what I have to do." I thought for a moment, then remembered the girl mentioning her father's powder, and said, "Cocaine would be even better. As a topical anesthetic, I mean. I don't suppose you know where we could get some of that?"

Some of the softness left her face. "Mister, if you're trying to trick me into something, I still got this shotgun. What I'm thinking is, you already tricked me once today. Did you call me on the phone this afternoon, talking about cemetery plots in an Alabama accent?"

"That was me, yeah. I'll explain why later. But this isn't a trick. I'm serious. It'd help your dog."

She left and returned a few minutes later with an ounce or so of white powder in a plastic baggie. I'd already placed two Acepromazine tablets on the back of the dog's tongue and massaged its throat until it swallowed. Then I'd used gauze and peroxide to clean the bare flesh around the tail and the missing ear. Now I dabbed the powder on liberally, listening as the girl told me what had happened.

There'd been thirty or forty men at tonight's fight. Shanay had been grounded by her father for some offense, so she had to stay on the property. She couldn't stand to watch or hear what happened to the dogs, so she'd remained in her room watching MTV, curled up in bed, her Lab beside her.

By midnight, her father was passed out on the living room floor. Around 1 a.m., she walked down to the river.

"I thought they was all gone, all his friends," she said. "And Daddy keeps his dogs locked in cages the nights there's fights, so I didn't have to worry about them, either."

Wrong. Two of her father's drunken "friends" cornered the girl outside the machine shop. When one of the men grabbed her, she screamed. Her old retriever, Davey, came charging to the rescue.

"He bit one of 'em, this motorcycle jock named Jason. So Jason let his pit bulls loose on poor ol' Davey dog. It was awful to watch, and there wasn't nothing I could do. By the time I got back here with the shotgun, they was gone. The bastards! I was hopin' you was one of 'em, mister, I surely was. I'd'a used it. I swear I would'a. So now it's your turn. Why are you here?"

I'd stopped much of the dog's bleeding by using dental floss sutures to ligate the open vessels. Then took the plastic tubing and measured the distance from the Lab's nose to its stomach and dented the tubing to mark it.

Davey had lost a lot of blood and was in shock. He needed to be rehydrated quickly or he would die. By touching the back of his tongue with my index finger, I forced him to gag the tubing down. Because it slid cleanly to my mark, I was pretty sure it was in his stomach, not his lung. Just to be certain, though, I laid my ear to the dog's stomach and blew gently into the tube. I heard a telltale *blub-blub*.

I took the funnel and began to pour the Gatorade into him. As I did, I told the girl the truth. A heavily edited version of the truth, anyway. I told her about my diver friends lost at sea. I told her I had reason to suspect that they'd been picked up by the *Nan-Shan*. I told her that aboard the boat was an albino man whose name might be Hassan Atwa Kazan.

When I spoke the name, she began to shake her head, saying, "That could be his real name, but it ain't what Daddy calls him. Those two freaks, I know exactly who you mean. The albino, nobody calls him Hassan, what they call him is Puff. I don't know why unless it's 'cause he's a doper. The guy he runs boats with, his partner, his name's Earl. Big fat colored man, only not like African colored, a different kind. He makes my daddy look skinny." She touched an index finger to her cheek. "This side of his face, the colored man I'm talking about, he's got a burn mark or something. His whole cheek.

"Both of them are pretty gross to look at, but the albino, though, he's the worst. Gives me the spooks just bein' in the same room with him. His face is so white, like the belly of a fish, and his eyes look like they're made out of yellow glass. He wears like a towel on his head, shaped like a tent. It ain't no turban, but something like a turban. I've seen 'em around here a few times, usually pickin' up and droppin' off the shrimper."

"Do they run the boat for your father?"

She thought for a moment, shrugged. "I don't know what it is they do. But it ain't shrimpin'. I don't ask. All I know is, they'll take the boat and be gone for three, four weeks at a time, and they never come back together. The colored man, he usually brings the boat back here alone. I guess the albino gets dropped off somewhere. Like he's the boss and the colored man does the dirty work. And stink? Man, that boat stinks so bad you can't hardly stand it."

"What about a man named Baker? Does he work with them?"

She made a flapping gesture of dismissal with her hand. "No-o-o-o. That's that idiot Timmy Baker, just an ol' boy that shrimps for Daddy sometimes when he ain't sleepin' on the dock drunk."

I had pulled the skin together around the Lab's ear as best I could, then around his ruined tail, and was stitching the wounds closed, applying Neosporin as I went. The tranquilizers had kicked in, and the dog was asleep, breathing rapidly. I said, "I need to find those two, Shanay. They may know something about my friends."

"Mister, you don't want to mess with those men. They're not going to tell you nothin' unless you make them tell you and, no offense, but you just ain't the type. You remind me of a algebra teacher I had back when I was still goin' to class. He played some weird, funny game. Badminton, I think it was."

"Would you tell me where to find the men if you could?"

"Daddy's probably got them down in his book. People that pay him money, he keeps track of where they live. The colored man, he's got an accent. I don't know where from. Same with the albino."

I said, "While I finish up here, why don't you go have a look. Write whatever information you find on a piece of paper."

She'd been sitting at the dog's side, stroking his back. Now she stood. I noticed for the first time that she had a small butterfly tattooed on her ankle, and she wore a bracelet of blue string around her wrist. She stared at her sleeping pet for a moment before she said, "Why is it people are so much meaner than dogs and such, but we call *them* animals?"

Tomlinson is fond of saying that a Godlike greatness is available to humanity only because we are balanced with an equal capacity for evil. My view of the world, however, is more clinical, so less certain. I replied, "I don't know. I'm more worried about how much blood he lost."

"Is he gonna live, mister? He's slept with me every night since my mama ran away. Never left me alone. I don't know what I'd do without my Davey dog."

I wanted to tell her that, sooner or later, her companion *would* die, leaving her alone in her father's nightmare world. I wanted to tell her that if she did not break away from that world soon, it would drag her in and destroy her.

Sometimes we get the urge to help even when we know we can't.

Instead, I said, "I hope he's okay, Shanay. He seems like a nice dog, and you seem like a nice girl. I really do hope the best for both of you."

I was waiting on the dock when she returned and handed me a sheet of paper. The security lights were bright enough that I could read her childlike printing: Hassan Atwa Kazan had a P.O. box in Tangier, Morocco.

Tangier?

Years ago, I'd been in Marrakech and in Casablanca. Just a week or two, then gone. But my knowledge of the region's geography wasn't good, though I'd certainly heard of Tangier.

Kazan's telephone number, however, had a familiar prefix: 57-5. It was the country and city code for Cartagena, Colombia. Same with a man named Earl Stallings. Not surprisingly, his address was the Hotel de Acension, Cartagena.

As I read the names, the girl said, "Hassan whatever-the-rest-of-it-is, I guess that must be the albino's name. He's sick-white looking, but his features ain't what you'd call American. He was in daddy's book under *P* for Puff."

I said, "Thanks. This helps me a lot. Something else, Shanay? I'd really appreciate it if you didn't tell anyone you gave me this information. You'd be doing me a big favor."

"I'm going to tell you again, mister: Stay away from them two. I think they even scare Daddy a lil' bit."

"I'll be careful. But it's not going to help if they know I'm looking for them. Would you promise me?"

Her voice had a touching, needy quality as she replied, "I don't even know your name, mister. I couldn't get in touch with you even if I just wanted to talk, so why would I make you a promise?"

I reached out, squeezed her shoulder, saw her face tilt upward toward me, felt her body soften. Sometimes, you have to operate on instinct, and I decided to trust her. I told her my name and that, if she was ever in trouble, day or night, she was welcome to contact me. As I talked, I opened my little waterproof pouch, stored the paper therein, and walked to where the *Nan-Shan* was moored to retrieve my mask and fins.

The girl said, "Marion? That's a funny name for a guy. You don't mind, I think I *will* call you. Just to talk some nights. It might be nice to have a man friend who isn't tryin' . . . well, it just might be nice to have a man friend."

Then she stopped as if stunned at the sight of my snorkeling gear, and added in a voice of surprise, "You're kiddin' me, dude — don't tell me you swam up this river?"

Her concern made me smile. "Not far, don't worry. My skiff's just around the first bend, less than a hundred meters from here. I've had a lot of experience swimming at night."

She grabbed my arm, pulling me back from the water. "Marion, you're nuts. Jesus Christ, I'm surprised you're still alive. Get in my little boat, I'll take you."

"I don't mind the swim. It's not a problem."

"Oh yeah? Hand me that little flashlight you got — no, look, don't even bother. There she is right by the dock. Lizzy Pig. You can see her in the light. I hate her. She still gives me nightmares."

Lizzy Pig? What kind of name was that?

Then I saw, and understood. Drifting alongside the *Nan-Shan* was one of the biggest alligators I've ever seen. Had to be close to fourteen feet long and so broad that it resembled an Australian croc — or the empty fuel drum I'd mistaken it for on my swim in.

When the girl took my fins and mask and stepped toward her little boat, I didn't protest. "Lizzy Pig, Daddy's had her for years. She gets real excited the nights he puts on dogfights. Big old fat lizard. She knows, next morning, he's gonna feed her the losers."

Chapter Nineteen

⊙—————————⊙

On Tuesday morning, December 16, I caught an American Eagle Flight to Miami International — not my favorite airport in Florida — and stood in line at the Avianca desk until I had tickets to Cartagena in hand.

Two tickets, not one.

I had an unexpected travel companion at my side: Amelia Gardner.

Early Saturday morning, just before dawn's first gray light, when I'd returned to my rental cottage at the Pelican Post on Bradenton Beach, her green Jeep was in the driveway, the hood cool to the touch. I tapped on the door before entering and found her curled on the couch, windows open, Gulf breeze blowing through the curtains.

When she asked where I'd been, I used the first alibi that came to mind, saying, "If

I'd known you were coming back, I wouldn't have stayed out so late snook fishing." It didn't account for being dressed in tactical clothing, but I'm not the most creative person around nor the quickest thinking.

She pursed her lips as she rubbed her eyes and said, "Bullshit." Then she reached, switched on the floor lamp, and held up the piece of notebook paper on which I'd made notes while talking to Dalton Dorsey.

Dexter Money's name was on the paper, as well as the name of his shrimp boat, the *Nan-Shan*. Stupidly, I'd left it atop the chest of drawers in the bedroom.

She said, "When you called the second time, almost two-thirty, I started to feel bad about not picking up. I know I've got a temper, and I work hard at controlling it. So I decided to call you back. No answer. I called a couple of more times, still no answer. By three, I was worried sick. So I got in my Jeep and came looking."

I crossed the room, saying, "Like I told you, I was out fishing. There was a great tide tonight at Longboat Pass." I opened the refrigerator and took out a bottle of Coors. I was exhausted but still wired.

"Sorry, Doc, I don't buy it. I deal with

professional liars every day, and you're no professional. You weren't here and your boat was gone. Your shaving kit was still in the bathroom — I could see it through the window, so Mrs. Post gave me a key. I found this note in the bedroom. I admit it, I'm a snoop. So who's Dexter Ray Money?"

"Nobody. A guy I wanted to see about a boat. What I'm wondering is, why are you so suspicious?"

"How do you know him?"

"Friend of a friend. Boaters are a pretty tight bunch."

"Really?"

"Yeah, really."

Amelia tossed back the thin bedspread and stood. She'd changed out of the black dinner dress into neatly pressed jeans and a white blouse. No makeup now, but her red hair still held the light. "I'm suspicious," she said, "because I'm a public defender in this county and I *know* who Dexter Money is. I know what a piece of trash the guy is. I've had to defend some of his sicko buddies. And I've heard the rumors about how he makes a living with his shrimp boats."

She took a step closer, staring into my eyes. "There's something you're not telling me, Ford. You had an appointment with him tonight, didn't you? Or someone. That's why you made me leave. You're not up here for a meeting with Bell Fish. That's bullshit, too."

"Would you feel better if I said yes?"

That made her smile; she couldn't help it. "Goddamn right I would! I've got feelings. But only if it's true. No woman likes throwing herself at a man, then being told thanks but no thanks. And only if you're not involved with some kind of illegal crap with that redneck slime. Which I wouldn't believe even if you told me yourself."

She was standing so close to me now that I could feel the warmth of her breath when she spoke. Her eyes *were* the luminous green of fresh mint. When I didn't answer right away, she put her hands on my arms and said, "You've heard something about them, haven't you? Our missing friends. It has something to do with Janet, Michael, and Grace. I can sense it. Why else would you be sneaking around at night, talking to criminals who own shrimp boats? Were you trying to buy information from Dex Money?"

I placed my beer on the table, still looking in her eyes. Touched my index finger to her chin, tilting it upward, then kissed her lips softly, then again, feeling her tongue move and moisten. When I felt her hands slide to my sides, when I felt her body begin to react, I pulled away long enough to say, "All I can tell you is, I think you were right. I think there's a chance a boat picked them up and took them to South America, maybe Colombia. I'm leaving Sunday if I can get a flight. Monday, maybe Tuesday at the latest."

Momentarily, her eyes had gone sleepy-woozy, but now they came back into sharp focus. "I'm going with you."

"Absolutely not."

She stepped back, holding me away with her hands. She was suddenly very serious again. "Doc, you don't understand. I *have* to go. If there's any chance they're still alive, I have to go and try to help them. Please don't argue with me about this. You don't know how important it is to me."

I was looking into her face, feeling, once again, that there was something she wanted to tell me but couldn't. I said, "This is the sort of thing that one person can do better than two. Colombia's a dangerous place. If you go, it'll only double our risk."

"I don't care! I'm going. I've got my reasons."

Sometimes you sense the need to push, and so I did. "Reasons? Why, because you feel guilty?"

Her face flushed. "Yes! I feel guilty. I've already told you that."

Now I was holding her arms, making her look into my eyes. "Yeah, you told me, Amelia, but you didn't tell me the rest of it. You haven't told anyone, have you? What *really* happened out there that night? You've got the courage to go to Colombia, but you don't have the courage to tell me the truth, do you?"

"That's not fair, Doc!"

"Fair? Unless you're playing some kind of game, why should there be rules? Just tell me what happened."

"Okay. Okay, I *will*. The truth is . . . the truth is . . ." She yanked her arms free of my grasp, turned her back to me, shuddered, and then began to sob as she talked. "The truth is I'm a worthless, cowardly piece of crap because I went off and I left them! Okay? I went off and left all three of them alone to die. I panicked. I've never been so scared in my life! *That's* what happened. Are you satisfied?" She'd been shouting, still crying, sobbing, and now she turned to face me, her eyes closed, and leaned against my chest.

I wrapped my arms around her, holding her close, patting the small of her back. I waited for what seemed a full minute before I said softly, "You didn't do anything wrong, Amelia. It's okay."

She was shaking her head. "No. No, it's not okay. That night, when we were trying to swim together, they were going so slow. I knew we weren't going to make it to the tower. Then I got hit by a really big wave and sucked down a lot of water. Then I got hit by another, and I just snapped. I lost it. I ripped my BCD off and started swimming. I could hear them shouting for me to come back, but I didn't. The last thing I heard Janet say was, 'Please don't leave us alone.'

"But that's exactly what I did. I left them alone. And they died. At least, I thought they died, and it's been killing me slowly ever since."

I stood there, letting her cry. Then I stooped and scooped her up into my arms and carried her into the bedroom. I laid her down on the bed, pulled her close. I waited until her sobbing had quieted before whispering into her ear, "You did the right thing. The smartest thing you could have done that night was to send the strongest swimmer off alone. It was the only way to be sure there'd be at least one person to tell searchers what happened and to keep looking. Without knowing it, you did the very best thing possible for the other three."

That surprised her. I could tell. "I . . . I never thought of it that way. Do . . . do you really mean it, Doc?"

Maybe I did. It really *might* have been the smartest thing to do. In light of what happened, it probably was. But I said, "Of course I mean it. If you feel guilty, you're wasting your time. You gave them their very best chance of being found. It didn't happen, but that's not your fault."

I felt her hand on the back of my neck, and she hugged me close. "You're still a terrible liar, and I love you for it. At least now you understand why I have to go with you."

I said, "Do I?"

For the next ten minutes, we argued back and forth. I despised the idea of her going. But she kept pressing, saying she had no choice, her conscience demanded that she make the trip. Her argument had the articulate professionalism associated with her craft, plus passion — so much passion that, ultimately, I withdrew and listened to her without responding until she paused, and said, "Doc? Hey . . . what's wrong? You look almost . . . almost on the verge of tears or something. I've never seen you so emotional."

"I'm not emotional," I snapped. "I'm concerned. I've had very bad luck taking friends to dangerous places. Please don't ask me to go into detail, but it's something I just won't do. I *can't* take you. I absolutely refuse to risk it again."

Lying there, she pushed herself away from me, framed my face with her palms, forcing me to look into her eyes. "I'm not asking you to take me to Colombia. I'm asking you to let me live my life as an adult." She tapped a finger to the side of her head. "Since the night I left them, I've been trapped in here, trapped by my own guilt. I'm sick of it. It's destroying me, so I have to go. I have no choice . . . and neither do you."

I was shaking my head — it was impossible to argue with her. "Okay, okay, *okay*. I don't like it, but okay."

Now she hugged me close. "It's settled then."

"Not until you agree to one thing. When we're there, you have to promise to do what I tell you to do. No matter what. I've spent a lot of time in places . . . in places like Colombia. Americans, people in this country, most of them don't realize how dangerous it can be once they cross the boundaries. I *do* know. So you need to trust my judgment without question."

Amelia whispered, "Deal," then touched her lips to mine. We lay there holding each other, kissing, and touching for what seemed a long time before my hands were on her blouse, fumbling with buttons, and her fingers were searching for me.

So now we were six miles high, sitting deep in leather seats, flying first class, the Caribbean Sea a canyon of blue beneath us.

Our relationship had changed irreversibly that early Saturday morning. We confirmed the change several more times throughout the day.

She was a healthy woman in her early thirties, and all that that implied. Sometimes the bodies of unfamiliar lovers simply do not fit. No explaining it, but it's true.

Our bodies *did* fit. They fit comfortably, passionately, and athletically. Amelia had that rare ability to abandon all inhibitions in sex while retaining her sensitivity to her partner's needs, as well as her sense of humor. Being in bed with her was fun and funny yet satisfying on a level of intimacy that I'd seldom experienced. Maybe *never* experienced before in my life.

Once, she whispered into my ear, "I feel like I've been waiting for you for a long, long time."

I was surprised to hear myself whisper in reply, "That's nice. I mean it. Very nice."

Why would I encourage such feelings? Ask Tomlinson, ask anyone at the marina, I'm the cold one, the one who believes that emotion is a waste of energy. But it really *was* the way I felt.

Overtly, she gave no sign that we were anything more than friends. I liked that. No public touching or hanging-on; no holding hands or nuzzling. I liked that, too. Outwardly, we were two individuals. Inwardly, though, we were already joined in some indefinable way, and I found that surprising as well.

I liked her. I trusted her. More important, I already felt totally comfortable with her. I hadn't told her about the satellite photos — that, I could never do. But I had shared with her my theories about what might have happened to Janet, Grace, and Michael if they'd been picked up. That included letting her read the State Department document that Dalton Dorsey had faxed to me.

Some of the data therein were as discomforting; some, I found fascinating. Why hadn't I heard the data before? The data read in part:

ECONOMICS OF THE INTERNATIONAL FLESH TRADE

According to [AGENCY DELETED] the global trade in the smuggling of humans is a $12 billion a year business, and the third largest source of profit for organized crime, including international terrorists.

The flesh trade is surpassed only by drugs and the illegal arms trade in estimated annual earnings. It has become a favorite investment of criminals and international terrorists because the profits are high, the risk of being caught low, and the punishments much less severe than some crimes that are not nearly as profitable.

The discovery of fifty-eight Fijians in the back of a refrigeration truck in Dover, England, all dead of suffocation, focused international attention on this brutal business. And, in late 1999, U.S.

Immigration officers arrested Algerian terrorist Ahmed Ressam when he tried to enter the United States with a trunk full of explosives. He had been smuggled into Canada where he applied for refugee status, and his financial backing has been linked to cocaine and a white slavery operation in South America and Brunei.

It is estimated that, each year, hundreds of thousands of illegals — many from China, North Africa, and the Middle East — pay up to $50,000 US per person to "Snakeheads." A Snakehead is often a Chinese-American or an Arab-American stationed in New York City or Bangkok. A Snakehead provides illegals with false identities and passports and transports them inside the twelve-mile limit that marks the end of international waters and the beginning of the United States's territorial sovereignty.

Like me, Amelia found the statistics very surprising. "I didn't know it was such a big business," she said.

The paper also touched on another form of the flesh trade that was even more astonishing. We both read:

Another very different, but related, type of business that deals in the buying and selling of humans is what is known, generically, as the white slave trade.

The term *white slave trade* has been passed down from a previous century, and it accurately describes what was then a booming illegal business: the kidnapping and transport of Caucasian women to foreign soil, where they were then sold to wealthy buyers. Over the last two decades, this business has grown faster than both trade in drugs and weapons, though Caucasian women are no longer the only acceptable form of human currency. Any woman who is young and attractive is a very valuable commodity.

The United Nations estimates that 4 million women throughout the world are trafficked each year — forced through lies and coercion to work against their will in many types of servitude, particularly as sexual slaves.

The International Organization for Migration has said that as many as 500,000 women from the former Soviet Union are annually trafficked into Western Europe alone, and then onto other foreign lands — most often North

Africa, Brunei, and the Middle East. Because some of the women have already immigrated illegally, and because some percentage of the women choose to work as prostitutes, statistics are difficult to assess.

Amelia whistled softly when she read that. "My God! Four million? I had no idea it was even going on, but four million women a year! Amazing."

In a way, though, we both agreed: The sobering statistics also provided us with some hope. If Janet and Grace had been kidnapped for profit, it explained why we had not heard from them. They were a valuable commodity. It meant that they could still be out there somewhere, alive.

Just as I could not tell Amelia about the satellite photos, there was a second letter I had in my possession that I could not allow her to read. Some of the information in it was from a consular research paper, but it also contained classified data that I could not share.

It was from a U.S. State Department intelligence guru named Hal Harrington. I'd met Harrington the year before when I'd helped get his daughter out of some trouble. Turned out that Hal and I had more in common than I was comfortable admitting. That meeting had resurrected aspects of my past that I'd thought were long behind me. Trouble is, the memories, the aftershocks, of a violent, clandestine life are impossible to forget, so they never really go away.

Harrington belonged to a highly trained covert operations team that was known, to a very few, as the Negotiating and System Analysis Group — the Negotiators, for short. Because the success of the team relied on members blending easily into nearly any society, each man was provided with a legitimate and mobile profession.

Harrington was trained as a computer software programmer and made a personal fortune by sheer intelligence and foresight. Other members of that elite team included CPAs, a couple of attorneys, one journalist, and at least three physicians. There was also a marine biologist among them, a man who traveled the world doing research.

Harrington is now one of the most powerful and influential staff members at the State Department, and he specializes in Latin-American affairs. Because I had his private numbers, and because we share a mutual interest in the well-being of his daughter, Lindsey, it was not difficult for me to get in touch with the man.

The night before Amelia and I left for Miami, Harrington's letter arrived via special courier. The first two pages were background, and it was good for me to refamiliarize myself with the complicated politics of the country we were about to visit. It was also good to be reminded that it is one of the most dangerous places on earth.

Colombia illustrates the stark contrast between the rich and poor, and the widespread neglect of human rights. This problem is compounded by extraordinary violence. Colombia has the highest murder rate in the world. Armed conflict has led to the mass displacement of innocent citizens by political violence — many thousands of Amazon Indians and farmers have been forced off their land as a result of conflict between the national, guerrilla, and paramilitary groups.

The main source of the conflict, of course, is strife created by the drug trade. In recent years, however, Colombia has also become a center of two other very profitable international businesses: the sale of illegal weaponry and the transporting of illegal immigrants and kidnap victims for sale.

I hadn't heard that before. Harrington had included the information for a reason. The paper went on to say:

Throughout the 1970s and 1980s, Colombia's illegal drug trade grew steadily, as the drug cartels amassed huge amounts of money, weapons, and influence. The 1970s also saw the formation of such leftist guerrilla groups as the May Nineteenth Movement (M-19) and the Revolutionary Armed Forces of Colombia (FARC). The violence continued, and many journalists and government officials were killed.

After going into specific detail about FARC, and the politicians believed to be associated with the movement, Harrington's paper continued:

The notorious Medellín drug cartel was broken in 1993, and the Cali cartel was later undermined by arrests of key leaders. Drug traffickers continue to have significant wealth and power, however, and many leftist guerrilla groups remain active, perpetuating a condition of instability.

In November 1998, the country's president ceded a state-sized region of land in South Central Colombia to FARC's control as a goodwill gesture, but the rebels negotiated with the government only fitfully and continued to mount attacks.

That region is now one of the most lawless and dangerous on earth. It has become the safe harbor for Islamic extremists and other terrorists. It has also become the center of a power struggle between the different factions of guerrilla groups, the paramilitary forces (vigilante groups formed usually by wealthy landowners protecting their own interests), and the state itself. Also sometimes involved in the fighting there are U.S. drug interdiction forces, the CIA and the DEA.

The conflict has become the dirtiest of wars, in which each side resorts to whatever tactics are necessary to gain an advantage. Summary executions, disappearances, extortion, intimidation, and torture are all part of daily reality.

Flying southward over the Caribbean in first class was not a good time to let Amelia read such a letter. But, once in Cartagena, if she insisted on accompanying me into the mountains, I would put the letter into her hands and insist that she read it.

The rain-forest mountains of Colombia. There was a pretty good chance that's exactly where I might be headed.

Harrington's personal, and classified, letter made that clear.

Harrington's letter read:

Hello, Commander Ford. This will be brief because I don't have a lot of time, and I suspect you are similarly engaged. I checked with our intelligence assets in Colombia and the U.S. Here is the result of that inquiry.

Earl Stallings. In the U.S., there are thirty-seven men of color over the age of twenty-one named Earl Stallings. In the last five years, three have included Florida as a part of their address. One of those three, Earl E. E. Stallings, has been arrested several times on charges that range from selling Internet pornography to assault with a deadly weapon to drug trafficking. On a charge of felonious drug trafficking, he spent twenty-seven months in prison, Raiford, Florida.

Hassan Atwa Kazan. Worldwide, there are 103 men over the age of twenty-one named Hassan Kazan. In the last five years, four have included countries in the Western hemisphere as a part of their address or in electronic communication outside the Middle East. One has included Colombia. Here is more information on that man:

Kazan is in our South American files as a suspected low-echelon smuggler of cocaine, weapons, people. He's known to associate with FARC sympathizers and known criminals. The bar at the Hotel de Ascension, Cartagena, is a favorite meeting place. I have yet to confirm if he is or is not an albino, as you described.

To be thorough, I also cross-referenced Kazan's name and additional specifics with our Middle Eastern files. I now provide you with this new information. A man named Hassan Atwa Kazan is suspected of participating as a freelance middleman involved in the financing of the terrorist cells of Jihad and Al-Qaeda, as well as the Kurdistan Workers Party, or PKK. The PKK, as you know, is one of the earth's most indiscriminately violent terrorist organizations. It is possible that Kazan can be linked to one or all of these organizations through a well-organized network of smuggling operations, most probably for his own personal profit.

I can't be certain it is the same man. However, there is sufficient evidence for me to take the following action: In light of your experience in these matters, and since you have a special interest in this suspect, I am authorizing you to investigate this individual as a sanctioned agent of our nation. I have upgraded your service status from Inactive Reserve to Active Special Duty Line Officer. I have also changed your pay grade from O-4 to O-5, which advances your agency rank from lieutenant commander to commander. Congratulations, and welcome back into the service of your country.

Furthermore, since the Executive Order of 18 February 1976 has now been revoked, and by the power vested in this body through the National Security Act of 1947 and the War Powers

Act, I also authorize you to use whatever means necessary to assemble evidence against the aforementioned individual (and associates) and I fully and legally license you to exercise Executive Action within the limitations and restraints with which you are already familiar.

Those were startling words to read: *Executive Action.* For me, they are a legal euphemism for a license to assassinate. I'd read those words before, in similar documents. For some reason, though, the phrase had never hit me so hard. Was it because I was now a different man? Or was it because I *hoped* I was now different?

The last paragraph was written in ink, the penmanship rushed, the wording far less formal. Harrington had added:

Doc, My Colombian pals tell me that there are two main camps where they warehouse kidnap victims. They keep them until they're ransomed or sold, then fly them out. One camp is near Cali on the Pacific Coast, outside a little village called Guapi, pronounced *WAUP-ee.* The other is in the state of Amazonia, way south in the jungle, a

410

camp called Remanso, pronounced *Ra-MEN-so,* which I've been told is an Indian word that means "still waters." Lots of Indios still in that area.

Good luck. I've notified a few of our friends that you'll be in the area, so you'll have some help. Also, keep in mind that your enemy, the late Edgar Cordero, still has his organization in place, and they get pretty good intel. So do the Islamic extremists, and they're all tied in together. Stay on your toes, watch your 6.

There was a final p.s.: "Lindsey is back on the drugs again. Dating a worthless beach bum. I love her so much, what can I do? H2"

Chapter Twenty

We passed through the customs gates of Cartagena's modern airport and exited out into the equatorial heat and glare of a December afternoon. There was a line of rusted yellow Toyota cabs, men selling lottery tickets, women in bright dresses hawking fresh pineapple, mangoes, bananas.

Amelia stopped, bags in hand, and said, "You're kidding. You have a limo waiting on us? I'm impressed."

Yes, there was a limo. She was impressed, and I was surprised. Among the taxis was a black BMW sedan and a man in a black suit standing beside it, holding a sign that read Dr. Marion Ford.

I was surprised because I hadn't ordered a car.

I told her, "Wait here for a second," then walked to the driver, and said to him in Spanish, "I'm confused. Who sent you?"

He was a stocky man, too wide for his jacket, with a weightlifter's constrained mobility. "The embassy sent me," he answered.

I said, "Which embassy?"

"Why, the U.S. Embassy, of course. *Your* embassy. I have papers if you wish to see."

He handed me a sealed envelope. Inside was a note with Harrington's familiar signature. It read, "Doc, welcome back into the business. One of my staff has arranged for you to use my personal driver, Carlos Quasada. You can trust him with anything, including your travel companion. He'll keep an eye on you while you're in the city. Carlos was one of the country's best heavyweight fighters for many years. Match the enclosed photo ID with the ID he is required to carry before you get into the car."

After I'd checked his papers, the man grinned at me and said in less formal Spanish, "Mr. Harrington has asked that I give you special care, Dr. Ford. I am here to serve as your driver, your bodyguard, your guide. The only exception is that I cannot go with you if you decide to leave our little state of Magdalena. The FARC rebels and their associates know me too well. I would be shot on sight, as would anyone unlucky enough to be with me."

The man had a grip like a hydraulic clamp, and I liked his easygoing, confident manner. "You must have given them good reason to hate you, Carlos."

His grin became even wider. "Oh, I have given them many reasons over the years, Dr. Ford. Sometimes, one of them decides to come looking for me to take revenge, and I give them yet another reason to hate Carlos!" Realizing that Amelia was walking toward us, he lowered his voice and said, "Does she understand Spanish?"

"No. A few words, that's all."

"Does she know that you are here in your government's service?"

"Of course not."

Quasada told me, "In that case, I must speak quickly. Mr. Harrington has supplied you with a special briefcase. It is in the trunk. You must not allow her to see the contents."

I said, "When we get to the hotel, walk her to the front desk and leave the car keys with me. I'll find a way to sneak it into our room. Later, I can tell her I bought it here."

He nodded, fixed the smile on his face again, and began to speak more loudly in a slow and careful English, "I am at your service, Dr. Ford. Anything you require, day or night. I will give you the number of my cell phone. Dial my number and I will appear!"

Sitting in the backseat of the BMW as Carlos sped us through the taxi and donkey-cart traffic of Cartagena, Amelia leaned her shoulder briefly against me and said in a low voice, "Why the special treatment? This guy's acting like you're a foreign dignitary and he's known you for years."

I cleared my throat before I answered, "I've been here a couple of times for conferences, research — things like that."

She seemed unconvinced. "As a biologist?"

"Yeah. In Latin America marine biologists are highly respected. Seafood. It's a very important industry here."

When I opened the briefcase that Harrington had left for me, I stood back and whistled softly, surprised and not a little apprehensive. Mostly surprised.

Did he really think I'd have a use for this *kind* of firepower?

I left the briefcase open and walked to the window of our third-floor suite. We were staying at the Hotel Santa Clara inside Cartagena's old walled city. Most of Colombia's dangers were known to me long before receiving Hal Harrington's briefing paper. I have tried to lock away a number of bad memories associated with the place. Even so, it is still one of the more interesting countries in the Americas, and Cartagena is my favorite city by far.

Cartagena is a Conquistador village built within a stone fortress six miles in diameter, and that fortress, in turn, is built within a perimeter of forts. The city was founded in the early 1500s. Gold and silver plundered from the Indians were stockpiled here prior to being loaded and shipped back to Madrid.

A city filled with gold attracted the attention of the world's pirates. French pirates kidnapped the governor and held him for ransom. English pirates such as Hawkens and Drake infiltrated the city under cover of darkness, burned the houses, sacked cathedrals, and sailed away with shiploads of treasure. Spain continued to build the walls around the city higher and thicker, but the pirates still came — just as pirates still continue to come to Colombia today.

In those years, some say that what is now the Hotel Santa Clara was a convent — a treasure trove of a different sort. So it too has walls as thick as those of a fort, four stories high, raspberry-colored, and impenetrable from the outside. But step through the hotel's double doors, and you enter a Castilian world that vanished three hundred years ago.

The ceilings are twenty feet high with rafters of black mahogany. There are gardens with palms, rare flowers, toucans, parrots, and fountains. The courtyards are tiled with bricks made by Indian slaves long dead. Today, the hybrid progeny of those dead, a hundred generations removed, wait and serve the descendants of the Castilians who enslaved their relatives. The hotel is built around a great plaza, and now there is a modern swimming pool in the middle of that plaza.

Amelia lay on a lounge chair by the pool, dozing in the afternoon sun. The garland sparkle of Christmas decorations seemed incongruous in the palms. She wore a green two-piece swimsuit, very modest. When I saw her naked for the first time, I'd realized that she was the type of redhead who tans.

She was out there tanning herself now. Which is why I could take my time with the briefcase, and its contents.

★ ★ ★

I turned back to the bed where the brief-case lay open and removed from it a small submachine gun. The weapon had a very fine balance and weight.

I have little personal interest in firearms, though I admire any kind of fine machinery. I've never been an outstanding marksman, and I seldom do much shooting anymore. However, because there was a time in my life when firearms were necessary tools of my trade, I possess a certain level of expertise.

The submachine gun I held was very familiar to me. It was, in the opinion of many, the most efficient and lethal hand weapon ever created. It was a Heckler & Koch MP5K submachine gun, a light-weight, air-cooled, magazine-fed weapon that, on full automatic, fires thirteen rounds per second with extraordinary accuracy. Ever needing to fire thirteen rounds per second accurately is an unimaginable situation.

Yet the weapon was tiny: only thirteen inches long, weighing slightly more than four pounds. You could hide it in the pocket of a trenchcoat, then clear an auditorium with it.

The H&K MP5 systems are modular,

which means you can mix and match accessories for almost any need. Harrington had included a couple of interesting options. From the briefcase, I now removed a length of beautifully machined aluminum stock — an integrally threaded sound suppressor. Fire the weapon next to someone's ear, he would hear a blowgun sound: *Phutt!* People fifteen meters away would hear nothing. There were also dual magazines that looked like twin twenty-eight-round magazines clamped together. But these would hold over two hundred cartridges. Squeeze the trigger on full auto and you could cut down a good-sized tree before having to reload.

Did the man think I was going into a war zone?

Perhaps that's exactly what he was arming me for.

Finally, the briefcase itself was an option: Made out of some space-age polymer, you could clamp the little sub gun into position, close the cover, walk it down the street, squeeze the trigger built into the handle, and fire through a hole in the side of the case.

I got no delight in seeing the weapon, felt no illusion of authority because I now had that firepower in my possession. From the look and weight of the thing, I got only a sense of loathing, and of dread.

There is an implicit dirtiness to machinery designed to maim and kill. Participate even once, and that dirt can never be washed away.

Harrington had included a couple of more conventional weapons as well, pistols. There was a Colt .380 semiauto Mustang, which was featherlight and smaller than the palm of my hand. It was a very easy weapon to hide in a boot or under a ball cap. There was also a much larger and more lethal SIG Sauer P226 9mm — exactly like the one I kept stored away in my old fish house back on Sanibel and had used over so many years.

It was no coincidence. Years ago, Harrington and I had been trained by the same people, on the same weaponry, and in the same way. Maybe he considered it a nostalgic touch.

I checked the magazine of each weapon. All were fully loaded. Inside the briefcase, I also found a "drop" weapon. A drop weapon is usually something silent and sharp that can be used in crowds. Walk up to your target, make the hit, and walk away, leaving the weapon behind.

There was a small plastic cylinder in

which there were a dozen or more Fukumi bari needles. Ninja warriors would hide the needles on their tongues and blow them into the eyes of their enemy. I am no Ninja, so judging from the tiny skull and cross-bones on the cylinder, these needles were dipped in something poisonous.

I broke the cylinder's seal and sniffed. The needles had a fruity, vinegar odor. Probably sodium morphate. Attach the cylinder to the tip of an umbrella, touch the needles to the leg of your target as you pass, and within thirty minutes or so, he will begin to feel a terrifying anxiety, then cramps, and soon will collapse with all the symptoms of both a heart attack and a brain aneurysm. A very nasty weapon and also illegal, according to the Geneva Protocol of 1927.

"This is a dirty war!" Bernie Yeager had told me.

I had no doubt of that now.

Finally, there was a military SATCOM telephone. SATCOM is a satellite-based, global wireless personal communications network designed to permit easy phone access from nearly anywhere on earth. Sixty-six satellites, evenly spaced four hundred miles high, made it possible. The phone was compatible with cellular systems worldwide, if the phone being called was equipped with a cellular cassette.

Hal Harrington's phone undoubtedly was.

I had to pace around the room a couple of times before I could bring myself to read the accompanying note from Harrington:

Commander F., Our intelligence now confirms that Hassan Atwa Kazan has financial links with terrorist Imad Mughniyeh, whom the Israelis consider a clinical psychopath. It was Mughniyeh who kidnapped Beirut's CIA chief William Buckley, videotaped his torture, then killed Buckley with his own hands. The tape was later sent anonymously to CIA headquarters.

Kazan works through terrorist cells in the Colombian city of Maicao, which is near Barranquilla on the Caribbean. Maicao is a Muslim extremist stronghold. Our government has yet to deal with anti-American organizations here, but it is time we started. Kazan is a low-echelon soldier, a freelance money raiser probably in business strictly for personal profit, but he may lead you to more prominent members.

When and if you conclude your private business with him, we urge you to take executive action against Kazan. If you have assembled sufficient evidence, you may also take executive action against any of his associates you deem an enemy of our government.

You have already been briefed on the restraints and limitations, and you are not authorized to exceed those limitations under penalty of military prosecution. We have no interest in Earl E. E. Stallings, and leave his dispensation to you.

As a personal favor, and with the help of our friend BY, we are hereby supplying additional classified information concerning your own private business in Colombia.

According to satellite imagery, as of yesterday's date, 15 December, 9:45 p.m. EST, nine women and two men were photographed in what appeared to be a wire-fenced area within a walled courtyard in the Colombian state of Amazonia, outside the village of Remanso. The fenced area was west of a large house, the entire compound four miles south of the village. Five of the women and both men appeared to be Caucasian. Good hunting, HH

I read the note a second time before tearing it into pieces and flushing it down the toilet. Then I went and sat heavily on the bed. I remembered obsessive Bernie Yeager saying to me, "Ours is a dangerous world. It would be good to have you back working with us again. We need you!" Remembered Hal Harrington once telling me, "I wish we could find a way to get you to come back."

I felt like vomiting, like running out of the room, jumping into a cab, and heading for the airport. I'd already done my duty; I'd served my time. My life was my own now. I was content to live quietly and alone on Sanibel Island, content to spend quiet, peaceful nights in my lab, doing my work. I didn't *want* to come back and participate in a dirty war.

But they'd found a way. I'd opened the door for them with my requests for help, baited my own trap. When I'd asked Bernie for information, was he already aware that these terrorist groups were involved in smuggling drugs, people, and weapons to finance their cause?

Of course. He had to know that the odds were good that the men running the *Nan-Shan* had at least indirect ties with enemies of our government.

Had Harrington known?

Certainly. He was an expert on South America. He knew who was doing what and where they were doing it. And the two of them had been in contact, obviously sharing information. They'd been smart enough to wait until I was already in Colombia to finally formalize the assignment. The obligation was implied but understood: They'd helped me. Now I was expected to help them.

"Dear God . . ." I said softly.

My voice sounded unusually hoarse in the silence of the air-conditioned suite. I stood, looked out the window, and saw that Amelia was no longer by the pool.

I rushed to the briefcase and began to pack the weaponry. I'd just gotten the thing locked and under the bed when I heard the door open and she came into the bedroom. Her skin was the color of fresh cinnamon, and there was a bawdy smile on her face that quickly faded. "Hey . . . Doc? What's wrong, you're so pale. You look like you've seen a ghost!"

I said, "I think I'm just thirsty. Let's go down to the bar and get a drink."

Chapter Twenty-one

That night, we showered together and dressed in our best clothes for dinner. Amelia wore a sleek beige dress that showed her body, made her look even taller, and left no doubt that she was braless, too. "When I'm outside the country," she laughed, "I always take the opportunity to show what little I have."

I wore khaki slacks, a Navy polo shirt, a light, silk sports coat I'd had tailored in Asia, and my old, soft jungle boots — which earned me a minor rebuke. "Just when I think you're halfway civilized, you prove me wrong."

I told her Colombia wasn't a particularly civilized country, and she smiled as if I were joking.

We walked the cobblestone streets west toward the Hotel de Acension, Hassan's hangout and sometime home. I didn't tell

Amelia why we were going there, just that I'd eaten in the restaurant and the food was very good. Nor did I tell her why I asked to have my new briefcase kept in the hotel safe.

It was a typical December night in Cartagena. A jungle breeze came off the water carrying aromatic little pockets of open sea, of jasmine and frangipani blossom, and of the city, too. It smelled of water on rock and diesel exhaust, of wood smoke and the shadowed musk of narrow alleys, and of cobblestone markets that hadn't missed a night in three hundred years.

Once Amelia hugged herself close to me, and said, "I love it here. We'll have to come back just to have fun. I feel so . . . relaxed."

Already, it seemed very comfortable to speak of us as "we," two people but one united couple.

I, however, did not feel relaxed. We were on our way — hopefully — to meet a man that I was now duty-bound to murder.

Earl Stallings was in the bar. I saw him when we walked through the great stone archway that was the entrance into the Hotel de Acension. The bar was to the left, ele-

427

vated above the marble lobby. Wrought-iron tables were crowded, people drinking and laughing, ceiling fans above stirring slow mare's-tails of smoke, while a very black man at a very black grand piano played and sang "Jamaica Farewell" in Spanish.

"My heart is down, my head is spinning around, I had to leave my little girl in Kingston town . . ."

Stallings stood beside the piano, dressed in white linen slacks and a white guyaberra shirt, smoking a cigar. Clinging to his waist was a woman wearing a purple blouse and a white Panama hat.

Shanay Money had been correct. Stallings made her giant of a father appear small. He dwarfed the piano and dominated the room. His head was huge, pumpkin-sized, and even from that distance I could see the yellow smoothness of a burn scar on the right side of his face. He appeared to be Polynesian, possibly Fijian or Samoan, and he had to weigh well over four hundred pounds.

"Doc, what's wrong? What are you staring at?"

I realized that Amelia was pulling me by the hand toward the restaurant, while I stood there taking him in, memorizing his features.

I said, "It's somebody I think I know. Let's get a table, and I'll come back and say hello to the guy."

The restaurant was in a smaller courtyard separated from a larger courtyard by palms and hibiscus in red and yellow bloom. From our table, I could see the moon through the feathered leaves, above the stone gables of the hotel.

Amelia took my left hand in both her hands and said, "Hey pal, we haven't known each other that long. I want to learn everything there is to know about you, all your moods, what makes you mad, everything, but I haven't had time. I want to. I *will*. The point is, I get the feeling that something happened this afternoon, that there's something wrong. Did I say something that offended you? Sometimes I talk before I think. You seem so distracted."

I kissed her hands, smiling. "No, I think you're wonderful. I mean that, Amelia. I'm a little preoccupied, thinking about how to get information on Janet and the others."

"You said you might know some people who can help."

"Maybe. That guy in the bar. I need to talk to him after we order. Alone."

Earl Stallings blew smoke toward the

ceiling fan before he looked down at me, and lied, "Kazan? Kazan . . . hmm. No, I've never heard of a man named Hassan Kazan. And if I had, why should I tell you?"

I'd introduced myself to him at the piano and endured his domineering handshake. Then I endured him saying, "I saw that redhead you're with. Kind of attractive. I've never slept with a redhead. They any good?"

Now we were standing in a quiet corner of the bar, him with a tall brown drink in hand, me with a bottle of *Aquila* beer in a brown bottle.

I said, "I'm surprised you don't know Hassan Kazan. He stays at this hotel regularly. That's what my friends tell me, anyway."

Stallings seemed to swell slightly. "You interrupt my evening, I don't even know who the hell you are, and already you're calling me a liar?"

His voice had a mellow, raspy quality that I associate with Hawaiians, but his English was occasionally clipped, guttural in a way that suggested Austronesian languages. I forced myself to smile congenially while my brain struggled to remember a few of the Samoan phrases I knew. *Laega, laega* — didn't that mean "sorry"?

I couldn't remember for certain, and then I decided, screw it, I wasn't going to bother trying to charm him. I said, "Yeah, that's exactly what I'm calling you. A liar. I've got a business proposition for Kazan. Maybe for you, too. But I'm not going to stand here and let you waste my time."

For a moment, I thought he was going to swing at me, smash the glass into my face, or maybe pull a knife. I watched his face blanch, then freeze masklike as he reconsidered. Stallings was used to bullying people, and bullies rarely have to use any force stronger than words. It was a struggle, but he got his temper under control. "If I'm included in your business, that might be different. Money. If there's money involved, I'm interested. You have American cash with you? Here in Cartagena? How much are we talking?"

I had brought a sizeable bundle of cash — about $5,000 — but I doubted if that were enough to tempt someone like Stallings. So I said, "All I could bring in legally, plus I have access to a little more, depending on how our negotiations go."

"You're going to need a lot more than that, but, okay, it's a place to begin. Why didn't you say so in the first place?"

A reasonable man — if cash were involved.

I said, "I wasn't thinking, Earl. Sorry. So let me start all over again. I want to discuss something that could make you both a profit. Sizeable money and very simple. So the question's the same: Where's Kazan?"

"No, no, no, Ford. The question is: What kind of business are we discussing?"

I said, "I think three friends of mine are being held captive somewhere in Colombia. I'm here to buy their freedom."

"How would I know anything about that? Now you're saying I'm a criminal, too."

"I know because they were adrift in the water the morning you ran the shrimp boat *Nan-Shan* into the Ten Thousand Islands. I know you saw them and stopped."

He did a good job of trying to hide his surprise. When he started to reply with a predictable lie, I held up a warning finger. "No more of your bullshit. I'm going to have dinner now. Think it over. Find your pal Hassan Kazan and meet me at that little restaurant, La Habinita. No . . . make it Plaza de Santa Domingo." I looked at my watch. "Let's say eleven."

Stallings wasn't used to being on the de-

432

fensive, but he was already regrouping. "I'll meet you — but not so early. Let's say midnight." He nodded toward the woman with the purple blouse and Panama hat as he grinned, his incisor teeth gigantic, the color of yellow ivory. "I hired her for the evening. I want to make sure I get my money's worth."

As I left the bar and was walking through the hotel's marble lobby, a tiny Arabic-looking man in a dingy white suit, his black hair pasted smooth, stopped me. He had a normal head, but his hands and his legs were dwarf-like. He was obviously very nervous, sweat beaded on his face, and his head swiveled constantly in a way that reminded me of a pigeon that has just heard a hawk. He was smoking a cigarette in a short black holder, and he took the cigarette from his mouth when he had my attention, and said with a Pakistani accent, "Señor, if I may be so bold as to offer you a warning. The man you were speaking with in the bar, do you know who he is? What he does?"

He was a humorous caricature of the sort of person one often meets in smuggler ports in the earth's darker places. They make a living off the scraps of larger predators, but I did not smile. "Why do you ask?"

"Because he is a very dangerous man. Extremely dangerous. And he has many dangerous friends. If you are here to purchase something — anything — I am a much better choice. Emeralds? Gold? Women? Whatever you want, even items I have not named. I'll leave those words for you to use." He touched a finger to one side of his nose and sniffed to illustrate. "I'll guarantee you fair market value, and I am not nearly so dangerous."

I told him I'd think it over, maybe another time. As I was walking away, he called after me, "In the jungles here, there are still savages! On the street, as well. Trust no one!"

Back at our hotel, Amelia stripped the beige dress up over her head, draped it on a chair, and walked on long legs, pelvis rotating, through the wedge of light that came through the doorway. Then she stood beside the bed in silken bikini underwear, her nipples very dark on the white, white skin of her breasts, and she said, "Every time I see your body naked, I love it even more."

I folded my hands behind my head, and said, "Same here, lady. I'm getting to be a very serious fan of yours."

She laughed as she lay down beside me, her fingers already encircled around me, moving on me, eager for me to be ready, and she said, "Yes, you *do* seem to be a fan, right there for the world to see. No denying it."

We made love quickly, both of us too eager and needy to attempt to slow ourselves, losing ourselves in a physical unity of belly-slapping, groaning, laughing without inhibition.

Then we held each other, saying private, silly things until slowly, gently, we were each ready again, and then we took turns pleasing each other, giving ourselves without restraint, and finally coupling to a final release that was simultaneous, and so powerful that I actually heard a ringing in my ears.

"You're amazing," I told her.

She replied, "No. We are. We're amazing."

Later, as we lay together in darkness, our bodies still wet, our legs tangled, Amelia pulled her face close to my ear and said in a tone that was touching for its uncertainty, "There's a word my heart keeps wanting me to use, but my brain won't let me."

I said, "I hope the word's not 'three.'

After that last one, I'm going to need a little more recovery time."

She chuckled. "That sounds wonderful. But you told me you had an appointment."

"People in Colombia are big on midnight meetings. They sleep 'til noon and have dinner at ten. I'll only be gone an hour or so."

She lay silently beside me for a long time before she said softly, "The word is *love*. I don't want to say it because it scares me. And it might scare you. Doc? It's true. I think I'm falling in love with you. It scares me because I've never truly been in love and, if it happens, you'll have all of me, everything about me. I don't want to scare you away by saying it, but it's true. I've never really given myself before, but, if I do, I'll no longer be just one person. Forever."

I nuzzled the hair away from her ear and kissed her cheek. "The funny thing is, what you just said *should* scare me. It always has. I've lived alone so long."

"What are you telling me, Doc?"

"I'm saying that maybe it doesn't scare me so much now. I'm not sure."

"Maybe?"

I kissed her again, and said, "Let's see how it goes."

Chapter Twenty-two

The Plaza de Santa Domingo is a wide park and courtyard of brick, open to the sky but walled by ancient, ornate buildings, including a massive, dun-colored cathedral that was built in the 1500s. During the Inquisition, people were burned at the stake here.

On this night, though, the only fire was from torches burning around the courtyard. They threw a yellow, oscillating light on the faces of men and women gathered beneath the black sky. People were still dining at outdoor tables, served by waiters in formal dress, while jugglers, street merchants, guitarists, and magicians moved from table to table, working for tips.

I arrived at the plaza nearly half an hour early. I bought an *Aguila* at Paco's, and bribed my way upstairs. There's a balcony there, closed to the public, and it gave me a good view of the narrow streets that entered into the plaza.

If Stallings was bringing confederates, I wanted to know who they were before they had a chance to get a look at me.

He was forty minutes late, but he came alone. I let him sit for a while, watched him order another drink and light a fresh cigar. He checked his watch repeatedly.

Twice he touched the right pocket of his baggy, tent-sized slacks.

It's a nervous mannerism. Something that people do when they're carrying a gun.

When I came up behind Stallings and touched his shoulder, he jumped slightly. The reaction was unexpected but encouraging. It showed me he was on edge, not as confident as he wanted to appear to be.

As I seated myself, he looked at his watch and said, "You're late. I've been waiting for nearly an hour."

I said, "No, I was *early* — which is how I know you're lying again. Where's Kazan? The guy you call Puff. He's the one I want to talk to."

The big man fixed an expression of amusement on his face and gestured with his hands: *slow down*. "*Taupou*, if you keep pushing me, you know what's going to happen? I'm going to reach across the table and pinch your little head off." He flashed his toothy smile. "I think I'd enjoy that."

Taupou, I didn't know what that meant, and I wasn't going to ask.

I held up my empty beer, signaling the waiter as I said, "You're not mad, Earl, you're just hungry. A guy like you needs lots and lots of calories. Let me get a menu."

He leaned toward me, his voice loud enough to cause people at nearby tables to turn and stare. "Motherfucker. You are *really* starting to piss me off!"

"I'm not here to please you, Earl. You need to lower your expectations. And your voice. I'm going to ask you again: Where's Kazan?"

He sat back, his cask-sized chest moving beneath the white guyaberra as he breathed, his hands flat on the table. "I know what you're trying to do. You're trying to make me mad, man, you *want* to get me pissed off. It's like a business thing, one of those deals the big shots on TV tell you to do. To get an advantage. Well, guess what? It's not going to work. Keep it up, I'm not going to help you find your friends."

"Don't help me find my friends, you won't get paid."

The grin was back on his massive face, the smooth skin of the burn scar wrinkling. "If I don't get paid, you're never going to see either one of those girls again. What was the white girl's name?"

His grin broadened when he saw my attention vector at that specific, telling bit of information because he knew that he was now back in control.

I said, "Why don't you tell me? Prove you're not wasting my time."

"I don't got to prove nothing to you, man! You think I'd bother with the name of a girl ugly as that? Chubby white girl with brown hair and a pretty black girl, only Earl doesn't do black girls."

I said, "I can hardly blame them, Earl. You can't fault their taste. So let's get down to business. Okay?"

Stallings sat there puffing away on his cigar as he talked, trying to blow smoke rings, showing me how relaxed he was. I wanted to play tough? No problem. He could handle it, not a big deal. He said, "Let's get something straight right off. I don't know anything about any of this. I'm just telling you what I hear. Okay? I'm not guilty of nothing, I'm not admitting to anything. You savvy?

"When I go back to the States, I don't want the feds grabbing me, carting my ass off to jail. Kidnapping's illegal — even here in Colombia, though just about every shithead you name out there in the jungle does it. I mean, it's a legitimate profession here. You got your lawyers, your plumbers, your fucking kidnappers, okay? So you and me, we're just sitting here discussing things that might have happened, talking . . . what-do-you-call it — ?"

"Hypothetically," I said.

He swung his head up and down. "Exactly. We're talking hypothetically. So you go first. Hypothetically, what makes you think I was on the boat that morning, sailing back to Florida?"

I said, "You had a lot of passengers, remember? The illegal variety. It was in the newspapers. I knew a fairly large boat had to be in that area at about the right time, so I went looking. I talked to a couple of the refugees before they got deported."

"Those spics, the Haitian trash, they gave you my name? I don't believe it. No way, not possible."

"Not your name. Just your description."

He said, "Those people are so fucking

dumb, what we should'a done was dump them all about a mile offshore. Done the world a favor."

It is an irony I've noticed before: It's not unusual for members of minority groups to be unrepentant racists.

I said, "No, the refugees told me that you stopped when you saw the swimmers. Dexter Money told me your name, where to find you, everything. He was so drunk the night I talked to him, he didn't even try to charge me for the information. Nice guy, Dexter. But he doesn't speak so highly of you."

I took a perverse joy in Stalling's expression. "That white whale, what he maybe needs is for someone to cut his tongue out. He flaps his jaws too much. Now I'm kind of looking forward to seeing him again. I owed him money, but now I think my debt's paid in full."

I said, "Sounds like a win-win situation for everyone involved. So now it's your turn, Earl. Where are my friends? Hypothetically speaking, of course."

Why did he continue to check his watch? It seemed to make no sense.

I should have known why. The depth of my occasional stupidities continues to be a source of surprise.

Stallings said, "What could'a happened was that the guys running that shrimp boat stopped and picked up all three people. They ran into shore, dumped the refugees, then boarded a larger boat out in open sea — the mother ship. That ship brought all of them back here to Colombia except for one, the guy who ran the shrimp boat back to Cortez."

I said, "That's the way I figured it could've happened. I find it very hard to believe, though, that you picked them up but still don't know their names. Or do you?"

He shrugged. "Don't know, don't care. If I was there, which I wasn't, I didn't take a personal interest. If the white girl had a body on her, yeah. They was just cargo to me."

"Are they okay? Are they hurt?"

"My guess is, they're happy as clams, but probably sick of living in a shack eating shit for food, wondering what's going to happen. Which is why we need to talk money. How much are you willing to pay per person? If I can find them, that is."

"I need some proof they're alive before we do anything. Are they at a place where there's a phone? We could call them."

"Fuck you. I'm the only proof you're

going to get until we see some money. They're your friends, not mine, so it's a seller's market. You know what you need to worry about? While you're sitting here playing word games, the humps got your pals up for sale. They're in touch with their hump friends back in Saudi Arabia, Brunei, you name it, talking price. How much will they pay for the white girl, how much for that pretty colored girl?"

I said, "Humps?"

His expression said: Are you stupid or what? "*Humps.* You know, the sand niggers, the ragheads. Like in camels — humps. In Colombia, if you got a woman to sell, the humps always do the negotiating because they're the only ones who have contact with the guys who have the real money. The oil sheiks, the big-time weapons dealers."

"Which is why I should be talking to Kazan, correct? Not you."

"That albino freak, he's not my boss. This deal's between you and me. But we've got to do it quick and clean. No more of your bullshit."

When he reached for his right pocket, I tensed slightly, ready to throw myself back out of my chair. But instead of bringing out a weapon, he brought out a pen. He took a paper napkin, then paused. "How much money do you have on you? I'll give you a big discount if we do a cash deal now."

"I'm not stupid, Earl. The way it's going to work is, I'll hand the cash to my friends, and they'll hand it to you."

He began to scribble on the napkin. "In that case, it's going to cost you this much per person. No questions, no more negotiations, that's how much it's going to be. You can buy one or all three. It's no skin off my nose."

I looked at the napkin and read, "$50K."

"I don't have that much."

He stood up. "Then find a way to get it." He tossed the pen on the table. "You may want to write this down. At the southern boundary of Colombia, there's a little airstrip at a place called Mameluco. It's not too far from Araracuara, where there's a bigger strip, but don't go there. Mameluco. That's the place."

I didn't bother noting the name. I'd already seen it on a map. Mameluco was very near the village of Remanso, the name that Harrington said meant "still waters."

He checked his watch yet again. "I'll give you two days to get the dough. Today's Tuesday . . . you've got to land at the airstrip before sunset on Thursday. Get off the plane and walk to the dirt road. We'll know you're there. Just you, alone, and the money in a briefcase. Cash. Bring anybody else, your friends are dead. Talk to anybody about this, your friends are dead. Have anybody follow you, we'll know about it. Same thing. Dead. Savvy?"

I told him, "I'll try my best to raise the money."

I didn't tell him I already had a briefcase.

Chapter Twenty-three

When I left Stallings, it was a little after 2 a.m. Amelia would be asleep, and I was feeling restless, so I stopped at a little hole-in-the-wall place called La Habinita, bought a beer to go, looking at all the photos of Che and Fidel on the wall as I waited. Then I took the long way back to the hotel.

I walked along the narrow street that follows the northernmost wall of the city, walked past lovers kissing on cannon parapets, passed vendors selling from munitions ramps — all the antiquated architecture of war now obsolete, nothing more than public furniture for modern life.

The great novelist, Gabriel García Marquez, has a fortress-sized hacienda across the street from the Hotel Santa Clara. There's always a lone guard outside the little door, predictably holding a 12-gauge shotgun. As I passed, I said hello and asked him how his evening was going.

I was surprised to hear him answer, "It's not been a good night, friend. It's not been a good night for anyone in our little quarter."

I stopped to face him. What did that mean?

When I hear something that truly shocks or frightens me, I feel an ether-like sensation move through the frontal area of my brain to my spine. I felt it now as the guard said, "There was an incident in the hotel. A man was shot, and a woman was kidnapped. I saw them turn the corner, a man on each side of her, moving as if she were very drunk." He slapped the barrel of his shotgun. "The *cabrones!* I wish I had known. I could have rescued her! One of them, I'll be able to recognize again."

I was already running toward the hotel as he added, "As I told the police: He was a tall albino man, but strange-looking. Not American, not Colombian. Colorless. He was *white*."

Carlos Quasada, one of Colombia's best heavyweight boxers, had fought his last fight.

His body was sprawled in the open air stairwell between the second and third floors of the hotel, surrounded by police and hotel employees. The police tried to stop me from entering what was now a crime scene, but I forced my way through the perimeter, shouting that I had information that could be helpful to them and demanding to visit my own room.

Or maybe they let me through because they saw the look in my eye.

I'd left Carlos standing guard in the third floor's open corridor. From where he was stationed, he had a clear view of the stairs, the elevator, and of San Felipe castle, built high on a hill outside the old walled city. Amelia didn't know that I'd asked him to stand guard there until I returned. I didn't want to frighten her.

Another stupid mistake on my part.

Whoever had killed him wasn't a very good shot. It'd taken them three rounds. One in the back, another just above his butt, and a third in the back of the head.

I knew the head shot was last, because Carlos was a bull of a man, and he'd done some crawling — probably toward his attackers.

He'd been well loved in Cartagena. I didn't realize how much, but I now knew. Standing in the little circle around the body, most of the hotel employees, in their neat beige uniforms, were weeping, as was one of the cops.

A woman who seemed to be the detective in charge said, "You knew the victim?"

I said to her as I pushed past, "Wait. I need to check my room," and ran toward the stairs.

I took the steps two at a time and threw open the door to our suite.

I didn't expect Amelia to be there, and she wasn't. But she had not gone quietly into the night with her abductors. There's a difference between a room that's been the scene of a fight and a room that's been purposefully ransacked.

There'd been a fight here. There were broken lamps, a shattered mirror, an overturned chair that she may have clung to rather than be dragged from the room. She had found weapons where she could. The most touching of them was a small, lignum vitae box, beautifully carved, very dense and heavy, that I'd bought for her that afternoon in the market. I stooped, picked it up, noticing that a corner of the box was moist and slightly darker than the rest of the wood.

Maybe she'd gotten a good blow in. I found myself hoping desperately that she had.

Something else I noticed was that the room had a strange, medicinal stink. It made my eyes burn, caused me to feel slightly dizzy. Probably some variation of chloroform.

I remember the guard telling me that, because of the way the two men were pulling the woman along, he thought she was drunk.

Behind me, a woman's voice said, "Is there anything missing?"

I turned to see the detective. She wore a dark blue skirt, light white blouse, and a badly cut navy-blue jacket. She had short, frosted blond hair, silver fingernails, and she was nearly as wide as she was tall.

Feeling sick, close to panic, I said, "Yes. I'm missing my girlfriend."

The detective said, "I'm aware of that. The redheaded American woman. Witnesses in the lobby already told us. Are you missing anything else? Did they *steal* anything, that's what I'm asking you."

The question was so asinine that I didn't reply. I was searching around the room and finally found what I hoped would be there. Murderers don't leave notes. Kidnappers do.

On the night stand, under the telephone, I found a folded sheet of hotel stationery.

Behind me, the detective demanded, "Sir! Please don't touch anything. My people haven't been through here yet. That could be evidence." I opened the paper and read words written there: "Bring the money. Come alone, or she's dead."

I stood there, my brain scanning for a quick, fail-safe solution. There was none.

I allowed the detective to take the note from my hand and read it. She folded the note and said, "I think this is very encouraging. In Colombia, kidnappers are also businesspeople. They keep their word. They keep their victims alive until they get paid, or they're out of business. I'm sure these men will be in touch with you soon. They'll provide you with a price and a deadline." She paused to look at me. "Unless you've somehow already been in touch with them?"

I answered, "No. Of course not," thinking of no reason why I should tell her the truth.

"Unfortunately," she added, "the note is now worthless for gathering fingerprints. This is a crime scene. I'm going to remind you one last time."

I told her, "Lady, your country is a crime scene," and walked out the door.

★ ★ ★

At the hotel's front desk, I retrieved my heavy briefcase and told the clerk, "When Señor Carlos's family arrives, if they need anything, anything at all, please charge it to our room. Perhaps you should call a physician as well. Tell him the situation, ask him to bring sedatives."

I walked outside into the early morning darkness of the park across the street and sat on a bench there. As I unlocked the briefcase, I could hear the *clip-clop* of horses' hooves on stone — wagons on their way to market. I heard roosters crowing, answering back and forth between the walls of the city. I took out the satellite telephone and dialed.

After a couple of rings, I listened to Harrington say, "Jesus Christ, Ford, do you know what time it is?"

I told him I knew exactly what time it was, adding, "I need your help. You need to sit up and pay attention to every little thing I'm about to tell you. Something terrible's happened, and we need to get moving. *Now*."

When I'd finished telling him how they'd managed to kidnap Amelia, he sounded sincere when he said, "I'm sorry, Doc. I shouldn't have been so abrupt. So the

453

question is, what do you think we ought to do?"

I knew exactly what I wanted to do. We had only two options. I needed to go alone and meet Kazan, as his note demanded, and try to free Amelia and the others on my own. Or I had to find a way to hit them so fast and hard that they wouldn't have a chance to react.

I'm not foolish enough or courageous enough to invest that much faith in myself. The latter option would be the best choice.

I said, "I want a SEAL team. I know SEAL Team Four operates in the area. Their hostage-rescue guys, that's exactly who I want, and we need to get moving right away." I checked my watch: 2:45 a.m. "We still have, what? about three hours of darkness left. You know Colombia better than I do. How far is it to Remanso, the southern border?"

"Remanso's about four hundred miles. The southern border is way beyond."

"Damn it! I didn't think it was that far. Well . . . if we really hustle, we can locate their facility and take them down while they're still having their morning coffee. And before the guys who snatched Amelia even arrive. The little airstrip near the village doesn't have lights. Stallings warned me about that. Kazan is going to have to keep her somewhere near here, then fly her out in the morning."

Harrington said, "So I need to have some of our people watch the local airports. I doubt if they'd be that stupid. There are plenty of private strips inland they can use. But you never know."

"Good idea. But a SEAL team, that's what you need to work on now. I want to be there waiting, in control of his facility, hideout, whatever it is when Kazan arrives. So make the call and scramble our guys. I'm going to throw some gear together. I'll expect to hear from you in ten minutes or so. No more."

He said, "I'll call when I have something to tell you," and hung up.

Half an hour later, now dressed in black T-shirt, camo field pants, and jungle boots, I answered the beeping satellite phone and heard Harrington say, "Okay, I've got a hostage-rescue team waiting for you. A chopper, too. Do you know where the Navy Amphib base is on the way to Boca Grande?"

Of course I knew where it was. Years ago, I'd been involved in an operation that had used the base as a staging area.

Harrington said, "Grab a cab, and you

can be there in ten minutes. I'll have one of our people at the gate waiting for you."

There was something about his tone that made me uneasy. He wasn't being evasive, but I got the impression that he hadn't told me everything, either.

I said, "You said you have a hostage-rescue team. You mean a SEAL boat crew, correct? Snatch and bag. A squad of seven or eight studs, fully tactical, fully trained, ready to go."

"Doc, SEAL Four is working way south and out of contact. I tried. Absolutely no way can they dump what they're doing and redeploy out of here. So I got you the next best thing. I've got a Colombian *Anfibio* team waiting to go."

I groaned loud enough for Harrington to hear me, so he raised his voice, continuing, "Now wait! Don't get pissed off at me. They're better than they used to be. Things have changed since you were in the business. What do you think SEAL Four spends half its time doing down here? Training their people, making them better so we don't have to invest so much tactical time in their country. It's not the same group that you used to deal with."

I hoped not. *Colombia's Grupo de Commandos Anfibios* or Amphibious Commando Group was a SEAL-type unit established back in the 1960s to work against drug trafficking, but it was also given other missions, such as naval counterterrorism.

I'd known some of their people and had worked with them once or twice over the years.

I was not impressed.

The *Anfibios,* or GCA as they are also known, are headquartered at the Cartagena Naval Base and are approximately one hundred men strong. Soon after the unit's inception, a Mobile Training Team from SEAL Team Two traveled to Cartagena to train them in basic swimming, demolitions, SCUBA, and land warfare. They were reportedly pretty good, but they lacked sound leadership — too often the case in Colombia.

I told Harrington, "You know what the last thing I heard about the *Anfibios* was? That their commanding officer got blown up testing a homemade limpet mine. Just a couple of years back. Is that true?"

I heard him sigh. "Yes, it's true. You know it's true. But they've gotten better."

"I hope so. I hope to hell you're right."

"Look at it this way, Doc. They're the only people we've got."

Chapter Twenty-four

The naval base ran for a mile or so along the busy four-lane highway that led to the beaches and tourist high-rises of Boca Grande. It was fenced the whole way, lighted guardhouses at the entrances and exits.

At this hour, there wasn't much traffic, mostly donkey and ox carts pulling wagons filled with vegetables and woven goods toward the markets of the old city. On the way, I passed the time by using fishing line to create a light and comfortable strap for my glasses — a fishing guide's trick. I also had a recent acquisition boxed and put away in my pants pocket: contacts. I didn't like to wear them, but it was good to have a backup.

Standing inside the guardhouse, with three Colombian soldiers, was a tall, blond man wearing dark slacks and a white short-sleeve dress shirt. He could have been a model for a catalogue company. As I stepped from the cab, he came out, shook hands, and said to me, "My name's Ron Iossi, Commander Ford. I'm with the embassy. I've been instructed to assist you on this mission."

I'd been expecting someone like him to be waiting for me. Was glad, in fact, that he was there. The word *embassy* was a euphemism for the CIA.

He had a Humvee, engine running, driver waiting. We drove through the tree shadows and beneath streetlights, through the military complex, on the road that parallels Cartagena Bay. Like many military bases, the architecture was repetitive, as if stamped from a mold, and dated well back into the previous century.

I only got a glimpse of the base's main docks. Among the Coast Guard cutters and light naval ships was a row of private vessels, both power and sail, anchored below powerful security lights. They'd probably all been seized because of some kind of illegal activity, so I was not surprised to see a black oceangoing motorsailer there, more than one hundred feet long. I recognized the boat as having once belonged to a man nicknamed the Turk by a transplanted Australian friend of mine.

The vessel had Istanbul registry and was christened *The Moon of* something. I'd forgotten exactly what.

That afternoon, when Amelia and I had had some free time, I'd tried to contact that Australian friend, Garret Norman, by calling Club Nautico, the local marina he owned. Garret's a smart, observant guy, and he could have provided me with some useful insights into Colombia's kidnap trade.

Instead, Candelaria, Garret's wife, gave me a surprising update on what had happened since I'd last been in Colombia. The Turk had been found shot in the back of the head, floating in Cartagena Bay. Garret had been arrested on unassociated — and bogus — charges. He'd escaped from jail and fled the country.

No one knew where he was.

"Garret always liked you," his wife told me. "He trusted you. You and your crazy old uncle. The one who beat up the Turk that time. What was his name?"

The way she spoke of her husband in the past tense gave me the uncomfortable feeling that Garret was dead.

No way of me finding out. In Colombia, people disappeared so commonly, so suddenly, that authorities no longer bothered to keep track.

★ ★ ★

The center for Colombia's counter-terrorism special forces, the *Fuerzas Especiales Anti-Terrorista,* is located on the bay side of the Cartagena base, not far from the old three-story tropical white house where the U.S. Drug Enforcement Agency and the CIA both keep offices.

We stopped briefly at that house, and Iossi — he pronounced it "Yohsee" — led me inside, then handed me several documents, including a laminated Colorado drivers' license that identified me as "Marion North."

I said, "You guys work fast."

"Not us, the computer. Press a couple buttons, then hit print. Presto. It's kind of what we do."

"This picture's at least ten years old."

"It's the only one we had on file. The other documents are important. Keep them on you at all times. They identify you as a privately employed mercenary for hire. A headhunter."

I said, "Headhunter?"

"It's a term we've come to use. There are still real headhunters out there in the jungle — don't let those little bastards catch you — but this means something different. It means you're an American sol-

461

dier of fortune. Up in the mountains, there are probably a dozen ex-SEALs, former Rangers, Delta Force guys. Maybe more. Came down here to make lots of money as bounty hunters."

"You're kidding."

"Nope. An absolute fact. They've been hired by the Colombian government, using a front business called Gin-EE Electronics out of Virginia, or a dummy corporation called SAIC. They're mercenaries hired to kill retreating FARC troops. They're hired specifically because of their backgrounds and the quality of their work in Southeast Asia, the Middle East, Central America, Africa — the world. They're each assigned their own little territory, kind of like gold claims back in the old days. The more successful they are, the bigger their claim gets."

I said, "And that's what I'm posing as?"

Iossi said, "Commander Ford, hopefully this evolution will go down so fast and hard, you're not going to need to pose as anything. But if something goes wrong, if you're captured or killed, the company can't be associated with you in any way. SOP — standard operating procedure. If someone asks us who you are, we'll tell them you're a gun for hire, you're a headhunter. Simple as that. You are not with us."

I nodded. "Killing people to get rich."

Iossi was walking toward the door. "Killing *killers* to get rich. Yeah, a couple of our people have made a ton of money."

The Colombian *Anfibios* all looked like teenage boys. There were four of them in full camouflage battle dress, faces painted, boonie hats pulled low. All together, they carried an M-16; some kind of stockless, sci-fi looking automatic shotgun; a 60-caliber machine gun; and a Knight's Armaments sniper rifle, complete with a complicated new generation of Startron night-vision systems that I'd never seen before.

Maybe they *had* gotten better.

Their commanding officer was Lt. Rafidio Martinez, a very short, squat wrestler type who wasted no time making certain I knew exactly who was in charge.

"Once we locate the facility, Commander, the helicopter will hover, and our team will fast-rope to the ground. You will stay in the stern of the ship, out of our way. We don't want to risk those lines getting tangled or someone accidentally knocking you out of the ship.

"Once we have secured the facility and taken down any resistance, we will signal the chopper to land. Then and *only* then can you enter the facility. Questions, sir?"

Nope. No questions. I liked the way the guy took command. In fact, I found it very reassuring.

The *Anfibio* had gotten better — or so I thought.

They walked me out through the early morning darkness to the helio pad. There I saw what appeared to be an ultramodern Plexiglas bubble attached to a khaki and camo fuselage. The aircraft had a six-bladed main rotor and a canted four-bladed tail rotor. There were infrared sensors in several places on the exterior, rocket tubes, a bristling of antenna and miniguns, plus twin external dismount planks.

I'd seen one of these choppers before. It was a high-tech, special-duty helicopter named Little Bird. Its principal role was to ferry commandos into tight situations. Troops rode on the two planks attached to the aircraft's sides, enabling them to dismount immediately upon touchdown.

Martinez had told me his crew would be fast-roping in — sliding down woven lines when the chopper was within seventy feet of the ground.

So we didn't need the planks, but I was inordinately pleased we'd been assigned such a craft. The chopper had to be massively expensive, which meant superiors would entrust the thing only to a first-rate pilot. Also, all the sensory systems suggested to me a level of electronic sophistication that would make certain the pilot was warned if someone opened fire on us with missiles or other guidance-system weaponry.

In other words, we wouldn't be a fat target as we flew low over the jungle.

There was a reason I was concerned. I hate flying in choppers. I'm not a particularly emotional person, but my fear of them approaches phobia. Maybe it's because they glide like a rock.

More likely, it's because I was once in a chopper that was hit with light weapons fire and lost its transmission. The pilot had to put it into an autorotation to get the ship down. It was one of the most sickening, helpless feelings I've ever experienced.

I much prefer boats.

As we walked toward the chopper, I told Lieutenant Martinez, "I'm impressed by your equipment. A covert Little Bird. I've never flown in one."

Martinez's voice had more than a touch of envy when he answered. "Me neither. That one's assigned to your SEALs. They won't let us touch it. We're going to be transported in that piece of shit."

He gestured toward a hangar. His men were just sliding back the big double doors.

Inside, was an old Bell UH-type Iroquois — "H" as in a Huey slick. It was painted desert yellow — an unlikely color for a country dense with rain forest. Even the main rotor was bright yellow — an old chopper pilot trick so that fighter aircraft overhead wouldn't accidentally drop a bomb on you.

I walked into the hangar to take a closer look. The place smelled of dust, diesel fuel, and paint. The chopper's large cargo doors were open, showing khaki bench seats inside and a single M-60 machine gun fixed in its harness on the starboard side.

I walked to the front of the craft and touched my hand to the landing light, knelt, and read the black and gold crest above it: BUSHRANGER.

I turned and looked at Martinez. "Jesus Christ! This is an old Australian Huey. It's got to be thirty, forty years old." I reached for the satellite phone in my pocket —

Harrington could certainly find us something safer than this.

The young commando was nodding, not pleased. "I know, I know. Let's hope we can get the damn thing started this time."

Above, through the Huey's open cargo door, the sky was a current of stars. Beneath us was an ocean of blue mist afloat upon canyons of shadow.

We were flying over jungle, the top strata of forest canopy awash in moonlight. The moon was at eye level, through the starboard door. It was huge, pocked by geologic cataclysm, white as winter ice. As we traveled at close to 130 miles an hour, there was the illusion that the moon was sailing along with us, gliding over the rain forest in pursuit, ghostly in its silence.

We had to stop and refuel at a military base near some large city in the mountains — I guessed it to be Bogotá. As the aircraft banked away, nose down, and gathered speed in the darkness, flying south, I watched the lights of the city fade, then disappear. After that, there were only small pockets of light: jungle villages, fires burning, the night strongholds of rural people linked by darkness, aglow like in-

467

cremental pearls, bright and solitary from half a mile high.

In the air a second time, I began to relax a little. Yes, I hated flying in helicopters, but the fact that we had now lifted off safely twice had increased my level of confidence.

Even Lieutenant Martinez seemed to noticed the difference. He slapped me on the shoulder and smiled, "You are not so sick-looking this time, Commander. Not so pale!"

I doubted if he was serious about my coloring — the cabin's interior was lighted with two overhead red bulbs. Very dim. The human eye contains two types of photoreceptors, rods and cones. Rods do not respond to red light, thus red lights do not alter our night vision.

I didn't doubt, however, that he and his crew perceived that I was a lot happier on the ground than off. Now, though, in the rare moments I wasn't worrying about Amelia and what Kazan's people might be doing to her, I could actually look out onto the jungle and take some small pleasure in the vastness of it, the pure wilderness that it implied.

I knew that we had crossed into the rim of rain forest and rivers that is the beginning of the Amazon Valley, one of the earth's last remaining wild regions. Below, there were many hundreds — perhaps thousands — of plants, insects, and even fish that had yet to be discovered or described scientifically. People, too — there were still dozens of isolated tribes that had had little or no contact with the outside world.

The thought of doing fieldwork here, of doing a fish count and finding a new species, made me long for my little lab back on Sanibel. I wanted to be back there. I wanted Amelia with me. I liked the image that played in my head: The two of us alone — her doing her work, me doing mine — joined by our proximity, but more than that, too. I liked the idea of the two of us creating our own isolated tribe and reducing our contact with the outside world. Maybe for a couple of months. Maybe a couple of years — or more.

That would be a good thing, too.

The thought that was always with me, though, was much darker. What if Kazan or Stallings had touched her? What if they'd done something to her?

The prospect made me nauseous.

If they had, I'd help put it behind her. She was one of the strong ones. Amelia would be okay. *We'd* be okay once we got back to Florida.

Before I could take her home, though, I had to find her.

When we were far away from civilization, we dropped down low, probably only five hundred feet or so above the tops of the trees, the pilot following the contour of the jungle. Through the open cargo door, I could feel the temperature drop as we followed, for a time, the course of a river. I could smell the musk of rotting wood and vine, the quarry scent of fresh water.

One of Tomlinson's favorite assertions is that for a certain type of person — both of us included — an external association with water is as important as internal consumption. Oddly, just knowing I was over water made me feel better.

But the feeling didn't last long.

From the cockpit, I heard the pilot shout *Shit,* a word that, in Spanish, has an ironic, musical sound. Then he yelled, "Those sons of bitches!" as the chopper twisted suddenly to port.

I knew then that we were in trouble.

The helicopter was equipped with some kind of a radar-detection system. As the craft turned, I began to hear a steady beeping noise. I leaned to look into the cockpit and could see a flashing red light on the control panel. If I hadn't known what the noise was, I could have guessed what it meant when the pilot began jinking wildly, making hard lefts and rights, as if trying to do evade.

The beeping alarm meant that something on the ground was tracking us.

For the *Anfibios*, it wasn't so bad. Except for the commando belted to the M-60 machine gun, the rest were strapped tight onto the bench seat across from me. From old habit, though, I chose to add an extra layer of protection between my butt and the chopper's thin armor. Any kid with a rifle can shoot up through the belly of a helicopter. From what I knew about Colombia, there were bound to be a lot of people down there with rifles. Probably eager to use them, too.

I was sitting on the briefcase that Harrington had provided me. I, too, wore a seat belt, but the surface of the briefcase was slick, and I began to slide violently one way, then the other, as the chopper jinked. I kept myself steady by holding on to the nylon strap overhead until, during an unbelievably sharp turn, the strap broke.

The fuselage of the chopper wasn't the only thing that was outdated.

From the flight deck, the beeping horn changed to a loud, high-pitched warble, as I heard the pilot yell, "They're firing at us, those sons of bitches just fired!"

And I thought to myself: *Stinger missile. You're dead, Ford. Dead.*

The Stinger is a man-portable, shoulder-fired, infra-red, heat-seeking guided missile that travels faster than the speed of sound. It weighs less than forty pounds and comes with a disposable firing tube.

In Afghanistan, mountain people used Stingers to shoot down a couple hundred Russian MIG fighter jets. For a computer-controlled missile sufficiently sophisticated to discriminate between background clutter and an actual aircraft, this old chopper wasn't much of a challenge.

Our door gunner had opened fire: a deafening staccato clatter, tracers streaming through the darkness, and spent brass casings ringing bell-like against the fuselage.

There was no way the gunner had a target. No way he could see what he was shooting. When the adrenaline is in you, when you're scared, you squeeze the trigger. That simple.

Chaos.

472

In the cockpit, the radar alert had changed again, this time to a loud and steady shriek. I knew the missile had locked on to us and was vectoring toward the exhaust pipes of the craft's overhead engines. There was now no escape.

We went into a steep dive, then the cabin began to rotate wildly beneath the rotor. It was a sickening replay of my previous crash landing in a helicopter. Now the nightmare was repeating itself. Could this really be happening?

I held tight to the handle of the briefcase, trying to stabilize myself, knowing that I was about to die, the realization of it roaring in my ears, feeling it as a weight on my chest.

"Hail Mary, full of grace! Hail Mary, full of grace!"

Across from me, one of the commandos was saying his catechism by rote, and I could see Lieutenant Martinez, wide-eyed, gripping his rifle for support, the centrifugal force tremendous. He held my eyes briefly: *Bad, very bad.*

Which is when my seat belt broke. I was ripped free, weightless, and clawed the air wildly as the velocity of my own body carried me backward, somersaulting, out the open cargo door.

Then I was tumbling in darkness . . . then in space, falling, falling, beneath an explosion so close that I could feel the heat, could feel the shock wave like an expanding bubble, my body tensing for impact when I would soon hit the earth.

Impaled on a tree.

That image was in my mind . . .

Then I did hit, crashed into a blackness, cement-hard, that crushed the wind out of me and nearly knocked me unconscious.

I came up splashing, spitting, completely disoriented until I realized what had happened: water. I was in water. I was *swimming.*

To my left and ahead of me, I watched the old Huey, already aflame, auger itself into the jungle. It disappear momentarily behind a silhouette of trees, then exploded, creating a bright halo of flame.

Chapter Twenty-five

It took me several long, bewildered seconds before I realized what had happened. When my seat belt broke, I'd been dumped out the chopper's cargo door. I'd fallen a hundred feet or so and landed in the river we'd been following.

The river seemed to be one of those deep and narrow, slow-moving rivers. The moon had drifted toward the horizon, but there was still enough light to see that the watercourse was fifty or sixty yards wide and was bordered by a high, abrupt canyon of forest.

Deep jungle has a density that muffles sound and magnifies odor. This was deep jungle, a biosphere of vine, limb, earth. It was cellar-cool, and the river created a narrow corridor of light through the mountainous tree canopy.

Drifting there, I heard a second loud explosion, then a series of smaller explosions: ordnance going off.

The silence that followed the explosions seemed a reflective pause.

It did not last long. Soon the night was filled with sound, wild with peeping, croaking frogs, humming insects, and the howling of monkeys from distant trees. The jungle's reply to an unusual intrusion.

I straightened my glasses, glad for the fishing line I'd used to tie them in place. Then I began to swim toward the bank where the chopper had crashed. As I did, my brain sent out the careful little search requests: Did I feel pain? Were all my body parts in place? Had I suffered some terrible injury that I was still too stunned to realize?

My left shoulder hurt like hell. I'd probably banged it on something when my seat belt broke. And my right ear was adding a tinny, roaring effect to any noise it processed.

I'd probably broken an eardrum when I hit the water.

Not the first eardrum I've broken.

Other than those few aches and pains, though, I felt pretty good.

As I moved toward the bank, I congratulated myself — I'd been damn lucky to survive.

The sense of good luck didn't last. I remembered that a day from now, I had to be in the village of Remanso with a couple hundred thousand dollars in cash, or they'd kill Amelia, and the others, too — if Janet, Michael, and Grace really were still alive.

I had no idea where I was or how far I had to go to get help.

I began to swim faster.

The briefcase had been catapulted out the door with me. I found it drifting high and dry, only a few dozen yards downstream.

I used it as a float, pushing it ahead of me toward shore.

The riverbank was steep, a congestion of roots and overhanging limbs. At one place, I grabbed a low branch and tried to pull myself out. As I did, I felt what seemed to be a heavy sprinkling of sand on my face . . . but then the sand began to burn like tiny hot coals.

Fire ants. I was covered with them.

I dropped back into the water and submerged until they were gone.

Finally, I found an opening, and crawled out. The first thing I did was take the satellite phone from my pocket and try it —

maybe Harrington had equipped me with some new generation of indestructible communications system.

But no. It didn't work.

I tried taking out the battery and drying it. No luck.

Tossing the phone into the river seemed to underline how completely cut off I now was from what I considered the civilized world. I watched water-rings created by the phone expanding in darkness, then I walked toward the orange glow that I knew was the burning helicopter.

As I did, the sky above me disappeared. No more moonlight, no more stars. I was in a cavern of trees, the ceiling a hundred feet overhead. The canopy was so tangled that light could not penetrate, so nothing grew below. The ground was springy with rot, and slippery, too.

Yet I could still see. It was as if the jungle generated a very low-voltage luminescence. The blanket of forest overhead was black, but the trunks of individual trees were gray or pewter.

It allowed me to walk fairly quickly.

Within a few minutes, I was close enough to the crash site to hear the roar of burning aviation fuel and the crackle of burning wood.

But then I heard something else, and stopped, frozen where I stood.

I heard voices speaking a loud, drunken Spanish.

Of course. The guerrilla troops or drug runners, whoever had shot us down, would be converging on the crash site, too.

How was I going to get around them?

There were six of them: five men and a young Indio girl. She couldn't have been more than sixteen or seventeen.

The men were older, in their twenties, a couple probably in their late thirties to forties. They wore mismatched military fatigues and carried both M-16s and old Soviet-designed AK-47 assault rifles.

The girl's skin was earthen, and she had thick black hair tied in a ponytail that hung to the middle of her back. She had a rough blanket folded over one shoulder and wore a copper-colored traditional blouse I'd seen before in South America, a garment known as a *huipil*. Her skirt was short, sarong-like, blue, and showed her thick legs. She was barefooted and wore bracelets on her wrists and around both ankles. On her ankles were also black decorative tattoos.

One thing I didn't doubt: The girl wasn't with these men by choice. She had a subdued look of fear and emotional resignation. It is an expression I had seen before on the faces of captives and new prisoners.

It would not be pleasant to be in the control of men such as this, especially for a girl her age.

I moved quietly from tree to tree, ducked low and kept in the shadows. When I was close enough to hear the soldiers clearly, I knelt and opened the briefcase. I was wearing my SIG Sauer on my hip, belted into a holster I'd borrowed from Ron Iossi. I was surprised that the force of my fall hadn't ripped it free, but the holster snap had held.

Now I took out the little submachine gun, locked the dual magazines in place, and pushed the little indicator switch until it was on full automatic.

I waited.

Not surprisingly, the guerrillas were looking for anything they could find of value among the wreckage. They'd collected a few things on the perimeter, not much: a couple of weapons and a can of ammo that had somehow been thrown clear of the fire.

I decided they sounded drunk because they *were* drunk. One of them had a bottle of cloudy liquor and was passing it around.

I listened as over and over they replayed

what had happened, how it had happened. Among male hunters, it is a very old ceremony: elevate and institutionalize the success of a hunt. I listened to them argue among themselves about how they'd first heard the chopper, how they'd run to get into position, and how the youngest of them — a kid named Marcos — had been so damn nervous to be shooting his first Stinger at a real live target.

"You made a mess in your pants!" they chided him. "But thanks to our help, you scored blood!"

That was bad enough, but then it abruptly became worse.

Suddenly, they all stopped talking at once, heads tilting in unison as if straining to hear.

Then I heard what had given them pause: a low, moaning sound from the nearby trees, louder than the bellows wind from a burning fire. The men grew more silent, weapons at ready, as the moaning grew louder, and then they all took a step back when, into the circle of light, stumbled what had to be a human being but who looked like no human I had ever seen.

One of the commandos had survived the crash. Or maybe it was the pilot. I couldn't tell. His clothes and his skin had been burned off him, and, but for one terrible bright and agonized eye, his face was gone.

Apparently, he'd been hiding but could no longer stand the pain, for he walked toward them, mummy-like, arms outstretched, still smoldering, calling, "I need a doctor, I've been injured! Please help me! Mother of God, please help me!"

When they realized what this aberration was, the rebels visibly relaxed, even seemed to find the situation funny.

One of them turned to the silent girl and yelled, "Where is your tribe of cannibals? We have a cooked meal for them!" as he stuck out his leg and tripped the injured man.

Hilarious.

I was already up and walking toward their group, moving before I realized what I was doing, the little submachine gun in my left hand, the 9mm pistol in my right. I stepped into the clearing, into the light of the fire. It was the only way I could instantly change the angle of my approach and put the girl out of the line of fire.

She was the first to see me. I saw surprise register on her face, then maybe just a flicker of hope.

Whap-whap-whap.

One of the rebels had touched his automatic weapon to the back of the burned man's head and fired the three-shot volley.

The man's body quivered, a muscle-re-flex response to severe trauma. I found my-self relieved when he finally lay still.

But there was no going back for me. I'd committed myself. So I continued walking toward them, the MP-5 at hip level, but sighting over the top of the pistol that I held outstretched toward them. I didn't yell, because I wanted my words to com-municate meaning, not emotion.

Speaking just loud enough for them to hear me clearly, I said, "Drop your weapons. *Now,* or you're dead."

I was surprised by the calmness of my own voice.

So were they. The men turned as one, the woman watching all of us, backing away, as her captors stood frozen, weapons slung over their shoulders or held low.

I fired a short burst with the machine gun, over their heads — but not by much.

They ducked reflexively as I yelled, "Drop your weapons!"

They all did — except for one.

The man carrying the liquor bottle was the same one who'd shot the burned com-mando.

Some people get a taste for killing. They like it.

He was a tall guy with a very black, very thick beard and baggy fatigues. He wore new Nikes — a modern touch. As the others slowly unslung, then dropped their rifles, black-beard remained motionless, staring at me, AK-47 in one hand, the bottle in the other. His expression was familiar, a mean-drunk look, defiant, dumb.

I fired another short burst, yelling, *"Do it."*

As I did, I saw his expression change, knew what was going to happen, understood the sudden decision he'd just made, and hated it. He tossed the bottle away, probably to divert my attention, as he snapped his rifle upward toward me, already firing.

I leaned toward him, squeezing off four fast shots with the pistol, and watched the rounds knock him backward, contorting his face and body as if he were taking blows from an invisible bat. He continued firing wildly as he fell.

I dived to the right, rolling as I did, still focused on their small group. Two of his own men — one of them the kid named Marcos — were backpedaling drunkenly, both of them hit by black-beard's fire. The other two had dropped to their bellies.

I screamed, "Get your hands away from those weapons!" as black-beard hit the ground and the firing stopped. I sprayed another short burst just above them to make my point. Then I got to my feet, heart pounding.

The girl was still there. I was surprised by that. Why hadn't she run — let these crazy men fight it out among themselves?

The two rebels who'd been hit were writhing in the dirt, crying for help. They'd both taken rounds in the back and legs. Black-beard was still moving, too, trying to get to his stomach, trying to crawl.

I could see that the two healthy rebels were giving it some thought, trying to decide what to do, so I walked toward them yelling, "Hands behind your heads! Hands behind your heads!"

As I repeated it a third time, black-beard tensed, then his body seemed to deflate.

I didn't want to get so close that they could use their hands to try to trip me, so I said to the girl, "Do you speak Spanish?"

In the orange light of the burning helicopter, her eyes were black pools, her face a brown mask. She nodded.

"Are you hurt? Did they hurt you?"

She shrugged.

"Okay. Then I want you to walk behind them, take their weapons, and place them over there, near the wreckage. Be careful, they can go off. Don't throw them. Put them down carefully."

She stared at me for a moment, thinking about it. Her voice was deeper than I expected to be, but still girlish. A teenager in the rain forest. "You're not going to kill them?"

I shook my head. "We get their weapons, throw them in the river, they're not going to bother us anymore. I'll help you. I promise. You can trust me."

Once again, she gave me a considered look that seemed void of emotion. Then she walked quickly to where the guerrillas lay on the ground. At black-beard's body, she paused, touching him experimentally with her bare foot.

He did not move.

I said, "I think he's dead."

Her response surprised me. "Too bad."

Then I watched her kneel and pick-up the AK-47 that black-beard had used. She looked at the barrel, looked at the trigger, then looked at me.

Why was she behaving so oddly?

"Hurry up! We need to get moving."

The two wounded guerrillas were still

groaning, calling for help, and she looked at them, rifle in her hands, before looking at the two men on the ground at her feet. Then, before my brain could process what was happening, she shouldered the rifle, and shot both of them in the back and head with short bursts.

"What are you *doing?*"

I was running toward her as she turned and emptied the rifle into the bodies of the two wounded men.

"Stop it!"

Then she looked at me, as if I might be next, but I could see her brain processing it. No, she would not shoot me . . . and so she threw the weapon away from her, her eyes staring into mine.

I stopped running, looked at her through the jungle's vacuum of silence, and heard her say. "Good. They're all dead now."

Then she turned to black-beard. "I wish you had not killed this pig. He was the worst. Him, I would have taken back to my village and given to the old women for a night. *They* know the ways to deal with bad men. Then I would have taken his head."

Chapter Twenty-six

Her name was a windy, guttural sound —
Kee-shew-ha-RA? — that I tried to pronounce several times, but couldn't get right.

Finally, she said, "The year that the missionaries came, they called me Keesha. I hated them, but it is a name that you may use for the time we're together."

At the wreck site, she'd insisted that I wait while she yanked a few strands of hair from each guerrilla. It was a compromise: She'd asked me for a knife. She wanted to decapitate black-beard.

When I refused, she told me, "The things he did to me I will never say."

After hearing that, waiting for her while she plucked out a few strands of her kidnapper's hair seemed a minor indulgence.

Now, as she led me through the forest toward the river, walking single file and fast, I listened to her explain that she was from an Amazon people called the Jivaros, but that her smaller tribal group was called the Shuar.

"My family would be very angry at me," she added, "if I did not exercise my right to *tsantsa,* or *untsuri suara.* Those men hurt me and my brother, so I killed them. But their spirit still remains in their hair. You would not allow me to take a head, so taking their hair is an acceptable alternative."

Back in her village, Keesha told me, she would use beeswax to attach the hair to gourds.

"In that way," she said, "I will still have taken their heads. When I marry, I will hang the gourds outside my door, and so continue to own my enemy's *muisak,* their avenging souls. My husband will show me greater respect because of it."

I told her, "That I don't doubt."

The guerrillas had crossed the river in what she called an *obada,* a large dugout canoe that looked to have been hollowed out using fire and an ax. It was pulled up on the bank, hidden among bushes.

"The sun will be above the trees in an hour or two," she said. "We must get as far down the river as we can. The dead men have friends only an hour's walk from here. A military camp. They will soon be looking for us. If they find us, they will shoot us."

I told her, "I need to get to a telephone. It's very important. Or a highway where I can flag down a car and get help. I have to hurry. Friends of mine, their lives depend on it."

"The soldiers control the only road. There are many of them. You can't help your friends if you are dead. We must go by river."

"Is there a telephone in your village?"

The slightest hint of a smile came into her voice. "If there were a telephone in my village, I would find a new village."

That morning, just after 6:30 a.m., the river was slowly transformed from water, to clay, and then molten wax. Then it became a tunnelway of brass streaked with golden mist. Overhead, the sky absorbed the river's incandescence and mirrored the gradual evolutions of color and light.

We were deep in a ravine of vine and leaf, two human specks riding a vein of silver. The forest walls were sheer as rock cliffs, matted with wildflowers and shadows, but hollow, alive inside.

I was in the front of the canoe because

the girl refused to let me take the stern, even though I insisted that I was very experienced in boats.

"All men say that they know boats," she told me. "I have been building and paddling *obadas* all my life. Can you make such a claim?"

She was a superb paddler, no denying that. No wasted effort, no unnecessary ruddering, and she could steer a straight line, too.

So I concentrated on paddling. Hard. For the first hour, we exchanged only a few words. With the aid of the river's steady current, we probably put seven or eight miles between us and the crash site.

Finally, Keesha stopped us, saying, "I have to make water."

I turned to see her standing nearly naked behind me, the blue skirt in her hand, brown thighs paler than her legs, the thin strip of pubic hair very dark. There was no shyness as she squatted over the side and urinated.

As she peed, she said, "If you need to make water, this is a good time."

So I stood, feet spread wide for balance, and did, feeling her eyes on me. There was no coyness in her. She was curious, wanted to look, and so she did. Unused to an audience, I took longer than usual to relax my bladder, and that seemed to amuse her.

As we resumed paddling, she became more talkative. The guerrillas, she said, captured her more than a month before. She'd been with her older brother, whom they shot, but she didn't know if he was dead or not, because he'd fallen into the river.

"He will be in my village," she said, "if he's alive. I hope he is there. I have seven brothers and sisters, but he is my favorite. His name is Bixa, though we call him Zarabatana, because of his skill at using a *pucuna*."

I said, "A *pucuna?*"

"What you call a blowgun. He is an excellent hunter."

Keesha told me that the guerrillas had used her as a slave, made her cook and clean for them, and also shared her body in bed. She'd tried to escape twice, but the guerrillas caught her and turned her over to black-beard for punishment. He'd beaten her as he raped her.

"I came to learn that it was his way," she said. "It was the only way he could perform as a man. He had me often, and so I was beaten many times."

"Not as a man," I corrected her. "That's not what men do."

"Perhaps. But it has created a problem I

did not anticipate, and caused me much fear. As soon as I get to a village, I must speak to the *curandeira,* the old woman who makes medicines."

I suspected what the girl's fear was — that she was now pregnant with black-beard's child. But I did not press.

I listened to her say, "I'm very glad that you shot him, but I wish he had lived so we could take him back to the village. The old women. Oh! They would have enjoyed punishing him. They have ways. They know many tricks."

I told her, "I understand now."

We paddled all morning and did not see another human being or any sign that humans had been on the river before us.

In daylight, the forest had a different sound. Birds were wild along the river-banks, chattering kingfishers, parrots, blue macaws, and screaming hawks. From the forest shadows also came a liquid, bell-like call — another type of bird, Keesha told me — and the grinding, chirping, cricket sound of toucans.

The electric hum and whine of insects were unceasing: cicadas and locusts and varieties of large wasps and bees that I'd never seen.

From deep in the forest and from the high sky canopy, monkeys used sound to impose themselves over other wilderness noises. Tribes of howler monkeys woofed and roared, communicating across the river. One tribe would scream as a group; a second and, sometimes, a third tribe would holler their reply. The tenor of their calls seemed territorial, combative. The rhythms were not unlike the drunken talk I'd heard among the guerrillas — men who now lay dead upriver.

The most spectacular thing I saw that morning, though, came tumbling toward us, following the course of the river as if the river's current were generating an opposing wind. It first appeared as a glittering, metallic blue haze in the far, far distance, a quarter-mile away.

I stopped paddling to watch. What kind of cloud was this?

As it swept closer, the cloud began to oscillate in terms of its height over the water. The way it moved and reflected sunlight reminded me of the spontaneous movement of baitfish in clear ocean.

Then the cloud was close enough for me to finally define what I was seeing. It was a mist of butterflies, their metallic blue wings shining like mirrors, many thousands of butterflies, rare morpho butterflies, as delicate as rice paper. As they passed over us, we were shadowed from the sun for several seconds, and I could feel the breeze their wings created.

To Keesha, I said, "That is amazing!"

She shrugged. "Why? It is something that happens here."

Later, as we saw a peccary charge into the water and watched a large cayman submerge in sync, Keesha said, "Food. We will soon need something to eat."

The distance we covered hour after hour increased as the speed of the river's current increased, and I knew that we were gradually ascending, moving downward through the forest, certainly toward some larger river, perhaps the Amazon.

Just as I asked questions of Keesha, she sometimes asked questions of me. Once she said, "The woman you seek. Amelia? Do you wish to keep her as a worker or take her as your wife?"

I hadn't thought about it, so I was surprised at the pleasure it gave me when I said, "As my wife, maybe. It's something to think about. I've never been married. Maybe it's time."

Later, Keesha said, "Someday, perhaps I

will find a man to marry. But there are so few of them with brains!"

She seemed perplexed by my laughter.

I'd become so accustomed to a world in which we were the only two existing humans, that I was a little surprised — and irrationally peeved — when we began to see other dugouts, men fishing with cast nets, women paddling canoes loaded with baskets of palm fronds, and even a couple canoes driven by small outboards.

"Are we near your village?"

The girl shook her head. "No, I would not live here. This is an evil place. We must go fast now. This is a place called Remate de Males, and a very bad man lives nearby. These people rely on him for their wealth."

"Will there be a telephone?"

I could sense that she didn't want to tell me the truth, but she could not do otherwise. "It is possible that there is a telephone."

"There's a village, then?"

She gestured with her chin. "Not so far. Two bends from here, where the *paranamirims* touch. The small rivers, that is our word for them."

Around the next bend, the river and the world were transformed.

One moment there was rain forest, the

next moment the hillsides became a muddy moonscape. A horizon of trees had been scalped off the bare hills, thousands of acres of forest had been clear-cut. Rain had dug gullies down the mountainsides. The earth was the color of Georgia clay here, so the erosion had turned the river a chalky, chemical orange.

To the girl, I said, "What's that smell?"

"Up the road from the village, there is a factory where they do something with the wood. I'm not sure what it is."

I said, "If there's a factory, then we'll find a phone."

The village of Remate de Males was the sort of South American slum that springs up on the perimeter of industry or around tourism centers. The workers have to live somewhere, and very cheap labor can afford only the cheapest of housing.

But this was no place for tourists. Remate de Males consisted of some heavy commercial docks — if there was a pulp factory nearby, boats would have to service it — a few plywood shacks, and dozens of huts made of bamboo, roofed with banana leaves.

Along the muddy bank were a half-dozen dugouts similar to ours. Keesha steered us in among them, and I pulled the boat up far enough so that it wouldn't drift away.

I asked, "Is there somewhere we can buy some food here? I'm starving."

She said, "Perhaps, but this is not a good place. It is an evil place. We must not stay long. Believe what I am saying to you."

"Keesha, I have to get to a phone. I'll be fine here. Take the boat, and keep going if you want. I'll understand."

"No. If I'm on the river alone, the soldiers might capture me again. I would rather die than let that happen."

I motioned to her with my hand — come on. "Then stay close to me."

From a woman cooking over a wood fire, I bought a loaf of flat bread, but she refused to sell a small can of beans she was heating.

"Money means very little," Keesha said, "when there is no food to buy. This village, these people, they stay because of the coins he gives them. I do not understand why."

Nor did I — though there was something I did understand. Something terrible had happened to the river here. The smell I'd noticed didn't come from some distant factory. It was the water itself.

I offered the bread to Keesha, then tore off a hunk myself, chewing slowly, troubled by something, but I wasn't certain what. Then I realized: There was no surface activity, no jump and slap of small fish, nor were there any wading birds. Why? I'd seen hundreds of egrets and herons upriver.

I watched an old man paddle his dugout to the bank and climb out with arthritic care. There was a handmade cast net in the bow of the boat, so I asked, "How was the fishing today?"

He shrugged. "Upriver, I took a few *cara-chama*, and an *acar*." He lifted the lid off a woven basket to show me the fish: One was long with a bony armor plating, the other two were a peculiar gray with large heads. "Downriver, though, it is dead. Even the *paranamirims* have been poisoned. There is nothing alive in the water there. A few turtles, perhaps. I've been told that a man must paddle several days, all the way to the big water before the river shows life again."

I asked, "Poisoned by what?"

He made a open-palmed gesture. "When I was a boy, we'd mash the roots of liana or a bush called *timbo*, and pour the milk in places of still water. All the fish would soon come to the surface, unable to breathe.

Perhaps someone has found all the *timbo* bushes in the world and boiled them." I helped him pull his canoe onto the bank as he asked, "Do you know something of fish?"

I said, "They are an interest of mine."

"Then you will find this unusual. Because the lower section of river has died, we're are now seeing for the first time many *botos* searching here for food. This far upriver, it is unusual. Our younger men have been hunting them with harpoons."

I said, *"Botos?"*

Keesha was eating her bread, listening. "They are hunting *botos?*" she sputtered. "Are they crazy? That will bring the worst kind of luck to you and all your people!"

The man ignored her, and wagged his finger at me. "Come. If you are a student of fish, I will show you."

Chapter Twenty-seven

The men of Remate de Males were hunting, harpooning, and butchering freshwater dolphins.

In a little circle created by bamboo huts, five Amazonian dolphins had been hung on a crossbeam wedged between two trees. Even after death, the animals were pink in color, bright as flamingos. They were hanging nose-down, tied by their tails. Gravity had engorged their heads with blood, so their small eyes bulged.

As children and women stood watching from the shade, three young men in ragged shorts took turns with a long, curved knife, gutting the animals and carrying the viscera off in buckets. They worked within a glittering ballroom of flies.

To the old man, I said, "This is a tragedy."

Misunderstanding my meaning, the old

man answered, "Yes. It is not a good thing. Only the man on the hill has ice. The flesh of these *botos* will soon rot, yet the women stand here, doing nothing! They should be constructing bamboo flats for salting. And a good fire for smoking the meat. But these young women, their brains have gone soft. They think only of owning a television set and living in the city."

Keesha glared at him but said nothing.

I asked permission of the three hunters before walking to the animals to get a closer look.

Supposedly, of the five freshwater species of dolphins in the world, the pink Amazon River dolphin, *Inia geoffrensis,* is the most intelligent. I say "supposedly" because the bottle-nosed dolphin has been so consistently imbued with compassionate, human qualities — even by biologists who should know better — that, these days, I doubt much of what I read about them.

But research on these rare, freshwater dolphins predated an unfortunate transition, for some, from science to wistful mysticism. Even early researchers described them as sensitive, intuitive mammals with a measurable brain capacity 40 percent larger than that of humans. At that time, they were considered to be one of the least threatened species of dolphins, though even then their numbers were small.

If desperate men were now hunting them for food, I doubted if the future of the species was still as certain.

I remembered reading that, because Amazon River dolphins had no known natural predators, they didn't need to live in large groups, or pods, for protection. As a result, they were solitary swimmers, though occasionally seen in small family groups of five or six.

These village hunters had managed to kill three females, a young male, and a very large, mature male that looked to be just over nine feet long and had to weigh at least two hundred pounds. There was no mistaking the sex. Death had freed the muscles that held their genitalia within their abdomens.

I touched my finger to the harpoon hole in back of the large male, then moved around the animal, noting the physiological differences between this freshwater animal and the dolphin I saw so often back on Sanibel Island.

He had a very long beak that was lined with tiny hairs, and small, almost piggish eyes — in water so murky, sight would not be so important. He had disproportionately large flippers, and a hump on his back instead of a fin. The pink color, I suspected, had something to do with the iron oxide color of the river.

To the hunters, I said, "Did you take them near here?"

"Yes! Very close. Only a few kilometers away."

"I've heard they are very intelligent. I'm surprised they let you get close enough to harpoon them."

One of the men stepped forward, very proud of himself. "Sir, you are correct in saying that they are the smartest of fish. But they are not so smart as *man*. I discovered a way!

"We found one of the *botos* in a narrow river, and used a net so that she could not escape. Are you familiar with the strange noise these animals make when they are hurt? We kept her wrapped in the net while she made these sounds. Soon, other *botos* appeared. Perhaps to rescue this female. It was easy, then, to use our harpoons." Laughing, he added, "Though it was not so easy to stay in our boats as they pulled us all over the river!"

Everyone in the circle of huts thought that was hilarious.

I opened the belly of one of the females,

using my hands to part the stomach panels as if opening a thin curtain. She had net burns on her delicate skin — this was the female who'd called for help.

They'd emptied everything out of her, but for one small oversight. There was a partially developed pup in her womb. I left the dead infant where it was, then knelt, and searched through the viscera. "Was there anything in their bellies?"

"One small catfish, nothing else. They were very hungry." The young hunter laughed and added, "Like our families. But not now. Tonight, we will have a feast!"

Keesha told me, "Do you believe me now? This is an evil place."

We were walking through the village, up a mud road. Among the huts, naked children played in banana thickets while scrawny dogs lay in pools of sunlight, cleaning themselves. We'd been told that a man who lived on the outskirts of the village was very rich and might have a cell phone we could use, so we were searching for him.

To Keesha, I said, "I don't know about evil, but it certainly isn't very attractive."

"No!" she said. "Evil! The *botos*, the pink ladies — they are sacred animals. How can you have lived and not know about them? At night, they grow hair and walk away from the Tefe River. They have magical powers — they're witches. They will punish this village. They'll destroy it. We must leave very soon!"

She was very agitated. Killing human beings didn't seem to bother her nearly so much. I told her, "I don't see much worth destroying. But, yeah, I'm with you. The sooner we get away from here, the better."

The wealthiest man in the village was a middle-aged Irishman with blood-bleary eyes who wore Birkenstock sandals, hiking shorts, a native shirt made of colorful patches, and a black beret over his long gray hair, which he wore tied in a ponytail.

Unlike the other shacks in the village, his house was made of unpainted concrete block and shingle, with a muddy yard protected by an out-of-place white picket fence. Parked out front, half in the road, was a new Toyota 4-Lux, a shortbed pickup truck papered with bumper stickers: *Vegetarians Are Delicious!*

To Become Master, Pose as a Servant.

Free Erin!

Life Is a Sexually Transmitted Disease.

He didn't open the door immediately

when I knocked. There was a blanket covering the house's main window. The blanket moved, and I saw a nose press against the glass. A few moments later, the door cracked opened an inch or two.

The Irish accent was unmistakable, even though he spoke in Spanish: "Who are you? Why are you here?"

Paranoia isn't paranoia if someone is really after you. This guy's voice had the sound of genuine fear.

I replied in English, "I need to use a phone. It's very important. I'll pay you, no problem."

The door cracked slightly wider, and I could see a wedge of his red Irish skin, and one dark eye. "Tell me who you are, what you're doing here. There're no gringos in this village. They don't belong."

I almost asked, Then what are you doing here?

Instead, I took refuge in an old, familiar lie. I explained to him that I was a marine biologist, here to do research on the rare Amazonian dolphin but that my boat had been stolen. Because I had friends in the village of Remanso, waiting on me, I had to contact them immediately.

I added, "If you drive me there, I'll pay you whatever you want. A couple hundred dollars? Three hundred? In American money. It's that important. Or let me use your phone. Please."

He looked at me, then looked at the heavy, plastic briefcase. "What'a you got in there?"

"Cameras, research equipment. A water-proof case is the only way to protect the stuff."

He thought for a moment, then nodded. "Wait here. I'll be out in a few minutes."

When he closed the door, I heard him lock it behind him.

I looked at Keesha. "You said there was an evil man in this village. Is that him?"

"No. He's a drunk. Could you not smell him? The evil man lives on top of the mountain. Up there."

I followed her gaze to the west. High above us, several miles away, atop the rain-scarred hillside, was what looked to be a clustering of big houses.

"He lives there," she said. "I have heard stories that people go into that house and never return. He's the one my people call the Bad Gift. He's an American — like you."

The Irishman came out carrying a beat-up Nokia cell telephone. "It's all charged up, but you can't get a signal here," he said. "I'll have to drive you to the top of the hill. Until we got all that goddamn jungle cut down, you couldn't even get a signal up there." He paused. "It's gonna cost you a hundred bucks, Yank. In advance."

As I paid him, Keesha said to me, "He's not going to take us to the big house on the hill? We must not let him take us there."

I looked at the Irishman, to see if he understood the question. He replied, "Take you to Tyner's place? You don't go looking for Curtis Tyner. He comes looking for you."

"He's an American?" I asked.

The Irishman replied, "He used to be. I'm not sure if he even knows anymore. Or cares."

When we were loaded in the pickup truck, Keesha between us, the Irishman lighted a cigarette, and told us his name was Niall, no surname offered. It reinforced the impression that he was afraid of something, on the run.

"How long have you lived here, Niall?"

"Too fucking long. This place is hell when it comes to civilized things, things we take for granted back in the world.

Women, though . . ." He swung his chin toward Keesha. "You can have all the girls you want, and as young as you want." As if she were not there, he added, "And a lot more comely than this one. She looks a little used up. The jungle girls. They don't flower for long. Give me another ten bucks, I'll find you two girls a hell of a lot prettier than this one."

We drove the rest of the way up the mountainside in silence, the back of the truck fishtailing on the slick orange clay. Once, the Irishman came very close to losing control completely, and we nearly slid over an embankment that would have dropped us several hundred feet into a gully.

The girl had reached for me involuntarily, her small hands tight on my arm, yet the stoic expression on her face did not change. Even when she said, "It is not so interesting as I thought it might be."

"What's that?" I asked her.

"Riding in an automobile. I thought it would be as interesting as paddling my *obada*. But it is not. It gives my stomach a sick feeling. Do people ever recover from this sickness?"

Thus I knew it was her first time in a car.

Several hundred feet above the village, near a ditch already overgrown with scrub bush and weeds, the Irishman braked to a stop. He handed the phone to me, and said, "Step out of the truck, you may have to move around a wee bit. But you should get a signal."

I walked away from the truck, taking a slip of paper from my billfold on which I'd written Harrington's number and a couple of others. The paper was sticky wet from being dumped in the river, though still readable.

But I never got a chance to finish dialing. As I straightened my glasses and began touching buttons on the phone, a half-dozen Latin-looking men, heavily armed and dressed in camo, stepped out of the bushes.

I stood there motionless, with no way to respond. I'd taken off my holster prior to entering the village, and I'd left the briefcase in the truck.

In Spanish, one of the guerrillas yelled, "If you move or try to run, we will kill you both!"

To my left, I heard the door of the Toyota slam shut, and I looked to see the Irishman drag Keesha out onto the ground as, in the far distance, a green Humvee sped toward us, kicking up a rooster tail of mud.

As I raised my hands above my head, I said to Niall, "You have me, there's no reason to hurt her."

In reply, the Irishman said to the guerrillas, "Search him while I see what the bastard's got in this case. Sergeant Tyner is on his way."

Chapter Twenty-eight

I'm not certain what I expected to see when the door of the Humvee opened, but it was not the astonishing figure that now approached me. Curtis Tyner — for it could have been no one else — was only slightly over five feet tall, and he had fire-bright red hair and bristling orange muttonchops of a type that I associate with Scottish bagpipers from a previous century. The hair of his beard was combed out away from his cheeks so that his face would have been orangutan-like in size and form but for the huge, waxed handlebar mustache that swept up toward his blue eyes.

Belted around his waist was a semiautomatic pistol and an attack/ survival knife in a leather scabbard. His tiger-striped camouflage tactical dress — pants the same as mine — were bloused perfectly into his jungle boots. He wore a black beret cocked low over his right eye, and carried a leather swagger stick, which he used to slap the palm of his left hand as he approached. The T-shirt he wore was dark blue with a bright-yellow inner layer. Golden letters over the left breast read:

British Royal Marines
Special Boat Service
M Squadron

Pinned on to the beret, I noticed, were a golden death's head, along with a dagger and wreath that may have been from the South African Special Forces Brigade. There was also a patch that read: 1st SFOD-Delta Force.

An eclectic and unlikely mix of associations.

Tyner stopped a few paces in front of me, looked into my eyes — a chilly look of appraisal and indifference — and said in Spanish as he continued to look into my face, "What did you find on him?"

Standing beside the truck, with Keesha on the ground at his feet, the Irishman spoke first. "He's got enough weaponry here to start his own fuckin' war. He's no bloody marine biologist, that much I promise you, Sergeant."

The guerrilla who had searched me walked through the mud with the papers and false passport he'd taken and handed them to Tyner.

Tyner was silent for a minute or two as he read through the papers, then he shoved them back toward the guerrilla.

"Your name is Marion North? Says here that an electronics corporation out of Virginia sent you down here to help us do a little housekeeping. That you're a retired commander, Navy Special Warfare. Is that true, Commander North?"

He was an American. The man's accent was rural Midwestern, pure farm country, and he communicated suspicion with the easy, breezy friendliness that I have heard many times before from people of that region. Sometimes you've got to follow your instincts and take a chance. My guess was that he'd been in Colombia long enough to know how the system worked, what papers were real and which were counterfeit.

It was not a good time to lie, but maybe not a good time to tell the truth, either. So I said, "It wouldn't make a lot of sense, them sending me into your territory, would it?"

"Exactly my point. And make no mistake Commander — if you really are a naval officer — this *is* my territory. I worked my ass off taking it — and *keeping* it. In the old days, they had a name for people like you — claim jumper. Or maybe spy. Who knows." He smiled at me, but his eyes glazed slightly as he added, "Either way, they executed them. Tradition! I'm a stickler for tradition. So tell me why you're really here. The truth. You've only got one chance, and I don't much care either way. For starters, are you here looking for me?"

I said, "No, I'm looking for two men. A Samoan named Stallings, and an albino named Kazan."

The little sergeant nodded. "One of those names is vaguely familiar. And why have you come to my territory looking for these two gentleman?"

I looked at Keesha, who was still on the ground, afraid to move. I thought for a moment before I said, "Tell that Irish Republican Army piece of shit to get away from the girl, then tell your men to leave us in private. They don't need to hear what I have to say. You have my word, Sergeant. I'll tell you the truth. But it's classified."

For some reason, Tyner found that funny. He looked at the Irishman. "You can't fault his ability to judge character, McCauley! And right he is!"

516

Still laughing, Tyner said to me, "The cowardly bastard, McCauley, blew up a bunch of civilians with a bomb. So he's scurried off to the jungle to hide. Hates it here. Always worried about snakes and diseases, and someone like me coming along and cashing him in. He's got a hundred-thousand-dollar bounty on his head, so he's paying me off a little at a time. Information, snitch work — grunt stuff that a man with any character couldn't stomach. Still got a long way to go, don't you, McCauley?"

Tyner pushed me toward the Humvee, waving for Keesha to follow, while behind us, the Irishman yelled, "I gave you two of them, Sergeant. No matter what you do with 'em, you still have to give me credit for both. That's our deal. *Two* heads, Sergeant. I want it applied to my debt!"

Standing at the rear of the Humvee, aware that, from a distance, his men had their weapons trained on me, I told Tyner the whole story.

The real reason for me being there was no threat to his own strange operation, so I risked nothing in telling him the truth. The only details I omitted were which people and agencies had helped me.

When I was finished, he asked a few questions about my life in Florida, a little bit about my lab. He wanted to confirm that I really was a marine biologist come in search of friends. He took pains to be certain of that. Judging from the articulate questions he asked, he, in fact, seemed to have a pretty good general knowledge of natural science.

Living on an eroding mountainside above a dying river, that surprised me. I'm not sure why.

Then he said, "So you're really *not* a commander with Navy Special Warfare?"

I shook my head slowly. "No."

"But your name *is* Marion North."

"Nope, that's a cover, too. It's Ford. Marion D. Ford."

"Marion D. Ford, huh?" He nodded, thinking about that, looking up at me through the framework of his orange mustache, blue eyes glittering. "So why'd the CIA geeks agree to set you up? Help you find your pals? I took one look at your papers, and I knew who'd made them. You wouldn't be the first they sent out to check on me."

I said carefully, "I can't and won't confirm that it was a specific agency. In the past, I did some work for the State Department. Foreign-service variety. Not directly for any agency; sort of a contract thing. But some people in high places owed me favors. My friends who've been kidnapped are important to me. I pressed until certain people agreed to help."

He slapped the swagger stick into his palm. "Okay, that's just vague enough to be the truth. I believe you, Ford. Copacetic. Everything is copacetic. You look like you could use some food and some sleep. But . . ." He looked toward the men covering us, and gave a hand signal — they could relax and go about their business. "But first things first. You say you left five bodies upriver? Let's go to headquarters, I'll get out a topographical map. I want you to show me exactly where. The Colombian government will be searching for that chopper, and my men need to get to the bodies before they do. That's money in my pocket."

I said, "What do you mean?"

He seemed surprised by the question. "The dead guerrillas, that's what I mean. I'll collect the bounty for them. It's what I *do* here. Business comes first, understand. I'll give you a percentage, if you want, but not much. Or maybe I'll pay you back by helping you out with your problem. Either way, you and the Indio girl may have done the killing, but I'm the one with the contract, all the permits. Without me, you could kill a thousand of the bastards, and you wouldn't get a cent. Consider me generous just to include you, Dr. Ford. I don't have to do a damn . . . do a damn . . ."

Tyner then paused, as if surprised by something, allowing the sentence to trail off before saying very softly, almost as if speaking to himself: "Dr. Ford? Marion *Ford*. Marion *D*. Ford."

He said it as if struggling to remember some lost bit of data.

Then he looked up at me, eyes wide, his face an illustration of what might have been shock, as he whispered, "My God! You're him. Dr. *Marion* Ford. I *knew* about you. You're one of the Negotiators!"

I was so surprised by his reaction that I couldn't speak for a moment, but then in a flat voice, I finally replied, "I have no idea what you're talking about."

He slapped the swagger stick into his palm again. "I'm *right*. I know I'm right. You're one of about ten guys with the W designation. You *are* him. I can see it in your face. Jesus Christ, man, you're one of my heroes! What you did in Cuba, your work in Cambodia, it's legendary. The way you took out the Soviet attaché in Managua, the way you set him up — 'Let's go spearfishing, comrade' — it was a masterwork. A piece of art. And that anarchist professor who disappeared from the bar in Aspen. Hell, man, I know a lot about you. I've *studied* your work."

In the same flat tone, I said, "Sorry. Mistaken identity. You're confusing me with someone else."

"Hey, Ford, you can *trust* me. A couple years back, a guy named Heller — you trained together, according to him. He was here, doing the same kind'a work I do. Blaine Heller. An amazing man. He told me if anything happened to him, I should destroy all his files. He bought it in a chopper crash, so I burned all his papers. But I read them first — hell, who wouldn't? That's how I know about you."

I waited but said nothing. Blaine Heller had been a good, good man. An intelligent, perceptive man who loved literature and fine art. What could have possibly driven him to come to this dark place?

Tyner stopped talking, grinned, and slapped his knee with the swagger stick, then thrust out his right hand to me. "Curtis Tyner, U.S. Army, Green Berets and Delta Force at your service, Dr. Ford!

This is an honor. Damn *glad* to meet you."

He began waving me toward the Humvee. "Come. I'll radio ahead, have my staff lay out some food for you. I've got a couple prime Kobe steaks from Japan I've been saving. Anything you want. Finally, I meet a man who's truly going to appreciate what I've done here. My place — it's a . . . well, hell, it's a warrior's palace." The little sergeant made an open-handed gesture of delight. "We have so much in common, you're not going to *believe* it."

Tyner didn't live in a house, he lived in a castle fortress. It was built on a mountaintop, at the end of a long series of muddy switchbacks, constructed of rebar and concrete, dug into the bare hillside like a sprawling bunker, a low-profile mansion built for luxury, comfort, and defense.

The complex had a half-dozen or more thick-walled outbuildings, some set far from the house — munitions warehouses, possibly — the entire compound consisted of at least ten acres, all of it contained by high, iron fencing — electrified, it looked to be — with a ribbon of concertina wire around the top.

As the driver steered us through the gate, onto the grounds, Tyner chattered away about the years of work it'd taken to get his complex properly built. How difficult it was to get good help out in the jungle. Told me about his redundant systems for generating electricity, potable water, communications, waste treatment, and the improvements he'd made to guarantee easy transportation by land, river, and air.

"The danger of living in the jungle," he said, "is that the goddamn thing never quits. It's always out there, pressing in. Stand too long in one place and the vines will grow up your legs, around your neck, and strangle you. The humidity seeps in and turns everything metal into rust" — he snapped his fingers — "that quick. If you don't fight it every single day, it'll swallow you alive. But why am I telling you? You *know* that."

When Ron Iossi of the CIA told me there were some retired special ops guys out in the jungle getting rich, he was accurately describing Curtis Tyner. The man had all the imported toys: satellite dishes, cellular communications mini-tower, new pickup trucks, ATVs, skeet range, three-hole golf course, a massive garden patio with built-in barbecue grill and wet bar, and a competition-sized lap pool with a three-meter diving board. On the bottom of the pool, in golden tiles visible through the chlorinated water was a Latin motto: *Vae Victis.*

When I asked about it, he translated, "*Woe to the conquered.* I'm surprised you don't know it. It's an old military expression. Dates back to Roman times."

I told him, "Military history was never a main interest of mine."

The man had an affection for maxims. Over the double doors that were the main entrance to the house, chiseled into the cement were the words: *By Way of Deception, Do We Make War* — that phrase, at least, I knew. Carved into the mantel over a wall-sized fireplace of raw stone was more Latin: *Mors ad Barbarii.*

This one, I didn't bother asking about.

Inside, the place was furnished as impersonally as a model home. It was as if he didn't live there. The building was a trophy — a thing to be shown, not used. The entrance hall was draped and carpeted, two stories high, and the dining room table was beautifully made, some kind of exotic black wood, and long enough to seat twenty or more beneath crystal chandeliers.

When I asked, "Do you get a lot of guests out here?"

Tyner replied. "Not yet. But I will. I've been making a few friends. I know a family in Bogotá that I like a lot. There's a priest there that I sometimes play golf with. But it's tough out here. Socially speaking, I mean. You don't want to associate with the locals too much. It undermines respect — I'm sure you understand what I mean."

I thought to myself: *This man's insane.* But I said, "Sure. In a place like this, a little distance is healthy."

Each time I reminded him that I was in a rush, that I had a deadline if I wanted to save my friends, Tyner made a dismissing motion with his hands as if it were a minor problem, as if all my worries were over.

Once, he said, "Remanso? I own a piece of a Bell helicopter. I'll call my pilot, have him pick us up. We can be there in an hour. There are two ways we can work it. We can pay the ransom in cash, make sure your friends are secure, then kill the bad guys. Or we can lure the bad guys out and do it surgically. That might be the most interesting way to approach it. As a classic problem — hostage rescue."

When I replied, "I don't have that much cash, so the ransom option won't work," Tyner seemed pleased that I'd opened the door to the subject.

"I've got cash, all you need," he said. "You won't believe how much money there's to be made down here. After you eat, get some sleep, I'll explain to you how it works. The way we could do it is, I lend you the cash. You give it to the turban — Kazan, you called him? — he gets the cash when your friends are safe. Then we pop him and as many bad guys as we can, get my cash back *plus* collect the bounty on the heads. See? We actually make a very sizeable profit. Outstanding! Something like this, I think of as an *investment,* man."

Another time, he said, "I don't know why you're so dead set on involving the Colombian government in this, or calling your friends at the State Department. You really think those idiot *Anfibios* can do a better job than us? Think about it. This is a chance for the two of us to finally work together. You and me!"

Tyner had a staff of a couple dozen or so people, most of them teenage Latino girls, and a few stoic Indio men. "See a girl you like?" he told me. "Let me know, and she's yours. The reason you need to talk to me is, I've got a personal relationship with three of them. All Castilian, all from Cali — where the prettiest women in the Americas come from. Other than those three, the choice is yours. But some things, a man won't share, *right?*"

He assigned a girl to me, then one to Keesha, too, though he was visibly disappointed that I was taking a personal interest in Keesha's well-being.

"Indio girls, man. The jungle's thick with them. They breed in the bushes like rabbits, drop babies like it's nothing. I don't see why you'd waste your time."

I told him, "This one may have saved my life. I kind of like her."

From Tyner's house on the mountaintop, I could look out the window of our guest suite and see a horizon of cloud forest, the black tree canopy silent, cavernous beneath a layer of white mist. It was a swollen presence, meticulous photosynthesis in relentless slow motion. Connected as they were, the forest and the eroding strip of mountainside, the yellow earth seemed an indecency, bare as private flesh, an exposure that needed covering. It drained into the only section of river that I could see, changing the water's color to a bloody orange.

The two servant girls — there was nothing else to call them — led Keesha and me into the suite, and showed us the full refrigerator, the closets of generic clothing, and a massive sunken marble bathtub. When I told them that Keesha would need her own room, the Indio girl grabbed my arm, squeezing, and shook her head. "I stay with you. Not alone. Not for a moment. In this place, we will be always together."

I could see that she was very frightened, and I didn't blame her. Houses, even some buildings, have a feel to them. Tomlinson would be able to explain it more completely, but it's true. Perhaps my impressions were colored by my subconscious assessment of Tyner's employees — they never made eye contact, and they spoke in whispers — but this house had a dark feel to it, a kind of chilly dread. Even as solidly built as it was, it did not seem a thing of permanence in this vast place.

One servant girl brought us a stack of sandwiches — ham and cheese, and rare roast beef with onions. The other filled the sunken tub with hot water and bubbles.

Standing in the doorway of the huge bathroom, Keesha looked at the tub and said uneasily, "What form of soup is it that she is making?"

When I told her it was a place for

bathing, Keesha thought about that for a moment, then nodded as if pleased — as if the bath were a good opportunity. Without commenting to me, she then told the servant girl to bring one of the Indio men to her immediately — a woman right at home giving orders.

Keesha's conversation with the man was in a tribal language I didn't understand, and very brief.

When I asked her about it, she said, "I asked him for the leaves and the root from a *lehuenka* plant. In this room's cooking place, I can make a strong tea of it. I'll drink it, then sweat myself in this tub of bubbles. It must be done soon, very soon, and you'll be here to help."

"Help do what?" I asked.

The girl walked to the stove, looking at it, scrutinizing the knobs, not sure how to use it. "I've missed my cycle by nearly seven days. The soldiers who raped me. One of them, I think he now lives inside my body."

Chapter Twenty-nine

I got a pot of water boiling, then went to the bathroom, stripped, and sat myself neck-deep in the tub.

It was now noon. I'd had no sleep for more than thirty hours, and I was physically and emotionally exhausted. I made a little pillow of a towel, and lay my head back.

When I closed my eyes, Amelia was there. Amelia with the copper hair and wildly green eyes. Amelia with the good laugh, and comfortable, communal silence. The tall woman with the vixen smile, whose hands and body had so quickly learned the likes and wants of my own.

I told myself that she was out there, somewhere, getting closer to me each and every minute, and I sent out a private and personal message to her, *Please be safe, my friend. Please be safe.*

Prior to our leaving for Colombia, nearly midnight and unable to sleep, I'd idled my skiff over to where the *No Mas* sat at calm anchor, lighted portholes creating golden paths on the waters of Dinkin's Bay. There I'd found Tomlinson sitting naked on the bow, a single candle stuck into his ear, lighted and flame flickering.

Because the candle was hollow, he explained, specially made for one's ears, it channeled heat into his auditory canal, warmed the back of his eyes, and also the lower, more primitive portions of his brain.

He'd said to me, "What I'm attempting is what the Hindus call *Klartraum*. I know you often doubt my rationality, old friend, but you have never doubted my honesty. Astroprojection. Soul travel, psychic navigation. That's what I've been doing nearly every evening since the sixth day of our search for Janet. Sometimes I find her. I can see her. I know *exactly* how she felt, what she said."

He added that there were five forms of soul travel: imaginative projection and trances were two that I still remembered. Something else he'd said also stuck with me: "The ashes of the average cremated person weigh nine pounds. The volume of the Earth's moon is precisely the same as the volume of the Pacific Ocean."

When I told him that I failed to see the connection, he nodded, very pleased with himself. "Exactly. Specialization is for *insects*."

Which made even less sense, though now the prospect of soul travel — as ridiculous as it was — seemed an appealing thing to try. So, as I lay in the hot water, I tried to imagine some inner sensibility soaring out of my body, over the horizon of rain forest to where, finally, I found my girl.

I watched as I touched my ghostly hand to Amelia's soft face, wanting desperately to draw all the fear and pain out of her, and then whispered my thoughts into her ear. *I'm coming for you. Hold on. I'll be there.*

Keesha said, "American man? Can you hear me?"

I'd fallen asleep in the tub. The water had been nearly too hot to endure. Now it was barely warm.

I looked at my watch. I'd been in there asleep for almost two hours.

Something was wrong with the girl. Her face was very pale, and she was not only trembling but also sweating.

"I made the tea from the *lehuenka* plant,"

she explained. "I chewed the root, just as the old women told us as girls to do if a stranger plants a creature in our bellies. Now I must sweat myself in this hot tub. I will need help. Will you help me?"

I pulled the plug, stood, and found my glasses, then found a towel. "Of course," I said. "I'll do whatever you want me to do. But my advice is let's get you to a doctor. You're in pain, this could be serious."

Keesha shook her head — no. No modern doctors — as she said, "I didn't know the tea would hurt my bowels so much. Perhaps the sweating will help."

I said, "I wish you could have waited a few days."

"Ten or twelve days past a woman's cycle, the tea no longer works. It may not work now. You saw the man who created the creature. Would you choose to carry it to birth?"

I answered, "You've got a point."

I refilled the tub with steaming water. As I did, the girl pulled the ornate blouse over her head, shed the cotton skirt, and stood naked, shivering, arms crossed over brown, heavy breasts. She was heavy-hipped, short-legged, and her nipples and aureoles, I noted, were an unusual clay-like shade of red.

As she lowered herself into the tub, she said, "It would be better if we had a sweat hut. Then I could lay back while you poured water on the rocks for heat. The *paje* would come and give me the juice of *murure* bark to purify my blood, and the women would massage my body to loosen the creature inside me, and let it know that it is not wanted.

"If the creature still refused to leave, the *paje,* or another man of my choice could then enter me, and deposit his seed. In that way, the creature would be replaced by a child of my own wanting."

I cleared my throat, uneasy with the direction the conversation was headed. "There's some herbal tea in the kitchen. I can make tea for you, or get you something cold, with ice."

The girl said she'd like something hot to drink, and some honey, too, if I could find it. Then she added, "When you come back, it will be necessary for you to rub my belly and make the creature move."

I sat naked in the tub behind the girl, her head and hair comfortable on my shoulder, her eyes closed, no pain now showing on her face, as my fingers kneaded her stomach and abdomen, and then lower on her body, too, the tendoned areas between her thighs.

She'd shown me exactly what she wanted me to do. Insisted on the familiarity. "Beginning at my shoulders, first the front, then the back, you must gently stroke downward, pushing everything in my body toward the place where a woman is open to the earth. Over and over, you must do this."

I massaged her for an hour. Longer, perhaps. There was no hint of sexuality between us, no escalating passion, despite what my hands were doing, the private place where my fingers touched.

She was sick, in trouble, in need of help. I felt a closeness to her, a very real intimacy, but no more.

Once, her eyes still closed, she reached beneath the water and encircled my penis with her hand. Holding me, she said, "If you wish, I can make you ready, and you may enter me. You have done much to help, and it would be good to replace the creature with your child."

I kissed the top of her head. "No, Keesha. I'm flattered, but no."

"Are you certain? In just this short time, your male part has told my hands that it would soon be ready." She squeezed me for emphasis.

I lifted her hand away. "Are you feeling better?"

"Yes."

"Do you think the medicine worked?"

"Not yet, but it may."

I pulled her body closer to mine. "Lay back. Try to sleep."

When I awoke, the water had once again turned cool. Even so, Keesha didn't want to get out.

She seemed in a sort of mild stupor, as if the drug she'd taken had made her slightly drunk. I got her out of the tub, rubbed her dry, then steered her into the bedroom, and tucked her in, naked, beneath the sheets.

I checked my watch: 3:15 p.m.

I dressed myself in the same clothes I'd been wearing, then went out the door of our suite, into the hallway of the main houses. My jungle boots echoed on the tile floors. There was no other sound. The place seemed deserted, silent as a crypt.

As I passed the dining room, I noticed that only two places were set: very fine-looking china and silver, and green cloth napkins. If Tyner was expecting to eat with me, why hadn't they set a place for Keesha?

I continued walking but then stopped: a telephone. There was a black cordless telephone atop the drink trolley.

I stepped into the room, looked around — no one there — then took the phone, pleased to hear a dial tone. I still had Harrington's number in my pocket, and I looked at it as I dialed. I heard two rings, and when a man's voice answered, I said quickly, almost whispering, "Hal. It's Doc. Our chopper was shot down, the crew's dead, and I need a pickup ASAP. I need help."

Then I listened to a man who was definitely not Hal Harrington reply, "We don't need help, Commander. I thought I had you convinced. We can do it ourselves with just a small team. Small risk and big profit — stay where you are. I'll take you to the war room and I'll show you."

A minute later, Curtis Tyner was standing there, grinning at me and wagging his finger — naughty, naughty for trying to call out — and he said, "Follow me. We'll take a look at some topo maps and discuss our strategy. After that" — he paused, looking at me as if assessing my worthiness — "after that," he continued slowly, "I think I'll take you down into the armory — the Vault, I call it — and show you something. It's something I've shown only to a couple of other white men. Ever. My collection. Not many would understand. I think you might. It's quite a thing to see."

"You collect weaponry?" I asked, feeling oddly uneasy, not certain I wanted an answer or to see what it was that Tyner collected.

"Oh, of course. Lots and lots of weaponry from all over the world. Fighting. It's my business, understand. One of my businesses, anyway. But I have other things, too. Unusual things that you may appreciate."

As we walked, Tyner told me, "To kill one of those jungle girls, you'd have to cut her heart out and put it in the freezer. Leave it there for at least an hour. The men aren't so bad. A mild case of the flu will do them in. But you can't hurt those Indio women. They're savages."

I'd told him about Keesha's condition and asked about getting her some medical attention. Where were the closest facilities?

I should have known what his response would be. Tyner had already made it clear that he considered the rain forest his enemy. As an enemy, he'd done an effective job of redefining it as inconsequential, and so also dehumanized the society which the forest had created.

"Commander, if you want a girl, we'll fly to Cali. You can pick out seven — any age you want — and bring them back here. One for every day of the week. The best thing you can do for the Indian girl is let her go back to her tribe."

It was a second negative reaction to a second request. The first had been no less reasonable, I thought: Why not contact my friends at the U.S. Embassy and at least tell them what we had planned? If we failed, who was there to back us up? I explained to him, "The people involved are very important to me. We need a second team. Just in case."

It infuriated me that he wouldn't even consider it, and I found his reasons revolting, though I couldn't let him know how I felt. So I listened stoically, as he said, "If we get the governments involved, the U.S. government, Colombian government — it doesn't matter. There are going to be rules. Heads counted, reports filed. Don't you understand? That's why they hire people like me to come here in the first place. I provide a necessary service.

"The bad guys don't play by the rules, so

the government types need a buffer. Someone to keep civilized people from getting strangled by their own stupid laws. Hell, Commander, they don't want to know what I do, just so long as I get it done. Lying to them is part of the deal. They expect it."

A few minutes later, he tried to reinforce his point. "The team we're taking is the best that money can buy, so money is the key word here. My men, that's all I care about. I trained them myself. They're like my own children. If we ask your pals to join us, we're not asking for military backup. We're inviting witnesses."

Chapter Thirty

Tyner's study consisted of a single upper-story room, with a massive wall of glass so thick that I knew it had to be bulletproof. It looked out onto the same horizon of rain forest as from the suite in which Keesha now slept, but from an elevated aspect.

The walls were lined with books, decorated with coats of arms and medieval weaponry. There was a giant-screen television and several computers.

"I built the cellular tower so I can have Internet access," he told me. "A couple of the guys out here have it, guys who do what I do." He chuckled. "Not as well, of course. But they've had the same mini-towers built. We stay in touch, send instant messages — I've got a bunch of e-mail friends back in the States who believe I teach high school in Iowa. Davenport — grew up there, love the place. Mostly, though, my colleagues and I trade intelligence. Kind of our own profit-sharing plan."

Which was how, he said, that he happened to have a low-altitude aerial photograph of the compound where, hopefully, Amelia, Janet, and the others were being held.

Davenport — I remembered receiving an order from a high school there. It now seemed a decade ago.

He sat at the computer, and I stared over his shoulder, as he said, "The photo's a couple years old, but the place can't have changed that much. It's an old rubber plantation estate. French people owned it for years, then the drug people bought them out."

I was looking at the roof of what seemed to be a very large hacienda, built around a courtyard and fountain, the entire estate enclosed by a high stone wall.

Tyner continued, "When the drug cartel went out of business, a corporation based in Saudi Arabia bought the place. They still do the raw rubber thing, plus they raise bees. My sources tell me they keep a fairly good-sized security team there — that's not unusual for private businesses out in the jungle, by the way. Hired guns are cheap, and that's what it takes to survive.

"So, yeah. It makes sense. The whole thing's probably a screen for some kind of drug operation, plus they dabble in a little kidnapping on the side. Cash business. Saudi Arabians? That's got terrorist cell written all over it."

Tyner twisted the waxed ends of his mustache, studying the photo, and smiling. "I'm going to enjoy this one, Commander. These days, the turbans bring a pretty good price, plus they're packrats when it comes to money. They keep a lot of cash on hand because the U.S. government has gotten very good at freezing their bank accounts. I ran 'em out of my area. They despise me. You know why?"

I said, "I could guess at a number of reasons."

"But you'd never get it. The reason they despise me is, when I go after one of them, two of them — a dozen, it doesn't matter — I have my men rub bacon grease on their rounds."

"Why? Infection?"

"Their religion, Commander. For a devout Islamic, pig meat is considered unholy, an abomination before God. Put pig grease in them, you not only kill the body, you condemn their soul to hell. They don't like that.

"Something else? Couple years back, some bigshot turban fundamentalist tried to start an organization in my territory. He and his group were from a Colombian city called Maicao. Cocaine, I believe it was. We used the greased rounds on his men, but we did something special with the bigshot. Every little farmer in the jungle keeps a couple of feral hogs. A wild pig'll eat anything dead, and most things alive if it's been wounded. The turban had already been shot in the thigh, had his leg broken. So my guys put a couple of more rounds in his knees, and flipped him into the pen."

His smile broadened. "Psy-War-Ops. Something like that, word gets around fast. Most of the turbans in this country, the fanatics, they live in Maicao. In that town, anyway, they know my name and my territory. People like that, they stay away from someone like me because they understand me. So this is a rare one for me. This one's got the smell of money. Yes, sir, outstanding!"

Tyner told me we would leave for Remanso by helicopter at 1 a.m. That way, he said, I could get some sleep, make sure I was rested.

"Down south, they're still farmer-types, so you don't want to attack too close to dawn, but they also like to stay up drinking *aguadiente,* so you don't want to attack too close to midnight, either. This whole country, it's a balancing act."

He'd sent his men ahead in a tight convoy consisting of two Humvees and an armored personnel carrier. We'd be in radio contact, but he'd already briefed them on the plan of attack.

A helicopter? Humvees and armored cars? I looked at the hundreds of books on the office shelves, at the careful crafting of the wood, at the expensive, imported furniture, his executive's desk, at the carvings and sculpture and the thick Persian carpet before I said, "Did you really get this rich killing people?"

I could see that the question irked him. Like many small, driven men, Tyner had small, nervous mannerisms. One was twisting the tips of his handlebar mustache. Another was an unconscious motion as if he were washing his hands over and over — a Freudian mannerism that could have meant something, or could have meant nothing.

"You sound as if you disapprove. Hah! Coming from you — of *all* people — that's almost funny."

I said, "I'm not making judgments, Sergeant. I'm just curious."

"In that case, I'll answer your question. Come here and take a look at this map of Colombia. See the middle section highlighted in red? It's the size of a large state. The idiots in the government here gave all that land to FARC, the guerrillas. That's like siege victims throwing ransom over the walls.

"FARC's region, it's got everything: timber, minerals, good farmland, and a potential for oil. If the bastards were smart, had some initiative, they'd have their own thriving little country going by now."

Tyner turned to look at me, still irritated. "But they aren't smart. And they're lazy. Instead of working, getting rich, they keep asking for more, more. They don't want political change, they want bribes. They want a free ride. See where I'm going with this, Commander?"

I said, "Sorry to be dense but, nope, not a clue."

He returned his attention to the map and pointed to a section southeast of the FARC area. It was highlighted in blue, not as large, but still sizeable. "This," he said, "is the territory I control. I've worked my ass off here for ten years, and every year the government gives me a little more for a very simple reason: I'm better at doing the things they don't have the stomach or the brains to do. I make them look good. And I make it safer. That's the main reason they don't hassle me, and why I'm making lots of money."

I said, "They pay you a bounty for the guerrillas you kill. I know that. But it can't be that much. Not enough to run the operation you have here."

He was smiling, proud of himself, once again twisting the ends of his mustache as he answered, "See? You're a smart man. Bounty-hunting, that's small time. Quick cash, but no future. I realized that from the start. So I'm going to tell you the truth. I haven't shared this with many others. What I've done is start several ancillary companies. As a group, I've incorporated nationally and international. A little thing called Backyard Enterprises. Can you figure out why?"

I risked angering him further by saying, "No. Back Door Enterprises, that'd make sense. But not Backyard. Where's the name come from?"

"Think about it. How often do you hear people say it in the States? People need oil, but they won't let the oil companies drill. They get hysterical — not in our backyard, they can't. People create waste, all kinds of waste: petroleum and plastic and —" He nodded as if he could see me catching on. "And they create nuclear waste, too. A major nuclear plant creates only about a dump truck full of spent rods a year. Hell, the French, of all people, have proven how damn safe it is — but same thing. People go ape-shit. Safe or not, no matter how much it's regulated, no one's going to let it be dumped. Not in their backyard."

Sergeant Tyner gestured grandly toward the bulletproof glass and the jungle vista beyond. "So welcome to my backyard. No regulations, no rules, no controls. The world needs lumber? I've got it. A dumping ground? I've got that, too." His voice lowered slightly, as if he were about to share a valuable secret with me. "Have you ever noticed, Commander, that the more sophisticated a society becomes, the more adolescent it behaves? Back in the States, they want all of the benefits but refuse the responsibilities. Let's face it, most people are sheep. And they're cowards, too."

Now the little man reached out and tapped his index finger on my chest, an intentional invasion. "You know why they're cowards? Because they know the truth, but they won't allow themselves to admit it. You know the truth. I know the truth. What we've done, our lives, our actions prove it. But the common person — they can't handle it. It terrifies them."

I looked at his finger until he took his hand away, and then I said, "The truth about what?"

Blue eyes glittering, Tyner used his head to indicate the doorway. "Follow me. You'll understand. I'll show you. You're one of the few."

Down two flights of stairs, dug deep into the hillside, walled with thick cement and barred by double sets of locked, fireproof doors, was Sgt. Curtis Tyner's armory — the Vault.

I followed him out of some perverse desire to prove he was wrong but felt a strange sense of unreality. He kept saying over and over that he and I had much in common, that we were alike in many ways. Even to myself, I could not prove how wrong he was until I had seen it all, whatever it was. It was the only way to prove

549

that I was right, at least, in my hope that we could not have been more different.

But if I were so certain, why did I feel such overwhelming dread?

He used three different keys to unlock the metal doors, and when the doors swung open, he reached into the darkness, touched a switch, and an apartment-sized room was illuminated with sterile neon. I'd expected some fashion of survivalist bunker — a safe place to sit out WW III — but, instead, I stepped into a precisely maintained little arsenal. The walls were lined with professional-quality gun lockers; the stainless-steel bench tables were as neatly kept as those in my own lab.

Tyner began opening lockers, handing me equipment: an Autovon voice-activated radio, with headset ("Tonight, we'll have to be in close radio contact"), Generation 5 night-vision goggles ("My team owns the night — it's our biggest advantage"), and several choices of body armor, or bullet-proof vests.

I accepted it all without comment, certain that he was creating a little mote of time, a period of linear decompression, before showing to me whatever it was he wanted me to see.

Perhaps it was to get a more pure reaction. There may have been something in my face he expected to read. Whatever the reason, I was right.

When I had all the gear piled in my arms, I said, "Well, I better get back and check on how Keesha's doing. And get some sleep."

He held up two index fingers — twin exclamation points — and replied, "Not yet. There's one more thing you need to see. My *collection*. Did you forget? It's why we're here."

On the far wall was the biggest of all the brown metal gun lockers, and he used another set of keys to open the double doors. Inside, on shelf after shelf, row after row, were what looked to be small glass aquariums but were probably terrariums because I didn't smell the familiar ozone odor that I knew so well.

Instead, the open lockers filled the room with an unusual leathery, musty smell, a slightly acrid air.

When Tyner touched another light switch, I saw why.

Inside the locker, inside the glass housings, were rows of tiny, shrunken, human heads. Dozens. A hundred. Probably more. All males, and every race represented. Each head was isolated, individualized, by its own thin, glass boundary. Eyes and lips sewn shut, the miniature faces were frozen in various expressions of horror or pain, but all shared a dumb look of final, abject submission.

As I stood, feeling the shallowness of my own breathing, surprised by my own calm, Tyner said, "That Indian girl you're with. Did you see the black tattoos on her ankles? She's from farther south in the Amazon. I know her tribe well. She's a Jivaro."

He smiled. "Her people are the ones who do this for me. Headhunters. The shrinking of human heads — it's their most devout expression of art. The ones who avoid contact with us, they're the ones who do it because they love it. Your girlfriend — she's almost certainly eaten human flesh. Still think she's worth the price of a doctor?"

I swallowed, trying hard to keep my expression indifferent, to show him nothing, allow him no private insights into my reaction — it would have seemed a violation of my person — as I replied, "Is there a difference between the craftsman and the collector?"

He laughed, and waved me closer.

"Touché! You're right, I'll accept that. Point well made." He paused before he added: "From one craftsman to another."

I listened to him tell me about some of his trophies. He had the swagger stick again and was using it as a pointer. I listened to his concise description of individual hunts as they related to a specific head. He had an expert, almost scientific, approach when describing the final shot that felled each.

He touched the swagger stick to a case that contained a tiny head with a face the size and color of a very small, angry mandrill, but it wore a disproportionately long, squarish beard. The head was mounted on a pillow-sized purple turban and over a white conical *kalansuwa,* both of which looked to be stained by blood.

"This is the guy I was telling you about, the one who tried to get into the cocaine business in my territory, but ended up back on the farm, feeding livestock. His name was Rashid, Rashad . . . something like that. I knew I wanted to take him alive, and when my spotter first found him in the scope, we were half a mile away.

"I was using a HK Weapon System, a PSG-1 on a kind of lark because, as you know, optimal firing accuracy can only be achieved with single-loaders. Dispersion diameters and acceptance specifications call for something a little better that those shitty 7.62mm NATO rounds, so I'd loaded my own — right here in this room. I loaded very hot, very heavy.

"But still, it was a cold-bore shot. You've been through the training, Commander. When the barrel's cold, you're never really sure where the first one's going to go, are you? Plus the air was dense. So I did all the required calculations — range, distance, wind, and refracted heat — but mostly used my intuition, my instincts, before squeezing off a round.

"It seemed to take two or three minutes, watching Rashad through the scope, before the round finally busted his femur out from under him and knocked his turban crooked. Rashid, Rashad — whatever his name was — he had this expression on his face: Offended! Absolute disbelief. A profound look of surprise beneath a crooked turban, hands flopping around. It was almost comical.

"I consider it one of the finest shots I've made — or witnessed. I'm not bragging, mind you. I'm a professional. Keeping an enemy alive is so *much* harder than killing him."

★ ★ ★

I stood there listening to Tyner talk — lecture, actually, for that's what he was doing — and I'm not certain why. I could have turned and walked away. I could have told him the truth about himself: that he was mad. He'd stayed in this place so long that it had strangled all the humanity out of him — if there had been an element of humanity in him to begin with. He said he had grown up in Iowa? I could have told him another truth: He had traveled much too far ever to find his way back to his home state.

But I didn't. I stood and listened. Listened to him tell me about Keesha's people, the Jivaro. That they were artists of the first magnitude. That they, above all others, were preoccupied with realism, and so took utmost care to maintain the original likeness of the slain victim's face.

Tyner explained, "They believe the power of a dead man's soul is still dangerous, and that taking and shrinking the head of an enemy is the only way to conquer and destroy his soul. Plus, it's a hell of an insult for a man's head to be perverted and owned by another man. To a Jivaro, an enemy's head is the equivalent of the Medal of Honor to an American soldier."

He explained the process to me. I refused to listen attentively, though some of the details still got through: A slit was made up the back of the neck, and the skin peeled off the skull, which was then discarded. Then eyes and lips were sewn shut with fine native fiber. The actual shrinking process was extremely delicate and precise. Heated stones and hot sand were used, and the head had to be constantly rotated to prevent scorching.

"Finally," Tyner said, "a hole is made in the top of the head, and a thing called a *kumai* inserted so that that it can be worn around the neck. The process takes weeks, and the artist is required to work twelve, fifteen hours a day." His tone became emphatic. "The collection I have, you couldn't put a dollar value on it. It's the best in the world. *Priceless*."

Tyner had been looking up at the rows of glass containers. He clearly took great pride in his collection, though I got the impression that he didn't visit here often. Perhaps it took some special occasion — the addition of a new trophy? Or an unexpected guest.

Which is probably why I was so taken aback when he said, "Choose one. Any one you want, pick it out."

"No, thanks. I don't want one of your shrunken heads, Sergeant."

"I'm not offering to give you one, Commander." He chuckled, then began to laugh. "Can you imagine the looks you'd get at customs at Miami International? No. I'm offering to let you wear one. Around your neck. You can see how it feels . . ." He jabbed his thumb at the rows of tiny, simian faces. "Because this *is* the truth. What it all comes down to. Find out what it's like, for a change, to wear honesty on the *outside* of your shirt. I think you'll be amazed at how it feels."

I shook my head as I said, "If we're going to leave at one in the morning, I need to get some sleep. Good night, Sergeant Tyner." I lifted my newly issued gear off the lab table, and turned to go.

Behind me, I heard him say, as if testing me, "Tonight, at that compound in Remanso, you know what my men have been instructed to do, don't you? For us, it's standard operating procedure."

I waited.

After a pause, I heard him say, "If it flies, it dies; if it's got a head, it's dead. We're going to kill them all. Everyone but the hostages. If you've got a problem with that — if it's somehow a breach of your per-

557

sonal ethics, tell me now. We'll leave you behind."

I said, "I'm aware of your methods. My friends are up there. I'm going."

Tyner said, "And *participating*. That's important, Commander. Not just because of the bounties my men will receive. People like that, people who visit violence on civilians, extermination is the only remedy. You're a biologist, you've studied Darwin. How did he put it? 'The struggle for life is most severe between individuals of the same species. Only the fittest can survive.' Something like that. I probably need to have a look at his work again, refresh my memory. But do you agree?"

I turned and looked at him, hating what I saw, hating him because he'd been right all along — about him, about me — and hating him now because he was right once again. I said, "Yes. I *do* agree."

He smiled, nodding — I couldn't be certain if it was because he was surprised or relieved. "Good. Frankly, I was a little worried about taking you on this mission. That you'd lost your . . . professionalism, let's say. Isn't it irksome when our heroes let us down? But it's still there. I can see it in your eyes. So there's one last thing I want to ask you, Commander. Do you mind?"

"Why would I?"

"Okay, we'll see. The question is this: from what I've heard, what I've read, you were directed to take executive action against seventeen people —"

"That's not true!" I interrupted, suddenly furious that he had such an intimate knowledge of my past.

His voice rose, to cover mine: "Though you actually carried out only thirteen of the orders, because you refused to execute actions against women. But of the thirteen men you eliminated, you used nothing but your hands on seven of them. No knives, garrotes, nothing. Just your hands." He had moved closer to me, looking up into my face, his eyes intense, fascinated. His voice was almost a whisper now, as he pressed, "Why? It was obviously your method of choice. *But why?*"

He knew too much for me not to answer — and it would also have seemed an infidelity to the person I hoped and believed I'd now become: the quiet biologist who loved to work in his lab, the guy who delighted in sunset beers with his many friends back on Sanibel Island.

I shrugged. "I don't know, because it was quieter, maybe." But I was already shaking my head, knowing that was a lie and an evasion, so I let myself think about it for several long beats before I said in a more reflective voice, "I chose that way, that method because . . . because it was more . . . because it was more *personal*."

I could see in Tyner's expression that he misunderstood completely, an obscene misinterpretation that I could hear it in his grinning, locker-room reply: "Outstanding! Yeah, man, up close and personal. Listen to their heart stop. It makes sense now. *Perfect*."

Chapter Thirty-one

At exactly 12:45 a.m., I heard the little Bell helicopter fire up out on the heli pad to the north of the complex, and I trotted all my gear up the hill to where Tyner stood far from the strobbing luminescence of aircraft running lights, backdropped by the paler incandescence of a copper Amazon moon.

He wasn't alone — which was not surprising, until I recognized the man with him. It was the ponytailed Irishman, Niall McCauley, wearing a jacket in the damp, night air, hands folded behind him — it seemed.

But then I realized that he kept his hands behind his back because he'd been handcuffed.

To Tyner, I said, "What's wrong? Why's he here?"

Tyner had been talking to the pilot, the two of them going over something on a clipboard, far enough from the chopper so that they didn't have to yell to be heard. "Mr. McCauley will be accompanying us, Commander — but only for the first part of the trip. I may hand him over to the authorities at the closest city of any size. Or maybe I'll save the British government some money and shove him out the door when we get over the jungle."

When Tyner said that — *shove him out* — the Irishman began to sob, his chest heaving, as he pleaded, "Don't, Sergeant, please don't even joke about such a thing."

Tyner thought that was humorous. "Joking? Hah! You know what this traitorous little coward did? When I was questioning you this afternoon, Commander, he overheard you mention the names of the two men you're after. Kazan and Stallings?

"One of my pals intercepted a couple of cell-phone calls McCauley made this afternoon. Guess who he was trying to contact? A man by the name of Hassan Kazan. Information for a price. This little sonuvabitch may have warned Kazan and compromised the whole operation. If he did, my men — you and me — we're all walking right into a trap. As to the hostages, they're probably dead by now. It comes under the heading of getting rid of the evidence."

McCauley was still sobbing. "I didn't, Sergeant! I swear to Christ I never got in touch with Kazan."

"But you tried!"

"I know, I know. I was that drunk and scared, and I hate this goddamn jungle so much I'm not in my right mind. I just want out. I want enough money to get out, and it's made me crazy. You're my friend. You've always been a friend to Niall McCauley."

I moved away from the Irishman, not trusting myself to be within arm's reach. I said, "Is he lying? Do you think he made contact?"

Tyner said, "He made five calls, one lasted nearly fifteen minutes. I don't know. If he told me the earth was round, I wouldn't believe him."

"Did you try to contact your guys?"

"Of course. They're way out of range for radio contact, and they don't answer their cell phones, which means they're too deep into the jungle to get a signal."

"We're still going to Remanso, though, right? We're not going to let this little worm stop us."

Tyner said, "Oh, we're going all right. As

of now, I think we'll do a little experiment midway. See if an Irishman can fly while handcuffed."

I was nodding — he'd get no protest from me. "Either way, there'll be room for the girl. We're taking Keesha. She's sick. You've certainly got medical supplies here. I want a full script of Septra or Cipro, or both. She needs to be back with her people."

I was surprised that Tyner didn't put up a stronger argument. Maybe it was the resolve in my voice. Or perhaps he'd already anticipated the request — I did not doubt his intellectual gifts. All he said was, "There's only one Jivaro village I know well enough to set us down at night. That'll have to do."

I said, "They're the ones . . . the ones who do the work for you."

He answered, "Yes. I've become a cottage industry, I'm afraid."

I told him, "Then that village will have to do."

Keesha was sick, no doubt about it, and there was very little I could do to help.

When I'd returned to our suite after touring Tyner's macabre armory, I'd found her asleep in the bedroom, sweating and slightly feverish, but in no obvious danger.

I'd stripped to my underwear, and climbed in beside her, holding her close because she was chilled, her skin cold to the touch. She'd awakened long enough to recognize me, and favor me with a weak smile. "The big man," she whispered. "I'm glad you've returned. The creature inside me is fighting and refuses to leave. You must rub my stomach and urge it out into the light."

I stroked her belly and thighs until she drifted off to sleep, then I pulled her tight into the crook of my arm, and fell asleep beside her.

I awoke nearly four hours later — a little after 11:30 p.m. — to the sound of her moaning. Her eyes were closed, and she'd drawn her legs up into a tight fetal position, a clear sign of pain.

In the bathroom medicine cabinet, I found Ibuprofen tablets and a thermometer. I got her awake long enough to get a couple of pills down her and take her temperature: It was 101 degrees, a low-grade temp, but still a matter of concern.

I was worried that jungle root tea had worked, that she really was pregnant and had miscarried — and all the dangerous possibilities that combination implied.

She would not, however, consider my pleas that she let me get her to a doctor. Became nearly hysterical, in fact, when I pressed the argument.

"Get me home," she said over and over. "Take me to my people. They will call for the *curandeira*, the old woman who makes medicines, and she will drive this evil thing out of me."

I felt terrible. Absolutely powerless in the face of her strident fear of the outside world.

Holding her, trying to give comfort, I'd whispered into her ear, "You must at least take the pills I give to you. Take them as I tell you to do, no matter what. As my friend and traveling companion, will you do this for me?"

She had nodded as I rocked her in my arms. "Yes," she said, "that I will do. Out of my affection for you."

I carried Keesha, wrapped in a blanket, up the hill and strapped her into the seat just aft of the pilot's, and next to my own. As I did, her eyes grew wide, and she yelled over the noise of the engine, "How will my heart stay in my body when this airplane leaves the ground?"

I patted her knee, making certain that

she could see my smile, how at ease I was. "It's just like riding in an automobile but louder. You're going to enjoy it!"

The Irishman had been loaded into the cargo area behind me. He lay on his belly, hands still cuffed. He tried to get my attention several times, calling my name, but I ignored him. Ingratiation is the last resort of desperate people, and I wasn't in a mood to cooperate. The idea that he had endangered Amelia for money — the callous self-absorption of such an act — had created in me a cold fury.

As I sat there, listening to him ("Commander? You seem like a civilized man, Commander. For God's sake, please answer me!"), I knew without having to give it much consideration or much wrestling with my conscience that if he had caused harm to Amelia, I would have a difficult decision to make. My instincts, all my training, told me to kill him.

A pilot himself, Tyner sat forward next to the pilot in his employ. I noticed that he'd combed his muttonchops and waxed his handlebar mustache, everything downward, perhaps so the facial hair wouldn't distract his vision — a tactical touch.

As we lifted off, he turned toward me and touched the earphones of the voice-ac-

tivated communications system he wore —
he wanted to talk.

I fitted my tiny earphones on and adjusted the microphone arm as I heard his voice say, "The Jivaro village I know is on our way, but I still want to make it quick. Drop the girl and go. It's at the confluence of two rivers. We'll see their fires, and let's just hope the men aren't too drunk. They drink this psychedelic swill called *chuchuwausee*. Gives them visions. A drunken Jivaro is quick to use his blowgun, and they dip their darts in *curare*. Or the frog poison. You know about that, don't you?"

I knew. The poison, curare, contains strychnine. Throughout South America, indigenous people made it from the wourali vine. I'd seen it done, once. The vine was boiled until it became a thick, gooey black mess — curare.

In the jungle, there are also many varieties of tiny frogs, only an inch or two long and always brightly colored — red, blue, yellow, strawberry — that, if roasted, produce a highly toxic alkaloid. Also a very effective poison if delivered into the bloodstream by an arrow or a dart.

I said, "I'll talk to Keesha, and make sure she warns them off."

"Do you trust her?"

Into my mind flashed an image of the little Pakistani man back in Cartagena calling to me, "Trust no one! No one!" Now it seemed almost funny.

I told Tyner, "Lately, she's one of the few people I do trust."

With my hand on the girl's knee, I sat back and watched the moon drift upward beside us, afloat on the rolling black hills of forest, the surface of which was layered with a yellow, fulminating mist. I felt the outside air turn cool, then cold, as we gained elevation and soared southward through the night.

Perhaps because I was filled with adrenaline and anxiety, it seemed a long time — though my watch said it was only twenty minutes — before the pilot circled over what looked to be a ring of campfires in the darkness.

In my earphone, Tyner's voice said, "This is it. See where the two rivers come together? It's a little trading outpost. The Jivaros and the Yagua, they use it because they both refuse to mingle much with the outside world. This is kind of a halfway point between what's civilized and what's not."

Below, I could now see two silver rivers,

an arrow-shaped spit of land in the blackness between them, in the body of which the fires had grown larger, the distance between them greater. Keesha had flown most of the trip with her eyes closed — terrified — but now she was looking out the window, too.

I pushed the microphone away from my face and said to her, "Below us, there's a village. He says these are Jivaro people. People who are part of your tribe. We're going to put you off here. They'll take care of you."

She answered, "The Bad Gift. He tells you that?"

"Yes. But I believe him."

"You will return before the sun rises?"

"No. Probably never."

In the red lights of the cabin, I saw her eyes expand with a sudden awareness. "You are leaving me? I will not be seeing you again."

I'd already given her my name, my phone number on a waterproof card — meaningless data in a place like this, but the only small offering I could make. "If you need me, if you need anything, look at the paper and dial those numbers. I'll come."

The chopper listed to port and starboard

as it landed, tail swinging like a horizontal pendulum. I shoved the door open when the skids touched down. I reached in, unbuckled Keesha's seat belt, and then took her up into my arms and ducked beneath the overhead blades, carrying her toward the campfire light.

I was aware of small, dark shapes in the shadows. In the strobing white explosions of the helicopter's lights, like the flash of a camera, a series of images were printed briefly in my mind's eye: naked men with rice-bowl haircuts, faces painted red or yellow, holding blowguns six feet long, watching me as I carried the girl past them. An old woman, her breasts sagging flat, as if they'd been deflated. Three young girls, black hair hanging down, babies strung across their bellies in little hammocks, skinny dogs yapping while naked children, boys and girls, hid behind their elders, peering at me, the strangest of visions.

The village smelled of wood smoke, roasting meat, river air, and something else — something powerful, important, and very intimate. It was an odor that seemed to register low on the back of my neck, not in my brain. It was very familiar. It created in me a curious yearning for *something* —

what, I did not know.

I continued walking toward the fires, feeling the girl's weight in my arms, the warmth of her breath on my cheek, and, for an instant, I felt an overwhelming but ludicrous desire to stay right here, in this village, with her. To tell Tyner to go on without me, leave me and never return.

Into my ear, Keesha said, "Do you see that old grandmother? That's her. How did she know I was sick? Our *curandeira,* the woman who makes medicines."

Standing before us, next to a blazing fire, was a woman in a grass skirt, wearing layers of beads around her neck, gray-haired, toothless. When I called out a greeting in Spanish, she looked at me as if she were deaf.

"The old people here don't speak Spanish," Keesha explained.

I put the girl on the ground and held her until her feet were steady beneath her. I waited until I was sure before I said, "Then tell the woman that you must take the medicine I gave you. You promised. Understand?"

The girl hugged herself to me, her body shaking, then held me away. "I will do this thing for you."

Then Keesha turned, held her hand out

to the old woman, and the two of them walked into the darkness with only the briefest of glances at me.

Back in the helicopter, I watched the village, the silver river, and then the campfires grow so small that they were finally absorbed by the overwhelming gloom of jungle. I rode in silence, trying to recapture that mysterious but oddly familiar odor that I'd recognized, which therefore had to be recorded in my memory.

I couldn't find it. I knew it was there, somewhere in my brain, but it was gone; it had ascended into some place that I could no longer access.

The nose of the chopper tilted downward, and we were under way.

It was awhile before I realized Tyner and I were alone with the pilot in the helicopter. Behind me, the cargo area was empty. Where was McCauley?

I had removed my earphones, so I was out of contact — didn't want to listen to anyone's chatter — but now I put them on again. "Sergeant? You there?"

The response was immediate: "Roger that, Commander. I thought you were asleep. Couldn't hear a thing. Or were maybe just lovesick and didn't feel like talking."

I said, "Neither. But I just checked the cargo area. What happened to the Irishman?"

I heard Tyner laugh and cover his microphone as he said something indistinguishable to the pilot.

I repeated the question: "What happened to the IRA guy?"

"Well . . . our bomb-making friend has gone native," Tyner replied. "He seemed confused when I told him he'd make an excellent necklace. Kind of smiled, like we were dropping him off at camp to learn arts and crafts."

Chapter Thirty-two

When we were still low over the jungle, but only ten minutes or so from the village of Remanso, Tyner switched radio frequencies and tried to raise his special operations team.

Nothing.

I listened to him try over and over, his voice always flat, indifferent, professional.

Still nothing.

Finally, he turned to me and said, "It's not looking good, Commander. The Irishman may have torpedoed us," anger evident in his tone for the first time. "My men aren't answering."

I said, "Two Humvees and your armored personnel carrier, plus, what? A team of sixteen? You think guerrillas could have taken out the entire platoon?"

He was tugging at his mustache. "A couple of stinger missiles, yeah, just like the one that brought down your chopper. My guys are the best, really first-rate, but they didn't know they were driving right into a trap. The bad guys could have set up on any hilltop over the road and zapped them." Now he rubbed his forehead, clearly distressed by the prospect of losing so many people. "Damn it!"

I was thinking about it, not wanting it to be true, hating the possibility that Amelia had suffered or been murdered because of one greedy informant — that little Irish bastard — and was now feeling a sense of desperation that was very, very close to dread.

I said, "Maybe communicating with you would compromise their position. They're too close to the compound to talk. Do you have a squawk code?"

I could see he didn't know what I meant. "Like in the Battle of Britain. When ground control picked up incoming planes on radar, the British fighter pilots had what they called a parrot code — just a series of taps on the mike key to tell gunners below not to open fire. Squawks. Try it. If your guys hear it, they might catch on."

Tyner pressed the microphone key several times, always in a series of three, then waited.

Still nothing.

He was getting frustrated, and I'd all but given up hope when, through my earphones, in reply to his signal, I heard three distinct transmissions of static.

"Try it again," I said.

Once again, he received a response: *Click . . . click . . . click.*

Smiling, Tyner said, "They're so close, they can't even whisper. That means they're on station, locked, loaded, and ready to roll. Outstanding."

I nodded, said nothing. But I was thinking: *if the person responding is part of our team.*

Matching the topographical map to GPS coordinates, the chopper pilot touched down just long enough for us to swing off the skids, then he was gone again, banking away into the night.

We were on a level patch of ground surrounded by forest, half a mile from the hacienda. I checked my watch: 2:40 a.m., on a very early morning, December 19, only six days before Christmas.

Oddly, Dinkin's Bay flashed into my mind, what it would look like at this hour, on this morning. I could imagine the holiday lights, red, green, and blue barbering up the masts of sailboats, and outlining the roof of the marina office and the Red Pelican Gift Shop. I could picture the soft yellow light of Japanese lanterns aboard the *Satin Doll* and hear the sump and gurgle of bilge and bait well pumps and the whine of automatic switches. Could see the *No Mas* anchored in darkness and the silhouette of my tin-roofed house, built over the water on stilts, backdropped by a long ledge of mangroves.

I wanted nothing more than to be there — to be there, safe, with Amelia and, hopefully, Janet, too. Soon, very soon.

"Time to switch to night vision, Commander."

I was following Tyner along a dirt path. The waning moon was low on the horizon, creating enough light to see as long as we were in the open. But when we stepped into the forest, it was as if we'd stumbled into a cave. I was wearing a black Tampa Bay baseball cap, and now I turned it around catcher's style, fitted the goggles over my head, and touched the power switch.

I'd used night-vision equipment before, but never anything nearly this good. I knew that the best you could buy on the open market was second- and third-generation stuff — each generation, presumably, representing an advancement in technology. And he'd said this was fifth generation?

The cave was instantly transformed into a bright world of phosphorescent green, minutely detailed with perfect depth of field. Except for the iridescent glow and the slight whirring sound, I might have been walking in the light of midday — an illusion, as I well knew. There are two types of night-vision optics: passive and active. Passive systems amplify existing light, while active night-vision systems project a near-infrared light source, then electronically enhance the picture, so what you are actually seeing is a video image of the scene before you.

This was the high-tech active variety, and I now understood what Tyner meant when he said that, in these jungle places, he and his people owned the night.

We were in a grove of rubber trees, row after straight row. Their pale trunks were scored with silver V-shaped wounds, metallic cups fixed below them to catch the bleeding latex. I was reminded of Southeast Asia, the French rubber plantations there.

As we walked, crouched slightly, his weapon pointed left, mine right, I heard his soft voice again in my earpiece. "Ford, there's one more thing I need to ask you. It's time for me to know."

"What's that?"

"The help you got from your State Department friends, they wouldn't do it unless they were getting something in return. These guys Stallings and Kazan, have you been ordered to kill them?"

I thought about it before answering. "Yes. Kazan."

"So you're back in active service."

"Not for long. As soon as this is over, I'm out. Forever."

His voice communicated amusement. "Really? That surprises me. My guess is, you're like Blaine Heller. You wouldn't be here if you didn't *like* it."

We came out of the trees from the south, through a translucent mist that seemed to boil from the rain-forest base. Ahead, I could see the hacienda's high stone wall, wedges of it illuminated by blue security lights. The goggles I wore were so sophisticated that the scene before me dimmed and brightened automatically as I looked from light to shadow.

We still wore the voice-activated transmitters, but now we communicated with standard military hand signals.

I saw Tyner raise his hand, fist closed, and so I stopped behind him. We were both carrying MP-5 submachine guns, each made only slightly longer with sound and flash suppressors.

We waited, watching the top of the wall for activity. I could hear a dog yapping in the far distance, coming from the direction of the village. Could hear the electronic chirring of insects, but nothing else.

We waited for more than a minute before Tyner opened his hand, fingers pointed upward: *Forward.* We began to advance again, moving slowly through the mist. At a hedge of what may have been coffee bushes, we paused once more, kneeling.

Still no activity along the wall, and no noise from inside.

We'd discussed our plan of attack thoroughly, so there was no need for us to speak now. It seemed a good plan because it was extremely simple.

If there were hostages inside, there would, presumably, be armed guards. At our signal, Tyner's men would open fire from a concentrated area outside the north wall to draw the attention of those guards. If possible, a first priority would be to destroy the outside transformer, and so cut off all electricity. For us, the darker it was, the better. If the transformer could not be located, the team's three snipers would shoot out the security lights.

Human nature being what it is, we anticipated that the guards would rush to congregate along the north wall and return fire or at least to see what the hell all the noise was about. A full minute after the opening salvo, Tyner and I would then climb over the south wall, locate the hostages, and free them while the guards were busy fending off our attack from the north.

"Nothing to it," Curtis Tyner had joked. "I've done this dozens of times. The trick, of course, is staying alive. But my men will do *their* jobs — that much you can count on."

Now, hiding behind bushes, waiting in the silence, I thought to myself: *Please let his men be there.*

In my earphone, I heard Tyner signal to his team leader, and then say in Spanish, "Red Team, we are in position. Let's make some bacon." He was telling them to open fire.

If Tyner expected a reply, he was disappointed because there was none.

We waited through a silence that seemed to originate in some dark place within me

— the place where fear resides, perhaps — and that silence ballooned out into the night, permeating shadows and magnifying the vibrations of air molecules. The inner ear bridges an ancient barrier between land and water, taking sound waves and translating them into waves of liquid before the brain can then read them as electrical impulses.

That yapping dog — why didn't someone in the village silence the damn thing?

In my earpiece, I heard Tyner repeat his order — "Red Team, we're in position . . . " Then, long moments later, I heard him whisper, *"Shit,"* convinced they could not hear.

He stood, about to signal some command to me . . . and that's when the world around us began to explode.

Tyner's men were out there, all right. No doubt about that now. Possibly, there'd been a delay because of a bad detonator fuse. No way of knowing, but the first signature of attack was a series of three powerful explosions to the north of us that filled the night sky with volcanic showers of sparks and flame.

Then all of the lights in the hacienda

compound blinked out.

In my earphones, I heard Tyner say in English, "It's about time, boys."

Then there was the rattle and whistle of small-arms fire, concentrated on the north end of the property, followed by shouts and one shrill scream from the direction of the main house.

I was standing and didn't even realize it. Was already moving toward the wall. Full of adrenaline, full of an overpowering desire to find Amelia and Janet, I'd completely blanked on our battle plan until Tyner caught me from behind.

I felt his small hand grab my shoulder. "Steady, Ford. We're going to give them the full minute. Let the guards clear our area before we go in."

Now, very close, I could hear answering gunshots from inside the compound. Automatic rifles and pistol fire. The guards had rejoined forces, apparently, and were fighting back.

Tyner threw the thick rubber pad he was carrying up so it hung over the wall — in South America, the tops of nearly all walls are protected by shards of broken bottles cemented in place — and he said, "Give me a stirrup up. I'll go in, secure the inside of the wall. When I whistle,

584

follow me. I'll go left, you go right."

I was so chemically charged, so eager, that I nearly threw the little man over the barricade when he put his boot in my hands. I heard a burst of three rounds from his weapon, distinctive because of the sound suppressor — *phuuut, phuuut, phuuut* — then a shrill whistle. I vaulted up onto the top of the wall, rolled off the pad, and came to my feet.

Through the night-vision goggles, I could see scattered whitewashed buildings in a broad courtyard. Ahead was the main house, a massive place with an ornate, tiled roof — probably red. To my right, or the east, was a grove of citrus trees and a couple of big mangos. To the west was what might have been a small horse barn, but it had been fortified with bars on the windows. There was a heavy concertina-wire fence connected to it.

The layout matched the satellite intelligence that Harrington had provided.

My heart was pounding so hard, the skin on my chest and neck was vibrating, and I could feel the rush of blood in my brain. If they had brought Amelia here, and if Janet were still alive, they would probably be inside the barn.

Tyner was to my left, kneeling over what

I realized was the body of a man. Whispering into his transmitter, he said, "He was a runner, trying to get out of fighting. Deserters. These are the ones you've got to watch out for because they're never where you expect them to be."

He had what looked to be surgical scissors in his hands, and he was doing something with the dead man's fingers. When I realized what, I turned away.

"Don't go soft on me now, Ford. You think the Colombian government takes my word for the casualties we inflict?"

I said, "You couldn't wait and do that later?"

"Absolutely not. We've got no guarantees we're going to secure this place. Money's money."

I was already moving toward the barn.

Chapter Thirty-three

Because we were separated from the plantation's north wall by the main house, we were protected from the main line of fire. Even so, I could hear the whistle of spent rounds ripping through the trees and ricocheting off rock walls. Ahead, there was a lot of screaming in garbled Spanish and some kind of Persian language, perhaps Pashto or Dari. When Tyner had caught up with me, I began to jog toward the barn.

"You see the light?"

I did. The back windows of the hacienda were suddenly illuminated by what must have been one or more kerosene lamps.

"If Kazan's here, the turban, that's where he'll be. Inside the big house, probably crapping his bloomers he's so scared. Now's the time to take him. Before the shock wears off."

I replied, "I don't give a damn about

Kazan. He's his own punishment. I'm going to find those girls and get the hell out of here."

"You got it back-assward, Commander. We pop the bad guys, then we snatch the hostages. Standard operating procedure."

"No way. I'm not going to risk it. My friends are more important than your damn head count."

"I'm warning you. Now's the time, not later. What about your orders?"

I ignored him and kept moving, even as he added, "You're making a mistake if you don't waste that guy now. A mistake. *Trust* me."

The barn was enclosed by common chain-link fence and topped with razor wire. At the gate was a heavy section of chain, which was padlocked. How the hell were we going to get that open?

When Tyner stepped toward it, I said, "Tell me you're not going to try to shoot it off. You'll kill us both. We're going to have to find a way to climb over it."

"No, we won't." From one of the cargo pockets, he pulled a metal device the size of a ratchet arm, fixed it onto the lock's shackle, and began leveraging the handle. I waited for a minute, no more, though it seemed longer, before he finally said, "Bolt cutter," and pushed the gate open wide. "Out here, when you knock on a door, lots of times people won't answer."

The barn was empty, though there was no doubt that it had served as a combination dormitory and prison. At one end, set inside a series of horse stalls, were a total of seven canvas cots, two or three to a stall. At the other end, in a larger stall, were two more canvas cots.

I remembered the intelligence provided me by Harrington: Seven women and two men had been photographed in a fenced area. This was the place. Presumably, the men had lived in one part of the barn, women in the other. The numbers added up. More telling that this place had been a prison, though, was its stench. It stunk of human waste, garbage, a festering unhealthiness. At each end were plastic five-gallon buckets. One had been spilled. The contents explained much of the stench.

To Tyner, I whispered into the transmitter, "Where *are* they? They were here. Hostages, their prisoners, they obviously kept them here. Where could they be?"

He was shaking his head. "Gate's locked. It doesn't make sense. Why would they lock an empty guardhouse?"

"I'm going to take a closer look around."

Tyner had stationed himself at the door. "Make it fast. It's been a little over eight minutes, and we only have a fifteen-minute window. My guys are going to start moving. They're going to spread out and close in. We don't want to be inside this place when that goes down."

I returned to the area where the majority of cots were located, what I assumed to be the woman's wing of the little prison. I ducked into one of the stalls. On the wooden walls, as if marked by a nail, was a calendar, the days marked off in columns of fives. Someone had been here for more than fifty days.

Couldn't be Janet, and it certainly wasn't Amelia.

Inside the second stall was another calendar, and a few blankets. The third stall, which contained three cots, was equally sparse. There was no calendar, no obvious method of keeping track of the days, but there was some graffiti:

Love Is God

Humanity Rules

Both were carved into the walls in big letters, the wood still raw.

I had to kneel to read a longer passage written over the bunk:

This Evil stands no chance against my prayers!

I reread the maxim more slowly, letting the words sink in, my memory banks scanning for some connection. It was familiar. I wasn't certain why. Who had I heard speak that phrase before?

Beneath the cot was a thin blanket, a metal cup, and a spoon. I removed them and inspected them individually, looking for some kind of distinguishing characteristics, but there was none.

As I did, that phrase repeated itself in my brain.

This Evil stands no chance against my prayers!

Where had I heard it? In my memory, the phrase was somehow associated with some event, something bad, a tragedy, but also the strength of the individual who'd endured it but had managed to go with her life.

Her life. A car wreck. A lost child.

Then I knew.

I stood, in slow realization, and pulled the microphone arm away from my mouth, calling a single name, as loud as I could: "Janet? *Janet!* Where are you?"

I waited in the silence and called her

name once more. Then, behind me, I heard a pounding, creaking noise, and I turned to see a door in the barn's floor being opened — the passageway to some kind of tack room or feed cellar, probably. Then the familiar face of Janet Mueller was peering out, her cheeks very gaunt, as if she'd been starved, her eyes hollow as caves, blinking in the darkness.

I heard her strong voice say, "Doc? My God! Oh dear God, please let it be, *please*. Is that you?"

The barn was so dark that she couldn't see me, I realized, so I spoke as I rushed toward her, saying, "It's me, Janet. It's Marion Ford come to take you back to Sanibel." Then I reached and pulled her up to look at her — nope, I wasn't dreaming — and then I hugged the lady mightily, feeling her thin arms, the warmth of her body against me. "You're safe now."

On the ladder below her, someone had lit a candle. I watched eight more haggard, emaciated people climb out, all naked but for rags of burlap or underwear or maybe a T-shirt. One of them, a tall, lean black woman, threw her arms around me, even as I still held Janet, both of them weeping in my ear.

The woman, whom I knew had to be

Grace Walker, said to me, "I'm not dreaming, am I, man? Man, tell me I'm not dreaming. I want to go home. Please take us home."

I pulled away long enough to say, "That's exactly where we're going. But first, where's Amelia?"

Grace said, "Who?"

I repeated her name, "Amelia," as I looked toward the cellar. "Is she still down there hiding?" Then I called, "Hey! Amelia. It's *me*."

Even now, in shock, Janet was still reactive enough to be puzzled. "Do you mean Amelia Gardner? Oh, Doc, something terrible happened. Our boat sank, and we got separated from Amelia, and we left her. I feel terrible. I feel so guilty. We couldn't find her, and we left her. She's probably still out there in the ocean somewhere. And Mikey, my God, poor Mikey." She began to cry again, and Grace Walker was now sobbing even louder. "This terrible man — a guy we call the albino — he shot our dear Mike for no reason, and he's treated us like animals."

In my earphone, I heard Tyner say, "Commander, there's something I need to tell you."

I felt my body numb slightly when he

added, "It's about that woman you're after. Amelia Gardner."

A weapons firefight is sustained panic interrupted by moments of raw terror, and the sounds of that fight — the shouts, the screams, the gunfire — had drawn closer. Tyner was crouched in the doorway, and he leaned and fired two short bursts out the door as I approached.

Expecting return fire, I turned and motioned for Janet and the others to get on their bellies, before I said, "What about Amelia, Tyner? Is there something you didn't tell me?" To my own ears, my voice seemed oddly pitched.

"We need to get our asses out of here, Commander. My men are on the move a little earlier than I expected. We don't have time to look for your other friend. We've got to go."

I told him, "Go without me. She's here somewhere. I'm not leaving."

"Looks like we've got eight or nine very weak people to take care of. I can't get them out alone."

"You'll have to try. The moment I find Amelia, we'll be right behind you."

His words seemed then to slow horribly and deepen into a spatial echo, as he said,

"Then you leave me no choice. I want you to get ahold of yourself, Commander. I'd have told you earlier, but I needed you gung-ho, with your full facilities because of what we had to do here tonight."

He said, "That woman? She never made it out of Cartagena. Maybe she put up too much of a fight, I don't know. The guys who kidnapped her shot her. They found her body in a motel. I got the word about an hour before we left."

I whispered, "They . . . killed Amelia? She's *dead*. You're sure?"

"Yes. The Intel comes from the U.S. Embassy. There's no doubt about it."

Emotional shock affects different people different ways. In that moment of comprehension, into my mind came an analytical clarity: They had murdered a woman about whom I cared deeply, and so there was only one rational response. I would kill them. I would kill both of them, Kazan and Stallings. I did not have time to indulge in overwhelming emotion or expressions of grief. Perhaps I would — but later. Now I needed to stay absolutely focused on the task at hand: Find those two, look into their eyes, tell them why I had sentenced them to death, and then eliminate them.

"Are you okay, Commander Ford?"

I had been down on one knee, but now I stood. "Yep. Hundred percent. I want you to lay down some covering fire. I'm going to bust into the big house and see who's there."

"No. It's too late. We've got to move out now."

"Sergeant, I've been given an executive order on Hassan Kazan, and I'm obligated to carry it out."

He was standing, waving Janet and the others to get in line and be ready to follow him. "The time to hit them was when we first got in. I tried to tell you, but you wouldn't listen. You missed your chance. They're gone by now."

He raised his night-vision goggles long enough to look into my eyes. "But I'll tell you what. Help me get these people out safely, and I'll come back with you and kill anyone who's left."

Behind him, Janet was helping to support a young girl who looked sick, near death. "Doc, please don't leave us. Please. We need you."

I noticed that my whole body was shaking, quivering, as I answered, "Okay, okay. Of course I won't, Janet. I won't leave you. I'm here."

That morning, in the jungle's first bronze light, Tyner and I returned to the remains of the rubber plantation. Janet and the others were safely on their way out via a private plane that we'd hired, so there was no rush.

We tallied nine bodies among the rubble — a profitable night's work for Tyner's team. We also found a wall safe in which there was a box of Colombian emeralds and more than $100,000 in cash.

I was more interested in inspecting the bodies. Six looked to be Middle Eastern, but neither the big Samoan nor the albino was among them.

Chapter Thirty-four

Back in Cartagena, I behaved as a modern, responsible adult is expected to behave. As with the heirs of the very wealthy, victims of crime are assigned many small, legal obligations by governments, as if to punish them. I busied myself taking care of those details for all involved. But that feeling of clarity, of pure purpose — *Stallings and Kazan* — stuck with me.

My first consideration was Janet, Grace, and their fellow captives. The FBI and the State Department wanted to debrief them, but both agencies agreed to wait until they'd had complete physicals and their health was back on track. That meant the nine of them had to stick around in Colombia for a few days before flying home, and they insisted on spending those days together, as a group.

So I got them rooms at the Hotel Santa

Clara. Made sure that the superb staff there kept them stuffed with gourmet food and local fresh fruit. I took paternal pleasure in watching them divide their time between the plaza dining room and the lounge chairs around the pool.

They had become extremely close, Janet explained. One of the two males was a boy in his early teens — the albino had killed his oil executive father — and she had taken the kid under her wing.

"Ronnie has become like a son," she said. "He hasn't seen his mother in years, so we've already discussed it. He's coming back to Captiva to live with me. If I can, I'm going to adopt him. You know how badly I've missed my child, Doc."

The change that had taken place in Janet was remarkable. She'd always been a solid person, but the quiet type, seldom outwardly demonstrative.

Not now. I saw in her a strength, a confidence, that positively glowed, yet both she and Grace Walker also exhibited a demeanor of inner peace that provided me with both courage and hope during what were among the darkest days of my life.

One night, standing on the docks of Club Nautico, looking out over Cartagena Bay, Janet confided something to me. She said, "The night we were adrift, lost at sea, I'd never experienced such fear. The chaos of it all, the wind, the waves, and those black stars. I remembered walking the beach on Captiva awhile back, at sunset, and telling someone that I felt at one with nature." She shook her head and squeezed my hand, remembering. "It's the sort of thing people say, but it was a lie. A fairy tale. I've never felt a union with anything other than another human being. I know that now. The people I'm with, the courage they all showed during some of the terrible things they did to us, their love and caring, like a family, that's what makes life not just bearable, but wonderful. Everything else seems as . . . well, as cold as the stars that night."

Something that Grace said also helped me through those days: "Out there, I learned that on the other side of every great fear is freedom. Even if we'd have died, our loved ones could have found comfort in that. We helped each other, and, after awhile, we weren't afraid."

On the day that I identified Amelia's body — she looked so tiny and alone in the refrigerated drawer, all of the youth leached out of her — I'd walked the streets of Cartagena like a zombie, walked for hours until I somehow ended up in Grace's arms, and then on her bed, wanting badly to cry but unable. I don't know if I'd have made it without her strength, and Janet's.

There was one dazzling bright and happy moment during that time. It was when we first got back to Cartagena, and I placed a call to the office of Dinkin's Bay Marina, Sanibel Island, and asked to speak with Jeth Nicholes.

When I heard his voice, I said, "Hey, you big ape, I've got a pretty lady here who wants to talk to you."

"The Family of Nine," as they called themselves, flew back to Florida on Wednesday, December 24, and I waved them away as their Avianca flight pulled back from the boarding ladder.

Then I hurried to another part of the airport where Curtis Tyner's Bell helicopter and pilot were waiting for me.

The pilot, whose name was Barry Rupple, told me, "The hotel sent your gear over, Dr. Ford, and I've got it stored aboard. Sergeant Tyner wanted me to offer you his help. Again. Whatever you need."

I said, "Transport back to the jungle is all I need," and strapped myself in.

I had the pilot land us at the convergence of two rivers — a *paranamirims,* in the Jivaro language — and I stepped out, seabag over my shoulder, into the smell of wood fires, roasting meat, and something else, something intimate and important, a memory that was instantly recognizable but, for some reason, impossible to anchor consciously in my brain.

Keesha wasn't there, but they found her. With the chopper gone, I ignored the bitter stares of the painted men, the suspicious chatter of women, until the girl arrived, smiling, and held out her hand to me. "You will stay with me in my *pacovas,* big man. The creature is gone from my belly, and I am healthy again. But you must bring me food."

Keesha's village was deep in the interior, at the confluence of two narrow, black-water rivers where, at dawn and dusk, I used a spear tipped with the barb of a stingray to take piranha, and red-scaled *pacu* and, once, a very large *arapaima* — it had to be close to fifty pounds — that fed the whole village.

Not that there were many people in this small branch of the larger Jivaro tribe. There were a dozen huts, home to three dozen men, women, and brown-eyed children, and an amusing variety of pet monkeys and macaws. The huts were framed with bamboo, built beside small cooking fires and roofed with banana leaves that fauceted off the afternoon downpours.

When it rained that way — a waterfall that crashed down through the forest canopy — Keesha would lead me to the big, woven hammock, and we would cling to each other there, and use our hands to explore each other's bodies, and give comfort.

I stayed a month. Longer. I don't know. I lost track. It was long enough to be accepted and, I hope, respected by the men. I hunted with them and learned to use the long blowguns with which they took howler monkeys and three-toed sloth, though I was not a good shot. I made certain, though, that I did more than my share of any unpleasant jobs that had to be done — a sure way to win allies in any survival situation.

One night, squatting around the communal fire, Keesha's brother, Zarabatana, handed me a huge gourd filled with what he called *cashiri*. It was a kind of beer made from the mandioca root, and slightly psychedelic. The village men — as men are likely to do — proceeded to get me, the cashiri novice, absolutely shit-faced. They thought it was hilarious when I tried to show them how to limbo by drunkenly imitating Tomlinson's artistry. Still roaring, they mimicked the sounds I made as I vomited into the bushes.

Two days after that, Zarabatana returned to the village, paddling his carved *obada*, and said to me, "Finally, our people have located the men you seek. They are in a village in the jungle where the tourists come to see the big river. I think they will not be there for more than two nights. Our people say they are running from something, hiding. They say that they get very drunk at hotel where they yell insults, then sleep."

Feeling a great stillness inside me, nearly whispering, I said, "Is this jungle hotel close?"

"Yes. A half-day's paddle. Hotels such as this, there are more and more of them near the big river."

I grilled Zarabatana for all the details I could assemble before asking, "I don't suppose anyone raises pigs in the forest near this place?"

He looked at me like I was insane — and perhaps I was.

"Pigs?" he said. "No. Of course not.

Why would our people raise pigs when we have peccary to kill and eat?"

That night, when I told Keesha what I must do, she insisted on painting my body. "You are in my heart, big man. It is the only way that I can protect you."

Another village woman, plus the *curandeira*, the old shaman, helped her. They built the fire high and stripped me naked as the rest of the village watched. First they smeared my face and body with a dark-red powder they called *carujuru*, and then kneaded it into my hair.

Then Keesha brought out a wooden bowl that contained dark-blue *genipapo* dye. With a brush made out of a twig, she painted my ankles in the fashion of her tribe, then began to paint my face with a series of parallel lines.

I didn't mind. I could picture the jungle resort where Kazan and Stallings were holed up. One of those travel-adventure outposts where people were boated in for quick bites of wilderness and prepackaged ecology lessons. For two murderers, it was perfect cover.

For a man painted like a Jivaro warrior, the same was true.

Zarabatana let me borrow his *obada* and

offered me his *pucuna,* too. I refused the blowgun but promised to return the dugout to him soon.

"It does not matter," he said, with the easy indifference of his people when it came to material items. "I can always make another."

Just before I pushed away from the bank, Keesha came trotting down the path, something in her hand. "Would you care to wear this, as your *muisak,* the avenging soul of your enemy? As a necklace for luck."

I looked into the tiny, wizened face of Niall McCauley, his eyes sewn closed, head suspended on a leather strap, and said, "No. That guy ran out of luck long ago."

The jungle hotel was not hard to find. In six hours of paddling through darkness, past the occasional village fire, it was the only human stronghold with a generator and incandescent lights.

The place consisted of a main hut and outdoor Tiki bar, then a series of little bamboo cottages, all set along a dock fronting this broad section of river. A place for the tour boats.

Nor was it difficult to find the cottage where Kazan and Stallings were staying.

From the darkness, after peering through half a dozen screened windows, I saw an open bottle of Moët on the kitchenette counter and a carton of Dunhill cigarettes.

All people create a personal spore, and this was the spore of Hassan Atwa Kazan, the man who'd murdered Amelia.

I went inside and searched the two small bedrooms. In one, I found clothing that would fit only a giant. In the other, I found the clothes of a very tall, very thin man, plus several linen kaffiyehs, in several colors, folded atop the chest of drawers.

I turned off all the lights, sat in a chair by the door, and unholstered the SIG Sauer. In my left hand, I held an obsidian knife with a mahogany handle, beautifully polished, that Keesha had given me as a present. I waited, expecting both men to return at the same time, after the little bar had closed.

They did not.

Stallings returned first, and I watched the surprise register in his face when he switched on the overhead light and saw me, a strange, painted vision, a big man wearing only a breechcloth, pointing a gun at his belly.

The bully in him came to the fore. "This better be some kind of joke, asshole!"

I hit him in the face with the heel of my open palm and dropped the full weight of my elbow on the back of his neck. Then I walked him at gunpoint out into the jungle. Once he said, in a tone of dawning realization, "Jesus Christ, it's *you*. I know who you are now!"

His last words were "I didn't kill her. I *swear* it."

When Kazan came in, wearing baggy pants and a crooked linen kaffiyeh roped around his head, he was so staggering drunk that his slow-motion reaction was the second disappointment of the day.

The first was the fact that there were no wild hogs nearby to which to feed a wounded man.

He had a surprisingly high voice and a stink about him, like curry, or toads kept in a jar too long. It is one of our oddities that, as humans, we invest in our enemies strengths they do not possess and qualities of evil that elevate them while diminishing us.

Hassan Kazan seemed weasel-like, not evil, and surprisingly frail — though why I was surprised, I do not know. Only weak people take pleasure in imposing on the vulnerability of others and causing them pain.

Out in the jungle, far enough from the camp so no one could hear, I slapped his face, hoping he would fight back. Instead, he began to cry and to chant a repetitive phrase — a prayer, perhaps — in a language I did not understand.

But when I asked, "Why did you kill her?" and he replied, "Because she bit my hand. I had no choice!" the cold fury in me returned.

I dropped both weapons, ducked under his arm, behind him, and locked my fingers beneath his jaw, tilting his head back, my right knee pinned against his spine. With teeth clenched, I said, "I have done this ten times, and each time I whispered something into their ear. I've never told another living soul what that was."

Kazan was crying again. "I'm sorry. Please. I don't want you to do this. I truly am *sorry*."

His words so surprised me that I heard myself reply, "*Yes.* Very close. That's almost exactly what I've told them. But not now. Not to you. This time, it would be a lie."

Then, with my hands still locked around his neck, I allowed my legs to collapse beneath me, my full body weight plummeting earthward, pulling Hassan Atwa Kazan down as if we'd both been dropped through the trapdoor of a gallows.

Epilogue

In what an editorial in the *Sanibel Shopper's Guide* would call "a clear conspiracy between the makers of Guinness beer, whiskey, and other strong drink," Florida's state legislature showed uncommon foresight and backbone by postponing the implementation of the so-called "manatee protection laws."

They postponed them, at least, until lawyers of Save All Manatees filed briefs explaining why they had "(allegedly) intentionally perverted and misrepresented certain scientific data to advance their organization politically and economically to the detriment of the economic well-being, and maritime freedoms, of the citizens of Florida."

The fact that the legislature made its announcement on Thursday, March 16 — the day before St. Patrick's Day — catalyzed the tongue-in-cheek editorial in the Sanibel newspaper.

The article went on to say, "Nowhere on the islands will this evil Celtic conspiracy be more self-evident than at our own Dinkin's Bay Marina and Fishhouse. Tomorrow, the marina's traditional Friday pig roast and cotillion — always popular — will reach gala proportions. The fishing guides, liveaboards, sad old hippies, and other misfits who have lived there, unproductively, for years will be celebrating the fact that the government will not be kicking them out of their slovenly, floating homes. Not yet, anyway."

The article even quoted Mack — and probably accurately. "According to Graeme MacKinley, the marina's owner, the local package stores have hired extra personnel just to deliver the massive quantity of dyed draft beer and liquor he's ordered. Hundreds of locals are expected to attend.

" 'There's only one thing that really scares me,' MacKinley told this reporter. 'We all know how marina people are when they get a few beers in them, and it's dark on the docks, and they have to relieve themselves. I'm afraid we're going to wake up Saturday and the whole damn Gulf of Mexico will be shamrock green.' "

★ ★ ★

It *was* good news. Even to my face, it brought a small smile — and I had not smiled much since returning from Colombia. There were a couple of obvious reasons. For one thing, in the rain forest, I had seen myself in another incarnation, and my name was Curtis Tyner. As much as I'd fought the truth, I'd proven it true. As much as I hated the truth, I now had no choice but to acknowledge it. It was not an easy thing to live with, yet I would have to find a way to do exactly that for the rest of my life.

Mostly, though, I missed my friend, Amelia Gardner. From her mother, I'd asked for and received several nice photographs of her. In my little house, I'd tacked the photos on the wall at eye level, so I could look into her eyes when I felt the need. It was the only way I knew to try to blot out the way her face looked the last time I saw her. I wanted to replace that sad, small image with the face of the person I knew and loved.

Sometimes, it worked.

I know enough about mental illness to have realized I wasn't doing well, or behaving normally. All people have emotional boundaries, limits beyond which there is no return. I was on the very outer fringes of mine. I recognized in myself certain troubling symptoms of depression — a malady to which I've never been prone. So, early on upon my return, I paid a visit to Dr. Dieter Rasmussen aboard his forty-six-foot Grand Banks and asked of him a favor.

In his heavy, German accent, he replied, "Yah! Of course, I will treat you. Doctor-patient confidentiality. I am a psychiatrist and a scientist. You haf my word!"

I didn't tell him everything, of course. But I did discuss my symptoms and my strange inability to cry.

After seven visits, I found his diagnosis amusing but not surprising. "You, my friend, will never be an entirely happy man because you are a *rational* man. In you, and people like you, intellect and spirituality will always be in conflict. My advice as your physician? Find a new good woman and make love to her. Drink more, laugh more, show your friends that you care. Concentrate on some of the many good things that have been happening lately! Remember what I've learned in all my years of practice: Freudian psychiatry is absolute bullshit. We are chemical, genetic creatures, but we still have the option of choosing our own direction."

So, wanting badly to follow his advice, I made a choice. Some good things *had* happened, and I decided I would focus my attention on them.

The return of a transformed Janet Mueller had had a healthy, happy impact on the whole marina family, as well as on more than a few individuals. The teenage boy she was in the process of adopting, Ron Collins, was among them. So, surprisingly, was my cousin, Ransom Gatrell. Ransom and Janet had both lost children in earlier years, and the two of them had become the closest of friends and confidants. Grace Walker — a truly gorgeous woman — had been included in their sisterly triad. In the three of them, I now saw a peace, and a sense of self-security, that I envied but that also pleased me greatly.

It was more surprising that Jeth Nicholes had not benefited in a way that most of us at the marina had expected. Oh, he was happy to see that Janet was back home, healthy and alive, but a curious thing had happened in her absence. He and Janet's sister, Claudia Kohlerberg, had fallen quickly, passionately, and devotedly in love. When he tried to tell Janet what had happened, he stuttered so badly that

Claudia had had to interpret.

Only Janet's great gift for understanding, and her new strength, saved what could have become an ugly, community-damaging situation.

She'd actually laughed as she told me, "Irony, Doc. Irony and love. Those are the only two things that separate us from the beasts."

Another good thing was Tomlinson — who was *still* Tomlinson, thank God. He continued to demonstrate his universal quirkiness, which is to say, he never followed the path that those of us who know him expect. The most resent example was that, while I was away, he hired an attorney, started a small corporation, and embraced — of all the strange disciplines available — the American free-enterprise system.

He was fascinated by chili peppers and had grown them for years. First, in pots aboard the *No Mas*. Then whole lots of them on land he leased near Periwinkle Boulevard. A natural extension of that passion was bottling and selling his own hot sauce. He said he had his sights set on a small catalogue company: sarongs from Indonesia, hammocks from Panama, things like that.

"The stuff I love," he told me, "from the places I've been and still miss."

Tomlinson also continued to demonstrate his kindness and his loyalty to our strange friendship by his concern for my mental health, his careful inquiries, his thoughtful gestures.

One night, sitting with a beer on my deck, looking out over the black rim of mangroves, he said, in reference to nothing that I'd mentioned (perhaps it was in reply to my long, moody silence): "Marion, the world would be a far worse place without you. Please don't doubt that. Not nearly so generous, and a hell of a lot duller."

A few days later, we both chuckled over another of his thoughtful gestures. It was a copy of *People* magazine with a story and photos about a new feud between Gunnar Camphill and his pointed-faced former agent, Lester West — the guy I'd lobbed into the water. Camphill was sueing West for spreading "slanderous lies" about the film star being bested in a fight by a hick fishing guide who resembled the star of *Gilligan's Island*. In reply, West had provided the magazine with a photo showing Camphill with two black eyes and a bandage over his nose.

"Two adolescents," Tomlinson said.

"Immature spirits always behave this way."

Now there was this additional good thing: The government was not going to close our marina after all. As a biologist, my immediate concern, though, was that this mandated review of "fraudulent" manatee data was, itself, based on greed, not science. There are now, without fail, parties on both sides of environmental issues who seldom hesitate to pervert science to advance their own cause, increase their own power.

But then I was much reassured when I read the name of the scientist whose work was most often cited: Frieda Matthews, one of Florida's best biologists and field researchers.

So maybe we'd get to keep our home after all.

Mack was right. That was a pretty good reason to celebrate.

Which is why, on this late Friday afternoon, St. Patrick's Day, I returned from the marina after spending a couple of very rugged hours helping Mack and Felix, Jeth and the other guides lug kegs of beer and platters of food and set up tables, decorations, a limbo pit, and a PA system for the bands — getting ready for the all-night party to come.

I was sweaty, dirty, and more than ready for a hot shower and my first cold beer of the day — which is why, as I hurried down my wobbly boardwalk, I was so pleased to see the girl standing on the upper porch of my house, frosted mug in hand, smiling.

She was another of the new and unexpected good things that had happened recently, and who had helped bring the occasional little smile to my face.

I listened to her call out to me, "So is this the way civilized people are expected to behave? Drink waiting. House cleaned. All your files, nice and neat. Anything else I can do for you, sir?"

I took the beer from her, nodding while wagging my finger, "You are learning, young lady. That is why you're here — to learn. Don't forget it."

She followed me through the door, telling me about her day, all that she had done, all that she had accomplished. The paper she'd written, the math problems she'd solved. Proud of herself, and with good reason.

In the lab, she said, "Oh yeah, and when I was dusting, this thing fell off the wall. Like it was already broke, just hanging there. What is it, like a security camera? I didn't know what to do with it."

As I sat at the stainless-steel dissecting table, she placed in front of me the little digital camera that Bernie Yeager had sent. I'd forgotten all about the damn thing. During my many weeks in Colombia, all of my stone crabs and calico crabs had died, and all of my octopi had disappeared. Right along with most of my fish and two of my biggest sharks.

I was too busy trying to restock to mess with a camera, which was why I hadn't thought to check the memory stick. But now I did. I opened the little viewing screen, pushed the on button, and then touched rewind.

As the little machine whirred, I heard the girl say from the breezeway, "A package arrived for you today. The box was torn a little, so I could see inside. It's some kind of small glass case, with like a little blackball inside."

I looked up from the camera, peering over my glasses. Trying very hard to keep my tone breezy, disinterested, I said, "Oh? Probably some kind of specimen. You better let me open that one." I wondered if it might be from Tyner. Had he somehow gotten my address?

I listened to her reply, "Okay, okay, I was just telling you, that's all. Oh, and I took your advice. I called the school counselor and told her I definitely planned to apply to college. Trouble is, I'm so far behind it's going to be tough for me to catch up. It's a lot harder than I thought it was going to be. So . . . well, I'll see how it goes."

Speaking slightly louder because she was outside, I said, "Just because it's difficult doesn't mean you can't do it. If it's harder than you thought, then work harder than you've been working. It's that simple."

"Oh sure, for someone like *you*. Maybe I just wasn't raised that way."

I didn't care for her tone of voice. I stood, walked out the screen door, then into my little house where Shanay Money, dressed in baggy shorts and T-shirt, was busy cleaning my kitchen.

She glanced up broom in hand, when I entered, and I said to her, "Look, young lady, when you called me bawling, the night they hauled your father off to jail, you told me that you felt like you were trapped in your father's life. Trapped by that kind of society. That you wanted out. Okay, so I agreed. We've got a deal. You're out. You have our full support, Ransom's and mine."

Shanay said, "I know, I know. That sister of yours, man, she's so great."

"Yeah, and she thinks you're a great roommate, enjoys having you around. You don't have a mother? Ransom might make a pretty fair replacement. But there are a couple of things neither one of us is going to tolerate. Among them is you speaking badly of yourself. You have a fine intellect, every gift it takes to succeed. I'm not going to let you quit something before you've tried. So stop whining, stop looking for ways to fail. I won't allow it. Any questions, Shanay?"

I liked the look that came into her face. It was a combination of gratitude, astonishment, and humor. "Damn it, Doc, when you're right, you're right. I *was* whining. Exactly what I was doing. You know what's weird? Kind of secretly, I wanted you to tell me just exactly what you did. That I was looking for excuses to quit."

Pleased, I said, "There you go. You are your own best barometer. Not me. Not anyone else. So when you talked to the counselor, did he happen to ask what you're interested in majoring in?"

She said, "He did, matter of fact. I told him pre-law. I've always found it kind'a interesting. Plus all the experience I've had with cops coming to the house, I figure I already know more than most."

I smiled, hardly trusting myself to speak. After a long pause, I said, "This state can always use another good lady attorney."

"That's what I figure," she said. "Plus they do some good. Help people. Like you did for my old Davey dog. I'd like that."

Janet's line came to mind, though I did not speak it: *Irony and love are the only things that separate us from the beasts.*

I'm glad I didn't. The irony I then witnessed would have made a mockery of her, of me — of everything, perhaps. Or maybe it was simply a confirmation of something that only Tomlinson would understand.

I returned to the lab, picked up the camera, pressed play, and a bright, digitized video began to run, everything colored as if shot through a green lens. For a while, there was nothing. Then the show began. I watched the little screen amused, then amazed, and then in a sort of chilling wonderment, as the largest of my Atlantic octopi used its tentacles to pry back the lid of its own tank.

Then, as if purposefully trying to be quiet, the octopus crawled slowly across the lab floor, moving like a Slinky, toward the tank in which I'd kept my stone crabs and calico crabs.

I whispered, "You brilliant little sneak!"

as, still methodically, the animal climbed up the leg of the table, to the top of the crab tank. There it carefully and expertly augered the little vise open.

The audio was good. The metal vise clattered when it hit the floor.

Then the octopus pushed back the lid of the crab tank and slid inside to feed.

But that was not the most astonishing shot. The last few seconds of the video consisted of a sudden, unexpected close-up of suction cups, very powerful suction cups, clamping on to the lense of the camera.

They were from the tentacles of a second octopus.

The tentacles flexed, suction cups flattening themselves over the glass of the lens — huge, throbbing a furious red — and then the body of the animal slid over the camera, and suddenly I was staring into one bright, yellow eye. The eye had a black, vertical pupil set like stone into lucent gold. The eye telescoped toward me, then away, focusing, goat-like, staring into the lens as if studying the construction of the camera — or as if studying me.

Then the lens shattered.

I sat back, holding the camera away from me, as the screen slowly faded into darkness.

Author's Postscript

Much of what you've just read is not fiction, it is fact. This novel is based on an actual event as well as political realities that exist in North and South America. To the best of my ability, that event and those complicated political circumstances are described here accurately.

The event: On Friday, November 1994, at approximately 7 p.m., four Canadian SCUBA divers were set adrift off Marco Island, Florida, when their swamped boat sank to the bottom. They were fifty-two nautical miles offshore, anchored over the wreck of the *Baja California*.

On Sunday morning, thirty-eight hours later, a Coast Guard helicopter spotted one of the missing divers standing naked on a light tower, waving his wet suit to get their attention. The search for the remaining three — all of whom were wearing inflated buoyancy compensator devices (BCDs) and wet suits — resumed. For six days, the search continued. In the body of this novel, the results of that search are portrayed accurately in every small detail. The Coast Guard combed more than 23,000 square miles of water on a carefully coordinated grid search, using the latest high-tech radar and heat-sensitive vector systems, but found nothing. No trace of the remaining three divers was ever found. They vanished as if they'd been drawn into a vortex, then swept over the edge of the earth. David Madott, Omar Shearer, and Kent Munro, all twenty-five years of age, and each a resident of Mississauga, a suburb of Toronto, left behind family and friends who still grieve for them.

It was during the search that rumors began to circulate. As Marion Ford observes in this novel, blame and reason are contrivances to which we cling for comfort, a way of imposing order. All theories as to why the boat sank relied on sinister motives. There were no exceptions.

Watermen also tend to be territorial. No outsider, some believe, can know the currents and quirks of their area like they know them — including the Coast Guard. Some critics said the Coast Guard was searching too far to the south; others said the Coast Guard was searching too far west.

As a longtime fishing guide on nearby Sanibel Island, I was as interested, curious, and suspicious as anyone else. Much of what I heard made no sense; some of what I heard seemed impossible. For instance, I am an occasional long-distance open-water swimmer, and the distance covered by the lone swimmer in the time reported seemed unlikely. There were other troubling improbabilities as well.

At the time, I was a columnist for one of the nation's great magazines, *Outside*. My editor gave me free rein to do whatever it took to find out the truth about the sinking of the boat. Exactly four weeks after the event, I accompanied several professional divers and a former FBI agent to the wreck of the *Baja California*. They'd been hired to bring up equipment and personal effects that had been lost when the boat sank. Ironically, the weather was nearly identical to the weather on the day of the accident, with a wind out of the northeast fifteen to twenty knots. Aboard our fifty-three-foot cruiser, the four- to six-foot seas were unpleasant. In a twenty-five-foot boat, conditions would have been miserable.

Like Marion Ford, I dived the wreck. Like Ford, I got into the water near midnight in an attempt to gain some understanding of the terror those divers experienced that night.

Over the next two months, I investigated every minute aspect of the event and interviewed many dozens of people, including the diver who was found atop the light tower. Investigators hired by the families and I were all seeking answers to the same questions: Why weren't the three divers found? If dead, they would still be afloat *somewhere*.

My story was published. I remained in contact with the father of one of the missing three divers, Bill Madott. He refused to give up hope. All of the families refused to give up hope. Because I travel a lot, I helped the families circulate posters in Cuba and countries in Central and South America. Perhaps a boat — a boat used in some kind of illegal enterprise — had picked them up and carried them off to a foreign land. Perhaps they were being held hostage, or maybe they were being used as slave labor.

Perhaps.

Years passed. I continued to stay in contact with Bill. Recently, when I called and told him I was considering writing a fictionalized account of the tragedy, he was enthusiastic.

"Anything to get the word out," he told me.

The story you've just read of their disappearance is precise and factual in every small detail, including actual quotes from many of the people associated with what happened. However, I have completely reinvented not only all four divers, but everyone and anyone involved directly or peripherally with the event. Why? The reason that all the characters in this novel must be fictionalized is simple: No one can write from the perspective of the divers but the divers themselves. Because I wanted to explore the possibilities of what might have happened in fiction, they and everyone else had to be newly minted. The only things the divers of fact have in common with the missing divers in this book are similarities assigned intentionally by me: All were strong, productive, intelligent, and decent people. All were capable of behaving and performing as well as others who have actually survived similar tragedies.

After voluminous research, after hours of interviews with their friends, families, and coworkers, I am convinced that all were capable of enduring heroically and that they probably did endure heroically — three lone stars out on the Gulf Stream.

The political realities of South America as portrayed here are also based on extensive personal research and are accurate in each detail, including information on the natural history of Amazon rain forests and the work of terrorist cells that have found safe haven in the South American country of Colombia. For instance, the fictional Hal Harrington speaks factually when he writes: "Maicao, Colombia, is an Islamic extremist stronghold. Our government has yet to deal with anti-American organizations here, but it is time we started." The same is true about the data on the international flesh-trade business, white slavery, and the smuggling of illegal aliens.

I should add, however, in fairness to Columbia and its 48 million people — most of whom are extraordinarily friendly, gifted, and generous — that this country remains one of my favorite travel destinations despite its troubles. Jamaica? The Bahamas? San Jose, Costa Rica, or Mexico? I feel much safer in Cartagena, and, in my opinion, it's a heck of a lot more fun and far more interesting.

The trick is choosing where you go outside Cartagena, and when. The same is true of all rain-forest countries and other wild regions — open sea, for instance — for, in these places, "civilized" people disappear every day.

Randy Wayne White
Hotel Santa Clara
Cartagena, Colombia